Jack approached and found an area of perfect blackness. A heavy steel grate had been moved aside, leaving a dark, empty square in the floor. Here was where H3 did its disappearing act.

He flashed his light down and saw foot rungs imbedded in the concrete wall. Jack didn't expect H3 back soon but had no doubt it would return, so he couldn't waste what time he had. Holstering the Glock, he slipped through the opening and clambered down the rungs.

Another tunnel but unlike the usual drainage pipe. Bigger, a comfortable six feet in height, and of more recent vintage than the one running under the Belt. Its floor was flat but its walls and ceiling angled this way and that. Like a German expressionistic design without a true vertical anywhere. He could imagine Dr. Caligari's somnambulist wandering by.

The tunnel curved to the left ahead. A half dozen feet around the bend his beam reflected off some plastic packing on the floor. Closer inspection revealed a *Star Wars* action figure: Ridley. Beyond that another plastic pack, this one with a doll's dress.

What was going on here? What was H3's attraction to these toys?

A few feet past that Jack found a cubic battery pack loaded with four D cells; a switch jutted from one end and wires trailed off into the dark from the other. A few feet away Jack's flash picked up a tiny bulb jutting from one of the wires.

Lights?

Weirder and weirder.

Feeling a little reckless, he flipped the switch.

The alcovelike space ahead came to life, brightening with multi-colored lights. It took him a moment to recognize what he was looking at. And then—

"Aw, no!"

ACKNOWLEDGMENTS

Many thanks to my wife, Mary; Dannielle Romeo, and Elizabeth Monteleone. Also to all the good folks at Gauntlet Press and Crossroad Press.

A Gordian Knot Books Production–Gordian Knot is an imprint of Crossroad Press.

First Trade Edition

—THE—
LAST
CHRISTMAS

A Repairman Jack Novel

F. PAUL WILSON

GORDIAN KNOT BOOKS

OTHER BOOKS BY F. PAUL WILSON

Repairman Jack*

The Tomb	*Harbingers*
Legacies	*Bloodline*
Conspiracies	*By the Sword*
All the Rage	*Ground Zero*
Hosts	*The Last Christmas*
The Haunted Air	*Fatal Error*
Gateways	*The Dark at the End*
Crisscross	*Nightworld*
Infernal	*Quick Fixes—Tales of Repairman Jack*

The Teen Trilogy*

Jack: Secret Histories
Jack: Secret Circles
Jack: Secret Vengeance

The Early Years Trilogy*

Cold City
Dark City
Fear City

The Adversary Cycle*

The Keep	*Reborn*
The Tomb	*Reprisal*
The Touch	*Nightworld*

Omnibus Editions

The Complete LaNague
Calling Dr. Death (3 medical thrillers)
Ephemerata

Short Fiction

Soft & Others
The Barrens and Others
Aftershock and Others
The Christmas Thingy
*Quick Fixes—Tales of Repairman Jack**
Sex Slaves of the Dragon Tong
Secret Stories

Editor

Freak Show
Diagnosis: Terminal
The Hogben Chronicles (with Pierce Watters)

* See "The Secret History of the World" (Page 356)

AUTHOR'S NOTE

I think a bit of orientation (or *reorientation*) might be in order.

Nightworld hasn't happened yet. What you're about to read takes place in the December after *Ground Zero* and a couple of months before *Fatal Error*.

The *Compendium of Srem* is still in Jack's apartment; Weezy just moved out to her own place near W. 72 & Amsterdam and left the *Compendium* with Jack until she finishes repainting.

The Lady, still weakened and stuck in old-woman form after *Ground Zero*, recuperates in an apartment in Glaeken's building.

Russ Tuit is still alive; Hank Thompson is still kicking; Ernst Drexler is still plotting.

It's been just over a year since Jack's dad's death on December 7, and just under a year since his brother Tom disappeared on Christmas Eve.

FRIDAY—DECEMBER 19

1

Jack suppressed a groan as Edward Burkes appeared in Julio's doorway.

Not again.

Burkes looked more like a bear than ever, but his brown hair and neat beard had gained a generous helping of salt since Jack first met.

Burkes and Julio arrived at Jack's table together. Julio still sported the goatee he'd started in the summer.

"Julio," Jack said. "You remember Burkes, right?"

Julio, short and muscular, maybe half Burkes's size, scanned him up and down. The pair of them looked like a little organ grinder and his dancing grizzly.

"Oh, yeah," Julio said. "You used to come in here back in the day."

"'The day'?"

"Yeah. Right after I took over."

"Aye. Our mutual friend here introduced me to the place." Burkes sounded more like Sean Connery than ever. "You had John Courage on draft, as I recall, and that kept me coming back for a while."

"Yeah. Can't get that no more. You drinking someplace else?" Julio made it sound like a challenge.

"I frequent a proper pub further downtown. They have Guinness. You don't."

"Do now. Replaced the Courage."

Burkes slapped the table. "Now you're talking! Be a good lad and draw us a couple of pints!"

Jack held up his Yuengling. "I'm good."

"Got Murphy's too," Julio said.

"Guinness it is, lad." As Julio strutted away, Burkes glared at Jack's glass. "What's this pish you prefer to a free Guinness?"

"America's oldest brewery. Want to try?"

"Wouldn't touch a drop of it to me lips."

Jack liked Burkes. He had a presence that said everything was under control as long as he was here. His Scottish burr and jolly Burl Ives exterior hid a dangerous man. He'd come to see Burkes as the type who'd stand his ground when it made sense and get the hell out when it didn't. But in retreat he'd be the last man onto the last helicopter leaving the roof.

Burkes had been chief of security for the UK's mission to the UN when they'd met back in the '90s. Still was. They'd butted heads during Jack's early years in the city, but wound up working together trying to foil what became the first Trade Center bombing. They'd failed but remained in contact.

In his position at the UK mission, Burkes sometimes came up against a situation he thought better handled by a local than a Brit. That was when he'd call on a freelancer like Jack.

Burkes was looking around, taking in the place. "One thing I'll say for Julio's: It never changes. Still has those dead plants in the windows, still that eedjit sign."

He'd never appreciated Julio's *"Free Beer Tomorrow . . . "* sign. Similar ones had popped up all over the city the past few years, but Jack couldn't remember seeing one before Julio's.

"That's its charm."

"And he still smells bad."

"His latest aftershave."

"Must he marinate in it? It's honkin'."

"You tell him."

"What? And risk a jab in the nose? He's got muscles on his muscles."

Yeah, Julio worked out a lot and liked to show off the results.

"No worry. He's a pussycat."

Julio returned then and placed a deep brown pint on the table.

"Guinness for Shrek."

"Here now, laddie. Am I looking green to you?"

But Julio was already moving away.

Burkes held up the glass, admiring the perfect half inch of foam. "Knows how to pour a stout, I'll give him that." He held it higher. "*Slàinte mhòr agad.*"

Jack clinked his glass against his. "Ditto."

Jack waited till Burkes finished a deep quaff and wiped his mustache, then leaned forward. "I'm guessing you didn't ask to meet because Julio's Guinness might be better than your pub's."

"Nae danger. Might have some work for you."

Burkes didn't call on Jack often—averaged once every year or so. But this was the third time this year.

"Not interested."

"Again?"

"Look, I barely survived the last referral I took from you."

Burkes looked surprised. "That Indian bloke? Bahkti, wasn't it? Wanted you to find his mother's necklace or summat, aye?"

Right. Two and a half years ago. Sounded like an easy fix at the time but . . . Jack rubbed his shirt, fingering the three diagonal ridges of scar tissue across his chest where Scarlip had tried to rip him open . . .

"It got complicated."

Burkes frowned. "Come to think of it, I never saw Bahkti again after that." His eyes narrowed. "You two didn't have a falling out, did you?"

"'Falling out'? What are you implying?"

"Well, we both know you can be, shall we say, intemperate when provoked. And don't y'be telling me otherwise. I've seen it."

Kusum Bahkti . . . the *late* Kusum Bahkti . . . Jack had been forced to fry him, but Burkes didn't need to know that.

Deflection time . . .

"'Intemperate'? Am I hearing correctly? The man who introduced me to that gentle flower of a woman, *La Chirurgienne*, is talking about intemperate?"

Burkes laughed. "Forgot about that. Point taken. By the bye, I hear she's semi-retired."

The scariest woman Jack had ever met. A Picasso of pain. What had she called herself? Right, a *nociresearcher.*

"Okay, here's the deal," Burkes said.

"I repeat: Not interested."

"Working something else?"

"Not working anything."

"Why not?"

Jack shrugged to hide his discomfort. "Things been slow lately."

Burkes gave him a hard stare. "Slow and yet you keep turning me down? What's eatin' you, lad?"

"Nothing. I'm fine."

"No, yer not." His burr thickened. "Yer in some kinda funk."

"Funk? As in 'smell bad'?"

"No, y'eedjit. As in depressed."

"Depressed? Me? Hell no."

He wasn't depressed. Other people got depressed. Not him.

He didn't want this conversation. He was fine. Really. He simply didn't feel like doing fixes lately. Didn't feel like doing much of anything lately. No biggie. Nothing to get worked up about. Just sitting and watching the wheels go 'round . . . wheels within wheels . . .

"At least give me a listen and see what you think."

Burkes wasn't going to be put off, it seemed. Oh, hell . . .

"All right. Shoot."

"There's a good lad. Now, last night I was approached by a pair of Americans who wanted to know if I could do—or arrange—a discreet search for a missing person here in the city."

Jack leaned back. "A pair of Americans? How weird is that?"

"I know. Locals asking a foreigner to search for a missing local. Makes nae sense."

"Well, you've been in the city for a long time—longer than I have, as a matter of fact. And, let's face it, you've been known to step off the reservation when the situation demands it."

Burkes looked uncomfortable. "That's known only in certain circles."

"But that doesn't explain why they don't contact the boys in blue or a PI."

"I think the key here is the 'discreet' part. They were adamant about that. Did not want local authorities involved. Did not want local police resources accessed. And let's face it, most PIs are either ex cops or have strong cop connections."

"So, they go to a guy who's unconnected to local officialdom but who's got his own police force. Makes a contorted sort of sense."

Burkes's personnel at the mission included some hard-ass SAS vets.

"To them, maybe. Not to me. If everything's got to be oh-so secret, it won't do to have my guys going around asking a lot of questions with their Glasgow burrs. It's just asking to be noticed. And if there's something minging on the end of their stick . . . well, I don't want my guys getting the stink on them."

Jack had to laugh. "So, you thought of good ol' Jack."

"Who better? I told them I know a guy who lives under the radar and hires out for this kind of thing for a living. He's got no connection to the cops—in fact, he avoids cops at all cost—so they could count on him doing everything on the down low."

"Missing persons aren't exactly my forte. You know that."

"Aye, I do. Indeed, I do. But you *have* found people, haven't you?"

Yeah, he had.

"Unless you've got something better to do," Burkes added.

"As a matter of fact, I do."

"What?"

"Stuff."

"Give me a for instance."

"Just . . . stuff."

"A funk, I tell ya. Yer in a blue funk. You need to get back in the ring and throw some punches."

Did he?

He'd lost his sister, his brother, and his father within a six-month period last year. And then earlier this year . . . Emma. All gone, all senseless. Somehow, he'd fallen into a holding pattern that had lasted all through the fall, wandering in some gray, featureless limbo. He'd been turning down pretty much every fix that came his way.

Hanging with Gia and Vicky, helping Weezy set up her new apartment, visiting Glaeken and the Lady. Directionless, purposeless . . .

Okay, a funk.

Maybe finding this missing person would serve as a baby step out of his narrowing gyre.

And maybe not. He didn't answer to anyone, and wasn't about to start.

"Well?" Burkes said. "Whatta y'say? Are y'game?"

"Nah. I'll pass."

"Just give them a listen. They told me they're free tonight."

"Even if I was interested, tonight's no good. Got a memorial service to go to this afternoon."

"Sorry. Anyone close?"

"My father and brother."

Burkes nearly choked on his Guinness. "Jesus! When did this happen?"

"Last December."

"Together?"

"A few weeks apart. You remember the LaGuardia massacre?"

"Bugger! Remember? How can I forget? We were all on high alert for weeks."

"Well, my father was one of those caught in the gunfire."

"I'm gutted. I had no idea!"

"No way you could know."

"Your brother too?"

"No, he just sort of . . . disappeared last Christmas Eve."

"What's that mean—'disappeared'?"

"It's complicated."

"You keep saying that."

"I mean it. Explaining what I know about it—and I know only part of it—would take a good hour. And when I finished, you'd say 'bollocks' or 'balderdash' or the like."

"I've never said 'balderdash' in me life. But I get your drift. Whatever the story, I'm sorry as all hell, Jack."

"Yeah, me too. But I've had a year to adjust."

Burkes's hard stare had softened. "And done a brilliant job of it, too, I see. But you've got reason to be in a funk, I'll grant you that."

Burkes didn't know the half of it. All the deaths, and how Jack had failed people like Dawn Pickering and the Lady, and then the hit and run that had left Gia and Vicky in comas.

And then his own situation. He'd spent most of his adult life trying to get to this place—a ghost within the machine. Dodging the system had been an end as well as a means. The cat-and-mouse game of staying one step ahead of officialdom had been a rush when he'd started, but the system had grown taller and wider and thicker, making the country a grim place. One by one it had plucked the good cards from Jack's hand, leaving him with junk. Staying under the radar had progressed beyond high maintenance into an unending daily grind. With the city's ubiquitous camera networks, Big Brother was indeed watching. He was beginning to weary of the upkeep. Was it worth it? Especially with Armageddon around the corner?

Yeah, even if Jack had wanted to, how could he explain to Burkes how human civilization was rolling toward the precipice of a new kind of hell and Jack was mired in the thick of it? Despite all he'd seen, he still had trouble grasping it himself.

"Get back in the field," Burkes said. "That's the cure."

He could tell Burkes wouldn't stop until Jack made some sort of concession.

"You could be right. Let me think on it, okay?"

"You're not just putting me off, are you?"

"Who me? Never."

They small-talked while Burkes finished his Guinness and parted with let's-get-together promises they both knew were bogus. Jack stayed at the table, nursing the dregs of his beer. He'd developed a premonitory sense over the past few years, and it was stirring now, as if the old witch were whispering in his ear.

By the pricking of my thumb, something wicked this way comes . . .

2

Tier Hill had just crossed Central Park West when he heard the tone. He'd been noticing it off and on for years, but faintly. Never this loud.

The sound began shortly after he'd moved to the city, usually a low-pitched hum. He had a history of ringing in his ears related to acoustic trauma from an incident in Afghanistan—high-pitched noises singing in his head after being too close to an IED when it went off. He'd been shielded from the shrapnel but not the boom. The doctors had called it *tinnitus*. But that had been high pitched, like crickets on a summer night. And temporary. It had cleared up and never bothered him again until he'd moved into his father's apartment uptown.

He did private investigations and was late for a meeting with his latest client, but he felt compelled to slow and listen.

So, what was this—another form of tinnitus? Maybe. But if memory served, his tinnitus had always been non-directional. The new sound seemed to be coming from somewhere. He lived in the West Seventies and the low-pitched hum, when it occurred, always seemed to emanate from southeast of the apartment.

The occurrences were random and more of a curiosity than an annoyance or distraction. They didn't last long so he hadn't worried about it. He'd never been able to figure out what triggered it. Like now. Just strolling down Broadway, hanging a left on Sixty-sixth. This was supposedly the last relatively mild day before the arrival of a cold front—an Arctic Express, as the weatherfolk were calling it—so he'd decided to hoof it instead of take a cab or Lyft. Tier had been raised in the Mohawk tribal homelands along the New York-Canadian border, so his idea of cold differed substantially from his neighbors'.

He'd been strolling east on Sixty-sixth, thinking about finding a use for his word of the day: *immure*—to enclose within walls, imprison. He'd been thinking about Han Solo immured in carbonite, but his rule demanded the use be related to something he encountered that day. So, he was still on the hunt when the sound struck him.

He stopped at the entrance to the park's Sixty-fifth Street Transverse and looked around, listening, trying to locate the direction of the sound. So damn loud now—a low-pitched hum that rumbled through his head and vibrated within his chest. He remembered as a kid going to this Montreal club where the band was playing so loud he had to cover his ears. That had worked for the higher tones, but the bass notes had vibrated through his whole body. Just like now.

He couldn't escape this sound. Covering his ears had no effect, just like with the bass player that night. He checked out his fellow pedestrians but none of them seemed bothered in the least. Was this some sort of regular occurrence here?

The sound came from somewhere ahead and to the left. A path led in that direction and so he took it, following it past the Tavern on the Green and across West Drive, the sound growing louder with every step. He stopped on the edge of the grassy field known as the Sheep Meadow.

Here . . . the sound originated here. Deafening, nauseatingly loud. He felt his gorge rise but swallowed it back. He had to find the source, had to stop it. So, he pressed on, forcing himself forward toward the center of the field. He began to stagger as the sound grew even louder. And yet all around him people were strolling by as if nothing was wrong.

He approached a young couple ambling hand in hand.

"Doesn't it bother you?"

The sound drowned out her reply, but he could read her lips and puzzled expression: "What?"

"You're joking, right? Don't you hear it?"

"Hear what?"

Her boyfriend looked pissed and mouthed, "Stop shouting and get lost!"

Tier backed off. They didn't hear it. Nobody around seemed to hear it. Was he going crazy?

Whatever, he had to get away from here. The sound seemed to emanate from the center of the Sheep Meadow so he broke into a staggering run toward the volleyball courts beyond it. And gradually the sound lessened. By the time he reached the Balto statue it became bearable. He slowed to get his bearings. He'd been headed for Fifth Avenue and—

The sound stopped. Like pulling the plug on a giant speaker system, it cut off. The sounds of the city rushed back in. He wandered back to the Sheep Meadow—the *silent* Sheep Meadow.

What had just happened? What was wrong with the Sheep Meadow? Or rather, what was wrong with him?

3

"I'm sorry this turned out to be so pathetic," Gia said.

Jack slipped an arm around her waist and hugged her close, hip to hip.

She'd put on a black-and-white print dress for the occasion that made her short, naturally blond hair and sharp blue eyes look blonder and bluer. She'd added a black cardigan against the chill. Eight Sutton Square might occupy a choice spot in one of Manhattan's toniest neighborhoods, but the place was old and drafty, and its heating system no match for a windy December afternoon like today's.

Gia lived here but neither owned nor rented it. Eventually it would belong to her daughter Vicky, but that day remained many years off. Three years ago, it had belonged to Vicky's aunts, Nellie and Grace Westphalen, both of whom had abruptly and mysteriously disappeared. Not a mystery to Jack and Gia and Vicky, but they weren't talking because no one would believe the truth. Nellie and Grace's wills left Vicky a nice piece of change, but everything else had gone to Vicky's father and Gia's ex-husband, Richard Westphalen, who had disappeared in England a year before the aunts, under equally abrupt and mysterious circumstances.

But Vicky's nice piece of change remained untouchable. She was the sole survivor of the Westphalen line and heir to the family fortune, but not officially. Not yet. Not until her aunts and her father were declared legally dead.

The executor, however, had thought it wise to let the future owner live in the house and maintain the property.

"'Pathetic'?" Jack said. "Not even close. You're doing a good thing."

"I thought so at the time, but . . . four people?"

"Well, seven counting you, me, and Vicks."

Gia had wanted to hold a memorial service for Jack's older brother Tom who had disappeared—quite literally—last Christmas Eve. Was he alive, dead, in suspended animation? No one could say. Only the Lilitongue of Gefreda knew, and it had disappeared with him. All Jack could say for certain was that Tom was *gone* and his return doubtful in the extreme.

Gia hadn't dressed up the living room for the occasion much beyond framing a photo of Tom she'd found online in a Philadelphia newspaper. Jack had seen the clipping before she'd cropped it—the lede had mentioned Tom being charged in a string of briberies and kickbacks. He'd confessed to Jack that the charges were mostly true and that he'd been "the finest Judge money could buy."

My brother the crook.

"You couldn't really expect his two exes to show," Jack said.

He didn't know their names because Tom had referred to them only as "the Skanks from Hell." And as for wife number three, he hadn't been on speaking terms with her nor any of his kids before his disappearance. Most likely they all assumed he was on the lam.

Here and there along the lurching course of his life, Tom had managed to burn just about every bridge he'd ever crossed.

Gia sighed. "I suppose not. Especially considering the awkwardness of the invitation."

Yeah, that had been a challenge because, like Nellie, Grace, and Vickie's dad, Tom wasn't legally dead—wouldn't be for years to come.

"At least Weezy and Eddie showed up," he said.

The Connell sibs had been Jack's childhood friends; they'd grown up knowing his brother and dad and had only recently re-entered Jack's life.

"Showed up separately," she said. "And they've stayed that way."

They don't seem to be speaking to each other—not even looking at each other. What's up between them?"

Jack bit back the *it's-complicated* reply. He was saying that too often. But it *was* complicated, damn it.

"A temporary falling out."

At least he hoped it was temporary.

"And then our huge turnout is rounded out by Abe and Julio, neither of whom ever even met your brother."

"They're here for me. And the food."

That earned a smile from Gia. He loved her smile and was glad he could brighten her down mood, however briefly.

Jack had added a photo of his father next to Tom's on the piano. Dad had been laid to rest next to Jack's mother last December, but no service had been held. The old soldier had fallen out of touch with his Jersey friends when he moved to Florida, and Jack had no idea who he'd hung with down south. It felt right somehow to include him in the mix today.

Gia squeezed his arm. "We should get this rolling. Do you want to speak first?"

He shook his head. "I've changed my mind. You go ahead."

"But you promised."

"I didn't exactly promise . . . "

"You said you'd speak at the memorial."

"Well, I meant it then, but I . . . I'm empty. Sorry."

He hadn't been able to come up with anything to say about Tom. They'd never gotten along. His deep love for his sister Kate had been matched by his antipathy for his brother.

And damn, he should have Kate's photo up there too. And Mom's as well. Mother, father, sister, brother—all taken from the world before their time. No natural causes, all by violence . . . all part of a plan.

A squeeze from Gia. "Come on. You can do it."

"You know I'm not one for speeches." He pointed to the two bottles of Balvenie Doublewood on the piano—one fresh and one missing a few drams—and the stack of six shot glasses beside them. "I'll start pouring after you speak."

His plan was to go around and pour each of the adults a shot so they could all drink a silent toast to Tom. That was the best he could do where his brother was concerned.

"Sure?"

"Very. I'm still processing what he did."

Jack had been slated to disappear via the Lilitongue—to die, most likely. For some unfathomable reason, totally out of character, Tom had stepped in and taken his place. Was it a way out of the legal troubles closing in from every side? Or maybe a mad, heroic impulse to undo the danger he'd brought into their lives, first threatening Vicky, and then Gia, and finally Jack. Tom's reckless desperation to evade prosecution had put all their lives in jeopardy and Jack had yet to forgive him for that.

"Okay," Gia said. "Here goes."

As she stepped toward the piano, Jack spotted Vicky standing next to Abe. Over the years those two had bonded into an unlikely duo. Whenever Abe was around, Vicky gravitated to his side and never left. Gia called them the Odd Couple.

He waved and she grinned and waved back. The newly ten-year old's dark hair was woven into its customary French braid.

"I'll be brief," Gia said and conversation died. "Jack's brother Tom is gone. We don't know where. He disappeared from this very house a year ago Christmas Eve. I spent his last minutes here with him and, while I can't remember his parting words verbatim, I remember the gist of them. I will always remember what he told me.

"He said going in Jack's place was the best thing he'd ever done in his life. He said he was so tired of living the way he had and needed a clean break. He was hoping he wouldn't die but go on to a different life, and that maybe because he'd done this one right thing here, he'd have a better life there—be a better man there.

"He said he hoped that at least one person in this world would remember him and speak well of him after he was gone. So, that's why I asked you here today. Because I guess I am that one person, and that is what I'm doing now. Tom led a troubled life and told me at the end how he regretted his many bad choices. And from what I hear, he made a slew of them. But for me none of that matters. Because at the end he stepped up and—"

Her voice caught and her lower lip trembled. Jack felt his own throat tighten.

"Because," she went on, "in the end he saved one of the two

people in this world who make my life worth living. And for that his name will always have a prominent place in my book of heroes."

A tear ran down her cheek as she said, "Thanks for listening."

Jack stepped up and wrapped his arms around her. She sobbed once against his shoulder, then said, "I'm okay."

"You were great."

"I wanted so bad to get through that without blubbering." She tightened her arms around him. "I know you two never got along, and I know he was as crooked as they come, but never forget: You're here today because of him."

Gia had never known the Tom Jack had known, and so she had a soft spot in her heart for him. Jack could have said that if not for Tom's reckless treasure hunt, the Lilitongue of Gefreda would have remained on the ocean floor where it couldn't threaten anyone's life, and no heroics would have been necessary.

But he kept that to himself.

Gia lifted her head and raised her voice. "And now, everyone, Jack has a few words to say."

"You rat," he whispered.

"Just holding you to your earlier promise."

"I hate you."

"No, you love me."

"True, true," he said. "With all my heart for all my life."

She smiled. "There you go." She pointed to the piano. "And there you go."

Well, he had promised. Sort of.

Jack released her and stepped to the piano where he held up the used Balvenie bottle.

"This belonged to Tom. It sat between us during our last moments together."

Last because Tom had dosed it with a roofie and fed Jack a couple of snorts to put him to sleep. Later on, it hadn't felt right to toss out the bottle, so he'd used Krazy Glue on the cork to make sure no one could sample it by mistake.

Jack lowered Tom's bottle and raised the fresh one.

"Even if you don't like Scotch—and you should know this is an especially tasty single malt—I think you can tolerate a wee dram for a toast."

He passed the jiggers around, then uncorked the bottle and poured everyone a shot while Gia handed Vicky a jigger of apple juice.

Jack raised his glass. "To Brother Tom. Wherever you may be."

Restless, Jack wandered the first floor.

Julio and Weezy stood in a corner in animated conversation as they munched the sandwiches Gia had made. And Eddie was . . . where was Eddie? Furthermore, where was Vicky?

He ran into Gia in the hall and asked.

"With Abe, of course. He brought cookies."

Jack laughed. "Of course he did. Let's go see."

"Look, Mom!" Vicky said, holding up a crescent pastry as Jack and Gia entered the antiquated kitchen. "Rugalah!"

She and Abe sat at the round oak table with a tray of chocolatey cookies between them. Abe's ample belly pressed against the rim of the table. Crumbs speckled his perpetual half-sleeve white shirt.

"Ruge*lach*," Abe said. "End it like you've got a sesame seed from a bagel in your throat and you're clearing it."

"Ruge*lach!*" she said, in perfect imitation, then took another bite. "Mmmmm, so good. I'm gonna learn to make these. Abe, you gotta give me the recipe."

Maybe she didn't realize Abe's expertise with food preparation was limited to ordering take-out. He'd undoubtedly bought these at a bakery on his way over.

Abe looked up at Gia. "For a mother, this little one's got a Midwestern Italian Catholic; for a father, a British WASP. So, how'd she wind up such a yentaleh?"

"She's a changeling, what else?" Gia said, not missing a beat as she dropped into Abe's accent. "Nu? Cookies you bring to my house? What, my dessert's not good enough for you?"

"Ah hah!" Abe said. "You've just answered my yenta question. And not to worry. Whatever dessert you have planned, I'll eat as well."

No doubt about that, Jack thought as he stepped over to where Eddie leaned against the wall under the old Regulator clock. He held a beer in one hand, a turkey sandwich in the other. A trim, athletic-looking guy with longish sandy hair, wearing a herringbone sport coat. He'd been fairly chunky as a kid when he and Jack had spent hours playing *Pole Position* on his Atari 5200 back in Johnson, NJ.

"Thanks again for coming, Eddie."

He swallowed and said, "Wouldn't miss it. Sorry about Tom. I don't remember him that well."

No memories of Tom. Jack understood. Tom had been ten years older, already in law school when they were entering high school, with nothing but disdain for Jack and his "little friends."

"I remember your father, though. Great guy."

"Yeah, he was."

"Did he introduce you to that Scotch? I want to take a picture of the label and find me a bottle."

"No, that was Uncle Stu. Say, um, are you and Weezy still on the outs?"

"I'm fine. She's on the outs with me. Kind of afraid to be in the same room with her. Afraid she'll go off on me again."

"I'll talk to her."

Mediating wasn't exactly Jack's thing, but he'd known these two so long . . .

Julio entered the kitchen then, saying he had to get back to the bar. He said his good-byes and Jack walked him to the door. Then he approached Weezy, still in the living room.

His best friend during his pre-teen and early teen years, Weezy Connell had disappeared from his life for decades, only to reappear last summer. She'd gained weight in the interim, going from the skinny Goth kid from the Jersey Pinelands to a chubby nerd in baggy sweat suits. She'd slimmed down again in the ensuing months, now all Christmasy in a white sweater and red-and-green kilt, wearing her dark hair longer than he'd ever seen it. No makeup. She'd long ago ditched the heavy eyeliner that had been her trademark as a teen.

"You still ticked at Eddie?"

"He joined the Septimus Order. Of course I'm still ticked at him. I'll be ticked at him forever."

"You've got to get over this, Weez. He had no idea what they're up to. He thought it was like the Elks or Linked-In, or the Royal Order of Raccoons."

He saw a smile struggle to break through and fail.

"Don't make light of it, Jack. They were out to kill me."

"But Eddie wasn't."

"He let them *brand* him!"

Jack could see he wasn't getting anywhere on this tack. He spotted his father's picture on the piano.

"See that guy there," he said, pointing. "I spent years and years avoiding him as much as I could." Jack had been sure his father would never understand or accept his lifestyle—"urban mercenary" was how someone had put it. How do you explain that to a straight-laced accountant? "And then we reconnected and I found out we could have an adult relationship—you know, as equals, something beyond the father-son dynamic. We bonded in Florida, and I enjoyed being with him down there. So last December I invited him up for the Christmas season."

Jack paused and swallowed.

"You okay?" Weezy said.

He'd been playing the *if-only* game ever since it happened: If only he hadn't invited Dad, he wouldn't have been in the line of fire at the airport . . . still be alive. He put the thought aside. His life already had a long-enough string of if-only moments.

He cleared his throat. "Yeah, fine. Anyway, I was looking forward to spending more time with him. And then"—he snapped his fingers—"gone. And now my greatest regret is all the time I wasted avoiding him."

She looked away. "I hear you. I know what you're saying and I appreciate it. But I'm still just too . . . pissed."

"You found out this summer. It'll be winter in a couple of days. When—?"

She held up a hand. "Don't push, Jack. Okay? You ought to know I don't let things go very easily."

He had to smile. "If at all."

Part of her bipolar thing, he guessed. She'd always been like that.

"I'll get past this. I'm just not there yet. Just like you're not there yet with your own brother."

Ouch. Was it so obvious?

"Touché."

"Gotta go."

Jack followed her into the foyer where she grabbed her coat off its hook and shrugged into it.

"Weez ..."

"Tell Gia I'm sorry but I had to leave suddenly."

And then she was out the door.

Jeez, could that have gone worse? His future as a mediator was not looking bright.

4

Tier Hill stood in a closet and observed the confrontation through a crack in the door. His client, Roland Apfel, had stipulated this when he called him over: *You will see and not be seen. Observe and nothing more.*

Tier understood. The woman was his quarry and it would complicate his job if she knew what he looked like.

Had to concentrate . . . usually no problem, but after that episode in Central Park on his way over . . . that sound. Though it no longer rang in his ears, it continued to boom in his mind. What did it mean? Some sort of PTSD from Afghanistan? A brain tumor? A—

Stop. You're on the job. Do it.

He focused through the door crack.

The woman he was to follow—for he earned his living following people—stood slim and straight before Roland, almost haughty in her demeanor. Her hair was as black as that of Tier's Mohawk kin, yet her eyes were pale amber. She seemed about his age—mid-thirties, he guessed—and he found her quite attractive. Attractive and yet . . . untouchable. He couldn't explain that last, but something within warned that he'd be wise to keep this woman at arm's length.

Roland cleared his throat, a rough, phlegmy sound, and spoke in a gravelly voice. "Madame de Medici . . . " Another throat clearing, brief this time; he tended to do it after every sentence. "We meet again."

"Bonham's, wasn't it?" She, on the other hand, spoke in a clear, calm, oddly accented voice. "You outbid me, I believe."

A throat clearing. "But not until after you'd bid up the price to an extraordinary level."

She shrugged. "I wanted it as a companion to another piece in my collection, but not that badly. *C'est la guerre.* But let's get to the point, shall we? I agreed to this meeting only because I wish personally to impress upon you that I do not have the Bagaq and to implore you to stop harassing me about it."

Tier weighed her words. The content was a plea, but her tone was defiant. Almost a warning. And he had not the slightest doubt she was lying. An excellent liar, no question there, but he could tell.

His interest stirred.

Nine years now as a private investigator and he'd found himself more than ready to hang it up and try something else. Tracking was his specialty, and he was sick of exposing tawdry trysts between people who, first off, should know better, and who, even worse, were unbearably clumsy at hiding their movements. Challenges had all but disappeared. He was running on empty and operating by rote.

He regretted sleeping through high school, he regretted joining the Army and his tours in Afghanistan. But his life experiences had gained him entry to John Jay and he was starting there in the spring semester, aiming for a criminal justice degree. No more sneaking around with a camera. No more hiding in closets and . . . wait: No more being *immured* in closets.

Got it!

Back to the matter at hand: At least this client was proving different from most. Roland Apfel wanted a woman tracked, yes, but not to reveal an infidelity. Instead, he wanted to learn where she'd hidden an ancient artifact he coveted and claimed she'd stolen. Something known as the *Bagaq*, whatever that was.

Judging from Roland's living room, he'd spent most of his life coveting artifacts—and acquiring them. The space was packed floor to ceiling with a dizzying array of antiquities from all over the world. "Diverse" might describe it, if one were in a generous mood. Tier thought "fucking mess" fit it better. He had little doubt the rest of the mansion was crammed to the same degree.

Yes, mansion. Tier didn't know how else to describe the five-story limestone monstrosity with a green copper top floor just a stone's throw east of Fifth Avenue and Central Park.

He didn't know how Roland planned to take possession of this Bagaq after Tier located it. Better not to know, better not to concern himself with those things. He'd agreed only to find it. His buck stopped there.

Tier could see that Roland was not a well man. He didn't know what ailed him, but he was totally bald and emaciated. He slumped with his skinny ass perched on a thronelike chair while an IV ran into his left arm. The nurses who usually hovered about like moths around a flame had been dismissed for this tête-à-tête.

The fourth person in the room—"person" being loosely applied but Tier was feeling generous—was Roland's right-hand gopher, a vicious little thug named Albert Poncia standing off to the side in a shadowed corner. Tier had met him once before and had disliked him on sight; then Poncia had opened his mouth and *dislike* had graduated to *despise.*

Roland cleared his throat at length again. "Madame de Medici, why must we do this dance? I know you have it. You know that I know that you stole it. But I'll let that pass. All I want to do is borrow it. I've made that quite clear, haven't I? I don't want to steal it back from you. I simply want to borrow it for one day, and then you can have it. After that, it's yours for as long as you want it. That's all I ask. Why can't you understand that?"

Wait . . . what was this? *One day?* What was he going to do with whatever it was for one day?

Interesting. Tier had known Roland was rich and eccentric, but this made no sense.

"I understand you perfectly, Mister Apfel. Why do you not understand me? I. Do. Not. Have. The. Bagaq."

"Let me handle the lying bitch," Poncia said through a snarl.

He stood about five-ten and had a penguin body. His plaid suit only emphasized the peculiarity of his shape.

Roland held up a hand. "Be calm, Albert. Madame is here at our invitation. We must be polite."

Spoken like a parent to an unruly child. Tier still hadn't determined

Poncia's place in the household. Gopher, yes. Perhaps pit bull too?

Roland leaned toward Madame de Medici. "And you, Madame, should not take me for a fool. I purchased the Bagaq in a lot in Teheran. I know it arrived by freighter from Iran last Tuesday. I know exactly what container and what warehouse it landed in. Security footage shows a turbaned man entering and leaving that warehouse on the night the shipment arrived. He carried something to a car and drove off. In the morning the crate was opened and the Bagaq was gone. Closer inspection revealed tampering."

She appeared unfazed. "I am sorry for your loss, Mister Apfel, but I assure you that whomever you saw on this footage has no connection to me."

"The man on the video wore a Sikh turban, exactly like your driver. The car he drove was a black Maybach S-650, with a curtained rear compartment. Exactly like the one you own."

Damning evidence, even if circumstantial. But the lady appeared unperturbed.

"Certainly, in this city of so many millionaires and billionaires, there is another such car."

"Not belonging to one possessed of such a ravenous appetite for antiquities as you."

She lifted her chin. "I must say I am insulted at your implication that I would be involved in the theft of a rare antiquity."

Hardly an *implication*, lady, Tier thought. Sounded more like a flat-out accusation.

And what was up with arriving at a robbery in a Maybach and sending a Sikh in to do the deed? She had to know the area was monitored—the whole damn city was under surveillance. Had she been taunting Roland? Purposely getting in his face? Sure looked that way.

"And further insulted," she added, looking Tier's way, "by the fact that you have someone spying on me from that closet."

Tier quickly stepped back from the crack in the door. How could she know? He'd hidden himself in here well before her arrival.

"Your paranoia is unwarranted," Roland said, his voice slowly rising toward a hoarse scream. "And as for the Bagaq, it is not merely *rare*, Madame, it is *one of a kind* and *priceless*! Especially to someone such as I with pancreatic cancer! But you know all that!"

So, that was his problem.

Tier made a mental note to get paid in advance.

"I do know all that," she said. "I even know the meaning of the word *bagaq*. Do you?"

"No, I do not. But not for not trying. The meaning seems lost in the mists of time. Would you care to enlighten me?"

"Not under these circumstances. But I will say it's from the Old Tongue. Pray you do not have the misfortune of learning the meaning first hand."

Roland's laugh degenerated into a cough. "You must take me for an idiot. The Old Tongue is a myth. And as for any 'misfortune' attached to the Bagaq, I'll take that risk. But first I must acquire it."

"I am afraid I can't help you there, since I do *not* know where it is. I–" Her attention seemed drawn to her left. "What have we here?"

She approached a six-inch metal tumbler on a pedestal and examined it closely, her face only inches from its rim.

"Bronze," Roland said. "From–"

"The valley of Gohar Rud. I recognize it. How much to part with it?"

"Why do you want it?"

"Sentimental value." She pointed to the rim. "See that dent there? That's because of me."

Roland's voice rose an octave. "What?"

"It belonged to a local chieftain with delusions of grandeur. He declared me his 'queen,' which meant he could rape me any time he pleased. When the opportunity presented itself, I poisoned him. When he realized it he threw the cup at me. He missed, and thus the dent." She smiled. "He died horribly."

After a long pause, Roland said, "You realize, don't you, that that cup is three thousand years old."

Three thousand? She had to be putting him on. Yet she spoke so off-handedly.

"Seems like yesterday. How much?"

"It's not for sale."

A sly look. "Would you trade it for the Bagaq?"

Roland raised a fist. "I knew you had it! The cup for the Bagaq? Done!"

"Except I don't have the Bagaq."

"Then why–?"

"Well, if you're willing to trade, that means the cup is for sale. Now we can start negotiating."

His voice rose to a scream. "You try my patience, Madame! I've tried reason. Must I resort to extreme methods?"

"So, you're threatening me?"

"Take that any way you wish. But rest assured that I *will* have the Bagaq."

"I can only take that as a threat." She started to turn away. "So, on that note–"

Poncia leaped forward and grabbed her arm. "No, you don't, bitch!"

She reacted quickly and–more importantly–decisively, grabbing Poncia's little finger and using it to lever his hand off her arm.

Tier reflexively reached for the doorknob to go out there and pull Poncia off her but she glanced his way again–this time with a quick, hard look that stopped him cold. He wasn't sure if it said *Don't even think about it* or *I've got this* or a combo of both. Whatever. He held back.

All this occurred in the heartbeat before she gave Poncia's finger a vicious twist. He cried out and dropped to a knee as the tendons and ligaments popped. When he tried to rise, she gave it another twist. He stayed on his knees and whimpered.

"Do not ever touch me," she said in the same calm, even tone as before. "Not. Ever."

She released him and strode from the room.

Wow, Tier thought as he stepped from the closet and approached Roland. I think I'm in love.

"Thanks for the help, Hill," Poncia said, still on his knees, his face gone all pasty and sweaty.

"You seemed to have the matter in hand."

"Oh, fine." He struggled to his feet. "He's a comedian now."

"You want serious?" Tier said. "Okay: I don't manhandle women. Neither should you and–judging by what we all just witnessed–especially not that one."

"She took me by surprise!"

"Enough!" Roland said. He motioned Tier closer. "Follow her. Follow her night and day, Mister Hill."

His was a one-man operation, so that wasn't going to happen, but he had options.

"You didn't tell me she was crazy."

"What do you mean?"

"That story about the cup. Does she really think she's three thousand years old?"

"She made that up to taunt me."

"Pretty convincing ad lib."

"Just follow her, Mister Hill."

"Might help to know a little about her."

"I've no doubt you have resources for that. I can tell you that she has a midtown apartment, but that's just one of her addresses. I'm sure she keeps her treasures elsewhere. I know beyond a doubt that she stole the Bagaq. Now it's just a matter of finding where she's keeping it."

"Might also help if I knew what this thing looked like."

Roland had a tablet on his lap. He lit it up and started swiping at the screen. After half a minute or so he turned it toward Tier.

"That's what you're looking for. The seller photographed it in Iran just before he packed it for shipment."

"You're sure he packed it?"

"Absolutely. I've had many dealings with him—a decades-long relationship. He's not going to jeopardize that. Especially since I have enough on him to get him in deep trouble with his government."

"But you *did* say it was priceless."

"Only to the rare person who knows its history. I happen to be one of them. Madame de Medici is another."

The photo showed a wrinkled metallic ovoid—bronze, judging by its color—running five inches along its long axis according to the ruler next to it. A bronzed avocado.

All this angst over a wrinkly lump of metal? Tier wondered if the tumor had spread to Roland's brain and made him crazy.

"Doesn't look like much."

"It and its six kin rarely do."

"There's seven of them? I thought you said it was one of a kind. If there's six more like this—"

He shook his head. "Seven related objects, no two looking the same, all with different purposes."

"And what's this one's purpose?"

Roland turned off the tablet. "Not your concern. Your only concern is to locate it."

Tier had a few more questions. Obvious ones, like, how old was it, who made it, and the most important: Had anyone ever seen it perform its purpose? But he had quarry to track.

"One more thing. Do you have that surveillance video handy?"

"Yes, why?"

"I want to get the license plate number off her car."

"I've already confirmed that it was hers."

"Fine, but I may want to make an adjustment to her car and need to make sure I've got the right one."

A slow nod. "I see. Interesting. I'll text you the number."

"Great. I'd better get moving."

"Yeah," Poncia said, still cradling his left hand. "Don't want to lose her."

No chance of that, fat boy.

In the Army, as a scout with Mohawk blood, Tier became his unit's go-to guy when it came to tracking. He'd tracked Taliban fuckers through their own mountains and always found their caves. He figured he could handle a pretty woman in Midtown Manhattan.

5

Jack stood outside Glaeken's building on Central Park West—*literally* his building—and gazed up at the one illuminated window on the eighth floor. Most of the windows were dark because the building was mostly empty. Glaeken wanted it that way. He was very choosy about his neighbors.

Jack had walked back from Gia's so he could drop in on the occupant of that eighth-floor apartment, as he did from time to time.

The Lady lived here . . . had since August when she'd been severely damaged. Rasalom and his minions in the Septimus Order had tried to destroy her. Her dog, her constant companion, had vanished defending her, but her enemies had succeeded in wounding her—severely—along with the Noosphere that fed her. The Lady persisted but in a crippled state, and the dog was gone. Jack missed the dog.

No doorman, so he stepped through the heavy glass double doors into the vestibule. The name *G. Veilleur* sat atop the spotty occupant list. Only fitting since he occupied the penthouse. Jack pressed the button and didn't have to wait long before the heavy steel inner door buzzed open.

Glaeken's voice came through the speaker. *"Anything important, Jack? We don't have a meeting scheduled."*

No, not a meeting—Weezy would have been included then.

"Just passing by and thought I'd drop in on the Lady."

"I'll join you."

He took the elevator up to the eighth floor and didn't knock on her apartment door. She never locked it. No reason. She didn't need to bathe or change her clothes, so no risk of catching her in a state of dishabille. Couldn't interrupt her at a meal because she didn't eat.

He found her where he knew she'd be, where she spent her days and nights, staring out one of the windows at the world she could no longer be a part of.

At least she could stand now. After the attempt on her life this past summer she'd been so weak she needed a wheelchair.

She used to be able to change her appearance in an eye blink—age, hair, face, race, weight, clothing. Now she was frozen as a thin old woman, able to change style of clothing and nothing more.

"Jack," she said without turning as he entered. "It's been a while."

They went back a long ways, Jack and the Lady. He'd first met her in his teens when she'd posed as Mrs. Clevenger. Everyone in his hometown—well, at least all the kids—thought she was a witch. From then on, she'd popped in and out of his life in different guises. For most of that life he'd had no clue, and hadn't learned until recently that all those women with dogs he'd met along the way were the same being: the Lady, the avatar of the Noosphere, the beacon to the multiverse that here dwelled sapience.

But she'd been so deeply injured last summer. It pained him to see her in this damaged state.

"Yeah, well. It's the holiday season. Christmas will be here Thursday."

He knew the holidays meant nothing to her, but she appreciated how important they were to humans.

"Busy buying gifts, I suppose?"

Only for Gia—she picked out the gifts he'd give Vicky on Christmas morning. All except one. An elderly gent's arrival cut off his reply.

"Good evening, Jack."

"Hey, G."

His name was Glaeken and Jack wasn't sure exactly how many thousands of years he'd been alive. These days he went by the name

Gaston Veilleur, and liked to be referred to simply as Veilleur. He'd been aging, although slowly, since World War Two and now looked to be in his eighties, with gray hair, a craggy face, and a cane. Still a big guy, bigger than Jack, still cut an imposing figure.

Glaeken seated himself at the western end of the heavy oblong table of dark-stained oak that dominated the room.

"To what do we owe the pleasure?" he said.

The Lady took her place at the eastern end. Jack dropped into a chair halfway between them.

"Just wondering what's up."

"The Otherness and its minions are seemingly quiescent," Glaeken said.

"I thought they were never quiescent."

Glaeken gave a half smile. "That is why I said 'seemingly.'"

"We should check the signals," the Lady said.

Glaeken nodded. "I have Burbank's reports but I confess I've neglected them."

In the past Jack had had run-ins with the signals—streams of electromagnetic energy beaming at different frequencies into the Earth from somewhere out in the void—but they'd remained simply one more thing in the cosmos beyond his comprehension until he'd met Glaeken and the lady. He still didn't pay them much mind, and maybe that was just another facet of his general loss of interest. Decades ago a fellow named Burbank in a penthouse just down the street had taken it upon himself to monitor them and send out reports. Their frequencies were somehow significant, but Jack left those concerns to Glaeken.

Glaeken said, "They're planning something—you can count on that—but obviously not ready to move yet."

"And so, we do nothing but wait?"

"The three of us are hardly equipped to go on the attack."

"I am. I can track down that son of bitch and—"

Glaeken held up a hand. "You gave your word, remember?"

Glaeken had extracted a promise from Jack not to make any moves against Rasalom. The only thing holding back Rasalom and the Otherness these days was the belief that Glaeken was still a powerful immortal, lying in wait, watching for them to make a misstep so he could pounce.

Glaeken said he couldn't risk them learning the truth.

Jack wanted to do the pouncing. But Glaeken feared that if Jack failed in an attempt to take out Rasalom, he might wonder why Glaeken hadn't been involved. And then he might learn that his ancient nemesis was nowadays simply an old mortal man who was no longer a threat to him. And then the Otherness would have no further reason to hold back. The end would begin.

And so, Jack would honor his promise, even though he now thought he'd made a mistake in agreeing. He didn't have a defensive mindset. His default was to get out there and make things happen. These two, however, seemed content to wait for Rasalom and the Otherness and the Septimus Order that served them to make the next move.

They discussed mundane matters—Gia, Vicky, Glaeken's ailing wife, Magda. Jack described the memorial service and how Weezy was still at odds with her brother.

Finally, Jack had had enough and said good bye. Sitting there with Glaeken and the Lady while they did nothing and planned nothing ...

It made him crazy.

6

Tier had had a bad moment following the Medici gal because she chose a route through Central Park, right along the edge of the Sheep Meadow. If that tone sounded again, he'd be incapacitated. For much of the trip he'd wondered if she knew about the sound and its effect on him. Was that why she chose the route? The question was answered when he saw her enter the Allard on Central Park West: She'd simply taken the most direct path home.

The Allard . . . of all places. His grandfather had helped build it back in the late 1920s. Not quite as well known as the San Remo or the Dakota–grandpa had worked on the San Remo as well–but still pretty damn impressive. He remembered his grandfather hinting that it held secrets in its foundation. He'd always play coy with the details, but Tier assumed he meant gangsters from the Roaring Twenties had found their final resting place in the concrete.

Both his father and grandfather had been skywalkers, making the skyscrapers possible by walking the high steel and riveting the girders into place. But grandpa had been gone by the time the Trade Towers went down, and Dad had developed cancer from working among the ruins to help rebuild the Trade Center.

As much as Tier had wanted to continue his family's skywalker tradition, he couldn't handle the heights. His father hadn't minded, hadn't insisted Tier follow in his footsteps. He knew skywalkers weren't immune to fatal falls. His big piece of advice had always been, *Find your place.*

Tier had never been sure where his place might be. He would have loved earning the skywalker designation, despite the inevitable *Star Wars* references it sparked. Better than being called an "Indian." As far as he was concerned, Indians wore Nehru jackets and saris and ate curry. Skywalkers kicked ass.

Find your place, Dad kept saying. *Find your place.*

At least Dad had never held his mother's death against him.

Both Tier and his mother had died during childbirth. The doctors had been able to bring Tier back, but not his mother. His grandmother always told him that coming back from the dead made him special. As far as he was concerned, the only thing it made him was halfway to being an orphan. But she insisted that being stillborn granted gifts. And maybe it did. He turned out to be one hell of a hunter, able to sneak up on game without its being aware—always close enough for an easy kill shot. Grandma called it "the Stealth."

If he had such a thing—and his experience in Afghanistan tended to bear out that he did—it had suffered an epic fail earlier when the Medici gal had sussed out his presence in the closet.

Whatever.

Somehow, through a circuitous route via the US Army, he'd wound up in the detective biz. A biz he'd be leaving soon.

But tonight, it had placed him outside the Allard's garage door where he was pretending to enjoy a cigarette. As much as he hated the smell of tobacco smoke, he had to admit the cancer sticks made great props. People see a guy standing alone, doing nothing, they wonder what he's up to. But if the guy's sucking on a ciggie, they assume he's on a break and he can't smoke inside.

The Allard's underground garage opened onto the side street. At 5:30—about an hour or so after sundown—he'd wandered from the front entrance on Central Park West over to the side where he'd watched the metal door roll up and down as the tenants' drivers or the tenants themselves pulled in and out. The door rolled up in response to a clicker in the cars and remaining open for a fixed interval.

During one of those intervals he slipped inside and down the ramp. The single level was packed with cars. Not enough spaces for every apartment, so he assumed each commanded a primo rental fee. He found the Medici Maybach—only one in evidence and its plate matched the number Roland had texted—parked next to a huge Hummer.

Tier opened his messenger bag where he always kept a couple-three GPS transmitters handy for when he was following a car. The models he used had a one kilometer range, more than enough for his purposes. Attaching one to a vehicle enabled him to allow extra distance between himself and the car he was tailing. Never a good thing to be a constant presence in the quarry's rearview mirror.

But he didn't need one of those now. He pulled out a combination GPS recorder / tracker beacon and attached it inside the rear bumper. This way he could leave the site and still keep track of where the Maybach was, as well as where it had been.

Now to head home to his apartment and do some in-depth back-grounding on the mysterious Madame de Medici.

7

Out on Central Park West again, Jack took in a few deep, bracing breaths of the cooling air and crossed over to Central Park where he stood at the wall, staring toward the Sheep meadow.

Glaeken and the lady . . . was their inertia contagious? Was that why he'd been turning down fixes? Or was he simply burned out? Whatever the cause, he'd been feeling dead inside. Taking on some work might make a difference or it might not. Maybe he was too far down to break the surface again.

He could think of only one way to find out.

He called Burkes, who must have had Jack's number programed because he answered the phone with his name.

"Jack, Jack, Jack. So, you've changed yer mind and yer gonna take the job, are you?"

"Yeah, why not."

Burkes barked a laugh. *"Now there's enthusiasm for you! I told them you weren't cheap, and they didn't seem to mind. Warned them you tended to leave collateral damage and were a cheeky bastart as well."*

"First time I've ever been called 'cheeky.'" He wasn't even sure what that meant. "Okay, so you told them about me, what can you tell me about them?"

Jack knew Burkes well enough to be certain he wouldn't bring anyone around without first doing a little probing. Not that it really mattered. Kusum Bahkti had been exactly who he said he was—a member of India's UN delegation. But that hadn't prevented him from being one of the looniest and most dangerous human beings Jack had ever met.

"They told me they work for the Bronx Zoo."

"Both of them?"

"Both. I checked and they're listed there as employees. One's a zoologist and the other's got a doctorate in genetics."

"Brainy types. I wonder who they're looking for."

"You'll have to talk to them to find out. Wouldn't tell me anything until I agreed to search—which I didn't. Want me to set up a meet?"

"Better if I do it. I'll let you know the when and where and you can join us."

"Nae good on that. They won't want me. Apparently, the matter is super sensitive and for your ears only—should you agree to take the job."

Why the drama? Jack wondered as the *Mission Impossible* theme started playing in his head.

He hated drama.

"Who's missing? Someone from the zoo? Marty the Mandrill?"

"Damned to bloody hell if I know."

"Give me the number and tell them I'll call them early tomorrow."

"Will do."

Yeah, he needed to get back in the saddle again.

SATURDAY—DECEMBER 20

1

The rising sun was attempting a Manhattanhenge when Tier stopped by the Allard's garage door and accessed the GS recorder on the Medici gal's Maybach. No movement during the night.

Next step was to grab a coffee and a bagel from the pushcart down near Columbus Avenue, and then set up shop across Central Park West from the front entrance. Half sitting, half leaning on the low wall that divided Central Park from the sidewalk, he sipped coffee and pretended to smoke another cigarette as camouflage. No matter what the weather—and this was one frigid morning—smokers had to have their ciggies.

He'd chained his Honda Forza to the bicycle rack a dozen feet away. After many trials and even more errors, he'd decided a motor scooter was the best way to tail a car in the city. He rarely had to worry about getting trapped behind stopped cars at lights, and the Forza could roll up to 95 mph if necessary. Best of all, the law required him to wear a helmet, so he made sure his was equipped with a heavily tinted, identity-concealing visor.

The helmet had become a super-important accessory. Yeah, concealing your features from your quarry was always important but, because of his heritage, especially so in Tier's case. His pure-blood Mohawk features—the black hair, the black eyes, the reddish skin, the high cheek bones, and hawk nose—tended to leave an impression. One of his Army buds had said he looked like a cigar-store Indian. Tier hadn't taken offense—truth is true.

He checked his email and saw that his Word of the Day had arrived:

Grandiose
Adjective—gran-dee-OHSS
1: characterized by affectation of grandeur
or splendor or by absurd exaggeration
2: impressive because of uncommon
largeness, scope, effect, or grandeur

Not too bad. He'd find a way to use that by the end of the day.

As promised by the weatherfolk, the Arctic Express had arrived. The average New Yorker might consider this a frigid morning, but Tier hailed from Kahnawake on the St. Lawrence River in Quebec. And prior to moving here he'd done a couple of tours in the frozen mountains of Afghanistan. Compared to them, today was positively balmy. So, he found it no chore to hang out along this stretch of Central Park West.

Besides, he loved the architecture, especially the Allard. His appreciation went beyond the family connection. A graceful twelve-story art deco tower, capped with an impressive, heavy-duty antenna, jutted from the roof of the blocky, sixteen-story base. The tower held the primo apartments, each taking up the whole floor with a three-hundred-sixty-degree view of the city.

So much for the good part about the Allard. The bad part was its location: overlooking the Sheep Meadow. He'd found himself experiencing a sort of adverse reaction to that simple open field. He never wanted to hear that sound again—at least not close up like yesterday.

Get over it. You're on hound dog duty. Eyes open, nose to the wind.

He checked himself out. Had he forgotten anything? Part of his line of work was being unobtrusive. So, he kept his hair short and dressed like the average white dude—khakis, LL Bean coat, work boots, knit cap. But still he got stares. Add the ruddy complexion to the cheek bones and nose and he stood out like, well, a classic cigar-store Indian.

Thus the cycle helmet whenever he could make it work. A chore sometimes, but part of the game.

His gaze roamed the façade of the Allard, trying to guess which apartment belonged to Madame de Medici. Had to have monster bucks even to think of living there. He wondered where she got her money and if she owned one of the tower apartments or just rented. The view … an apartment with a city view wherever you looked had to be something else.

No, wait. It had to be *grandiose*.

Yes! Not yet 9 a.m. and he'd already found a use for it. Gonna be a good day. He could tell.

At least he hoped so. This Medici gal was not his typical quarry. He subscribed to a number of in-depth criminal databases and dark web search engines that could ferret out damn near anything about anybody. But his searches for Madame de Medici had come up pretty much blank.

Considering how he didn't know her date of birth, her place of birth, not even her first name—unless it was "Madame"—he felt lucky to have found her at all. Fortunately for him she was consistent with using that unique designation and so a search for "Madame de Medici" did trigger a few hits. Very few.

Those hits revealed no direct Internet presence, but a mostly passive involvement. From all appearances she limited her web-based activities to subscribing to newsletters from Internet auction sites that specialized in Old World and Middle East antiquities and occasionally browsing their websites. Beyond that, nothing. No Facebook, no Twitter, no Instagram, no Pinterest. Her email had an AOL address. Those tended to belong to early-adopter Boomers who started using the Internet in the '90s, and she didn't look at all like a Boomer.

Tier didn't trust anyone with such a sketchy identity. He had no doubt she'd stolen Roland's Bagaq, and he was going to find it.

All he had to do was wait.

He'd never had a problem with waiting. Waiting had been his forte as a kid when he'd go hunting deer in Kahnawake and, later on, hunting Taliban in the A. Both of those waits tended to end in death—animals in the former, human beasts in the latter. Tier didn't miss killing deer, but he did miss killing Taliban. Oh, how he'd loved killing Taliban.

Too much so, the Army had thought, the shrinks pressing him for some sort of guilt, some kind of PTSD.

Nope.

Wanted really bad for him to be suffering nightmares.

Nope.

After all, a guy with that many kills had to feel *some* guilt, didn't he?

Nope.

Would he kill again?

Nope. Not unless he came across Taliban in America.

Thoughts of the Taliban triggered memories of Lamiha.

Tier had been assigned to the Tora Bora base at first, just outside Jalalabad. While patrolling past a small village he came upon a little girl named Lamiha. Her forehead was a mass of scar tissue reaching down and into her left eye. The Taliban had intended to blind her for trying to learn to read. They'd only half succeeded.

A loner by nature, the Army was where Tier discovered how much he disliked other people. He pretty much loathed on sight everyone he'd met in his battalion. Esprit de corps? He couldn't imagine it.

But after seeing little Lamiha, he realized he didn't hate his fellow soldiers, he merely hated being with them. He reserved his hatred—nurtured it, stoked it—for the people who had scarred that child. He loathed no beings on this Earth more than the Taliban.

Which was why, when assigned to Combat Outpost Keating in Nurestan Province, not too long before they closed it down, he decided to hunt the Taliban like he'd hunted deer back home in Kahnawake.

Soldiers weren't allowed to go wandering off on their own, especially at night, but Tier would sneak off into the mountains and hunt down camps of Taliban. They never knew he was there until he opened fire.

And after they were down, he'd go from one to the other with his 1911 and send a .45 slug through the left eye of each, point blank. Then he'd leave them there to be found the next day or whenever, but not before taking a picture of the bodies with his phone. Whoever found them had to wonder about those left eye hits. It became Tier's signature.

When his superiors finally caught on to his night-tripping, they wanted to know what the hell he was doing out there. He showed them the photos.

Why the left eye coups de grâce? they wanted to know.

For Lamiha, of course.

The story got around the outpost, and the good fallout was that the guys tended to give the crazy psycho killer a wide berth, which was fine with Tier. He kept going out, but he didn't have to sneak anymore.

The Taliban may have sussed out that the left-eye assassin was operating out of Keating. Maybe that was why 300 of them overran it in 2009. But he'd shipped out by then.

He was done with all that now. These days he limited his hunting to wild game, and didn't do much of that. Though he had a carry permit, he wasn't interested in killing. Today he was hunting Roland's Bagaq. Locate and report—no more. In the process of tracking it down, he'd learn all about the mysterious Madame de Medici. And when he did, she'd be a mystery woman no more.

2

They'd said to look for a silver Honda Odyssey parked on Seventy-first Street just east of Amsterdam Avenue. Coincidentally, just a hop and a skip from where Weezy recently had rented an apartment.

He'd placed the call around noon and spoken to a guy who'd identified himself as "Dr. Hess." Jack had suggested Julio's but Hess said the information was too sensitive to risk discussing in a public place where they might be overheard. Thus, the assignation in the soccer-mom van.

By 6:30, sunset was already two hours old, leaving the windswept streets dark and cold. Jack didn't think he had anything to fear from two scientist types who hadn't known he existed until Burkes told them. And Burkes still hadn't mentioned his name. So, to these two he was just a "lad" who could get the job done.

But that didn't stop Jack from removing the Kel-Tec backup from its ankle holster and palming it. He found the van just where they'd said; he checked out the cargo area and the rear seats before tapping on the passenger window.

The guy on the other side jumped, then lowered the window an inch.

"Burkes's man?"

"That's me. Hess?"

"No, I'm Monaco."

The rear door popped and did a slow rearward slide. Jack got in and sat in the middle of the rear seat as he waited for it to reclose. Both men half turned to face him. The courtesy light was off but enough light filtered in from the street and passing cars to give him a look at their faces. Not much to see. Both clean shaven. The driver wore a wool knit hat and had a big nose. The passenger was nondescript except for his Yankees cap.

"What do we call you?" the driver said.

"Jack'll do."

"As I've already told you," said the passenger. "I'm Doctor Monaco. This is Doctor Hess."

What was it with guys with doctorates? Always wanted to be called "doctor." Was that what their mothers called them? Their wives? Their kids?

Nobody asked for Jack's surname and nobody offered to shake, all fine with Jack.

"Well, let's get to it," he said. "Burkes tells me you've got a missing person problem."

"Before we get into the specifics," Monaco said, "we must insist that what we say here be held in the strictest confidence. Can we count on that? Because loose lips sink ships."

"I'm not about to sign an NDA," Jack said. "But confidentiality goes without saying. I'm your priest and this just became my confessional."

They looked at each other, then Hess nodded.

"Good enough, I suppose," Monaco said. "Here's our problem: The missing person isn't exactly a person. It's an animal."

"Whoa! You've just wasted a lot of my time. I'm not equipped for anything like that."

He searched for the door-open button. This was total bullshit. Wait till he got hold of Burkes. He'd—

"Wait-wait-wait," Hess said. "Just hear us out."

Jack paused. He was barely equipped to find a human being and not at all to track down an animal, but he'd come this far, so why the hell not?

With a sigh he leaned back and folded his arms. "All right, but be quick about it."

Monaco said, "I'll do my best. The creature—"

"Why are you calling it a 'creature'? It's gotta fit somewhere in your zoo. Bear, wolf, lion, tiger—what is it?"

"That's just it: We don't know."

"How the hell can you not know?"

"It's something new," Hess said. "It was trapped in Manitoba, up near Hudson Bay. Nobody knows what it is. A new species, we think— we hope. We have a grant from the Museum of Natural History to study it and identify it—you know, map out its genome, work on its taxonomy. We *live* for that stuff. It was on its way from Canada to the Bronx zoo where we planned to cage it and start the testing."

Monaco took over. "Only it never made it to the Bronx. We had it tranqed—I mean, *heavily* sedated—but somehow it woke up, broke out of the transfer van, and ran like the wind."

"Well, I'm sorry for your bad luck, but this changes nothing. I'm not an animal tracker." Hell, he didn't even consider himself a people tracker. "What you want are the cops, or at the very least, animal control."

"No-no, please," Hess said. "It's a delicate matter. That's why we went to Burkes. We need help outside the usual channels. He recommended you."

"I understand that, and under different circumstances—you know, *people* circumstances—I might be your guy, but—"

"If word gets back to the museum that we've lost its specimen, our grant is toast."

"You guys aren't listening," Jack said, getting annoyed. "The discretion you need, the threat to your grant—none of that matters where I'm concerned. Because none of it makes me more capable of tracking your missing animal. It's not my thing. I wouldn't know where to begin."

"Not even if we gave you a tracking device?" Monaco said.

Okay, this was interesting . . . mildly so.

"How's that?"

"Before transport, the creature was electronically tagged."

"You mean like they do with Great Whites?"

Hess said, "Oh, no. Those SPOT tags they use on sharks are much too big; they need to be detectable from satellites. The one we used is much more compact—small enough to be inserted under the skin between its shoulder blades. The downside of that is it has a much more limited range."

Monaco reached through the space between the front seats, extended something that looked like a cellphone. "Here's the tracker."

A glowing street map of the Upper West Side occupied the screen, dotted with dozens of little pings.

"All these dots . . . ?" Jack said.

"New Yorkers love to tag their dogs," Monaco said.

"Then what good—?"

"Swipe down from the top of the screen." Jack obeyed and a list appeared. "Now tap *H3*."

When Jack did, the map reappeared, but sans dots.

"What happened?"

Hess said, "Our beastie is tagged 'H3.' Its official designation is H3730, but we call it H3."

"According to this it's not here."

"That's because it escaped in Queens," Monaco said. "You'll never get a ping at this range. But if you were driving around Queens, you'd eventually see a blip on the screen, and you'd have its location. H3 can run, but it can't hide."

"Why aren't *you* driving around Queens?"

Hess said, "Because we have jobs and we have to be on the job pretending that everything is just fine and the creature's transport has been unavoidably delayed."

"Besides," Monaco said, holding up a pistol, "we're lousy shots."

Jack reacted without thinking—the muzzle of his backup pressed against Monaco's forehead.

"Are you tired of living?"

Monaco's jaw worked soundlessly, then, "J-j-just a tranq gun—for you."

"Yeah? Hand it here." Jack took it, then leaned back to inspect the pistol. "You shouldn't wave a gun around a stranger."

Monaco's voice was hoarse. "I'll remember that."

Jack had never handled a tranquilizer pistol before. This one had a Lugerish look.

"CO-2 powered?"

"Right. We've had it hanging around the lab for years—you know, just in case. Never had to use it, so we put in a fresh gas cartridge just to be sure."

"It doesn't have much range," Hess added, "so you're going to have to get within a dozen feet or so. Tell you the truth, I'm pretty sure I'd miss within six feet. That's why we went looking for someone like you."

"Got darts?" Jack said.

"Of course."

Monaco handed over something that looked like a pub dart, but instead of vanes on the tail, it had what looked like a mini feather duster. After half a minute of experimenting Jack had it loaded and ready to fire

Monaco handed him three more, saying, "They contain a fast-acting neuromuscular agent that causes profound weakness."

"How fast?"

"Up to five minutes."

"You call that fast? An animal can cover a lot of ground in five minutes—as in charging the guy who shot it."

"It's usually quicker, but H3 might not respond quite the same as other mammals."

Well, at least they're talking about a mammal.

Hess added, "The agent in the darts acts about as fast as they come. Sedatives can take much longer. The more active the creature is after it's shot, the faster the agent will circulate and do its work. So, the farther away you are, the better. Which is why neither of us is a good choice."

Jack could buy that. Both of them looked wimpy and myopic.

Monaco said, "I suggest hitting it twice. We don't know how susceptible it'll be."

Twice?

"Swell."

Something missing here . . . a feeling these guys weren't leveling with him.

"What aren't you telling me?"

Hess looked offended. "I beg your pardon?"

"Why do I get this feeling you're leaving something out?" When they stonewalled him, he added, "Fess up or I walk."

After an exchange of glances, Monaco said, "We haven't been

able to do an in-depth evaluation of H3, but it seems to be relatively intelligent."

"Aggressive?"

"Only when provoked. The tranq dart will sting but I can't see how it will be perceived as an attack."

Jack was running a few scenarios through his head and, despite certain nagging doubts, beginning to think this job might be doable.

Hess said, "But we can't emphasize enough the importance of discretion along with a speedy resolution to the problem."

"Yeah, your grants and all that."

"More than that. H3 is a unique creature and, well, a bit unusual in appearance."

"That was my next question," Jack said. "What's it look like?"

"I was afraid you'd never ask." Monaco fiddled with his phone, then handed it to Jack. "We knew you'd need to know, so we came prepared."

Monaco had a way with the clichés. One for every occasion. Sometimes two. Jack looked at the screen, squinted, and looked again.

"What the–?"

H3 looked like a cross between a wolf and an ape.

"Yeah, we know," Monaco said. "Ugly as sin, right? If you swipe, you'll see more."

Jack swiped. Big … hairy … and not just ugly, H3 was *uuuuuuugly*.

"And no one's spotted it yet?"

"It's probably scared half to death," Hess said. "Imagine living your life in the North Woods and then escaping from a moving vehicle and finding yourself in Queens. Luckily for us it's nocturnal– does its foraging at night."

"Still," Jack said, staring at the screen, "you'd think someone would have spotted it by now."

"Apparently not. And that's our big worry: that sometime very soon it'll be spotted by a dog walker and attacked by his dog. It'll defend itself–much to the ruination of the pet–and that's when the shit will hit the fan. Someone will offer a reward, dead or alive, and the hunt will be on. We don't want a bunch of crazies with shotguns running it down and shooting it to pieces. We need it back *alive*."

"You said you lost it in Queens?"

"Not *we*. The rank incompetents transporting it. But yes, Queens."

Which happened to be the biggest of all the boroughs—by far.

"Can you be a little more specific?"

Monaco said, "It jumped out in a traffic jam on the Belt Parkway in the Howard Beach-Aqueduct area."

A traffic jam on the Belt—go figure. Like when wasn't the Belt jammed?

He mulled the project. A lot not to like here—especially the guys hiring him. But he needed a kick in the butt.

"Okay. Here's what I'll do. I'll take this tracker and run it around the Howard Beach-JFK-Ozone Park area, but it may be too late already."

"And maybe not. You know what they say: It ain't over till the fat lady sings."

Really? What a way with words.

"I'll give it a couple-three days. If I find your H3 and manage to tranq it, I'll call."

"Use the number Burkes gave you," Hess said. "That's mine. We'll come and pick it up."

"Fine. But if I get no hits by Monday night, I'll pull the plug and call it quits."

Jeez, now he was doing it.

"That's just two days," Monaco said. "Not enough. Keep digging and you might hit pay dirt."

"No hits means it's not there. For all we know, your H3 could already be headed back to the North Woods."

"Let's hope not," Monaco said. "Can't you start tonight?"

"I don't know those neighborhoods all that well and nighttime's not the time to learn. Even if it's nocturnal, it's got to spend the day somewhere. Besides, I got something else to do tonight. But I'll be on it early tomorrow." For Monaco's sake he added, "Early bird catches the worm, right?"

"Absolutely."

They did some business—Jack taking half his fee in advance—then he stepped out of the van and watched the door slide closed.

3

"Think he bought it?" Edward Hess said as they drove away.

Monaco shrugged. "I see no reason why he shouldn't—lock, stock, and barrel."

"I see plenty of reasons, prime among them being the whole spiel was pure bullshit."

"Yes, but it's good, carefully crafted bullshit."

Ed wasn't so sure.

"I don't know . . . he seemed a little hesitant."

"Wouldn't you be after a look at those photos? I know I would."

"Oh, they're scary, no argument there. But somehow I don't think it was the photos."

Monaco waved his hands toward the windshield. "What are you saying—or should I say, *not* saying? That we shouldn't have paid him? That we should go with someone else? Who? Beggars can't be choosers, Ed. We're between a rock and a hard place."

"I'm well aware of that. Look, I know you don't want to hear this, but I wish you hadn't given him that tranq gun."

"You're not going to start beating that dead horse again, are you?"

"H3 is better off dead—*we're* better off with it dead."

"Earth to Ed: After the years we've invested in H3, we're expected to produce results."

"We *have* results. But we're so damn dirty on this. We'd be better off if this Jack guy just killed it and we cremated the body and were done with it."

"And what do we show DoD in return for all the years they've been funding us? 'Sorry, Agent Greve. We cremated our greatest success. But you can have the ashes.'"

"We've had a whole string of failures. H3 would be just another. We tell them melis is a failure."

"But it's not a failure. Okay, yeah, we've had only one success, but what a success!"

How many years? Ed thought. How many years since that first sample of melis arrived? Nineteen? Twenty? Melis—weird, scary, and miraculous at the same time. And what made it even more intriguing was the aura of mystery about it: No one would tell them where it came from. A clandestine lab? Outer space? The latter possibility no longer seemed so farfetched. The stuff was strange enough to come from another planet.

But with all that had gone down with H3, he wished he'd never heard of goddamn melis.

"You know as well as I do, we need H3 alive to keep the project going."

That was just it: Ed wasn't sure he wanted to keep the project going.

"Is that really such a good idea?"

"You know damn well we're not the only game in town. Other labs are working with melis. I want ours to be the star atop the tree. But we need H3 back for that. Burkes has a sterling reputation, and he says this Jack is skilled, discreet, and reliable."

"That could be another problem. Let's just say he finds H3 and manages to tranq it—"

"I think we can safely assume that if he finds H3, he will tranq H3. Did you see how fast he was with that gun?"

Ed would never forget. The pistol seemed to appear out of nowhere with its muzzle against Monaco's head.

"You looked like you were going to faint."

"I'm not the fainting type." He laughed. "But I did damn near crap my pants."

"My point is," Ed said, "when he tranqs H3, he'll be able to get close, maybe close enough to get suspicious."

"Let him be as suspicious as he wants. He'll call to tell us to make the pickup, we'll pay him the rest of his exorbitant fee—can you believe he has the nerve to charge that much?—and never again shall the twain meet."

"But what if he guesses the truth?"

A scoffing grunt from Monaco. "Guess the truth? No one will guess the truth, let alone that troglodyte. It's too fantastic."

Ed couldn't let it go. It haunted him at night.

"But what if, by some chance, he does?"

"Ease your mind, Ed. That guy's not smart enough to figure it out. And even if he does, so what? No one will believe it. I hardly believe it myself."

"But still . . . "

"But still *nothing*. Remember, Ed, I'm the people person here, and I've got this guy scoped out. He's tied to an old-fashioned work ethic that'll drive him to get the job done. He'll give us the two days he promised and will work his butt off to bring home the bacon. We're the ones with the doctorates here, Ed. He's just a working stiff with a special skill set. As long as he gets his money, he'll be happy as a clam and buy into whatever line we feed him. Just because he's got great street smarts doesn't mean he's got great intelligence. He's just as gullible as the next guy."

4

What a load of crap, Jack thought as he watched the Odyssey drive away along Seventy-first Street.

Had they told him one true thing?

Okay, the photos on the phone were probably real because they'd want him to be able to recognize the quarry, but the rest . . .

The beastie jumped out on the Belt Parkway during its ride from Canada to the Bronx Zoo? Do I look like an idiot?

The Belt didn't lead to the Bronx. If they were coming from the north as they'd said, they'd hit the Bronx long before the Belt.

Yeah, he'd told them he couldn't start tonight because he had something else to do: Follow those two lying bastards.

He spotted a cab and hailed it.

"See that Honda van up ahead?" he said as he slid into the rear seat. "Follow it."

He'd used cabs to follow people in the past, and could usually count on a wisecrack ranging from "Are we in a movie?" to "For reals?" This guy said nothing, just put it in gear and followed.

He always chose a Yellow Cab over Uber or Lyft. Had never used either of those because they required an account and a credit card. Even though the identities attached to his cards were bogus—bogus identities who always paid their bills—their movements would be on file somewhere. No thanks.

The Odyssey turned downtown on Broadway to Fifty-seventh, where it headed east and over the Queensboro Bridge. The city wanted everyone to call it the Ed Koch Bridge now. Koch's reign as mayor had preceded Jack's arrival in the Manhattan and so he had no opinion of the man, but for Jack the span would always be the Queensboro. It would always be a special bridge for him because it ran damn near directly over Gia's place. Some folks liked to call it the Fifty-ninth Street Bridge; the Paul Simon song had fixed that name in a lot of minds. Either was fine with Jack.

"I do not want to go too far," the driver said as they eased onto the Long Island Expressway.

Jack got it. Cabbies didn't want to drive way out on the island and have to make the trip back with no fare.

The ID up on the Plexiglas divider said he was Nakale Ejiofor.

Jack pulled out a C-note and pushed it through the opening in the divider.

"Don't worry. I'll be using you for the return trip too. Just don't lose them."

Nakale held the bill up to the windshield for a better look, then tucked it inside his shirt.

"They shall not escape me."

Goody.

5

Saturday night in Ozone Park . . . fun-fun-fun!

Not. Maybe because Christmas was less than a week away. Maybe because the temperature was like minus ninety. Maybe because –

"Ay, Artie, you see that?" Hector said, his breath steaming in the glow of the streetlight as he whacked him on the arm.

Artie rubbed the spot. Hector was a chunky couch potato but he had this thing about hitting. Always bashing Artie on one arm or the other. Wouldn't be so bad if he had Hec's padding, but he had a bony bod. No matter how much he ate, he stayed skinny.

"See what?"

"Some guy was just dumpster diving – on my street!"

"Ain't no dumpsters 'round here."

Artie wished he lived on this street rather than in his Mom's crummy apartment over on Lefferts. Not that Lefferts was terrible or anything, but here on 114th Street was so much nicer. All the houses had neat brick fronts and trimmed lawns and mulched gardens. People here took care of their places. The only bad thing was they faced one of the Aqueduct parking lots. Trees along the fence across the street blocked sight of the track. Mostly. When they was running the horses at night, the sky above the trees kinda glowed from all the lights around the track. But when no races was going on—like now—you didn't even know it was there. Quiet as a graveyard. Just like the rest of the neighborhood.

Hector whacked him again. "You know what I mean. Garbage can. He had his head stuck in one of the garbage cans."

"Where?"

"Half way down to Conduit—the one right under the streetlight there."

Tomorrow was garbage day, so big wheelie rubberized trash cans lined the curbs like soldiers on guard.

Artie squinted into the dark. "I don't see nothin'."

"That's 'cause he ain't there now. But I saw him clear as day."

"How can you do that when it's night?"

"Not funny."

Hec went to whack him again but Artie was ready and dodged. Hec was his best friend but the kid had no sense of humor. They were both eighth graders at Virgil Grissom. Artie had lots of friends—lots more than Hec—but he hung with Hec. Wasn't sure why. Guy had a permanent chip on his shoulder. Maybe he stayed around because he never knew what that chip was gonna make Hec do next.

"Prolly just some homeless guy. What's the big deal?"

Another swat, another miss. "The big deal is we don't need no homeless fuckers around here stealin' shit an' all, that's what."

"It's *garbage*, Hec. Prolly leftovers."

"Yeah, leftovers today, maybe Sara tomorrow."

Artie didn't like him bringing his little sister into this, but . . . shit.

"Where'd he go?"

"Saw him heading toward Conduit. Bet he's in the park."

The park . . . Southern Park . . . basically a fenced-in field between North Conduit and the Belt Parkway. Trees, some benches, the usual crap. The only good thing was a couple of soccer nets. Artie wasn't a big fan of watching soccer, but he liked to play.

"So, you think he's practicing penalty shots?"

Another whack, this time he didn't miss.

"Not funny."

Yeah, well, what did Hector *ever* think was funny?

He grabbed Artie's jacket and pulled him the opposite way.

"Where we goin'?" Artie said.

"Gonna let this guy know he needs to do his dumpster diving somewheres else."

He led Artie half a block to his house—brick front, brick-lined gardens, brick-lined driveway. Brick-brick-brick. Hec's dad had a thing for bricks. And for his lawn. The winter-browned grass looked like he'd trimmed it with nose-hair scissors. Big Hector was really into his house.

Artie waited outside while Hec sneaked into the garage through its side door. He returned a few minutes later.

"Let's go."

"Where?"

"The soccer field." He held up a large can of charcoal lighter fluid and sloshed the contents. "It's a cold night. Gonna warm him up."

Artie stopped in his tracks. "No way!"

"Just gonna scare him. C'mon. Tonight, we're the Neighborhood Watch."

Bad idea, Artie thought, but followed Hec anyway.

They crossed North Conduit and entered the park through the gate that was supposed to be locked at night but never was. He couldn't understand why the parks people surrounded the place with a ten-foot chain-link fence but never bothered to lock the gate. Streetlights on Conduit and traffic crawling along the Belt Parkway on the far side offered some illumination, but not a whole lot.

"Looks empty," Artie said, liking this less and less. "Let's go."

"Wait a minute now, just wait a minute. He was heading this way. He's here. Gotta be."

Artie didn't know about that. And then he saw something silhouetted against the headlights on the Belt, moving between two of the trees along the fence there. He was hoping Hec missed it—

"You see that?"

—but no such luck.

"See what?"

"C'mon. He's down there."

"Hec . . ."

His voice sounded whiney and he hated that, but this was stupid and dangerous.

Didn't stop him from following, though.

They found him crouched under a tree with a banged-up pizza box. Had somebody left some slices, or was he just eating the crusts? Poor guy . . .

"Hey, you!" Hector shouted. "You ain't allowed in here, and you ain't allowed to steal no garbage!"

None of the light from the streets or the traffic reached these shadows, so Artie couldn't tell much about him. He was bundled in a big shapeless overcoat over a hoodie sweatshirt; under the hood he wore an oversize trucker cap pulled low over his face. He smacked his lips as he chewed on what he'd found, but didn't look up.

"You hear me?" Hec said.

When the guy still didn't react, Artie said, "Come on, Hec. He ain't hurtin' nobody."

"Fuck that!"

He popped the top on the can and sprayed it at the guy, hitting his sleeve. Then he lit up one of those long-barreled butane lighters designed to look like a gun, and touched the flame to the sleeve.

The guy made some sort of growly noise and jumped up as the lighter fluid caught.

The flames lit his face.

Artie screamed like a girl, just like Hector not more than a foot away. They started to turn as one but the thing caught them by their necks—were those claws at the ends of its fingers? It smashed their heads together. Artie had heard of seeing stars—had seen it in cartoons—but never believed it happened. But now bright flashes were popping everywhere around him as his knees turned to mush and he dropped to the frozen ground.

He tried to focus, tried to get up but was too dazed. Nearby he had a foggy impression of the thing in the coat slapping at its arm, putting out the flames.

And then, beside him, Hector struggled to his knees. But before he got any further, the thing did something to his throat—like, swiped at it—and Hec started coughing and gurgling as he collapsed again.

Artie lifted his head. "Hec?"

But then the same hand slashed by his throat and he felt something tear the skin—one of the claws, maybe. He sensed something running out of him. He reached to his neck and felt a hot gush.

Not blood . . . oh, please, not blood. Not so much blood. I'll die.

Artie didn't want to die. Not with Christmas so close.

Nearby, he heard the sound of chewing—sloppy, noisy chewing, followed by grunting swallows.

Naw . . . it wasn't eating Hec. Just the pizza. It couldn't be eating Hec. Could it?

Soon Artie stopped wondering about anything.

6

Jack slumped in the backseat of the cab as the ride dragged on and on toward the east end of the island, passing signs for all sorts of–*ogues*: Patchogue and Quogue, then onto the North Fork past Aquebogue and Cutchogue until they were running out of road and island as they approached Orient Point.

Oh, crap. Were they planning to hop the ferry to Connecticut?

But Hess and Monaco turned off the road before the Cross Sound Ferry dock and parked in a marina lot.

"I drive past and come back," Nakale said.

"Good thinking."

Nakale returned him to the lot in time to see Hess and Monaco ambling toward one of the docks. A thirty-foot cruiser bobbed on its moorings, as if waiting for them. They hopped on board and it took off. Jack spotted what looked like a boat owner standing on the dock.

"Wait here," he said. "Be right back."

The fellow had cultivated an Old Salt look, with a pea coat, a sailor hat, and a silver gray old-Dutch beard that spared his upper lip. Even had a pipe.

Jack hurried up and put on a worried expression as he pointed to the retreating cruiser.

"Was that the ferry to New London?"

The man laughed. "No way. You're at the wrong dock. But you're close. It's at the end of the road, maybe five hundred feet farther on."

"Thank God! Much appreciated!" Jack turned away, then turned back. "Just curious. Where's that one go?"

"Plum Island."

Jack couldn't hide his surprise. "No shit?"

"No shit."

He'd heard stories about Plum Island, none of them good.

When he returned to the cab he said, "Home, James, and don't spare the horses."

"Excuse please. I am not James."

"Right. Back to the Big City, Nakale."

As soon as they were rolling, he called Abe.

"What do you know about Plum Island?"

"Better you should ask what I don't *know about Plum Island."*

"Okay, what *don't* you know about Plum Island?"

"Nothing. Why you ask?"

"I'm close to it—as in Orient Point—and I'm heading back to town. Wait for me. I want to talk."

"Orient Point? You've seen the Montauk Monster maybe?"

"What—hello?"

He'd hung up.

Montauk Monster?

7

Jack ignored the CLOSED sign on the front door and entered the Isher Sports Shop. He locked the door behind him and headed for the rear, navigating a narrow aisle between precariously loaded shelves. Finally, he reached Abe who sat in his customary spot behind the counter, looking like Humpty Dumpty perched on a three-legged stool. Instead of the usual newspaper—he read every paper in town—he was peering at a laptop.

"At last he arrives," he said, looking at him over the top of his reading glasses.

"Long trip in from Orient Point." He placed a six of Yuengling and a white paper bag on the scarred counter. "Besides, I stopped at Basone's first."

"Nu? Gifts he brings?"

"I figured you'd be in need of sustenance by now."

Abe withdrew a foil-wrapped bundle from the bag.

"Hot. Is this what I think it is?" He parted the foil just a crack and the odor of olive oil and garlic erupted, carried on a cloud of steam. "Yes!" He ripped open the foil to reveal a baker's dozen garlic knots. "You didn't!"

"I did."

Jack twisted the top off one of the lagers and slid it across the counter, then opened one for himself.

"But my diet." Abe stared at the steaming array as Parabellum landed on his shoulder.

Jack laughed. "Yeah, right. The See-Food diet."

"You denigrate my efforts to eschew culinary excess?"

"You know damn well I waved the white flag months ago."

He loved the guy like an uncle, but officially he'd given up on reducing his oldest friend's waistline. Years of trying had failed. Despite all Jack's pleas and exhortations, Abe ate whatever was convenient and tasty.

What he didn't say was that while the knots were heavy on carbs, the olive oil had no saturated fats. And garlic was supposed to be good for you. Or so he'd heard.

"And increased my guilt in the process."

"What guilt?"

His hand went over his heart. "You say that to a Jew? We invented guilt!"

"I thought the Irish did."

"The carefree Irish were running around their glens and moors in fur breeches while the Sanhedrin were laboring in Jerusalem to perfect the nuances of remorse and culpability."

"I'll have to take your word for it. So, what are you guilty about?"

"What else? That I might die young and leave you without guidance—rudderless and adrift in a sea of uncertainty."

"You're young?"

"In my head—like a thirty-year old."

"And in your body? Never mind. They're getting cold. And they aren't so bad for you as they look."

His fingers waggled in the air above them, as if casting a spell. "Well, maybe just one."

As a knot disappeared whole into Abe's mouth, Jack pointed to the laptop and said, "No newspapers? Switching to digital?"

Abe shook his head, unable to speak around the hot, doughy mouthful. Jack took a bite of a knot and savored the oily rush of flavor. No question, Basone's made the best garlic knots in the city.

"The papers I've read already," Abe said, wiping his hand on his shirt after a convulsive swallow. "This is to catch any breaking stories."

"And are any? Breaking, that is?"

"The usual. The mayor's got another bimbo eruption, lots of big contracts flowing to the governor's big contributors, two middle schoolers have gone missing, a bicycle hit-and-run on an old lady just up the street here but she's going to make it."

"No monster sightings in Queens?"

Jack pulled a half dozen paper napkins from the bag and dropped them on the counter. Abe ignored them, preferring his shirt. He always preferred his shirt. By day's end it served as his food diary.

"No. Why? You're expecting monsters?"

No news was good news, he supposed.

"Just making small talk while you fortify yourself before starting your dissertation on this Montauk Monster you mentioned."

"Well, maybe one more."

Abe tore off a tiny piece and offered it to Parabellum. The blue parakeet cocked his head as if considering, then grabbed it with his beak. The rest of the knot vanished into Abe's beak.

The remaining knots quickly disappeared, Jack washing down five with two beers, and Abe and Parabellum downing a total of eight along with half a bottle.

"So," Jack said as he packed up the detritus and Parabellum policed the counter of crumbs, "tell me about this Montauk Monster."

"To appreciate the Montauk Monster you must first know the secret of Plum Island. How much do you know?"

Jack shrugged. "Germ warfare . . . animal experiments . . . anthrax . . . secret labs."

"So, you know the stories already."

"No, just the words. I never listened much to the stories."

Back in the aughts—2006 or thereabouts—he'd had a run-in with a guy who'd stolen a super-deadly toxin from Plum Island. Jack had come oh-so close to not walking away from that one. It also involved one of the most dangerous women he'd ever met. Or hoped to meet.

"Plum Island," Abe said, rubbing his pudgy hands together. "Such a tale. You'll love it. First off, like a pork chop it's shaped, and maybe the size of Central Park. Just ten miles off Orient Point. After World War Two, Fort Detrick—a name you of course recognize as our biological warfare research center down in Maryland—set up a satellite lab on Plum Island. Lab 257, as it was called, and headed by Erich Traub, a Nazi brought over by the Department of Defense."

"A Nazi?" Jack said, holding back a laugh. "This sounds like something for Bad Movie Night."

Abe's expression remained grim. "I should joke about a Nazi? I don't joke about Nazis."

"Sorry. It's just that it sounds so ludicrous. I mean, who'd bring a Nazi scientist over to the US and put him in charge of animal disease research?"

He couldn't help flashing on schlock films like *Shock Waves* and *Red Snow* and *Frankenstein's Army*.

"The United States government, that's who. The program was called Operation Paperclip. It was most interested in the V2 rocket scientists, but it wasn't saying no to bio-scientists either. Look him up. Erich Traub headed the Nazi bio-weapons lab on Insel Riems in the Baltic Sea. His immediate boss was a fellow named Himmler—of him you've heard maybe? Their aim was to find a way to infect the cattle and reindeer in the Soviet Union with foot-and-mouth disease, which would have devastated the herds. So, when the US decided it should know more about that particular virus, they turned to an expert—Traub."

"You're serious?"

"Serious like a krenk. All sorts of diseases they research there, testing them on animals. They say no animal ever leaves the island, that every single one is eventually put down, but the place is beloved by birds who come and go as they please."

"Uh-oh."

"Yes. Uh-oh. How do Boy Scouts on Long Island, just a few miles from Plum Island, come down with malaria? What was the strange flu that swept through Block Island, also a few miles from Plum Island? Where do you think Lyme disease was developed?"

"Oh, no . . . "

"It's not a coincidence that the first case was discovered in Lyme, Connecticut, a mere ten miles across the Long Island Sound from Plum Island. A nothing trip for a seagull."

Jack knew that Abe had never met a conspiracy theory he didn't like, and the loopier, the better. He even had a bunker buried deep in the wilds of Pennsylvania for shelter during the inevitable apocalypse. He poo-pooed a zombie apocalypse, but he truly feared an economic meltdown. Jack was glad for him, because he knew something much worse than walking dead and runaway inflation was waiting in the wings.

"Okay," he said. "Scary as all get out, but you've been talking viruses and ticks and the like. I want to know about hideous mutations like this Montauk Monster."

"Why this sudden interest? A trip he makes to Orient Point and suddenly monsters fill his kopf."

Jack gave him a quick rundown of the scientists' story and the results of birddogging them.

"So, they lied to you," Abe said. "Such a unique occurrence with your clientele."

Yeah, pretty much par for the course.

"Tell me about it. From the pictures they showed me, I've got a bad feeling this beastie isn't from the North Woods but Plum Island instead."

Which put a whole different spin on the tracking and tranquing involved in this fix.

Abe's eyebrows oscillated. "And related to the Montauk Monster, maybe?"

"Well," Jack said, letting his growing impatience snark his tone, "maybe I could answer that question if someone would stop dancing around the subject and get around to actually telling me about it like he promised."

"All right, already." Abe fiddled with his laptop, then turned the screen toward Jack. "This is what they found on a Montauk beach in the summer of oh-eight."

"Holy crap."

A sharply focused image of a creature like Jack had never seen filled the screen. It lay on sand, well-lit by full sunlight.

"What the hell is that? It looks like some mutant creature."

"You want the story spread by officialdom and its running-dog lackeys in the press?"

"Might as well. I get the feeling I'm not going to be able to avoid it."

Abe subjected him to a long dramatic pause, then tapped the screen. "A raccoon."

"*What?*"

Jack had grown up on the edge of the Jersey Pine Barrens where raccoons had been regular visitors to the neighborhood garbage cans. Many a night he'd come out with a garbage bag to find a 'coon had ripped the lid off a can and was sifting through the contents in search of goodies. Instead of running off it would sit there and stare at him through its Beagle Boy mask, as if to say, *You looking at me?* Or *Move on, kid . . . nothing to see here. And besides, I got here first.*

Jack said, "I know raccoons and that's no raccoon. Doesn't look *anything* like a raccoon."

"They explain the differences as the result of decomposition and long immersion in salt water."

"'They'?"

"You know . . . the usual suspects. All connected one way or another to the government. Others, not so connected to the government, have maintained it's a new species of cryptid."

"Meaning . . . ?"

"A creature whose existence is questionable."

Jack pointed to the screen. "Assuming lots of people saw it on the beach, that thing's existence seems *un*questionable. Was Plum Island ever mentioned?"

"Immediately. It's only a few miles north of that beach."

"Where'd the thing wind up? Some museum?"

"The carcass disappeared."

Like an *X Files* episode . . . jeez.

"So, nobody actually got to examine it? How convenient."

Abe smiled. "Indeed. It is not at all beyond the realm of possibility that someone from Plum Island sneaked in and spirited it away."

Jack mulled all this. "So . . . you think these two scientist types have me chasing a cryptid or something?"

Abe gave one of his shrugs. "I should know?"

"In the photos they showed me it looked like a cross between a wolf and an ape. Can you cross a wolf and an ape?"

"You're asking me, a lowly shopkeeper?"

"I'm asking someone who is privy to information that bypasses normal channels, and hears whispers that no one else hears."

"This mythical person you mention has heard nothing about crossing a wolf and an ape. So, from him, the answer is *no.* But for someone on Plum Island, the answer is maybe *yes.*"

If that was the case, Jack could understand Hess and Monaco's need for secrecy. Nobody wanted to think hybrid monsters were being created just a few miles offshore.

Jack shook his head, annoyed. "They could have leveled with me. It wouldn't have scared me off."

"Not scared of an ape crossed with a wolf?"

"Okay. Maybe a little. Maybe more than a little. But I still wouldn't blab it. Not like I run a blog or a podcast or anything."

"They don't know you're not one for shmei drei, that the Sphinx is a loudmouthed yenta compared to you. Especially where your customers are concerned."

"Still, I'm curious about what they did to this cryptid I'm chasing before it got loose."

Abe said, "For all we know, Plum Island could be the Island of Doctor Moreau."

Swell.

On the ride in from Orient Point he'd been half ready to call those two and tell them to make a suppository out of their money and their tracker. But now . . . now he was intrigued.

And something dormant within was stirring.

8

The gal in the third-floor apartment had her door open and must have spotted Tier on his way upstairs. Slim, pretty, with long dark hair, her name was Laurie, or maybe Lori—he'd never seen it spelled.

"Hey," she said, smiling as she stepped out onto the landing. "I've got some people over. You're welcome to hang out if you want."

Another invitation. She must like him or something.

"Why, thank you, Laurie. I appreciate it but it's been a long day and I just need to crash."

Her smile faltered just a little. "Yeah, well, okay. But if you change your mind, the door's open."

"I'll remember. Thanks again."

He was sure she was a nice person. They'd spoken in bits and pieces in passing, and he knew she'd acquired her rent-controlled apartment just like he had: inherited it. She from her mother, he from Dad. So, they had that in common, but not much else. Not that he had anything against her, but he didn't want to get friendly with a neighbor, male or female. Get familiar and they started thinking they could drop in whenever the mood struck them just to hang out and shoot the breeze. Tier could think of few things he liked less than hanging out and shooting the breeze. He cherished his solitude.

As for romance with a neighbor? Never.

Inside his apartment he shucked his coat and the holster with the snub-nose Chief Special .38 and hung them by the door.

Dad had found the place back in 1965. The Upper West Side had been pretty crummy back in its pre-gentrification days, with lots of rent-controlled apartments. He'd moved into this West Seventy-fifth Street one-bedroom, fourth-floor walkup west of Broadway and stayed four nights a week while he worked the high steel, then he'd train up to Kahnawake Friday nights with his fellow skywalkers to spend the weekend with his family—Tier was living with his grandparents then. Early Monday mornings he'd be heading south again to NYC.

When Dad learned he had cancer, he stopped coming home. Tier moved in and lived with him the last couple years of his life, sleeping on the couch and ferrying him back and forth across town to Sloan Kettering for his chemo and radiation treatments. Toward the end, Tier built up a lot of muscle working the old guy's almost dead weight up and down those seemingly endless flights of stairs.

When Dad finally passed on, Tier learned that, as his son, he qualified to take over the apartment. The place was cramped, the building old and decrepit, the plumbing and electricity antiquated, but the rent was such a bargain, and the location so perfect, he couldn't say no.

Before Dad became incapacitated, Tier would accompany him to the Beacon Theatre—an easy walk from the apartment—to catch the Allman Brothers Band whenever they were in town. How he *loved* the Allman Brothers. Duane and Greg were gone but, wherever they were, Tier bet his father had found a way to hang out with them.

He pulled his bottle of Patron Silver from the freezer and poured himself a couple of fingers, then dropped into Dad's old La-Z-Boy and grabbed the remote.

Surprise, surprise, the NFL was running a game on a Saturday night. Probably because Thursday was Christmas. Giants vs the Redskins. Who cared?

Okay. He admitted he was frustrated.

Today's wait had proven fruitless. Madame de Medici hadn't shown her face, and her car had never left the garage. The only good news was that the Sheep Meadow had remained silent . . . as it should.

He'd made his report to the increasingly frustrated Roland who reprimanded him for not being more creative, but really, what else could he do? B&E was a last resort, though hardly feasible considering the Allard's inaccessibility. All he could do right now was watch and wait.

Was she even there? Had she somehow sneaked past him, or slipped away during the night in a cab while her car remained in the garage? At a time like this, he could use an extra hand—or set of eyes. But he shuddered at the idea of taking on a partner this late in his game. He worked best alone, at his own pace, using his own methods.

As a teen, he'd take his rifle and go hunting alone. That was what he liked best about the hunt—he did it alone. Even after he'd filled his grandparents' larder, he'd go out with his rifle and sneak up on a deer, an elk, or a moose, and dry fire. Killing wasn't the point back then, nor was the hunt. Solitude was the point.

In the A, he'd go out hunting Taliban alone, but in that circumstance, the solitude was practical. Alone, he could approach game—human and non-human—without being detected. Having someone else along would ruin that.

Same with the PI game, to some extent. But he had personal reasons as well. He'd yet to meet anyone, male or female, that he cared to spend any significant time with.

Take Laurie/Lori's gathering just below him. The music wasn't loud, but he could hear the bass notes vibrating through the floor. People hanging out and talking. Ten minutes of that and he'd be casting longing looks toward the door.

Alone was better, always better.

9

"*Hello, Jack. This is Madame de Medici calling. We've never met but I've heard of you. In fact I recommended you to Mister Chastain last spring. I have a simple job for you. Please call me back.*"

After walking back from Abe's, he'd stowed the three remaining beers in the fridge and called his voicemail service. This was the only message.

Madame de Medici . . . Jack vaguely remembered Jules Chastain mentioning the name, but not as someone who'd recommended him.

Whatever. Chastain had flown him down to New Orleans and proceeded to double-cross him. Not a great reference. However, she had said "simple work," so maybe she was worth a call back.

If one fix was good, two might be better. He called her on his current burner and she answered on the second ring.

"*Hello, Jack. Thank you for calling back.*"

She had a soft voice with a vague accent he couldn't place.

"More out of curiosity than anything else. As I recall, Jules Chastain told me he'd stolen something from you. The Sydney Necco-wafer or something."

A melodic laugh. "*Cidsev Nelesso. I'm sure you've realized by now that he was lying—just one of the many lies he told you.*"

"I heard he lost it, along with part of his arm. Know where they might be?"

"Not a clue. However, I was telling you the truth when I said I recommended you."

"And how would you know to do that?"

"My main residence these days is in New Orleans—its climate is more to my liking—but I own an apartment in Manhattan. I shift between the two. I like the contrast in cultures. Your name came up in a conversation and intrigued me."

Her voice sounded young—thirties, maybe?—and yet he sensed age, or at least experience behind it.

"What conversation might that have been?"

Another laugh. *"Come now. A woman needs her secrets. But to the point: I called because I have an object I wish to give to you for safekeeping."*

Now here was a new wrinkle. No one had ever asked him to guard an object before.

"Keeping it safe from whom or what?"

"I shall explain when we meet."

An object she wished to give him . . . which meant he wouldn't have to go someplace and stand guard over it . . . which meant it wouldn't interfere with his hunt for H3.

"Okay, I'll meet you at a place called—"

"Oh, no. I do not wish to inconvenience you. I shall bring it to your home."

"But you don't know where I live."

Only a select few—those very close to him—knew where he lived.

"Of course I do. I shall arrive at nine a.m. sharp tomorrow. Illa al-liqa."

"No, you—hello?"

Damn. First Abe, and now this gal. Everyone was hanging up on him tonight.

And how the hell did she know where he lived?

SUNDAY—DECEMBER 21

1

Morning found Tier once again leaning on the Central Park wall across from the Allard, pretending to enjoy his cigarette, with his Forza chained a dozen feet away. He'd accessed the GPS monitor on her car and it indicated the Maybach hadn't budged from the garage. If today were anything like yesterday, he'd have plenty of time to work on his Word of the Day. He'd never heard of this one, so he checked his phone again.

Spavined
Adjective -- SPAV-ind
1: affected with swelling
2: old and decrepit: over-the-hill

His high school had given him a diploma because they were as sick of him as he was of them. He'd gone straight to the army. But just because he'd practically flunked out didn't mean he was a dumbass. And the last thing he wanted to do was sound like a dumbass. So, he worked on his vocabulary. Throw out an offbeat word, use it properly, and suddenly you sounded educated. Suddenly people had respect, suddenly they were listening. That was all it took.

As for this "spavined" ... no problem. He had little doubt the passing parade of New Yorkers would produce hundreds if not thousands of spavined people. But he cut off his search before it began.

Madame de Medici had stepped out of the Allard's canopied front entrance. She'd outfitted herself for the Arctic cold with an off-white fur coat—real or faux, he couldn't tell from here—a white fur Cossack hat, and knee-high black leather boots.

Immediately he began removing the chain from this Forza, but paused when she started walking uptown.

Well, damn. He'd expected if she traveled anywhere, she'd go via her own car or a taxi. Walking hadn't been in the plan.

Oh well . . .

He donned his helmet and, sticking to the park side, began walking the Honda along the sidewalk. A bit early for brunch—wasn't that what One Percenters did on Sundays? Maybe she was just headed for coffee. Whatever, he wasn't letting her out of his sight.

But she kept walking, passing the Museum of Natural History and on up until she finally turned into the West Eighties.

Tier debated his course as he waited for the light then pushed the Forza across CPW. He'd brought the bike along just in case she changed her mind about walking and grabbed a cab.

She strolled westward along the tree-lined, brownstone-bordered street like she hadn't a care in the world. Odd attitude for someone who had to know she was in Roland's sights. Wasn't she concerned about being followed? Not from what Tier could see. She hadn't looked back once since leaving the Allard.

He waited at the corner to give her a half-block lead then followed, keeping to the opposite side of the street. He closed in on her as she waited for the crossing green at Columbus Avenue and noticed how her little triangular shoulder bag bulged as if packed full. The Bagaq would fill it like that. Could she be bopping around the city with a supposedly priceless antique in her pocketbook? Who was this lady?

She crossed Columbus and kept heading west. Where on Earth was she going?

Halfway down the new block she climbed the dozen or so steps to the front door of a brownstone and stepped inside. As he passed, he saw her pressing a button on the vestibule wall.

Tier kept walking.

Now what? This was a residential street. The cigarette-break ploy wouldn't work here.

2

Jack stood at the bay window of his apartment's front room and watched for Madame de Medici, or whoever she was.

So much not to like about this situation: He didn't know her but she knew him; he didn't know where she lived but she knew his address—or said she did.

That was his hope: She was BS-ing him. A vain hope, he figured. She'd sounded pretty damn sure.

A glance at the Shmoo clock—approaching the witching hour. And now down on the street an elegant looking woman strolling in a cream colored polar bear coat with a matching Zhivago hat, carrying a small shoulder bag. She wasn't looking at the numbers on the brownstones so maybe—

Damn. She was climbing the front steps.

He scanned the street, east and west, checking to see if she'd brought anyone else along or had been followed. Early Sunday morning here on the Upper West Side tended to be quiet. One car passing and three people strolling—two of them walking dogs—and one guy pushing a dead motorbike along the opposite sidewalk. He didn't like the helmet that obscured his face, but as best he could tell, the guy didn't seem the least bit interested in Jack's visitor.

Okay, no red flags.

The buzzer from the vestibule sounded. He could ignore it but that would only delay the inevitable.

He pressed the intercom button and said, "Nobody's home."

That melodic laugh again. *"I am here as promised, right on time."*

"I don't do business at home. I meet in—"

"That scruffy bar. Yes, I know. I do not wish to go there. I prefer here."

"Sorry. Julio's opens in an hour. Meet you there then."

"I will wait here for as long as it takes. I am a very patient person. I have nothing but time."

Jack believed her. And since she was already here . . .

Crap.

He buzzed her in, then looked around the room. Had he left any weapons lying about? No, but the light from the window caught the metallic cover of the *Compendium of Srem* lying in plain sight on the paw-foot oak table. That would never do. Weezy had left it here for safekeeping while she was painting her apartment. Jack grabbed it and hauled it to the TV room where he tossed it onto the bed and dropped a pillow atop it.

He pulled his door open just as an attractive woman in her mid-thirties with the most intriguing amber eyes arrived on the third-floor landing. Her straight hair, black as interstellar space, was cut in a chin-length bob. A slim, black triangular bag hung from her shoulder.

"Mister Jack," she said, extending a gloved hand. "I am Madame de Medici."

"So I gathered. Come in. I guess."

"Such a warm welcome," she said with a smile. "I know this is not your routine, but I did not want to display the Bagaq in a public place."

"Bagaq?"

"The object I wish you to safeguard for me."

He pointed to her bag. "In there?"

"Yes."

She made no move to show it.

"Well, can I see it?"

"In good time." She moved past him and began to wander the front room. "Interesting. You appear to be a collector."

Was this how the meet was going to go? Was she trying to get a feel for him? Well, all right. Maybe he could use the occasion to get a feel for her. Because ... well, he couldn't exactly pinpoint why, but she intrigued him.

"I wouldn't call myself a collector. I don't have a want list. I see something that interests me, I buy it."

She removed her gloves and he noticed a wide gold ring inlaid with onyx in the head of a cat. She dragged her fingers along his Victorian wavy-grained golden oak furniture, inspecting the gingerbread-laden hutch, the secretary, the crystal-ball-and-claw-footed end tables. She smiled at the framed Shadow Fan Club and Doc Savage Fan Club certificates, studied the Daddy Warbucks lamp, and poked a finger into the soil in his Shmoo planter.

The ring seemed to sparkle as she said, "This needs water."

"I give it a good drink every Sunday."

He'd tend to that upon her departure–which he hoped would be soon.

She stopped at the bay window and stared out at the street. The line from *Life During Wartime* about staying away from the window because somebody might see you ran through his head. Why would he think of that now?

"You have a nice view here," she said.

"I suppose ... if you find the sight of Upper West Side brownstones interesting." Which he did.

After a long look she turned to him and said, "Unless you are much older than you appear, everything I see in this room is from a time before you were born."

"What of it?"

"That gives all this a theme, which makes you a collector of antiquities–of a sort–which in turn gives us something in common."

"You're a collector?"

She frowned. "Unfortunately, yes."

"'Unfortunately'?"

"It is a disease, a mania. I do not collect antiquities for their value, I collect them sometimes for nostalgic value, but mostly just to have them–to be the *only* one who has them. I can see from your expression that you do not understand."

"Well, not the exclusivity part. Much of what I've got here–which most folks would label junk—was mass produced."

But still it all somehow managed to speak to him down the decades.

Gia had often quizzed him on his "accumulation," as she called it, wanting to understand the appeal. He'd never been able to give an answer that satisfied her. In fact, he'd never found an explanation that satisfied himself. Maybe it came down to the personalities of the objects. His hand-carved furniture had personality. The old Bakelite radio with the Art Deco design had it. His utilitarian objects like lamps and furniture and even his fireplace screen had it. All the cars he most admired—like the 1949 Delahaye roadster or the 1925 Rolls Royce Phantom—had been designed with an eye that looked far past mere functionality. They became works of art.

"Nostalgia then?" she said. "How well I understand that."

"Hardly nostalgia. As you said, I wasn't alive when these things were everyday objects."

"That is where we differ."

What did that mean? But the sparkle from her ring caught his attention again.

"Your ring . . . part of your collection?"

She held up her hand to admire it. "I suppose. It belonged to an Egyptian princess."

"Nefertiti? Cleopatra?"

"They were queens. This princess was devoted to Bast, and thus the god's image in the gold. Anyway, my collections are—"

"Collections—as in more than one?"

"I have them broken up into subsets here and there around the world. I had a major subcollection in Egypt until the revolution made it impossible for me to keep it safe. After the looting, I moved what was left of it to your country. Most to New Orleans, but I keep some items in my place here in New York."

"Care to you tell me where?"

"The Allard."

He felt his eyebrows lift of their own accord. Pricey real estate. "Nice."

"It has good security and my tower apartment will afford me a front-row seat for Ragnarok."

Jack hadn't expected that. "What do you mean?"

A weary look. "Let's leave it at that and suffice it to say that the Allard is protection enough for the pieces I've used for decoration. The loves of my life are elsewhere."

"You're talking about things. What about people?"

"People are transient. They invariably depart. Things, however, are more loyal. Things remain. And speaking of things . . . "

She reached into the bag and removed something that looked like a large bronze avocado. Its surface reflected rainbow highlights, like from an oil spill.

She held it out to him. "The one and only." When he hesitated to take it, she thrust it closer. "Here. It won't bite."

Despite its appearance, the surface wasn't oily; warm and dry, in fact. Its weight surprised him—much heavier than he'd expected. But ugly. Why would anyone want to own this, let alone steal it?

"This needs to be safeguarded?" he said, rotating it in his hands. "Really? From whom?"

"When I said 'the one and only,' I was not exaggerating. It is unique. There is only one Bagaq."

"No offense, but I could go into a mine, pick up a lump of coal, and that too would be one of a kind. I could give it a goofy name and say, 'There is only one Whatever.'"

"Ah, yes, but it wouldn't be one of the Seven Infernals."

Jack fumbled and almost dropped the damn thing.

"*What?*"

He quickly placed it on the oak table.

"I know you had a bad experience with another Infernal but this one won't harm you."

Bad experience? Right up there with the worst experiences of his life. But wait . . .

"How do you know about that?"

"I have this and one other Infernal in my collection."

"The Lilitongue wouldn't be that other, would it?"

"The Infernal you encountered?" She raised her hands in a stop gesture. "Never would I have anything to do with the Lilitongue of Gefreda. It is monstrously dangerous."

He'd learned that the hard way. He'd managed to look up the Seven Infernals in the *Compendium of Srem*. Before today he'd seen four of them. The Lilitongue, of course; as a kid he's seen Jacob

Prather's "Mystery Machine," officially known as the Phedro; the Infernal that looked like a mini Tesla tower in the basement of the Ehler house in Monroe; and the Cidsev Nelesso last spring in New Orleans.

The Bagaq made five.

"But how do you know any of this?" he said.

"The Seven Infernals are interconnected. When you have access to one you can learn things about the others. I know you found the *Sombra* and recovered the Lilitongue from where it had been safely tucked away from human contact. Inevitably, tragedy ensued."

"Damn right it did." His brother was missing because of it. "You know, if this were six months ago, I'd be looking around for a dog."

She looked startled, then laughed. "You think I'm the Lady?"

Not really, what with the Lady still recovering. Wait—

"You know the Lady?"

"I know *of* her. We've never met face to face."

She knows of the Lady and she collects Infernals . . .

"Who are you?"

"I believe I introduced myself. I'm—"

"Madame de Medici. Or so you've said. But those are just words."

"They are words that will have to suffice."

Jack stared at the Bagaq—an ugly thing with a dumb name. "I don't think I want to do this."

"It will not harm you."

"They don't call them 'Infernal' for nothing."

"An excellent point, but you will not have to carry it around with you. You need only find a safe place for it—a location you will not share with me—and leave it there until the time is right for me to take it home again."

"And when will that be?"

A shrug. "I cannot say. Until a fellow collector named Roland Apfel no longer wants it."

"Why would he stop wanting it? If he's a collector like you, the mania won't go away."

"No, but Roland will. He is dying—terminal cancer of some sort— and he believes the Bagaq has a mystical power to heal him."

"Does it?"

"I have absolutely no idea. Rumors abound about each of the

Infernals, but often they are false, or only partially true. The simplest, most superficial and intriguing parts of the story are passed on, while the deeper part, the part with all the caveats, is lost to time."

"So, you're hiding it from a dying man? Kind of cold."

"Not necessarily. One should never expect to benefit from an Infernal."

"No kidding. But where's the harm in giving this Roland a chance to use it?"

"Because it's mine."

"Not even a loan?"

"Absolutely not."

Jack sensed he was dealing with an immovable object here, but he pushed her anyway.

"Afraid he'll scratch it or contaminate it?"

"Because he has threatened me. And if by chance the Bagaq should work some miracle cure—or if Roland merely thinks it has—he will never give it up. The Bagaq is mine and a key part of my collection. I do not lend pieces of my collection. Especially to his sort. He has intimated that he will kill to acquire it, and if he comes to believe that it will help him next time he falls ill, he will kill to keep it."

"In a way, you're 'lending' this piece of your collection to me."

"To keep it from Roland."

"I don't know . . . "

He would forever regret the last time he'd allowed an Infernal into his home.

"The Bagaq is harmless."

"That might be one of the partial truths you mentioned."

"The only danger is from Roland. No one can connect you to me. All you have to do is hide it away while I visit one of my homes abroad—I'm thinking of my place in Luxor to escape these frigid temperatures."

"Is Egypt safe?"

"Safer than here. If I stay around I fear Roland might abduct me and try to extract the whereabouts of the Bagaq through, shall we say, unpleasant means. He is a ruthless and cruel man. Much easier if I simply disappear and wait for Roland to die."

"Why not take the thing with you?"

She frowned. "That sounds like the obvious solution, but frankly I'm afraid to fly with an Infernal. I don't know what it might do. No one does. That is why it was shipped by sea from Iran."

Good reason . . . if true.

But none of that mattered. Bottom line: Jack didn't want to be responsible for an Infernal, didn't even want to be in the same room with one. He needed a graceful way to bow out of this. How about pricing himself out of the market?

"All right, I'll help you out, but seeing as it's an Infernal, I'll need two thousand dollars a day."

She didn't blink. "How much in advance?"

Oh, hell. This wasn't good.

A sinking feeling began as he said, "A week will do."

With a sly smile, she reached into her bag and produced a handful of gold coins.

"I believe these will cover the first week."

He hid his shock. When she held them out, he had no choice but to take them.

From their weight he knew they were definitely gold. And definitely old, despite the sharply engraved eagles.

"What are—?"

"Ptolemaic—from the first century BCE. Before Cleopatra. Collector's items and, if I may say, worth more than their weight in gold."

"Awfully good shape for over two thousand years old."

"The gold coins tended to be hoarded, and were rarely circulated. Any rare coin dealer will be overjoyed to take these off your hands."

Yeah, Monte down at Municipal Coins would need a drool cup when Jack showed him these. *If* he showed him. Might want to keep them for himself.

"What if I'd said four thousand a day?"

Another sly smile as she jingled her bag. "I came prepared. I can afford it. I just want to be assured that you will take proper care of it."

She certainly looked like she could afford it. And he looked to be stuck with the Bagaq.

A different story if she'd been asking him to safeguard her, which would have been a much more complicated proposition. But this lump of metal? Nothing to it. He knew just the place to hide it.

"How many weeks do you think this will go on?" He'd feel guilty taking sixty Gs from her, month after month.

"I don't think Roland will survive the year."

Which came to less than two weeks.

"Oh, well, that's good. I mean, I don't mean 'good' in a—"

"No, it *is* good. The world will be a better place when he is no longer polluting it with his presence."

Obviously, no love lost between Madame and Roland.

She returned to the bay window for another gaze outside. He saw her stiffen.

"Jack . . . would you come here and look at this man?" She sounded alarmed.

He stepped up beside her. "What man?"

"That one with the bald head across the street, in the flannel shirt and short pants. I thought he was looking up here."

Jack recognized him immediately. Didn't know his name but . . .

"He's a neighbor. Owns that brownstone with the green door. He's okay."

The guy never appeared in long pants. Always wore shorts, no matter what the temperature. Jack had watched him shoveling snow in shorts.

His attention was drawn toward the fellow he'd seen earlier with the Honda, still out there. He was parked by the hydrant and had the engine cover off, ratcheting something down inside. Couldn't see his face because, though his visor was up, his head was down.

"And what about that old one—staring up at us with that shocked look on his face?"

Oh, hell. Glaeken. He tended to go for extended walks when Magda's nurse was tending to her. Sometimes he strolled Jack's street. But his expression did indeed look shocked.

"He's a local too."

"But his reaction . . . "

"Maybe seeing me with a woman."

"You are homosexual?"

"He knows I rarely have company."

"That is a relief. I thought he was watching me." She drew him from the window. Jack gave Glaeken a little wave as he moved away. "I am leaving, but I have one request before I go."

"And that would be . . . ?"

"I wish to see your copy of the *Compendium*."

Another stunner. His mouth felt a little dry.

"How do you know so much about me?"

"I know about the *Compendium*. I used to own a copy."

"A *copy*?"

She nodded. "Yes. There were more than one—quite a few, in fact. But only a handful now remain, if that many."

How did she know all this? How did she know he had it?

"Well?" she said, tapping her booted foot. "May I see it?"

He hesitated. "How do I know you won't try to steal it?"

She smiled. "I'm quite sure you're capable of preventing that. But in truth, I have no need of one. My copy was lost in . . . I guess you could call it a flood. I have no desire to replace it. As I said, it is not one of a kind. I collect only unique objects."

Uneasy, he said, "Maybe you should go now."

She looked offended. "Why?"

"Because you know too much about me and I know nothing about you."

She laughed. "Dear boy, I know about antiquities—*all* about them. Infernals and the *Compendium* are antiquities. I keep track of them. Don't flatter yourself—I find them far more interesting than you."

Jack had to laugh. "Burned!"

"I will show you the entry about the Bagaq and you can read for yourself."

Since she already knew about the *Compendium*, he couldn't see any harm in letting her see it. He retrieved the thick tome from the TV room and placed it on the oak table.

"This is in poor condition," she said, opening the cover.

The text in the *Compendium* appeared in whatever language the reader grew up speaking. Jack wondered what language she saw.

She began muttering angrily in some strange tongue as she flipped through it.

"The pages are out of order." Her amber eyes flashed. "This has been sorely mistreated."

"It's changed hands quite a bit recently."

Jack had stolen it from a cult, then had it stolen from him, then stole it back.

She seemed more angry than annoyed. "I won't be able to find the Bagaq entry so you'll have to take my word. Even if I did wish to replace my copy, I would not want this one. It is useless."

Not if you have an eidetic memory, Jack thought.

Weezy had one and she was mentally indexing the *Compendium* as she read through it, page by disconnected page.

She slammed the cover closed. "I find this very distressing."

"You wouldn't happen to know how to fix it, would you?"

"No. Sorry. I must go now and pack for my flight to Egypt."

"How do I reach you?"

"You do not reach me. I reach you."

He wasn't sure he liked this. No, he was quite sure he didn't like this. She was turning the tables, keeping the upper hand.

She thrust out one of those hands. "Good bye, Mister Jack."

Their hands met. She'd been wearing gloves when she'd entered. Her hands were bare now and she squeezed his, maintaining her grasp.

"Something about you . . . "

Uh-oh. She knew an awful lot. Did she know *that?*

"My scintillating personality?"

Without missing a beat, she said, "Well, delusional people do tend to be more interesting than the perfectly rational."

He decided he liked her.

"No," she added, "it's something else." Finally, she released him and began pulling on her gloves. "It will come to me. Take good care of my Bagaq."

He couldn't help thinking of Bobby Vee's *Take Good Care of My Baby* as he let her out onto the landing and watched her start down the stairs. After closing the door behind her, he grabbed the Bagaq and placed it on the top shelf of the front closet where it joined a katana with a damaged blade, known as the Gaijin Masamune, leaning at an angle next to his main-carry Glock 19.

He'd have to find a better place for it, but at the moment, on a Sunday morning, this was the best he had to offer.

Right now he had to go hunt a lost cryptid.

3

Tier watched Madame de Medici leave the brownstone. He stiffened as she turned his way. He'd expected her to walk back in the direction she'd come, but she continued west. She'd pass within arm's reach.

Fortunately, the cover he'd prepared for hiding in plain sight would work for him now. He'd parked the bike at the empty curb before a fire hydrant and opened the engine cover. He had his tool kit out and was pretending to work on it.

He kept his face averted as she approached, but checked out her shoulder bag after she passed. The triangular leather sack that had bulged before entering the brownstone now lay flat against her.

Obviously, she'd dropped something off in that third-floor apartment. He knew she'd visited the third floor because she'd been good enough to stand in the bay window up front. Not once but twice—the second time with whomever she was visiting. Couldn't have done a better job of pinpointing her location if she'd been working for him.

He quick-quick stowed his tools, replaced his helmet, and started pushing the bike after her. He hurried to catch up as she hung a left on Amsterdam Avenue, but when he reached the corner seconds later—

No Madame de Medici.

What the hell? Where'd she go?

Not like she could hide in a crowd, because a crowd didn't exist at 9:40 on this frigid Sunday morning. Scattered people—most of them walking their dogs—wandered Amsterdam Avenue, but very few of the stores were open, so no one had much of a reason to venture out in the cold. And even if scads of people had been milling about, she'd be hard to miss in that coat and hat.

He started pushing his bike downtown past a computer place, a dry cleaner, and a restaurant—all closed. And then he came to a little park with empty tennis courts behind it. The branches of trees and bushes inside the park's wrought iron fence were bare; no place to hide in there, even if she'd managed to get in. He backed up to the buildings and tried the door that led to the apartments above street level but found it locked.

Tier propped the bike on its kickstand and did a slow turn. No subway entrance in sight for blocks around, so she hadn't ducked into one; she hadn't had time to cross the street without his seeing her, so where the hell did she go? People didn't just vanish into thin air, but Madame de Medici seemed to have done just that.

Okay, this was embarrassing.

She'd practically led him to that apartment, but now she'd managed to ditch him after half a block. How?

An old woman with swollen legs and a cane was trudging his way. She definitely qualified as spavined, but he took no pleasure in using his Word of the Day.

"Excuse me, ma'am," he said. "Did you happen to see a woman in a white fur hat just a few moments ago?"

"Fur hat?" she said in a thick accent he couldn't identify. "I have fur hat but my daughter won't let me wear it. 'Fur is dead!' she says. Over and over, 'Fur is dead!' I know it's dead. Of course it's dead, but that's all she says, over and over whenever I bring it out."

"I'm sorry about that, but did you see—?"

"Will you come home and tell her that I know fur is dead?"

Tier shook his head. "I'm kind of busy right now—"

"Then what good are you?"

He backtracked toward the brownstone she'd visited and was a couple of doors away when the guy he'd seen at the window with her came out and hurried down the front steps to the sidewalk. He turned east and headed away toward Columbus Avenue. He wasn't carrying a package of any sort...

Well-well-well... maybe fortune was smiling on Tier Hill after all.

He walked past the brownstone and chained the Honda to the nearest tree. He always kept his lock-pick set in the bike's storage compartment, so he grabbed that and, keeping his helmet on, trotted up the steps and into the vestibule. He raised the visor enough to see that this particular brownstone had only one apartment per floor. The tenant on 3 was listed only as "Jack."

After receiving no response to three long rings on the buzzer, he found a suitable bump key that had the inner door open in a flash. As he ascended to the third floor, he considered his options after retrieving the Bagaq.

A) Disappear and wait for Roland to die, then sell it to a dealer. Tier would receive only a fraction of its value, but a fraction of "priceless" could mean heavy bread.

B) Hide the Bagaq and keep charging Roland a hefty per diem as he supposedly continued the search, then turn it in for an additional bonus.

C) Tell Roland he'd found it and extort a huge price for it.

D) Simply turn it over and collect the finder's fee, hoping it was truly "generous."

The aces part of finding the Bagaq meant he wouldn't have to 'fess up about Madame de Medici somehow giving him the slip. Still couldn't imagine how she'd managed it, but the fact remained that his rep was based on his ability to track without being seen. If this got out...

Damn her.

As for his various choices, he knew he'd wind up with D. He had a sterling reputation in a field acrawl with lowlifes. That meant something to him. He didn't want to wander into Poncia's zone.

However, upon reaching the third-floor landing, all his choices were rendered null and void.

"Aw, shit."

The guy had a 14-button combo lock on his door—ten numbers plus four freaking letters. The possible combinations ran into the millions.

Good*damn* him!

Tier's lock kit contained a small tempered steel pry bar which he dutifully tried. The fact that the door was steel wouldn't have mattered much if it had been hung in a wood frame—he couldn't get over how many people did that. But this guy had his steel door set in a steel frame, with a super-thick latch guard. He was pretty sure he'd need a battering ram to get through, and even then . . .

Double damn him.

Okay. Time to get out of here and figure his next move . . . which would mean going back to the Allard and keeping watch for the Medici gal's return. His report to Roland would somehow omit mention of losing her trail this morning.

4

Jack slowed when he saw the flashing lights of the cop car behind him. A wasted day—at least so far. And this cop could make it a lot worse.

The dashboard clock read *4:40.* The sun had just set, leaving him in the growing dark after a day of cruising the streets of Ozone Park, South Ozone Park, and Howard Beach. He'd passed through every imaginable variety of neighborhood, from mansions to blocks of middle-class houses with dauntingly fastidious yards to trailer parks to abandoned buildings to empty, overgrown lots. He'd been around Spring Creek Park half a dozen times. To cover all bases, he'd even made a couple of side trips along the western perimeter of JFK Airport.

But all the while he'd obeyed every traffic sign, stayed at or under the speed limit. So why the stop? Broken tail light? What?

He pulled to the curb on Ninetieth Street in Howard Beach and the cop pulled in behind him. He wiggled his driver license free of his wallet and removed the registration and insurance cards from the glove compartment. All three cards and the license plate on the rear bumper were as real as a politician's promises. But also the best that money could buy, courtesy of Ernie's ID.

That didn't prevent a little extra acid from pooling in his stomach.

They'd been tested before and passed, but no guarantee they'd pass this time. He shouldn't worry. The Tyleski identity was solid. The real John L. Tyleski was dead, but officialdom had no record of his passing. He'd never broken the law and had no outstanding debts—he paid off both his credit cards in full every month with money orders.

Jack's main worry was the tranq gun. He'd wired a large canvas holster with a snap flap under the driver seat. The tranq pistol rested in that. No way a cop outside the car could get a hint of its existence.

Still . . . every once in a while, *no way* became *yes way*.

Not illegal to own a tranq gun, but how to explain it?

It boiled down to the simple fact that he couldn't allow himself to be arrested. Because once they took him in and started digging into his identity, his carefully constructed house of lies would start to crumble and they'd never let him loose—talk about a flight risk. He'd never take another free breath.

He rolled down the window and placed both hands in plain sight at ten and two on the steering wheel as he waited for the cop to come alongside. If memory served, the areas Jack had been searching came under the jurisdiction of the 106th Precinct. The guy took his time, no doubt running a computer check on the plates. They would come up as belonging to one Vincent Donato of Canarsie, Brooklyn, maybe a half-hour drive from here. But the local constabulary had to be relatively comfortable dealing with the likes of Vinny Donuts, seeing as John Gotti and Junior Gotti used to call Howard Beach home.

Jack had cloned Vinny's car a couple of years ago—same make, model, plates. He'd first met the big man shortly after arriving in the city. Vinny wouldn't remember Jack, but Jack remembered Vinny. Neither side of the law had any issues with the Donut. He belonged to a branch of the Gambinos and ran a legit scrap/salvage business up front. He made the right donations to the cops, paid a respectful percentage of his gross to his capo, and kept his games and loan-sharking close to the ground. Vinny Donuts liked a low profile. The cops and the other families wished they had more like him.

Jack got stopped now and again, and when the cop thought he was dealing with Vinny's car and driver, he never wrote a ticket and didn't ask too many questions. *Never* asked to look in the trunk. Some things you didn't necessarily need to know.

Jack's problem here would be explaining his presence, criss-crossing the area all day. The truth—well, part of it—offered a perfect excuse.

Finally, the cop appeared at Jack's window and shone his flash-light all around the interior.

"Good evening, sir. May I see your license and registration, please?"

Jack handed them over. "Is there a problem, officer?"

Had to strike the right balance here: Cool, calm, respectful but not obsequious. He worked for Vinny Donuts, after all.

"We've had a number of reports from concerned residents about a car like yours lurking in their neighborhood."

"I don't know about 'lurking,' officer. I've been searching for a lost dog."

"Your dog?"

"My employer's"

"Would that be the owner of the vehicle?" He had the flashlight on the registration card. "Vincent Donato?"

"It would, sir."

"And you're John Tyleski?"

"Yessir. I was driving Mister Donato back from a business meeting this morning and we stopped to let the dog do his business in that little park off Conduit, just past Linden."

Jack had been through there twice today.

"Tudor Park."

"It's got a name? I guess all parks got a name, right? Whatever, the dog somehow got off its leash and bolted."

"Big dog?"

"Little. Maybe eight pounds. A mix called a Bijou."

The cop made a face. "Bijou . . . no kidding?"

"Yeah. One of these new breeds—half Bichon and half Shih Tzu."

"Bijou." He seemed to like the word.

"I had a theater in my home town called the Bijou," Jack said, making it up as he went along. "Coulda been worse for the dog: Coulda called the breed 'Shitzon.'"

He saw the cop's lips twist toward a smile. Jack knew about Bijous because Vicky wanted one. So far Gia had resisted.

"Anyway, the little guy's name is Zorro."

"Zorro?" Now he cracked a full smile. "Vinny Donuts has a Bijou named Zorro?"

"Yes. He doesn't advertise it, if you understand my meaning, but Mister Donato is quite attached to Zorro."

The cop cleared his throat. "I'm sure. And you've spent the day looking for it?"

"After dropping Mister Donato at his office, I returned with this." Jack held up the tracker Hess and Monaco had given him. "Zorro has a chip embedded under his skin and this is supposed to locate him, but I haven't got a hit all day."

"Well, that being the case, maybe you should call it a day. People around here are on edge."

"Why is that, may I ask?"

"Two local kids went missing last night."

He recalled Abe mentioning them between garlic knots . . .

"I heard something about that. Not found yet?"

"No, sir. And as for Zorro . . . " The smile turned serious. "He might have been picked up. Certain types of people are always on the lookout for little dogs. Grab any stray they see. They're never seen again."

Jack knew what he was talking about. The subhuman slugs who ran dog fights were always looking for live fodder to train their killers.

"I appreciate what you're saying. Would you mind if I took another hour? I'll stay out of residential neighborhoods like this."

"I'm going to run your license. If it's clean, you'll get your hour."

He sauntered back to his unit and stayed there for what seemed like an awful long time. He finally returned and handed back the cards. Which meant they'd passed. Good old Ernie, his product never failed.

"You got till six. I'll have to ticket you if I catch you around here after that."

"Understood," Jack said and gave a little salute as he rolled up the window and cruised away.

And of course, that was when a blip lit on the screen.

"Well-well-well. Sun goes down and out you come. Let's see if we can arrange a meeting."

The tracker placed the blip to the east. He made the turn and headed that way, ending at Cross Bay Boulevard, four lanes running alongside a boat basin and lined with local businesses. Not his first time here today. He'd had a hot pastrami on rye for lunch at the Cross Bay Diner. The blip was now south of him so he turned and crawled along with his hazard lights flashing until he came to a Popeye's.

The blip was just about centered in the screen so this looked like the place. He turned into the lot and eased toward the rear until he found a dumpster. Scrounging for food? Had to be it.

At least H3 had good taste. Popeye's spicy chicken was a fave.

He pulled the tranq gun from under the seat and hid it inside his jacket as he jumped out of the car. Finger on the trigger, alert for any sign of movement, he eased toward the dumpster. When he reached it, he found the top open and the area littered with scattered trash, but no H3. Whoever or whatever had been going through the garbage had left a mess but was gone now—along with a supply of discarded biscuits and chicken tenders maybe? And some popcorn shrimp as well?

But the tracker had said . . .

He hurried back to the car where the tracker showed the blip north of here.

Just missed it.

H3 must have been moving fast because it was already nearing the Belt Parkway opposite Aqueduct.

Jack started rolling again, figuring H3 wouldn't be able to cross the Belt without getting killed, so it would have to turn east or west. All Jack needed was a little proximity and a clear shot.

As he neared the Belt he checked the tracker again.

Blank.

What?

Had the tracker gone dead?

He pressed the button to show all chips and it lit up with a dozen or more dots. He switched back to H3-specific mode and was rewarded with a blank screen again.

Three options here: It hopped a truck and rode out of range, the chip had died, or H3 had found a hidey hole that blocked the signal.

The last one made the most sense. H3 could very well have spent the day underground in a sewer or drainage pipe that not only kept it relatively warm but blocked the chip's signal. After dark it came out to forage, then returned to its lair to eat.

Yeah. That fit the facts, explaining Jack's wasted day and the brief tease just now.

So, H3 had gone to ground–*under*ground. But where? The tracker had nowhere near the precision needed to pinpoint the chip's position even when it was receiving a signal. And now, with a blank screen, Jack was out of luck.

Further complicating matters was Officer Krupke's warning to be out of town by six.

He pulled to the curb on 155th Avenue and idled the Vic.

Something wrong here. No, make that a *lot* of things wrong.

Exactly *what* was he chasing? It moved fast and unnoticed. How could that thing in the photos Hess and Monaco had shown him move about without raising alarms? His Crown Vic–certainly not a rare car in these parts–had been reported to the cops, but no mention of H3. Granted, H3 had waited till dark, but it wasn't six o'clock yet. How could it move from Popeye's to the Belt unseen?

He knew of only two people who could answer those questions . . . .

5

Hess and Monaco arrived around ten-thirty. Jack had been watching from the living room's picture window and let them in the front door.

"Wow," Hess said as he stepped inside. "I know Long Island pretty well but this is in the middle of nowhere."

"The Incorporated Village of Nowhere," Jack said.

"Seriously," Monaco said, "Google Maps is mostly blank here."

"Welcome to my country place. That smell is mildew. I don't spend much time here."

In truth, he spent no time here. He'd accepted the old two-bedroom farm house years ago as payment for a fix. It remained on the books in the customer's name but Jack paid the taxes and utilities. His country place, so to speak, but Jack used it exclusively as a decoy house.

After losing H3 in Queens, he'd called the number Hess had given him. He told them he'd captured H3 and brought it to a safe place to make the exchange—final payment for the beast—away from prying eyes.

"Looks haunted from the outside," Hess said. "And what happened to that truck in the front yard? Looks like it exploded."

"It did. Killed a number of people."

Hess laughed, but when Jack didn't crack a smile, he and Monaco stared in disbelief.

"It's true," Jack said. "Happened two years ago, almost to the day."

If anyone had heard the explosion–unlikely, what with everyone's windows sealed against the cold and the considerable distance to the next house–they never reported it. Certainly, the murderous crew that had invaded Jack's place that winter night wasn't about to tell anyone about it. They'd carried off their dead and wounded and never returned.

Rubbing his hands together Monaco finally said, "Well, that's fascinating, but where is H3?"

"In the spare bedroom, sound asleep."

He grinned. "The n-m agent worked like a charm, I take it?"

"Took two doses but he's out cold."

"Well, let's haul him out and get this over with," Hess said.

Jack held up a hand. "Not so fast."

"Ah, yes," Monaco said. "The balance payment."

Jack pulled out the Glock and pointed it at them. "Before we do anything else, we're gonna have us a little talk."

They made all sorts of shocked noises and blathering protests as Jack herded them into the kitchen where he had them shuck their coats. Next, he made Monaco duct tape Hess into one of the straight back chairs, then taped Monaco into another himself.

Next step was to go through the coats. The usual miscellaneous items dropped from Hess's pockets, but two pairs of nickel-plated handcuffs fell out of Monaco's.

"Into some kinky stuff, are we?"

Monaco made a face. "They're for H3. Maybe you can use duct tape on us, but it won't work on H3. It'll chew right through it."

Good point. Something to remember.

He dropped into a third chair and laid the Glock on the wobbly kitchen table. "Time for a heart to heart. Time to come clean."

"We've been totally honest with you," Monaco said. "Honest as the day is long."

"What do you do on Plum Island?"

Two pairs of eyes widened.

Hess said, "Plum Island? We have nothing to do–"

Jack picked up the Glock and pointed it at his face to shut him up.

"No more bullshit. You give me the straight story or I drag your pal H3 out here and leave you to deal with it when it wakes up."

Both went pale.

"You wouldn't do that!" Monaco said.

"You can't!"

Both looked panicked. Clearly, they feared H3.

"I'm getting the feeling you two aren't on the best of terms with your beastie."

"It's not th-that," Hess said.

"It's what? It wakes up cranky? What? Tell me now what you left out of your original tale or I go get it."

They looked at each other, then Hess said, "You tell him."

"Me?"

"You're the 'people person,' remember?"

Monaco glared at him, then sighed. "All right. But no interruptions, Ed. I'll tell it my way and you stay out of it."

Hess said, "Fine with me."

Monaco gave Jack a pleading look. "How about untying us first?"

"Not a chance." He wanted to concentrate on the words, not monitor their actions. "But warning: My bullshit meter is on high alert. You set it off and you can tell the rest of your story to H3."

He didn't know what he'd do if they called his bluff. Maybe fire off a few rounds.

"Okay, okay. It started back around the turn of the century."

"No-no-no. Start with H3. We can get to ancient history later. What. Is. H3?"

Another sigh. "H3 is a human-wolf hybrid."

Jack was about to call *bullshit* but Hess spoke first.

"No!" Hess cried, glaring at Monaco and looking like he wanted to kick him. "You can't!"

"Do I have a choice? We're between a rock and a hard place here. Unless you want to take over explaining."

Hess said nothing but looked genuinely upset. Terrified even.

"That's what I thought. So just leave me to it and zip your lips."

"Let's stop right there," Jack said. "I don't know much about biology, but I know you can't interbreed a wolf and a human."

"Of course you can't. Did I say anything about interbreeding? Did you hear the word *breed* pass my lips? No. That's because we haven't been *breeding* anything. We're part of a project that's intro-ducing human stem cells to various non-human species to see if any-thing useful develops."

"Come on," Jack said. "The non-human will reject the stem cells."

Hess laughed. "Looks like he's not as dumb as you thought."

"Hold your tongue!" Monaco looked at Jack. "The stem cells are specially treated."

"Who's paying for all this? Homeland Security?"

Jack had done a little homework after talking to Abe. Homeland security was now in charge of the animal disease studies on Plum Island.

"Yes and no. The Department of Defense is behind it, via DHS."

"What does Defense want with human-animal hybrids?"

"Think about it: The Army's got dogs as non-human assets and what else? Nothing. But if we could give, say, a mountain lion cer-tain human characteristics—greater intelligence, greater ability to follow instructions, and maybe even the ability to improvise as it searches for insurgents in the towns and mountains—what an asset that would be. Silent, agile, and ferocious. Much more effective than a dog. Same with wolves. Set a pack of human-wolf hybrids loose at night in the hills? The Taliban's worst nightmare."

"You're talking wolfmen? Is that what H3 is? A wolfman?"

Unbidden, Maria Ouspenskaya's voice started droning in his head. *Even a man who is good by day . . .*

Monaco looked uncomfortable. "We hate that term. Technically, if you called it a wolfman, you wouldn't be wrong, because it's a wolf with a lot of human cells in its brain and body. But 'wolfman' inevitably brings Lon Chaney and lycanthropy to mind, right? H3 is not by any stretch a werewolf. It doesn't change with the full moon. It's the same thing all the time, day in and day out, twenty-four / seven."

"Gotcha."

"But the possibilities are endless. Imagine hybrid rats or even mice with mini go-cams strapped to their backs invading an occu-pied building to show you exactly what the occupants are up to. Greatest things since sliced bread."

Jack found Monaco's parade of clichés distracting.

"Sounds great for the SyFy Channel, but you glossed over how you keep the wolf's or mountain lion's immune system from attacking the stem cells."

"Okay," Monaco said, looking anxious. "That's a problem."

"Damn right it's a problem."

"No, I mean the explanation is a problem. We had to sign some heavy-duty NDAs before we could work on this project. And by 'heavy duty' I mean revealing anything about the methodology will be considered an act of treason."

Hess added, "You've already told him enough to get us hung."

"I don't know about the 'hung' part," Monaco said. "We've been assured there'll be no trial, we'll simply disappear."

"Just a wee bit melodramatic, don't you think?"

"I sure as hell hope so. And I can pretty much guarantee that if they find out about this conversation, you'll disappear too."

"Really."

Gotta find me first.

"Yeah. DoD was serious as all hell about keeping the stuff secret.

"What stuff?"

"The goop they gave us to experiment with."

"Careful . . . " Hess said.

Monaco nodded without looking at him. "Right. Don't ask me what it is because I don't know and couldn't say a word even if I did. It's got a strange little code name which is not a fraction as strange as the stuff itself."

"What's the code name?"

A vigorous headshake. "Nope. Can't say it. Its name's not germane to the story and I've no doubt NSA has it as a key word in its ECHELON monitoring. If it ever pops up in a search, they'll come looking. My lips are sealed."

Jack waved him to continue with his tale. He'd extract the name later if he thought it mattered.

"Okay, long story short: We found a way to coat human stem cells with the goop before we inject them into the animals. We don't know the specific immune protection mechanism but the coating not only shrugs off all rejection reactions from the host but makes the stem cells aggressive as all hell."

"They cause aggression?"

"No, the host doesn't become aggressive—the cells, the stem cells become aggressive in replacing the host's cells. First they replace damaged ones, then they start replacing heathy ones, changing the body."

"Making it more human?"

"Exactly. We couldn't believe how quickly the changes occurred. Structural remodeling in *months*."

This was scary—if true.

"Let's back up here. So, you've got a lab full of part-human creatures out there on Plum Island? Like a modern-day Island of Doctor Moreau?"

"No way," Hess blurted. "Moreau was a crazy vivisectionist. We're nothing like that. We don't cut on anything."

"Easy, Ed," Monaco said. "Sadly, we have no Moreau-esque menagerie out there. I mean, it could have been something like that. The results we get are miraculous . . . but the hybrids don't survive. At varying points along the way, the stem-cell infiltration triggers an autolytic reaction and their cells start to lyse—all of them."

Lyse . . . Jack wasn't familiar with the term.

"What's that mean? "

Calmer now, Hess chirped up. "Lysis is when a cell is destroyed. Often the cause is from outside, but it can come from within. For some reason we haven't determined, the cells of the hybrids begin to destroy themselves, rupturing their cell membranes and releasing their contents. It's called autolysis."

"It's cell suicide, plain and simple. When we started this project at the turn of the century—"

They'd mentioned that before.

"Since 2000?" Sheesh.

Hess nodded. "Right around then. That was when the first sample of melis—" He caught himself and gulped. "The goop arrived."

"'Melis'?"

Monaco's expression turned furious as he shouted at Hess. "Now you've done it! Now you've fucking done it!" He gave Jack a pleading look. "Forget you heard that word. Erase it from your mind."

"I don't think so."

"Seriously. Burkes told us you live off the grid. You want to stay off the grid? Forget that word. You want the grid laser-focused on you? Then throw that word around. Go ahead: Google it. See what happens."

"What do you care?" Jack said, hiding his unease.

"Because when they find you, you'll tell them where you heard about it, and then they'll come for us. And don't think you can hold out on them, that your lips are sealed, because they'll unseal them."

A nightmare scenario. Jack put it aside.

"I'm not interested in what your goop is called. I'm interested in what it does. And you say all your test animals have died?"

Monaco paused and seemed to regain his composure. "All except H3. At least not yet."

"But you think it will?"

"It's lasted far longer than any of the others, but no reason to think it won't."

"When?"

Monaco shrugged. "I wish we knew, but we don't. We've inoculated all sorts of species with the supercharged stem cells but H3 is the only one that's survived past six or seven months."

"And Defense keeps funding you?"

Another glance at Hess. "We don't think our funding comes through the usual appropriations route, if you know what I'm saying."

Jack could guess—black funds for off-the-books research.

"Gotcha."

"So far H3 is the exception. Our golden child. It's broken new ground. No hybrid has lasted this long or come this far. We're over-joyed you found it before it began to deteriorate."

Jack was starting to feel a little guilty about his ruse. Just a little.

Hess said, "One of the reasons we chose that particular wolf for inoculation was that it had liver cancer. We wanted to see how the stem cells would respond when they encountered a malignancy."

"And?"

"Cured it. Gobbled up the malignant cells and replaced them with normal liver cells. We've never heard or seen anything like it."

"Wait-wait-wait. How does a human stem cell become a wolf liver cell?"

"Our supercharged stem cells are pluripotent, which means they can become pretty much any kind of cell. And they don't morph into wolf cells, they use some of the wolf's DNA to become cells that are part human and part wolf."

Jack shook his head. Sounded like bullshit—too good to be true was usually just that—but these guys seemed genuinely excited, like they'd stumbled onto some magic cure.

"So, you've found a cure for cancer."

"Unfortunately," Hess said, "it's a cure that will kill you."

Jack couldn't help a rueful smile. "Yeah, just that one little side effect."

"It's doable," Monaco said. "That's why getting H3 back alive was so crucial. It carries all sorts of medical secrets under its skin. Its blood contains antibodies of incalculable value. Its immune system has the potential to open a whole new avenue of cancer therapy. Can we see it now?"

This wasn't going to be easy . . . or pretty. But first . . .

"Just a couple more questions. This is a federal government project. If H3 is so important, why not have the FBI and the CIA and the DEA and ATF and ICE involved? You could have all of them and the US Marshals to boot looking for it, but you hired me? Doesn't make sense."

"Sure it does," Hess said. "Because we can't let them know we've had another escape."

"Wait. Another?"

That conspiratorial glance again.

"Back in 2006 we had one of the subjects get loose and—"

"The Montauk Monster? That was one of yours?"

"Unfortunately yes. We were able to retrieve its corpse before anyone could do a decent post mortem. If they had, they'd have found some odd anomalies."

"The thing is," Monaco said, "if DoD learns that we've had another escape, we'll be off the project. Over two decades of our blood, sweat, and tears will be dropped in someone else's lap. You've heard of Alexander Fleming?"

"The penicillin guy? Sure."

"Jonas Salk, Watson and Crick?"

"Polio and DNA. Yeah."

"Well, Hess and Monaco will be right up there with them if we can make this work."

"And we can," Hess said. "I know we can. The treated wolf stem cells replaced the cancer cells. Human blood cells can be transformed into stem cells now. Do that with a cancer patient's blood, treat them with the mel—I mean the secret goop—and inject them, they could do the same. At least the potential is there. We can make it work. We just need time and funding and, most of all, H3."

Monaco said, "We've worked too hard to let that be taken away and given to someone else. That's why we didn't bring in the alphabet soup agencies. And we're glad we didn't. We hired you and you got the job done totally on the Q-T. We'll take H3 back to the lab and all will be as before with no one the wiser."

Jack took a step back. "Yeah . . . about that . . . "

6

After the dramatic displays of outrage, the cursing, the shouting, Jack finally cut them free.

"I'm very disappointed in you," Hess said.

Jack shrugged. "Should've been straight with me from the git-go."

Monaco snarled. "How could we be? The nature of our funding made it necessary we tell you as little as possible."

"Well, then, you should have worked a little harder on your lies. Bronx Zoo?"

"Our legends have us officially listed as employees there."

"So Burkes told me. But you shouldn't spin me your tale and then head straight for Plum Island. H3 escaped in the lower end of Queens on its way from Canada to the Bronx? Did you think I was that gullible?"

"Not anymore," Hess said.

Monaco still looked royally pissed. "I'd fire you on the spot if you didn't know too much now. And if it wasn't too late to find someone else. But beggars can't be choosers."

"If it makes any difference, I got two hits on the tracker tonight."

"You did?" they said in unison.

"Started at a Howard Beach fast food joint where your pet raided the garbage. I followed it up to the racetrack area where the signal disappeared."

"How can that happen?"

"I'm thinking it's hiding underground. But getting hits in Howard Beach opens a new batch of questions. Why there? How did H3 get from Plum Island to Aqueduct Racetrack? And don't tell me it's got a gambling problem."

Hess closed his eyes and shook his head. "Can we *not* tell you?"

"You mean it's gonna be harder to believe than your super-duper stem cells?"

"No. It's just better that you don't know. There's no *need* to know."

Monaco said, "I'm afraid I'm going to have to disagree with you on that."

Hess's jaw dropped. "*What?* You can't be serious!"

"Trust me on this, okay?"

"But—"

He raised a hand. "Trust?"

Hess looked like he had something more to say, but instead he shook his head and dropped into one of the living room's ratty easy chairs where he buried his face in his hands.

"Okay," Monaco said. "All along we've made it sound like Hess and I were the only two involved in this project. I should tell you now that there was a third man, a DIA agent named David Quinnell."

Hess raised his head to stare at Monaco. He gave it a slow shake, then lowered it again.

The acronym didn't ring a bell for Jack.

"DIA?"

"Defense Intelligence Agency—DoD's own version of the FBI or CIA."

"You said 'was.' No longer on the project or passed on to his Greater Reward?"

"The latter. The late David Quinnell was—and in this case I do not hesitate to speak ill of the dead—a real son of a bitch. I mean he had a cruel streak a mile wide. He used to torture H3—burn it, cut it, just to see how fast it would heal. And because of the stem cells, it healed *very* fast."

"And you guys allowed this?"

"We didn't have much say in the matter. We objected, of course, but DoD had put Quinnell in charge of the project. And he never hurt H3 when we were around. We only found the evidence of the injuries later. For some unfathomable reason, he hated H3. And after a while, H3 came to hate him back."

As Monaco paused—to catch his breath and gather his thoughts, maybe?—Jack had a pretty good sense of where this was going.

"I'm getting an idea as to why you referred to this Quinnell as 'late.'"

"Oh, he got his just desserts, I suppose, but not before he did the unthinkable two weeks ago."

"I'm afraid to ask."

"He took H3 off-island."

Okay, that didn't exactly strike Jack as "unthinkable" but he'd go along.

"For why?"

"We're not sure, but we think he took H3 to a dog fight—at least that's what we surmised from the nature and pattern of wounds we found upon its return. But as usual they healed quick as greased lightning."

Jeez, listening to this guy was like reading a gun catalog with Gia turning the pages.

"Is there a caboose to this train? What's any of this got to do with H3 being in Queens?"

"I'm getting there. The backstory is important."

Jack couldn't see why.

"Can we just say that H3 killed Quinnell and get on with it?"

"Yes, we could. But then we'd be leaving out the really good parts."

"Like?"

"Like H3 killing Quinnell in a very nasty way—by tearing open his abdomen and letting him bleed out."

An ugly way to die.

"It also ate part of his liver."

"I still don't see—"

"Then it pulled clothes from the man's locker and stowed away on the shuttle to Orient Point."

Jack heard the words but it took a while to fully process them as he looked from Monaco to Hess and back. Hess's head was still down, still in his hands. And Monaco looked like a man who didn't know what to say next.

Jack said, "You expect me to believe that?"

"I'm not sure I believe it myself," Monaco said, "but Quinnell was dead, and his change of clothes was missing along with his overcoat. With the tracker showing no trace of H3's chip on the island, we could only assume it sneaked onto the ferry. It was raining cats and dogs that night and perhaps that's how it got aboard unnoticed. It made it to the mainland before anyone had a clue it was gone."

"Wearing a dead man's clothes?" Jack tried to picture it. "How is that possible? What *is* this thing?"

"I believe I mentioned that the altered stem cells affect the brain along with the somatic tissues. H3 is not pure wolf anymore. It's part human, and part of that humanness includes increased intelligence."

Jack was almost afraid to ask . . .

"How much of an increase are we talking here?"

Monaco shrugged. "We did some testing along the way which indicates it's probably at the level of a twelve-year-old."

A pre-teen? Jack wanted to flatten Monaco's nose.

"And you didn't think I might need to know something like that?"

"Frankly, no. You find H3, you shoot it with a dart or two, it falls down and can't get up. End of story. Doesn't matter how smart it is—it's *down* and that's all she wrote."

"I'm more concerned about *before* its down. Its intelligence makes it more dangerous than a dumb animal, not to mention harder to find. And none of this explains why it's in Queens."

"That's why the back story is important. When we reported Quinnell's demise, the DIA of course investigated the death of one of its own. We told them that Quinnell had killed H3 before he died and that, in the interest of security, we'd cremated its body. They weren't happy with that, but couldn't undo the cremation. It was *fait accompli*—water under the bridge. Which worked for us because, as we've already explained, we can't let anyone know H3 is free."

"Keep going."

"They traced Quinnell's steps when he took H3 inland. And yes, as we'd surmised, he took it to a dogfight. The investigators learned that he'd arranged for it to enter the pit with not one but three pit bulls. He won big money when it killed all three. But that wasn't the only stop Quinnell made. He visited his ex-wife and daughter before the fight to show off his 'pet.'"

"Sounds like a swell guy. But what's this got to do with—?"

"They live in Howard Beach. I have a terrible feeling H3's desire for revenge on Quinnell might extend to his family as well."

"Christ. And you've said nothing?"

Unbelievable.

"I said 'might.' We don't *know*. It's only a guess. But I think you might do well to keep an eye on Quinnell's house . . . just on the chance that H3 shows up there."

"Does the ex know Quinnell's dead?"

"No idea."

"You haven't told her?"

"That's not our business. That's DoD's bailiwick. They decide who knows what. And her being his "ex" may be a reason they feel no pressing need to tell her."

"What about H3? No one told her it's loose?"

Monaco gave him an incredulous look. "Haven't you been listening? No one in the public can know H3 *exists*, let alone roaming the streets."

"So, she doesn't know she might have this wolf thing stalking her?"

"Of course not."

Monaco's matter-of-fact tone made Jack want to kill him. Monaco must have sensed that because he took a step back. Jack balled his fists and forced a couple of deep breaths.

"How old's the daughter?"

"Three."

Shit!

"Get out," Jack said in a low voice.

"Beg pardon?"

"Out. Both of you. Out of my house."

"But—"

"*Now*. Before I do something you'll regret."

They got. But on his way to the front door Monaco scribbled something on a card and tossed it onto the couch.

"What's that?" Jack said.

"Quinnell's address. The wife's name is Jelena and the child's is Cilla."

7

"Do you think he bought it?" Hess said as he drove into the night.

The Odyssey's navigation program had guided them in and he trusted it to lead them out. Good thing he had it. These county roads out here had no streetlights and signage was non-existent.

Just get me to the LIE and I'll take it from there.

Monaco snorted. "Bought it? Of course he did. Hook, line, and sinker. I was fucking brilliant, even if I do say so myself."

"You *always* say so yourself."

He laughed. "Somebody's got to say it!"

Hess had to give Monaco credit: He'd taken a wild farrago of fact and fiction and whipped it into a credible presentation.

"Did you have *any* of that prepared? Like, were you thinking somewhere along the way that this guy might put us on the spot and we'd need a better explanation?"

Monaco shook his head. "Not at all. I thought he was just a street punk with a certain useful skill set. I was convinced I had him fully reeled in during our first meeting. I mean, he didn't ask any of the right questions so I figured he was in the bag."

Monaco's hubris was astounding. "Were you ever wrong."

"I wouldn't go that far—"

"You wouldn't? What did he do right after we left him? He followed us. We should have come up with something better."

"You're a great Monday morning quarterback, Ed."

"I'll admit none of that occurred to me till I had that gun pointed in my face."

Trapped in that isolated farmhouse with an angry, gun-toting psycho. His bladder had almost emptied.

"Yeah, we both underestimated him," Monaco said, "but let's face it: He may have street smarts, but he's still no match for us in the brain category. We can think circles around him—as I just demonstrated."

"You still told him too much."

"I had to tell him *something*. We'd already failed with a whole-cloth fabrication. I had to mix some truth in with the fiction."

"But you told him about melis."

"Not by name. I didn't say the name—*you* said the name."

"I know, I know. It just slipped out."

Ed had wanted to grab that word out of the air and shove it back into his mouth.

"Everything was going fine, Ed, until you spilled the beans. How we're using it in the lab could be written off as some crazy science-fiction scenario. But not the word itself. You know as well as I it's on the ECHELON list."

At least they assumed that was case, and Hess had to figure they were right. If "melis" popped up in an email or a phone conversation anywhere, NSA would report it to Defense and DIA would track down the source and make it disappear.

"But then you mentioned Quinnell . . . " Hess couldn't suppress a shudder. "I couldn't believe it. I almost puked. I thought you'd gone crazy."

Monaco grinned. "Crazy like a fox, you mean."

"Really. Transforming Quinnell into a DIA agent and then—"

"Killing him? I couldn't resist. A mangled DIA agent was no doubt wishful thinking on my part."

No lie about a DIA man overseeing their project, but his name hadn't been Quinnell. In February of 2001—Hess would never forget that day—Agent Benjamin Greve had appeared with the first sample of melis and instructions from DoD to find a way to alter human stem cells so they could be added to certain mammals.

And that was it. No analysis of what this melis might be, no past research results, or why it might have any effect on human stem cells. No guidance at all. Just see what you can do. Oh, and never, ever, ever mention the existence of melis or what you were doing with it.

From the very start they knew they'd been handed an enigma. The slimy goo was an impossibility. Melis had mass–it poured, gravity influenced it–but it had no weight. They could fill a flask with it and the flask weighed the same full as it did empty. Greve wouldn't tell them anything about its origins. They might have high security clearances, but not that high.

After that initial visit, he made a practice of stopping in once a month or so to check on their progress.

Agent Greve had been demanding and imperious and seemed to gain great satisfaction from threatening to terminate their project if they didn't produce the results he wanted.

Well, nothing seemed to work. Monaco had told Jack the truth about the autolysis in their experimental subjects. One after another they died, and they would keep on dying unless he and Monaco determined the cause of the cell lysis. But the cause eluded them.

With the looming threat of their funding being diverted elsewhere, Monaco came up with a desperate, last-ditch proposal. To their shock, Agent Greve had agreed. In fact, he'd been quite supportive, providing everything they needed.

Then something odd happened: Agent Benjamin Greve stopped coming around. This past August was the last time they'd seen him. He missed his September meeting, and October and November as well. And no replacement had arrived to take his place. They'd tried to find out about Greve–alive, dead, what?–but DoD never responded. Oh, the checks were still deposited to the proper accounts, but no word, no oversight.

As it happened, that turned out to be a very good thing. They would never have been able to keep H3's escape a secret with a DIA agent nosing around.

"If nothing else, mentioning Quinnell will start him watching Quinnell's house. I don't know if you noticed, but I left him the address. That's where he'll have his best chance for success, after all."

"Maybe," Hess said, "but is Jack still on the job? I mean, he seemed pretty pissed—pissed enough to kick us out of his house."

"But ask yourself *why* he was pissed. Because he blames us for putting Quinnell's wife and kid in danger. He's not the kind to throw in the towel. He'll go after H3 just to protect her."

"You seem pretty sure."

"I'm very sure. You'll see. The proof will be in the pudding."

Hess spotted a sign pointing to the Long Island Expressway. Civilization again. At last.

8

The sons of bitches.

Hands in his pocket to keep them from breaking things, Jack paced between the living room and the kitchen. He spotted the handcuff they'd left on the kitchen table. They might come in handy—*if* he stayed with this fix. A big if right now.

Those two . . . so concerned about their goddamned hybrid they'd put a woman and child in jeopardy.

Or had they?

Jack couldn't put his finger on exactly what, but something about Monaco's tale didn't ring true.

He broke it down:

The Department of Defense had delivered a mysterious compound called melis to those two clowns and told them to experiment on animals with it. Okay, he could buy that. Plum Island was home to animal experiments and investigations. Also, he'd sensed a hardening in Monaco when he'd asked him about the mystery stuff. He'd been genuinely afraid to give up the name, and deeply upset when Hess had slipped up—both good signs he was telling the truth about it.

So far, so good.

Hess and Monaco had been mixing human stem cells with the

melis and injecting them into various animals, causing changes in those animals. The Montauk Monster had been one of them. The experiments had been going on for over two decades with no lasting success because the cells start killing themselves. But finally they get this wolf-human hybrid that survives, and it escapes.

He could buy it. Far-fetched to some, maybe, but a bit prosaic compared to a Rakosh and other weirdness Jack had encountered over the past couple of years.

Monaco's story about the DIA agent—what was the name? Quinnell?—was the stumbling block. Not only the story itself, but the way Monaco had told it.

A member of the Defense Department's in-house intelligence agency—something Jack hadn't even known existed—had spirited an experimental animal off Plum Island to enter it in a Long Island dogfight so he could make a few quick bucks? After he'd exposed this top-secret beastie to his ex-wife and child?

Uh-uh. Couldn't buy that.

Here's a cliché for you, Monaco: I might have been born at night, but it wasn't last night.

Why add the Quinnell story and the threat to his family if it wasn't true? To suck Jack into staying on the job?

He glanced over at the end table by the door where Monaco had left the card.

And why leave an address?

Obviously, they wanted Jack to go there.

He kicked a chair across the room and it felt good. Felt good to be pissed off. He hadn't felt much of anything beyond frustration for too damn long.

He felt . . . alive.

He grabbed the card off the table. An address in Howard beach.

All right, you sons of bitches. I'm still on the job.

9

"So, you are certain she left the Bagaq at this apartment," Roland said.

His male nurse or orderly or whatever he was called had got him out of bed and into a wheelchair which he'd rolled into the high-ceilinged library. The chair had ended up behind the heavy, pool table-size desk. A tube from a suspended bag of slightly yellowish fluid ran into his arm. Shelves crammed with beat-up-looking books and folios ran up toward the ceiling and disappeared into the shadows.

"I am not certain of that at all," Tier said. Hadn't he been listening? "I said I'm certain she dropped something off—something the approximate size of the object you seek. I did not see the object itself."

Had to be precise here.

"You say you tried to enter his apartment after you saw him leave?"

That was exactly what he'd said.

"Yes. With no success."

"I'd've gotten in," Poncia said from where he stood off to the side with his left little and ring fingers splinted and swathed in bandages.

His presence annoyed the hell out of Tier. He did not so much as glance at him when he continued speaking to Roland.

"The apartment is protected by a thick steel door—"

"I'd've gotten in."

"—secured with a complex combination lock."

"I'd've—"

Roland raised a hand. "Enough." To Tier: "Your job is merely to find the Bagaq, not retrieve it. Why didn't you follow the occupant?"

Tier shrugged. Had to be careful here. "He left empty handed. I had a possible location and saw an opportunity to confirm or deny while he was out. I took it."

Roland studied him in silence.

Suspicious bastard, aren't you.

As the scrutiny reached an uncomfortable point, Roland said, "It appears we now have two people who require observation."

"Correct. And since I can watch only one, I suggest—"

"I will make the suggestions here, Mister Hill. Albert will watch the apartment while you will continue your watch on the Allard."

No-no-no-no-no! In recounting the events of the day Tier had edited out mention of the fact that he'd lost the Medici woman. She might be back in her apartment but he doubted it. Standing outside would be a complete waste of his time. He needed to watch the brownstone. Assuming its occupant "Jack" had the Bagaq, tomorrow—being Monday—would be the perfect day to move it to a safer location.

"I believe you would be better served if I watched the brownstone."

Poncia sneered. "'Better served.' Listen to this guy." He turned to Tier. "You already had your chance to get the Bagaq and totally blew it. Now it's gonna be in the hands of someone who knows what he's doing."

How dearly he would have loved to set this scumbag straight but he stayed focused on Roland and bottled his anger. But not before letting a little escape.

"I fear Mister Poncia's spavined physique might prove too conspicuous."

Yes!

Poncia huffed. "What'd he—?"

"Be that as it may," Roland said, cutting him off. "You stick with the woman."

Hiding his frustration, Tier said, "If I am to stay focused on Madam de Medici then, perhaps you could fill me in on her. My usual lines of inquiry have not borne much fruit."

"I'm not surprised," Roland said. "She remains something of an enigma in the collecting circles. No one had ever heard of her until she bought an old Garden District mansion in New Orleans. Moved in a collection of antiquities from her home in Egypt but apparently displays it only for herself. At least so we've gleaned from various workers she employed to set it up."

"So, she's Egyptian?"

"Who is to say? You've seen her. Some sort of mixed breed, I imagine. I don't know what she is. She made the acquaintance of a New Orleans collector named Jules Chastain who came into possession of another Infernal called the Cidsev Nelesso."

Cidsev Nelesso . . . where did they come up with these names?

"You've lost me."

"The details are confusing, but apparently Chastain lost the Cidsev along with part of his arm."

"I'm seeing a pattern," Tier said. "Does the Madame possess Chastain's Infernal now?"

"Who can say? For all we know, she might possess the missing part of his arm as well."

Tier blinked. "Pardon?"

"The severed section was never recovered. But I am joking. No one has seen her collection. But I don't need to see the Bagaq to be sure she has it. I suspect she's after all seven Infernals and will stop at nothing until she completes her collection. Which is why she stole my Bagaq."

Stop at nothing . . .

"Is she dangerous?"

Another sneer from Poncia. Was that the limit of his expressions? "Getting the jitters, Hill?"

A boor and a bore.

Tier continued to ignore him, saying, "I believe my question is reasonable considering how someone who possessed something she wanted is, as you said, missing the object along with part of his arm."

"Yes, a practical concern, I suppose. But I've heard nothing to that effect, though I'm told she has some people on her staff who appear to be of rather dubious character."

Look around, Roland. You too.

"One curious thing," Roland added. "I found a mystifying refer-ence to a Madame de Medici as a person of interest in the theft of an ancient inscribed sapphire from the Egypt Exploration Society in London. Of course, the police didn't use the term 'person of interest' back then, but they were on the lookout for a young woman named Madame de Medici whose description is uncannily similar to our own Madame's."

"Why 'mystifying'?"

"Well, the year was 1912."

10

Jack inspected the scratches on his apartment door lock. They centered around the latch and hadn't been there when he'd left this morning. Obviously, someone had tried to break in, but he couldn't imagine why. He lived a low-profile life with nothing of value in there except some quality weaponry. But no one knew that. So why—?

Oh, yeah. That Infernal that Madame what's-her-name had left with him.

Damn. Someone must have followed her here. And since they'd failed to break in, they'd be watching the place, waiting for him to leave again—hopefully with the Bagaq. Because if they had half a brain, they'd know they weren't getting through this door.

So, what would he do if he were after the Bagaq and knew it was out of reach in here?

He'd have no choice but to wait for someone to bring it out.

Which was exactly what he planned to do tomorrow morning. In the meantime, though . . .

He punched in a six-digit code and entered, then—he couldn't help it—he checked the top of the front closet. Yep. Bagaq still there.

He'd planned to start a Peckinpah festival tonight, skipping *The Deadly Companions*, which Peckinpah had pretty much disowned. He'd seen it once and that was more than enough—good start, but the last forty minutes or so were a chore. He was starting with *Ride the High Country*, even though he'd seen it maybe fifty times already. Never tired of that one. *Major Dundee* would be next, but first . . .

After grabbing himself a Yuengling, he plugged the Internet cable into the back of his desktop—no wi-fi for Jack—and started a search for David Quinnell. Success . . . too much success. A ton of hits. He tried putting it in quotes but even so that garnered about four thousand hits. He tried adding "defense department" and "DIA" and "Defense Intelligence Agency" to the search but they didn't help. No surprise there. DoD might not want their agents listed in search engines.

The David Quinnell who got the most hits was a guy who was convicted of killing a DEA agent and doing life in the federal pen in Canaan, Pennsylvania. Looked like he'd been a big story a few years back but Jack had missed it. No surprise there. He didn't keep up on murders.

But this Quinnell had also popped up on the "+defense" search so he opened it. Turned out the "defense" hit was triggered by his plea of self-defense. No help there. But as Jack was about to click the article closed he spotted *"resident of Queens"* at the end of a paragraph. Reading further he learned nothing more. Queens was a big place with lots of residents. And anyway, this guy was a lifer.

Jack figured Abe was his best bet for info. Abe knew people who knew people who knew people. He'd planned to stop by tomorrow anyway. Now he had two favors to ask.

Which would make a food stop doubly necessary.

He moused over the power button, ready to shut down, when the word popped into his mind.

Melis.

Strange word. Most likely a shortened form of a long, complicated scientific name.

He popped DuckDuckGo back onto the screen and began typing the letters into the search box. Wait. One "L" or two? He'd try one first, and if that got nothing, he'd give two a try.

m-e-l-i-s

His finger darted toward the ENTER button but hesitated over it. Hess and Monaco had seemed genuinely upset about letting the word slip. Beyond upset: terrified. Monaco's words came back:

Burkes told us you live off the grid. You want to stay off the grid? Forget that word. You want the grid laser-focused on you? Then throw that word around. Go ahead: Google it. See what happens.

Was the word really on the ECHELON watch list? If so, he was courting disaster by doing this, especially from his home.

He leaned back. This was what America had come to: afraid to type a word into a search engine.

He remembered the first time he'd used one, back in, what, the late '90s? He'd gone to the New York Public Library and sat at one of their new computers to look up . . . he'd forgotten what. But he did remember the wondrous search site called AltaVista that would look up anything he wanted—an electronic go-fer with instant access to all the world's knowledge. English, biology, chemistry, astronomy, the news, the weather, the spot price of gold or silver . . . anything he wanted to know at his fingertips.

And never a worry about someone watching. Maybe someone was, but hardly anyone worried about it. Nowadays you *knew* someone was watching—everywhere. Cameras up and down the block, all along the shopping aisles. And in your home computer: Do a casual look-up on a knife or a pair of boots and soon ads for knives and boots would pop up on your screen for days afterward. The retailers were keeping track. So was Google—and selling the info. Who else?

Jack stayed under the radar as best he could, but anonymity was becoming harder and harder to maintain. Privacy was a myth . . . a bit of fond nostalgia.

Sighing, he backspaced until the word disappeared.

Maybe he'd try it someday from an Internet café or the like. But if the stuff was so secret, he'd most likely find nothing. And in exchange for that nothing he'd galvanize officialdom into a search for him, poring over CCTV recordings to see who was where when the miscreant dared to enter that word. With cameras everywhere, odds were high they'd catch a look at him, enter his image in facial recognition software, and image analyzers around the world would be on the lookout for him day and night.

Nope. Not worth it.

He powered down, unplugged the cable, and headed for the shower.

11

Tier sipped his Patron in his father's La-Z-Boy as he watched the weather report on the 11 p.m. Eyewitness News with the sound off. No need for words. The weather map said it all as they tracked the huge snowstorm aimed directly at the city and due to arrive early Tuesday.

He had to find the Bagaq tomorrow. Not only because the storm would complicate everything, but settling this tomorrow meant only one day associated with Poncia.

Even that was too much. The prospect repulsed him. At least they weren't working side by side. He didn't know if he could take that.

Not that he couldn't use the money. He was building a nest egg for when he started college. But he wasn't desperate. When Dad developed a small-cell tumor in his lung, he'd applied to the September 11th Victim Compensation Fund. He'd smoked better than a pack a day most of his life, so maybe 9-11 had nothing to do with it, but he'd worked in the ruins and so he qualified for a nice hunk of change.

He hadn't lived long enough to spend any of it, so it had all gone to Tier. Tier kept a little cushion for himself and gave the rest to the grandparents who'd raised him. But they led simple lives and the dough was sitting in a money market account collecting interest. When they passed on, it would come back to Tier.

So, he'd soldier through and keep as much distance as possible between him and Poncia.

The only good thing about today was something that hadn't happened: that sound. Tier was beginning to wonder if he'd really heard it. Because no one else had. Its volume near the center of the Sheep Meadow had nearly driven him to his knees, so how could anyone nearby—and he'd seen a good number—*not* hear it.

Unless it was all in his head.

But it had a definite location *outside* his head—centered in the Sheep Meadow, dammit. It didn't make sense.

The possibility that he had something amiss in his mind or his brain nagged at him. He wouldn't do anything about it now. But if he heard that sound again, he'd have no choice but to seek out a doctor for a diagnosis. But where to start? A neurologist or a shrink?

Maybe it wouldn't happen. Maybe he'd never hear it again. He couldn't let it distract him. He'd simply go on with his life.

Which right now consisted of sitting here alone, sipping his Patron, and planning his next move.

And yes, a plan was forming ... a sneaky way to learn the whereabouts of Madame de Medici.

MONDAY—DECEMBER 22

1

Waiting for Jack . . . whoever he was.

Albert had found a spot out of the wind that gave him a good angle on the front door to the guy's brownstone without being seen: hiding behind the steps of another place just like it across the street.

Easy peasy.

Gonna be a good day, he could tell. If not for the constant throbbing in his wrecked finger, it might be a great day. The doc had said it wasn't broken but better if it had been because it would heal better. The torn ligaments might never heal right. Man, he'd love to get his hands on that Medici bitch—in more ways than one.

Whatever. He was here to show the boss he didn't need no hotshot Indian PI with a badass rep for tracking folks. All he needed was Albert Poncia. Good ol' Albert wasn't no Big Chief Indian like Hill and didn't have no P-I license, but what he had was instincts. All you needed was good solid instincts and you could get any job done, and done right.

All he had to do was wait till this guy left his place. Tonto had said his name was Jack—no known last name—and he lived on the third floor. When Jack was out of sight Albert would bust in and toss his place. Tonto hadn't been able to get in, but what did he know? Albert was ready to show him up.

If the fucking Bagaq was there, Albert would find it and return it to the boss. If it wasn't there, Albert would wait for this Jack guy to return and put the screws to him till he gave up the Bagaq. Either way, the boss would get his weird goody.

Roland Apfel didn't like to be called "boss," so Albert always called him "Mister Apfel" to his face. But "Apfel" was a dick name. Sounded like that computer company. And "Roland" was totally dick. So, in the privacy of his head Albert called him "boss."

The boss treated him right and paid him good. Even let him live on the second floor, which was a good thing and a not-so-good thing since it meant the boss could call on him anytime day or night. Not that he did so very often, but every once in a while he wanted something done right away, no delay, and expected Albert to hop to it.

Which Albert did. Basically, his job boiled down to doing whatever the boss told him to do. Some of it wasn't legal, some of it left people bleeding. Not a good thing to get between Roland Apfel and something he wanted. No matter. Albert did what needed doing, whatever it was.

Small price to pay for living rent free in the mid-Sixties right off Fifth Avenue. Couldn't beat that. Room plus board. Not that he ever ate with the boss—wouldn't want to, uh-uh, no way. But most days the house had a cook who fixed Albert something whenever he was hungry.

He had a sweet deal and wasn't about to let anything mess it up. So any time he could do the boss a solid, he was on it.

Like now. Find that fucking Bagaq thing. He had no idea why the boss wanted it, but the why didn't matter. If he wanted it, Albert would get it and—

"Who are you and what are you doing here?"

Albert looked up to see a baldie in a sweatshirt and shorts staring down at him from the top of the brownstone's steps. The house's green door stood open behind him.

"Just standing here. Who wants to know?"

"The owner of this house wants to know, that's who. And he happens to be me. And what you're doing isn't 'standing,' it's called loitering. Now move on before I call the police."

"You don't own the sidewalk, mister."

"I own the area around my front steps, right where you're loitering."

Rich people. Some of them, like the boss, were okay, but others were real assholes.

"Move, I said! Or you can explain it to the NYPD."

Okay, that wouldn't be good. Even if they just told him to move on, cops would attract all sorts of attention. He'd have to find another lookout.

"Awright, awright. I'm moving."

As he stepped away from the steps, he saw a guy coming out the door of the other brownstone. Hill had said Jack was *medium all over—medium height, medium build, medium brown hair.* The description fit this guy perfect.

Awright! Albert wasn't going to have to find a new lookout after all.

And then he noticed the package in the guy's hand: the same size and shape as the Bagaq. He was moving it!

This hadn't been the plan, but Albert saw no choice but to follow.

2

"You can't park that there. Can't you read?"

Tier finished chaining the Forza to the *NO PARKING* sign and turned to the Allard's liveried doorman. He raised his helmet's tinted visor just enough to clear his lips.

"First off, the bike's on the sidewalk, and second, I'll only be here long enough to deliver a package to one of your residents."

Releasing the box from the bungees that held it down, he approached the doorman. Despite the heavy ornate coat, his hat and gloves, the guy still looked cold.

"You got a Madame de Medici here?" Tier said.

"Lemme see your face."

"What?"

"Lemme see who I'm talking to."

He seemed pretty serious about that, so Tier raised the visor.

"Better?"

His nametag said *Simón* and he gave Tier a long look before answering. "Who you looking for again?"

He'd heard loud and clear but Tier would play the game.

"Does a Madame de Medici live here?"

"Yes and no."

"What's that supposed to mean?"

"Yeah, she lives here, but she's away for a while."

Shit. Tier kept a neutral expression.

"Away where?"

The doorman gave him a practiced *Are-you-kidding-me?* look. "Even if I knew, you think I'd tell you?"

"How long?"

"She didn't say." He held out his hands. "But we're holding her mail."

Tier hesitated, then handed it over.

The doorman hefted the box, saying, "What's in it?"

Tier's own *Are-you-kidding-me?* look wasn't quite as nuanced, but he put it on before he turned away. "Even if I knew, you think I'd tell you?"

"Ay, c'mon. I gotta know if it's perishable!"

"No worry. It's not."

Just a bunch of old magazines.

Tier unchained the bike and rolled it off the curb. He'd confirmed what he'd suspected. The Medici gal had skipped town. But with or without the Bagaq? Tier suspected the latter. His money was on Jack's place.

It bothered him that they knew so little about her. Usually when he took on a case, he had a thorough background on the quarry. This gal, though . . . total mystery woman. And that story of someone with the same name and an "uncanny" resemblance to the current Madame de Medici stealing an ancient sapphire back in 1912 . . . he'd never admit it aloud, but that gave him the creeps. Because this gal had anything but run-of-the-mill looks. Those amber eyes . . .

If she had any connection to the sapphire thief, it had to be her grandmother or some relative like that. Stupid to think it might be the same gal. She'd be pushing 150 now.

Away for a while . . . Roland said she had places to crash all over the globe, which meant she could be anywhere, but Tier had instinctive doubts about the doorman's veracity. Something about the way he'd delivered those lines. Like he said them every day. Maybe she traveled a lot. Maybe it didn't matter if she was here or gone. He was pretty sure she'd left something at that guy Jack's apartment, but had it been the Bagaq?

He'd watch the Allard a little longer.

3

Jack took another look out Costin's sooty, smoggy front window. The mom-and-pop had been here forever—a proto-convenience store that had opened back when the Permian Extinction was still a fond memory. Jack had been a regular since he'd moved to the Upper West Side.

"That's the third time you've looked out the window," Liz said from behind the counter. "Something interesting going on out there?"

Yeah, Jack thought. I'm being followed by a pear-shaped man.

"Saw a guy with a weird-looking dog. Wondering if he'll come back this way. Gotta find out what kind of mutt it is."

Over the years old man Costin and his wife had adapted their fare to the times, adding flavored coffees to their lineup of urns and, most recently, breakfast sandwiches. Lately their daughter Liz had taken an interest in the place. As a vegetarian—Jack thought he remembered her calling herself a lacto-ovo-vegetarian or some other multi-hyphenated variation—she'd been expanding the menu to her own liking.

He returned to the sandwich counter where she was finishing the four vegetarian breakfast burritos he'd ordered. She'd trapped her wild, frizzy brown hair under a net. When she forgot the net, she looked ready to break into a flashdance any second.

After finding the scratches on his front door last night, no surprise to find someone watching his place this morning. Jack had spotted the squat, dumpy guy in the Rangers jacket and knit cap from his front window. He'd looked cold out there, shifting from one foot to the other.

Jack decided to lead him on a mini tour of the UWS.

So, when he'd left the house, he'd taken the Bagaq along, tightly wrapped in a flimsy yellow plastic shopping bag so its shape and size would be obvious. If the guy had gone up the brownstone's steps instead of bird-dogging him, Jack would have been forced to return for a confrontation. But the lure had worked. He followed Jack all the way to Costin's.

"Sorry this is taking so long," Liz said.

"Take your time. I've got all morning."

He certainly didn't mind if his tail had to spend a little extra time on the frigid windy corner where he'd set up watch on the store.

"I still can't believe how good that fake sausage tastes," he said, making conversation. "Just like the real thing."

No lie. Her textured vegetable protein tasted exactly like spicy sausage meat.

"You wouldn't believe what they're doing with TVP these days, but that's my own special mix of spices. I think these'll fool Abe."

"Maybe. Maybe not. But you know what? He'll eat them anyway."

"What's not to like?" she said. "Scrambled TVP sausage, egg whites, and low-fat cheddar wrapped in a flour tortilla. Tastes just like the real thing except without all that animal fat."

That was the idea. Jack needed to arrive with an offering for the non-immortal deity perched behind the rear counter, but one that wouldn't shorten his life.

"Don't know why you bother, though," she added.

"Just doing my part."

"Maybe I shouldn't say this then."

"Go ahead."

"Just between you and me?"

Jack held up two fingers. "Scout's honor."

"You need three, Jack."

He added a third. "Promise."

"Abe likes to stop in on his way home."

Hoo boy.

"And?"

"Well, last night he bought a gallon of cookie dough ice cream."

Yeah. Why do I bother?

Shaking his head, he paid her and left the store carrying two bags instead of one.

He wondered if his tail planned to jump him. He hoped so.

But no such luck. Cars crawled the street, people scurried along the sidewalks. Too many witnesses.

So, he led him straight to Abe's. After entering, Jack paused a few feet inside the door in case the tail followed him in. But again, no such luck.

"Breakfast anyone?" he said, approaching the rear counter.

Abe looked up from the array of newspapers he had spread out before him.

"Nu? Who said I was hungry?"

"You'll be hungry for these. From Costin's."

His face lit. "Sarmale?"

Cabbage rolls for breakfast?

"No. Breakfast burritos."

"I've never had. But I'm not hungry. Maybe Parabellum will try."

As if answering a call, the blue parakeet fluttered to a landing on Abe's shoulder, cocking his head back and forth as he considered the two bags Jack laid on the counter.

When Jack unwrapped the burritos, Abe gave in and tried one.

"Just so Parabellum won't go hungry."

The bird didn't go hungry. Neither did his owner who downed two and pronounced them quite tasty.

As they were finishing, the front door opened and a man and a boy entered.

Abe rolled his eyes. "Oy, customers." Wiping his hands on his shirt, he raised his voice. "Look around. If you need help—"

"We're from Colorado and we're looking for skis," the father said. He was bundled in a red Gore-Tex jacket and a knit cap.

Jack leaned back to watch the show. Though his cover was a sporting goods shop, Abe hated to sell any of his upstairs stock. His stock in the downstairs armory was a different story. His stated goal was to try his damnedest to have every sporting customer leave emptyhanded.

Abe's accent thickened. "Gevalt! You're from Colorado and you don't have skis?"

"Not with us. With a big storm coming, I figure we'll head upstate and get in some runs."

"Snowpocalypse!" the kid cried, pumping a fist. He was about Vicky's age and dressed like his dad but in blue. "Snowmageddon!"

"Too many weather reports," the father said, smiling.

Abe pointed. "All we have are over against the wall."

As man veered off, the boy grabbed a basketball and banged it on the floor—where it stayed.

"Hey, this doesn't bounce."

"Bounce? You want it should bounce?"

Abe hated people bouncing balls in his shop.

The father said, "It just needs air, Billy."

"Of course it bounces," Abe said. "Like a Spaldeen it bounces."

"Hey, dad, he talks like Yoda."

"No, he doesn't." The father approached, carrying a pair of skis. "*Wooden* skis?"

Abe looked puzzled. "There's other kinds?"

With an I-can't-believe-I-have-to-tell-him-this look: "Yeh-uh. Like aluminum and fiberglass and composite. These things here are solid wood—not even laminated."

"I confess, when it comes to skis, a maven I'm not. But these are classics."

"They weigh a ton."

"Like a Viking you'll ski." Abe turned to Jack. "I'm kwelling about tradition, he's kvetching about weight."

"How about snowboards?"

"Snowboards? Snowboards we don't have."

"See?" Billy said. "He talks like Yoda."

Dad said, "I know Yoda, Billy, and he doesn't talk like Yoda."

"When have you ever seen a Viking on a snowboard?" Abe said. "But if such a thing exists, Ski World will have it."

The father's expression brightened. "Ski World? Now we're talkin'. Where's that?"

"I should know from Ski World? I'm sure you can find a place called Ski World somewhere in your phone."

The guy leaned the skis against the counter. "Okay. We're done here. Come on, Billy."

"But Da-ad!"

"Your Uncle Bob warned me about this place," he said as they headed for the door. "He said, 'Don't go. The owner's crazy.' But did I listen? Noooooo."

And then they were out and gone.

Jack laughed. "Another satisfied customer! You really laid the Yiddishisms on the poor guy."

"My grandfather used to read *Forverts* every day and what Yiddish I know I got from him. Sometimes I'm not sure myself what I'm saying." He frowned. "Who's this Yoda I supposedly sound like?"

"You don't. But better than a Jabba reference."

"Jabba?"

"Not important."

Abe jutted one of his chins toward the plastic shopping bag. "What's in there?"

Jack pulled out the Bagaq. "Need you to hide this for me."

"Hide for why?"

"So somebody can't steal it."

Abe considered it from various angles, all looks askance.

"*Mieskeit*. You think someone would steal this? You shouldn't worry. I should maybe put it out front to scare away customers like the last two."

"No-no-no. I'm keeping it for somebody. Just stash it downstairs until I come back for it."

Abe hefted the Bagaq, nodded, then placed it under the counter. "Next trip down."

"Excellent. Thanks."

Jack bunched up the burrito wrappers and the bag they came in, then stuffed them inside the plastic shopping bag. It looked like it still held the Bagaq.

"Why for you do that?"

"I want the guy who followed me here to think I still have it."

"Already someone's after it? He's blind, maybe?"

"Long story. Can I ask you to do a couple of look-ups for me?"

Abe rolled his eyes and looked at Parabellum. "What do you

think, my friend? Two assignments for two burritos? Sound fair?"

Parabellum deposited a multicolored load on Abe's shoulder and flew off.

"Well, you can see Parabellum's vote," he said wiping it up with a paper napkin. "I shall ignore that. Whom do you seek?"

He handed him a slip with Hess's phone number. "See if you can find where this guy lives. He's one of the researchers from Plum Island. I trust his partner less but this is all I've got."

"And you think it might become necessary to pay a surprise visit sometime?"

"Might. I'm hoping it doesn't become necessary, but it's not a bad thing to have in reserve."

"That's easy. You could do it yourself."

"But you've got all the software." Abe did a deep background check on every new customer. "The second one might not be so easy."

Jack told him about David Quinnell, his possible connection to the Department of Defense, and the address of his ex-wife in Howard Beach.

"Defense contacts I got," Abe said. "Shouldn't be too hard."

"Excellent. Meanwhile, time to lead my bird dog on a chase."

Jack waved as he headed out onto the bustling sidewalks, then over to Broadway, making sure to keep the plastic shopping bag in plain sight. His tail dropped in behind him, staying maybe fifty feet back. Time to run a little game on this guy.

4

Tier leaned against the Central Park wall in his usual spot across the street from the Allard, sipping some bitter food-cart coffee. Madame de Medici had not shown. Maybe she really was out of town.

He checked his phone and noticed his word-of-the-day email had arrived.

Inchmeal
Adverb—INCH-meel
little by little, gradually

Now there was an odd one.

He was pondering how he could work inchmeal into his day when a low-pitched hum began rumbling through his head and thrumming in his chest.

Not again.

He covered his ears but as before it had no effect. He couldn't escape it. He turned in the direction where it seemed to originate—the Sheep Meadow again.

And then another sound: a high-pitched scream. Somewhere in the park a little girl was screaming at the top of her lungs. Her piercing distress kicked him into motion. He hurried the short distance to the entrance at Sixty-ninth Street and trotted down the path.

The screams seemed to be coming from the direction of the Sheep Meadow. And as before the sound increased in volume with every step he took toward it. His entire skeleton seemed to be vibrating.

He spotted a teenage girl, dark haired, skinny, maybe fifteen or sixteen, running from the Meadow. Two others, her mother and an older sister maybe, chased after her. The younger one slowed and staggered in a circle with a finger in each ear. Her circular, tortoise-shell glasses gave her round face an owlish look.

She turned toward her mother and screamed, "Don't tell me you can't hear it *now*?"

Why were they just staring at her? Her distress was palpable. And why wasn't that goddamn noise bothering them?

"I don't know what else to tell you, Ellie," the mother said, stopping before her. "I don't hear anything." She turned to the older sister. "Do you?"

The sister shook her head. "I hear the traffic up on the street but that's all. What's it sound like?"

"Like a moan—a long moan that never stops. And so *loud!* Not as loud as it was back in the field, but—" She clapped her hands over her ears. "I can't *stand* it!"

Back in the field . . . she must have been in the Sheep Meadow when it began.

The mother hovered beside her. "I don't know what to do!"

"Make it stop. Please, Mom, you've got to make it stop!"

"We can't hear it, Ellie. That means it's in your head. Does covering your ears help?"

"No, it's all around."

"You hear it too?" Hill blurted. He hadn't meant to speak.

The teen nodded as her face paled, and her cheeks . . . they seemed to be sinking.

"It's making me sick. I wanna go home!"

"You mean like back to Mizzou?" the sister said.

Ellie retched. "I'm gonna puke!"

"No, don't! You know I hate that smell. It makes *me* wanna puke!"

"Hush, Bess!" said the mother.

Tier started to turn away. He felt sorry for the kid, but she was with her family and he needed to get away from that sound. God, his head was going to explode.

And then, as she'd warned, Ellie hurled. Tier had seen projectile vomiting before and that was what Ellie did.

Except she vomited blood—bright red blood. A long stream of it.

"Oh, no!" the mother screamed. "Ellie, no!"

And then Ellie dropped to her knees and did it again. So much blood...

Like a chopped tree, she fell onto her side, but never took her hands from over her ears.

"Make it stop, Mom," she gasped, her face white as a cloud. "Make it stop!"

And then her eyelids fluttered and she passed out.

Tier couldn't stand by any longer. He knelt and slipped his arms under her back and her knees. As he lifted her, he said, "Call 9-1-1!"

"What are you doing?" the mother cried as he started carrying her away. "Put her down!"

"The sound's not so loud up by the street."

"What sound?"

He couldn't believe this. "You really don't hear it?"

"No! And put her down!"

"Just follow me, lady. She'll be better on the sidewalk."

He increased his pace and heard the mother start to scream for help as she chased after him. He reached the sidewalk—the sound had definitely dropped in volume—and made for the nearest bench where a young couple sat worshipping their phones.

"Move-move-move!" he shouted, and they moved. He laid Ellie on the bench and began gently slapping her cheeks. "Kid? Wake up, kid. The sound's not so loud here."

She was all bundled up and he thought he should be loosening her coat, but no way was he going to do anything like that. The mother grabbed his shoulder and pulled him away, then pushed herself between him and her daughter.

"Get away from her!"

"Did you call the EMTs?"

"I was too busy chasing you!"

Idiot. He pulled out his phone and stabbed 9-1-1. As he waited for an answer, he glanced around at the crowd that had gathered out of nowhere and recognized Madame de Medici, Cossack hat and all, staring at him with a puzzled expression.

"What is your emergency?"

"Little girl vomiting blood at Sixty-Ninth and CPW."

"What exactly—?"

He hung up and looked around again. Madame was gone. He pushed through the crowd and searched the street and sidewalks but no sign of her. Damn! How did she disappear like that?

As Tier waited around for the cops and EMTs to show up, Ellie woke up.

"The noise . . . " she said.

The mother kissed her forehead. "It's gone now?"

"No. But it not as loud. It's not making me sick anymore."

The mother looked up and her eyes met Tier's. "Thank you. I'm sorry I panicked. I just—"

He shrugged and smiled. "A strange man carrying my daughter off? I'd panic too."

"But what's this sound she's talking about? I thought it was in her head but you seem to hear it too."

Tier looked from the sister to the mother. "And you don't? Neither of you?" When they both shook their heads, he turned to the crowd. "Who here hears that noise, that low-pitched hum?"

Not one person raised a hand. They looked at him like he'd grown another head.

"What is it?" the mother said. "Where does it come from?"

Tier shrugged. "Wish I knew. Heard it Friday, now today."

"Thank you again. May I ask your name?"

Instinctively he hesitated, but could see no reason not to tell her. "Hill . . . Tier Hill."

And just then, as suddenly as it had begun, the noise stopped. Same as before.

Tier turned back to Ellie who had started to sob.

"What's wrong?" the mother said.

"It stopped! It finally stopped!"

And then she passed out again.

Although he felt sorry for the kid, Tier swayed in a wave of over-whelming relief. He wasn't the only one. This kid had heard it too. He wasn't crazy. He didn't have a tumor.

As the EMTs and cops arrived with their usual flashing fanfare,

Tier wandered back toward his Honda. He froze in shock when he found Madame de Medici waiting for him.

"You heard the signal?" she said.

Unprepared for this sort of confrontation, he fumbled for an answer.

"Signal? What signal?"

Her amber eyes bored into him. "Did you or did you not hear the signal?"

"If that bone-melting hum is what you call 'the signal,' then yes, I heard it."

She stared at him for a long, uncomfortable time, then, "Come with me."

As she started toward the curb, he stayed put, not sure what to do.

"You followed me before," she said over her shoulder.

Chagrined, he said. "You weren't supposed to know that."

"You'd be surprised what I know. If you like to follow me so much, follow me to my apartment."

Shit.

So, he did as she said—followed as she jaywalked Central Park West to the Allard Building. The doorman grinned as they entered.

"Hello, Simón," she said.

He tipped his cap. "Good day, Madame."

"I guess she's back from her trip," Tier said

The grin widened. "She most certainly is."

Madame said, "To visitors I am always away. Those are my instructions to the doormen."

Tier stopped in the middle of the lobby and did a slow turn.

"Something wrong?" she said.

"The woodwork . . . it's magnificent."

The lobby was a riot of laminates and burled wood veneers and multicolored inlays in intricate, graceful designs.

"Yes, it is. I've grown so used to it I barely see it anymore. But it's one of the reasons I bought a co-op here. No one does this kind of work anymore."

"My grandfather helped build the Allard. Not the woodwork, the steel."

"Well, so far, so good," she said, continuing toward the elevators.

"My compliments to him. It hasn't collapsed yet."

She led him to the central set of doors, labeled TOWER. Inside, she pressed the 26 button, right below the P.

"Not the penthouse?" he said as the elevator began to move.

She looked at him askance. "That's Burbank's level."

"Oh." Who the hell was Burbank? Was he expected to know? "Tell me about that noise you called 'the signal.'"

"In due time. That is not why I asked you up to my apartment."

"Why then?"

"I want you to search it."

What?

"Are you serious?"

"Yes. I want you to search for the Bagaq as thoroughly as you wish in order to assure yourself that I do not have it."

Which meant he could be pretty well assured she'd hidden it elsewhere.

"But that will prove only that you don't have it in the apartment. It could be a million other places. I'm told you own homes all over the world."

"This is true." She was staring at him. "I have not been this close to you before. There is something about you. Something special."

Was this going to be some sort of seduction to distract him from finding the Bagaq? Well, yeah, he could get down with that. The seduction part, okay. Better than okay. She was one hell of an attractive woman. And she seemed as much into relationships as he.

But as for giving up on the Bagaq? Uh-uh. He could multitask in that regard.

"Special in what way?"

She leaned closer. For all he knew she was sniffing him.

"You have a destiny." When he stiffened she cocked her head. "Is something wrong?"

Destiny . . . that shook him. His grandmother used to say that. Well, not that exactly, but close enough. She'd talk about a purpose in life—a "mission." That was the word she'd used: *mission.*

He knew he had a mission this week and that was the return of the Bagaq. But a mission in life?

"No, no problem, except destiny is a weighty word. A lot going on there."

"Well, there *is* a lot going on—a lot more than anyone realizes. And your destiny might not lead you to a place you wish to be. And then again, it might."

The elevator stopped and they stepped out into a small vestibule where she used a pass card to open an ornate, inlaid door.

He felt as if he'd stepped into a museum—paintings lined the walls, statues crowded the floors. Tier knew nothing of art and antiques but he had an innate sense of design and order, and he sensed neither here. She made Roland look focused and organized. Her taste could best be described as . . . it had once been a Word of the Day . . .

"An *eclectic* collection," he said. Eclectic in the extreme.

She nodded as she removed her fur coat and draped it over a large stone Olmec head. "That's a good word for it. I like what I like and I'm long past making excuses for my taste. Some pieces aren't art at all, they're simply old. But they're all here for me. I don't care what anyone else might think. What's your name, by the way?"

"Tier. Tier Hill."

"Well, Mister Hill, search to your heart's content. I'll be making some tea."

"I'd have thought you'd have someone to do that for you."

"I do. But I sent them out so they wouldn't be in your way."

He waited until she'd strolled out of sight, then looked around. He crossed the huge living room to the front windows and parted the sheers to reveal a breathtaking view of the Central Park Sheep Meadow directly below.

He did cursory searches of the huge living room, the dining room, the office, and each of the three bedrooms. He had an idea which one might be hers but couldn't be sure. The apartment spanned at least three thousand square feet. It took up the entire width of the tower, affording 360 degrees of city views, with every room crammed with artifacts from all over the world and every period in history and sometimes prehistory. Even the Museum of Natural History might be jealous here.

Had she been screwing with his head, telling him to search to his heart's content? The Bagaq might well be here, but he'd never find it alone. Like searching for a particular beetle in a rain forest. He'd need a team.

He wandered back to the living room where he noticed her discarded fur coat. Was it possible? As soon as he lifted it off the stone head, he knew from the weight that he'd find nothing. He checked the pockets anyway: no Bagaq. That would have been way too easy.

Last stop was the kitchen where he found her leaning back against a black counter and languidly stirring a cup of tea.

"Well," she said with a mischievous smile, "what took you so long? I thought you'd never get here."

"I was searching—"

"And finding nothing."

As he began searching through the cabinets, she said, "I sense you are a disconnected person."

"Disconnected?"

"Yes. You don't have friends, only acquaintances. You're not estranged from whatever family you have, but you don't stay in touch."

Disconnected . . . yeah, that pretty much summed it up. He saw no use in denying it.

"I guess so. What's the point? You analyzing me?"

"Simply assessing your suitability."

"For what?"

She put down her cup. "I'd like you to meet someone."

"Where?" The place was empty.

She led him out of the kitchen toward the apartment door.

"Upstairs."

"This is a duplex?"

She had a throaty laugh. "No. Burbank is in the penthouse."

Burbank again.

She turned on a lamp and a panel in the wall slid open to reveal a spiral staircase.

Damn.

He followed her as she climbed the narrow winding steps to the next level where they stepped into a brightly lit, sparsely furnished room, nondescript except for the exquisite woodwork. No one here but the two of them.

"I don't get it."

"Follow me."

She led him down a hallway lit with stained-glass sconces to a darker, cavernous space crammed with rows and stacks and racks of blinking, glowing electronic equipment, most of it old—like 1930s / vacuum-tube old—but some of it state of the art. Although what art, Tier wasn't sure. A huge flat-screen TV, silent and black as onyx, hung on the wall. Whatever space the electronics didn't fill was littered with books, hundreds of them, most of them old and dusty, in ramshackle piles threatening to keel over at the hint of a breeze. In a near corner, something that looked like a coffin lay on the floor. Its lid, intricately carved with primitive symbols, stood against the wall behind it.

Figuring it couldn't be, Tier veered toward it for a closer look and, yeah, an ancient-looking coffin.

"Seriously?" he said with a glance toward Madame.

She nodded. "Burbank doesn't like to be far from his desk."

What?

He glanced in and saw sheets, a blanket, and a pillow. He'd heard of people sleeping in coffins but had never seen . . .

He pointed to the lid. "Some kind of native carving?"

"A small, reclusive South American tribe."

This was moving further and further into the weird.

"Why . . . ?"

"You can ask Burbank some time."

Shaking his head, he rejoined Madame.

A hanging Tiffany lamp, its chain disappearing into the darkness above, illuminated a bent old man, bald as an egg, crouched before a keyboard and a huge, sixty-inch monitor. A big, old-fashioned, slotted-chrome microphone was seated between him and the keyboard. A world map outlined in white filled the otherwise black screen. The map—continents and oceans alike—was peppered with glowing dots.

"Good morning, Burbank," Madame said.

"Twilight has come. Night will follow." He spoke without looking around, his voice as soft as a shovel digging into snow.

"Yes, I know." She lowered her voice to Tier—"His mantra"—then raised it again: "I'd like you to meet Mister Tier Hill."

"Why would you like me to meet him?"

"Mister Hill can hear the Sheep Meadow signal."

"Oh?"

The old man's neck barely rotated as he swiveled his chair to stare at him.

Damn, he was old. Wild gray eyebrows, the bags under his cloudy eyes dragging down his lower lids. Jowls like a bulldog. A wizened gnome in an island of light on a sea of darkness.

"This is true, Mister Hill?"

"I'm not sure. I heard something out there just now. This is the first time anyone's ever mentioned a 'Sheep Meadow signal.' Signal for what?"

"Twilight has come. Night will follow."

She said, "He'll need something more specific, Burbank."

"You tell him, dear."

"Very well," Madame de Medici said. "We don't know for what. And we don't know *from* what. We do know that only rare people—very rare—can hear the signals."

"'Signals'? You mean there's more than one?"

"Hundreds," Burbank said, pointing at his screen. "Hundreds all over the world."

"One of them—the signal from the Sheep Meadow—emanates *from* the Earth," she said. "The rest come from out there and go into the Earth."

"'Out there'? Out where?"

"The Void," Burbank said. "They form no pattern and they all have different frequencies and amplitudes."

"All right. Fine. Who's sending them from 'the Void'?"

She shrugged. "We don't know."

None of this made any sense.

"All right then, how long has it been going on? Judging from the look of this place, I'm going to guess you folks have been monitoring these signals for a long time."

"No 'folks'," Burbank said. "Just me since the spring of 1941. Other signals followed, but the Sheep Meadow tone was the first. It began at 8:56 p.m. Eastern Standard Time on April 23rd, 1941, to be precise."

"That sounds . . . pretty damn precise," Tier said.

"I never knew that," Madame said.

"You never asked."

"The date must mean something," she said.

"Not to me. But I remember it well, because I too can hear the signals. Also, it happened during the month of my tenth anniversary here."

Tier's grandfather used to talk a lot about the Allard. He loved the building and took such pride in raising the steel, especially this tower. But . . .

"Wait. This place was completed in 1930."

"Exactly. I moved in shortly thereafter."

"But that means you must be . . . "

"Over one hundred years old? Yes, I most certainly am."

"How far over, may I ask?"

Burbank turned his head about ten degrees. Tier figured arthritis had pretty much frozen his neck. "I'm not sure. You keep track of these things, dear. Tell him."

Madam de Medici leveled her amber gaze at Tier and said, "He was one hundred and eighteen last month."

Tier felt his jaw working. How . . . how was this possible?

"And you sleep in a South American native coffin? Is that the secret?"

Burbank's chuckle disintegrated into a cough. "It has a mattress and is quite comfortable. And convenient, of course. Mostly I take naps."

Tier jumped as a voice from a speaker somewhere in the dark said, "*Sector four-seven-two reporting.*"

With that, a white line began undulating across the map on the screen.

Burbank tapped on his keyboard and *472* appeared below it. He leaned forward and pressed a button on the mike's base.

"What is the frequency?"

"*Eleven point-seven-five megahertz.*"

He tapped that in, then said, "Recorded."

Tier looked at Madame. "What the—? That's in the normal hearing range."

He'd learned a little about hearing after suffering acoustic trauma from that IED in Afghanistan. Luckily that was all he'd suffered that day. A couple of his fellows lost limbs.

"You're thinking of sound waves," Burbank said. "These are electromagnetic transmissions. Quite different."

"You mean like microwaves?"

"Quite so."

"Then how come I can hear it? You can't hear microwaves."

"These signals don't follow the usual rules. Rare people like you and me can hear them. We're special."

Tier didn't know if that was the kind of special he wanted or needed. Young Ellie sure as hell didn't want it.

Burbank added, "The signal just reported happens to be medium frequency with a wavelength of over one hundred meters. As you may or may not know, wavelength is inversely proportional to frequency."

Tier did the conversion—a meter ran a little over three feet, so . . . No.

"You're talking a wavelength longer than a football field?"

"Exactly. The signals are all below the visible spectrum. They started out fluctuating between one hundred gigahertz with a wavelength of a fraction of a centimeter at the high end, and ten kilohertz with a wavelength approaching 100 kilometers at the low end. All fluctuating, that is, except the Sheep Meadow signal. That remained a constant thirty megahertz."

Jesus.

"I heard the same thing—signal—a few days ago."

"They all recur sporadically, at seemingly random intervals."

"And you're gonna tell me you keep track of all the signals and their frequencies?"

"Not all," Burbank said. "I don't have the resources for that. Just a hobby at first. My original job here in the thirties and forties was coordinating communications for a rather eccentric fellow—quite eccentric, actually—who let me pursue these curious signals during my downtime. I think he thought I'd gone crazy, and frankly I thought he might be right since I was the only one I knew who could hear them. But he humored me by buying extra equipment which I modified to pick up the signals and pinpoint their locations. He's long since retired but he lets me stay here."

"And you've been monitoring them since 1941?"

"Mostly just cataloguing them. Monitoring them made no sense, what with their frequencies and amplitudes randomly fluctuating all over the place. I send a monthly report to subscribers—by post in the beginning, now email."

"Subscribers? Who would—?"

"You'd be surprised," Burbank said. "People make decisions based on the frequencies. Just like a horoscope."

"But back in the sixties," said Madame de Medici, "everything changed."

Tier caught an ominous tone.

"Changed how?"

Burbank said, "In early 1968, on February eleventh by my best calculations—I wasn't paying all that much attention at the time—each and every signal stabilized its frequency. They still showed wide variations between them, but each one locked into a consistent cycle. And they held those frequencies for decades . . . until this past August."

He paused, wheezing.

"What happened in August?" Tier said.

Burbank huffed. "You tell him, dear. I'm out of breath."

Madame said, "In August, the signals suddenly began changing. Each signal—all except one—began increasing or decreasing its frequency. A rapid rate of change at first, which has gradually slowed to a crawl. But they still seem to be moving toward a common frequency."

"Progressing *inchmeal*," Tier said.

Yes!

After a brief, questioning look, she said, "We have no idea why they're moving toward synchronization."

"Twilight has come," Burbank droned. "Night will follow."

Tier said, "The Sheep Meadow tone today was the same as I heard Friday."

She smiled. "You have a good ear, Mister Hill. The Sheep Meadow signal—the only one that originates on Earth—is not changing."

"That's why I call it the Prime Frequency," Burbank said.

"Yes," Madame continued. "The other signals are gradually moving toward it. But I don't think it's a good thing. In fact, I think it will prove to be a very bad thing."

Tier said, "Why does it have to be good or bad?"

"Consider the reality," she said in an exasperated tone. "All these signals shooting into the planet, originating from who knows where. That's not normal. Neither is being able to hear them, yet rare people can."

"Well, it's odd, but—"

"A dark time is coming, Mister Hill—"

"Twilight has come. Night will follow." Burbank again.

Madame finished: "And these signals may be harbingers."

"Of what?"

"Of the beginning of a nightworld and the end of everything. Or at least the end of life as we know it, or wish to know it."

"Oh, come on . . . "

"They await a signal," Burbank wheezed.

Tier repressed a laugh. "The signals are waiting for a signal?"

"Exactly." He seemed to have caught his breath. "A signal to complete their synchronization. And when that happens . . . "

"What?"

"Night falls."

"Night? I don't—"

"Why are the signals placed where they are?" Burbank said. "They never waver from their original position. Why, for instance, does one emanate from the center of the Sheep Meadow out there?"

Tier shrugged. "I can't even hazard a guess."

"Nor can I. But when synchronization occurs, something will happen where those signals are located. Something nasty, I fear."

"You mean, like for instance, in the center of the Sheep Meadow? Something 'nasty' will happen there when the time comes?"

He nodded. "When night falls. Very nasty."

His certainty gave Tier a chill.

"It will begin in the heavens," Burbank added, "and it will end in the Earth. But before it begins, the laws will bend and break."

"What laws?"

"The laws of reality. And if I'm lucky, I won't be alive to see it." He cleared his throat. "We're owned, you know."

Was he serious? Yes, he was.

"Well, as the saying goes, everybody gotta serve somebody."

"I mean, we're property."

Okay, he'd play along.

"Whose?"

"That's in contention. One of them, you know . . . " He shifted his gaze back and forth to the ceiling. " . . . out there. One of them owns us but may lose us to a competitor. That will not be good for us. The game's got rules but not everybody plays by them. The one behind the signals has been cheating."

"And you know this how?"

"I've had almost a hundred and twenty years to learn a few things. I've tracked down books . . . lots of books. I've read them and kept them all. I still don't know the exact purpose of the signals, but I believe we can use them as an early warning system about the end."

"End of what?"

"Everything."

"On that happy note," said Madame de Medici, "it is time for Mister Hill to leave."

"Oh?"

"Yes. I really am going on a trip. I leave for Egypt tonight."

"Egypt?"

"I appreciate Egypt. It changes, but very slowly. Some areas change not at all. I like that. Besides that, an Ugaritic tablet is coming up for auction that interests me. But I want to examine it first hand before I bid."

He wasn't sure what to believe. Was she staying, was she going? She'd been so upfront about her apartment. Why? To put him off balance? And then showing him Burbank's bizarre penthouse setup. Another push to keep him off balance?

Well, if that had been her plan, it worked.

Add to that the signal in the Sheep Meadow and he was positively wobbly.

He gathered his coat from her apartment, rode the elevator down alone, and returned to the relatively safer and saner reality of the street.

5

Isher Sports Shop? The fuck did that mean? Owned by a guy named Isher? But then it'd be *Isher's* Sport Shop, wouldn't it?

Albert had thought this Jack guy might've went into the sports store to drop off the Bagaq, but then again, he might've just been dropping off the food he bought. So, he decided to play it careful like and wait outside. Which meant freezing his ass off. Hadn't been so bad by the brownstone because he'd been out of the wind there. Outside the food store had been bad, but out here in the open . . .

At one point he got so cold he considered going into the sports store to warm up while he pretended to be shopping for a hockey stick or something. But he shit-canned that idea real fast. He didn't want Jack to make his face. The Ranger jacket was good camo 'cause they was all over the city, but if the guy connected Albert's mug with the jacket and saw him again—busted.

So, he kept crossing streets and stalking sidewalks, but always with an eye on the front door of the sports shop with the dumb-ass name. Desperate, he risked losing sight of the door to hit up a push-cart for a cup of coffee and a hot pretzel.

The Arab-looking guy—probably a terrorist on the side—took the pretzel from the oven and held it up. "Mustard?"

"No. Ketchup."

The guy frowned, grabbed the ketchup, and squeezed out a piddly red line.

"Gimme that."

Albert grabbed the squeeze bottle and applied a righteous amount. No such thing as too much ketchup. Then he hurried back to where he could put eyes on the door of that sports shop again. Along the way he spilled ketchup all over his hand and his splint and on the sleeve of his Rangers jacket. No biggie about the sleeve since it was already red, but damn that splint made it hard to do anything right.

Finally, after like forever, the guy came out without the white food bag but still carrying the yellow Bagaq-size bag. Albert had been hoping the Isher place was the drop-off point, now he guessed not.

Jack made tracks uptown and Albert fell in behind him. Man, he'd thought the street outside the sport shop was cold, but when he turned uptown on Broadway, he felt like he was in a freakin' wind tunnel at the North Pole.

Okay, decision time: Keep following the guy or flatten him from behind and snatch the Bagaq? The second was dangerous, what with every fucker on the street with their phones out and itching to record any damn thing on a second's notice. But if he timed it right . . .

Yeah, wait till Jack was passing a subway entrance, then run up behind and hit him real hard, maybe slam his head on the sidewalk for good measure, then duck down the subway stairs and out of sight. Catch the first train to come through and bing-bang-boom—gone.

The boss would have his Bagaq and Albert would have a very grateful boss, plus the bonus. Win-win, baby.

Except for the Jack guy. Lose-lose for him. He'd be hurtin' bad—hurtin' in his head and hurtin' in his soul. Yeah, he'd—

Jack veered and entered a TD bank.

No-no-no! Please say you're just gonna make a deposit or withdrawal.

Albert tried to watch through one of the windows but couldn't see much. He did see some manager type take Jack out of sight into the rear section. Not too long after, they both returned, but Jack didn't have the bag no more.

Albert screamed and started kicking the concrete wall. But not for long. He hurt his foot and had all sorts of people looking as they passed.

"I'm okay, I'm okay," he said, waving off their stares.

Shit! He's got a safety deposit box. Now what?

Albert knew what he wanted to do: Grab the fucker and beat the shit out of him. But that wouldn't get him the Bagaq. Only get him arrested.

He backed off to a spot across the street as Jack exited the bank. A plan was forming. He'd follow the guy back to his apartment and brace him there. He was wiry, medium build, but Albert outweighed him by a good fifty pounds. Easy peasy. He'd overpower him and make him cough up the deposit box key and then . . .

And then what?

Too soon to go back to the bank and open the box. What if the same guy took care of all the box customers? Jack had just been in there. The guy'd know Albert wasn't Jack. He'd—

Hey! Jack was flagging a cab. Shit-shit-shit!

He hailed his own and followed to Eleventh Avenue in Hell's Kitchen where he got out at a BP station. Albert made his own driver wait till he could figure out what was going down.

After like twenty minutes, a guy from the station led Jack to a white Econoline van. They did a walk-around, then Jack hopped in and drove off.

Albert told his driver, "Follow that van."

Jack headed toward the East Side and the driver did a good tail job for about three blocks, then Jack pushed a yellow light and got across Sixth just ahead of the uptown traffic.

Albert wanted to wring the driver's neck but that would only complicate the situation. He had him drive over to Jack's place and circle the block, looking for the white van on the chance he'd brought it home, but no luck.

At least he had the plate number, whatever good that was gonna do.

He'd have to go back and tell the boss. The boss would come up with a solution.

6

Oh, damn. Cilla was doing it again.

"Cilla, stop, honey. You'll make yourself sick."

She kept spinning. Either she didn't hear or was ignoring her.

"Cilla, please!"

Still the three-year old spun—arms out, going around and around, whirling like a dervish. It might have been different if she was giggling or the like, but her expression was blank, just like her eyes.

If Jelena didn't do something, breakfast would be all over the floor. So, she put on a happy face and forced a laugh as she picked up her daughter and swung her around.

"Wheeeee!"

But Cilla only fought to get free and back on the floor, grunting and whining, "Down!"

Jelena held on while bending to grab her spinner top. She pumped the handle to start it spinning then sat Cilla down before it.

"There! Look, it's your top!"

Cilla sat and stared. Spinning fascinated her, spinning herself as well as watching things spin. The good news was that Cilla had learned how to work the handle to spin the top. The bad news was that she could sit there endlessly watching it go.

The clock on the microwave read *9:35*. Where was Tihana? Her sister was late again, even on Jelena's late-start morning at work. Sometimes she wanted to scream at her, really let her have it, but that might result in another walk-out, leaving Jelena for days with no one to watch Cilla. So, time after time she swallowed her frustrations.

Two years younger and still living with their mother, Tihana had grown into a flabby, slovenly pot head who'd dropped out of school, had no regular job, and no desire to find one. The only income she had was what she could cadge out of Mom and what Jelena could scrape together to pay her for babysitting.

Tihana knew Jelena had to be at the office by ten on Mondays—her day to work late—yet more often than not she arrived late enough to force Jelena into a mad rush up to Woodhaven.

She went to the window—no sign of her.

Damn!

She leaned her head against the glass. David, David, David . . . if only you hadn't screwed up so bad, so often. If only you could have found a way to stop. Maybe we could have . . .

What was the use? He was gone and he'd left her with a terrible mess.

And not as if Mom would ever let her forget choosing an Irishman over a nice Croat guy.

Movement outside caught her eye: Tihana's car pulling to the curb. Jelena gritted her teeth. Finally. Damn, she was annoying.

Okay. Keep it cool. The last time they'd fought she'd had to eat crow to get Tihana back, and had almost lost her job in the meantime.

Straining to keep her voice down and her expression neutral, she opened the door as her sister came up the steps.

"Morning. Have a good weekend?"

"Hey, sorry I'm late," she said as she entered. "Traffic's a bitch this morning."

Oh, right, especially now, after rush hour's over, leaped to her lips but she bit it back.

Jelena quickly pulled on her coat. "Gotta run or *I'll* be late."

Tihana was staring at Cilla on the floor. "I see she's got the top going again."

"Yeah, she loves it." She hurried over and got no reaction as she kissed Cilla on the cheek. "Bye, hon."

Cilla kept staring at the top.

"Jelena . . . " Tihana cleared her throat. "You do know she's not right, don't you?"

"I can't get into that now. I'm late as it is. Just keep an eye on her and try not to get too stoned, okay?"

With that she rushed out the door and down the steps. She had a sense of Tihana making some sort of gesture behind her back but wouldn't give her the satisfaction of turning to see.

Once in her Celica she jammed the key into the ignition and sent up a prayer as she turned it.

"God, please make it start. Pleeeeease!"

Her old car had grown increasingly temperamental in the cold weather and this morning was cold as hell. For a few seconds it seemed her prayer might not be answered, but then the engine caught and stuttered to life.

As she sat and shivered and gave it half a minute to warm up, she thought about what her sister had said.

Yes, Tihana, I know Cilla's not right. You don't have to remind me. And I know I have to do something about it, but I don't know what.

She'd had what she thought was decent health insurance until Obamacare came along and said it wasn't good enough. *Bam.* They canceled it. Her new policy cost more and had a sky-high deductible. Living paycheck to paycheck like she had to, that was like having no insurance at all.

Cilla needed a neurological evaluation to confirm whether she was autistic or something else was going on. But that consultation fee would have to come out of Jelena's pocket—her *empty* pocket. She was sure the city or the state health departments had programs and services, she simply had to hunt them down. But between work and school and cooking and cleaning and trying to be a good mother, where was the time?

Had to make it a priority.

She admitted she'd been in denial for a while now, but she couldn't talk herself out of it any longer. Cilla wasn't right. Jelena had been distracting herself with the accounting course she was taking at the community college—she wasn't going to be an insurance agent's file clerk forever—but now she had to start searching out children's services. She paid taxes. She deserved to get a little back.

My husband's dead, the bank's taking my house, I'm in a low-paying dead-end job, and my precious little girl who hit all her early developmental milestones now seems to be slipping into autism.

What else you got in store for me, God? Is today the day I get fired for being late again?

What a nice Christmas gift that would make.

7

Jack sat in his Econoline van in Howard Beach and watched the house at the 156th Avenue address Monaco had given him—supposedly the home of DIA Agent Quinnell's ex. Most likely was, but he wasn't taking anything from the Plum Island duo as the real deal until he'd checked it out himself.

He'd decided to leave the Crown Vic home this time. Vinny Donuts or no, that local cop wasn't going to cut him much slack if he spotted the Vic lurking around again.

The Econoline was a beast but had been the only van the station had available. He could have gone to Hertz or Avis but the BP station asked fewer questions and wasn't linked to any of the major car-rental databases. His John Tyleski license worked just fine, no questions asked.

The amateur who'd been following him earlier had been almost too easy to lose. But first Jack had led him to a bank where he'd rented a safety deposit box. He'd put nothing in the box, but his tail didn't know that. Afterward, even with this clunky van, giving him the slip had been a breeze.

He pulled out the receipt and the box key. As soon as Madame de Medici retrieved her Bagaq, Jack would cancel the rental. He folded the key in the receipt and shoved it into his wallet.

He shifted in the van seat. Felt like the springs were broken. But the van might come in handy. No side windows, heavily tinted rear windows, and an empty rear section. If he bagged H3 he could tie him down and transport him in the back.

He'd made one pass past the Quinnell address before parking and idling in front of a deserted-looking house. From what Jack had seen of Howard Beach yesterday, 156th Avenue was not in the most desirable part of the town—about as far as you could get from the water and still be in Howard Beach. As for the house itself, the property backed up to the Belt Parkway. Practically on top of it. He figured you either got used to the noise or went nuts.

But that might work to his advantage. A woodsy buffer zone had been left between the last row of houses and the Belt, offering possibilities if he needed an observation perch.

Sometime after 9:30 a battered Nissan Sentra pulled up and parked in front of the house. The driver—a heavy young woman with unevenly bleached hair—got out and sauntered up the walk. A slimmer, dark-haired version opened the front door before she reached it. She looked annoyed.

The two disappeared inside for a moment, then the brunette reappeared and hustled down the walk to an equally battered Celica. The blonde flipped her the bird and went inside . . .

Time to make a few assumptions. They could be wrong but, if so, he'd revise them on the fly. Assume, as Monaco claimed, that the brunette was Jelena, Quinnell's ex. Assume that the rather slovenly woman was Jelena's sister—the facial resemblance backed that—and had the job of looking after Cilla while her mother worked.

Speaking of work . . . might not be a bad idea to know where Jelena spent her days. Before popping the van into gear, he checked the tracker: blank.

He followed Jelena back to the Cross Bay where she headed north. He tracked her up to Queens Boulevard in Forest Hills where she pulled into the lot of an insurance agency called Tibbett & Son. Maybe she was an agent, maybe a secretary. Typical single mother story, he bet. She'd probably got by okay with alimony and child support from her ex, but now he was gone and the money cut off. Even with help from her sloppy sister she was no doubt living paycheck to paycheck.

He made a mental note of that, then headed back south. He'd stay in the area but avoid the Quinnell house for now—didn't want anyone to call in a suspicious van roaming the neighborhood.

8

Tier's hairless, skeletal client received them in his wheelchair in the living room. He'd arrived at the mansion expecting to face Roland alone, but apparently Poncia had arrived just ahead of him.

Roland's voice rasped more than ever. "I must conclude that, since you both arrive empty-handed while the day is yet young, the news is not good."

"I got some good to report," Poncia said eagerly. "Well, kinda good."

"I await on tenter hooks."

"I know where the Bagaq is—or at least I've got a pretty good idea."

"Where, pray tell?"

"In a bank safety deposit box on Broadway."

Tier refrained from telling him that the proper term was a *safe* deposit box.

Roland frowned. "If true, that is not good at all. What leads you to this conclusion?"

Poncia launched into an overly detailed discourse on following the surnameless Jack from his place to a deli-type store to a sporting good shop to the bank.

"He left his place with a bag containing something the exact size and shape of the Bagaq and had it with him all the way till he came out of the bank emptyhanded."

Tier had detected an odor coming off Poncia. He leaned closer and sniffed.

Poncia stepped back. "The fuck you think you're doing?"

"Why do you smell like ketchup?"

"Up yours."

"Mister Hill?" Roland did one of his ugly throat-clears as he looked at Tier. "What is your tale of woe?"

"Madame de Medici has skipped from the Allard."

Roland didn't look surprised. "And you know this how?"

"I delivered a dummy package to her today and they told me she's gone and they're holding her mail. The doorman didn't have a return date."

Roland's smile made his head look more like a skull than ever. "She's waiting for me to die." This seemed to amuse him. But the smile faded as he added, "But you didn't see her leave?"

"On the contrary. That's when this gets interesting . . . "

Leaving out mention of the signal and Burbank—and also about how she'd ditched him yesterday morning—he related how Madame de Medici invited him up to search her apartment.

Roland reacted with a shocked look and said, "And you found nothing?"

"I found plenty of things—her apartment makes yours look Spartan—but no Bagaq. I doubt she'd have let me search the place had it been there. As I left, she told me she was heading for Egypt today."

"Like I been telling you," Poncia said, "it's in that safety deposit box. We gotta get into it. But how?"

"We don't know for sure the Bagaq is there," Tier said. "She and Jack might be playing us."

"But I saw—"

"You probably saw exactly what you were supposed to see: a guy entering a bank with something in a bag and leaving emptyhanded."

"But it was the same shape and size as—"

"Could have been balled-up newspaper. How would you know the difference? And he could have just chatted up one of the managers and dropped the bag in a wastebasket."

Poncia reddened. "Fuck you, Hill! You—"

"Albert, Albert," Roland said. "A little decorum. I insist."

"Sorry."

"I fear Mister Hill here has a point. We don't know that Madame gave it to this Jack in the first place, but I believe we must operate on that assumption."

Tier didn't agree that they "must," but it seemed the logical way to go.

"Why wouldn't she have a secret compartment in her apartment where she could hide it?" Tier remembered how that wall slid open. "It would be safe there. The Allard looks pretty secure, after all."

"My sense of her is that she would want someone watching over it. Remember: She has an affinity for Infernals, and they are more than inert objects. They . . . "

His voice trailed off.

"They what?" Tier said.

"They have purposes—uses and misuses."

Whatever that meant.

"Okay, then," Tier said, "why wouldn't she just take it along wherever she went?"

"Because if she's left the Allard, you can be sure she's not hiding around the corner. She'd want to be where she can move freely without worrying about being stalked. She told you she's leaving for Egypt, and that makes sense. She has a large house in Luxor, which puts her out of reach."

And how, Tier thought. No way was he traveling to Egypt. But . . .

"All the more reason to take it with her."

"I'm sure she would have loved to. However, Infernals are sensitive to atmospheric pressure. Tradition has it that they cause bizarre effects at high altitudes. Which was why I shipped it here via sea."

Tradition . . . in Tier's experience, tradition had a spotty record of accuracy.

He didn't like operating on assumptions, and Roland was not only assuming that the Bagaq wasn't in the Allard, but that the Medici gal had given it to Jack instead of taking it to Egypt or wherever she really went.

She could be playing them. In fact, he was pretty damn sure she

was. It had occurred to him post facto that he'd had no problem following her to Jack's but she'd shaken him within half a block after
she'd left his place. Almost as if she'd led him to Jack. And that worried him.

What's her game?

He couldn't come up with a viable alternative to Roland's plan
off the top of his head. And after all, Roland was paying his per diem.
That meant Tier would play the good soldier, pay lip service to all
the assumptions, and give the man his best shot.

"That leaves us with this Jack fellow."

Roland nodded. "Find out all you can about him."

That wouldn't be easy without knowing his last name. But Tier
had ways . . .

"And then what?"

"We may have to resort to force."

Tier knew what that meant and didn't like it. He'd lived by his
wits since returning from the A, without putting the hurt on anyone.
He preferred it that way. Besides, he had his license and his future to
protect. So, he wasn't going to allow Roland to leave anything unsaid.

"Exactly what do you mean by that?"

Poncia gave one of his patented sneers. "Read between the lines,
Hill."

Tier didn't bother looking at him. He spoke to Roland.

"I don't read between lines when it comes to breaking the law
and risking jail time."

"Pussy!"

Still speaking to Roland: "Exactly what do you mean by 'force'?
How much and to what end?"

"To the end of securing the Bagaq."

"Specifics, please."

Roland glared at him. Tier could tell he didn't like coming out
and saying it. So much easier to leave it hanging, leaving it up to the
imagination.

Poncia said, "He means we may have to grab him and go caveman on his ass until he tells us where it is."

"Crudely put," Roland said, "but on the mark."

No surprise there, but they weren't finished.

"Okay, so through torture we learn that it's in the bank vault.

How do we make him get it for us?"

Again, Poncia saved his boss the discomfiture of issuing indelicate instructions.

"We grab his wife or his kid or his girlfriend or his boyfriend and tell him we'll trade them for the Bagaq. What, I gotta draw you a map, Tonto?"

Tonto?

Tier had grown up with racial slurs and had learned how to hide any reaction. A reaction was seen as a reward and only incited further insults. Tier had learned to consider the source. For an insult to mean anything, he had to respect the source. And in this case, the source was a fat douche bag.

No, he would not react. Now. But later, when this was all over, he might just pound Albert Poncia into the dirt—get "caveman" on him.

"I hope none of that will be necessary," Tier said.

But he didn't have a backup plan. At least not yet.

"I don't care how it's done," Roland said. "I just want results. And fast. My remission may not last much longer. And because of that, I want you two to work together."

Tier blurted, "You can't be serious!"

"What's the matter?" Poncia said. "Afraid I'll show you up?"

"I do my best work alone," Tier told Roland.

"If the zero results I've seen so far are your best work, then it appears you need help. I don't *want* the Bagaq, do you understand? I *need* it. Learn all you can about this Jack. Follow him. If he doesn't lead you to Madame or to the Bagaq, then I authorize you to take whatever measures necessary to secure it. The bonus you will receive for successful completion of your task should act as a balm on whatever moral wounds you must endure to succeed."

So, it comes down to this, he thought. Knuckle under or walk away.

He was tempted to hit the road and leave it to Poncia to handle the whole thing. But quitting wasn't a real option. Seriously . . . wimp out because he found Poncia repulsive? He came from a family that strolled high steel the way most people strolled sidewalks, ate lunch sitting on a beam thirty stories up.

He'd walked away from jobs before, but always from the high ground. He didn't feel like he had the high ground here. After all, he'd lost track of Madame de Medici yesterday, and even though she'd contacted him today, he still didn't know if she'd truly left the country. Which meant he'd let Roland down.

He'd get this done, but on his terms.

"If it's findable, I'll find it. But I must have the lead."

"I ain't taking no orders from you," Poncia said.

"Then I walk. Non-negotiable."

Roland turned to Poncia. "Mister Hill is the more experienced investigator. You will follow his lead."

"But—"

"You *will* follow his lead." To Tier: "Tonight you will research this Jack and learn whatever there is to know about him. First thing tomorrow you two will meet here and begin your quest. By tomorrow night you will have the Bagaq. Are we clear?"

"Very," Tier said.

Tomorrow was going to be a very long day.

9

Jack guided the van through South Ozone Park. He'd been killing time until the sun went down. H3 was supposedly nocturnal, so the dark hours gave him his best chance of finding it. The dashboard clock said 3:30, leaving him still an hour till sunset.

He was approaching the Aqueduct periphery when a blip lit on the screen . . . the south end of the racetrack grounds. He stopped and watched it head south until it disappeared again.

What the—?

Had it been heading toward Howard Beach? Maybe.

He steered onto Cross Bay Boulevard and cruised under the Belt Parkway. He'd just entered Howard Beach when the blip reappeared on the right side of the screen. He turned onto 156th Avenue where the tracker led him straight to the Quinnell address.

Looked like Monaco and Hess had been right. H3 was headed for the Quinnell family.

He pulled onto a scrub brush area opposite the end of Eighty-seventh Street, grabbed the tranq gun, and jumped out.

Christ, it was cold.

Still a lot more light in the sky than he liked as he entered the woodsy barrier, but he didn't have to worry about anyone hearing him over the roar of traffic rolling along the Belt just a hundred feet away.

He entered the woods and pushed through the leafless under-brush. Most of the trees were bare as well, which meant he wouldn't have much cover except from the red cedars and cypresses scattered among the oaks and elms. All the backyards were fenced in—one of the bigger lots even had a pool—and all were empty except one.

Jack counted the houses from the end of the row until he neared the one he'd been told was Quinnell's. Bare spots pocked the scruffy backyard grass. A little girl spun in a circle in the center of the yard.

A young woman, the same slovenly blonde who'd arrived at the front door this morning, sat on the back steps sucking on a joint. Jack squeezed in behind a cedar and watched her toke away, then tuck the roach into what looked like a red-and-white Altoids tin.

"Time to go in, Cilla," she said, standing. Her voice echoed faintly through the cold air.

Cilla kept spinning.

The sister approached Cilla. "Silly Cilla."

She grabbed her hand and stopped the spinning. Cilla let out a horrendous scream and the sister let go and backed away.

"Suit yourself. You got ten more minutes and then you're coming in whether you like it or not."

Cilla started spinning again.

Didn't she get dizzy?

As soon as the door closed, something moved in the woods. It looked like a man in an overcoat but didn't quite move like a man.

According to the Plum Island pair, H3 had stolen Quinnell's over-coat. This guy looked to be wearing a hoodie under the coat, with the hood up and over a low-slung trucker's hat. The shape under the coat seemed off—not definitely wrong, just... *off*.

He checked the tracker and if it was accurate, he was looking at H3.

As it approached the four-foot chain-link fence that ringed the Quinnell backyard, Jack loaded a dart into the tranq gun. Whoever it was, human or H3, he couldn't see how anything good was gonna come of this situation. At four feet, the fence was high enough to keep a child inside, but not to keep an adult out.

Jack sidled closer. He wished he'd had a chance to practice with the tranq gun. He had no idea how accurate it might or might not be.

He adopted a Weaver stance and was ready to spring if the figure started over the fence, but instead it crouched and placed its hands against the links.

The little girl stopped spinning and swayed like a drunk as she stared. She didn't seem afraid. In fact, a grin lit her face as she made a weaving approach. She stopped about three feet away and seemed to be speaking, but he couldn't make out her words. Unlikely she'd have a conversation with a wolfman.

What the hell? Maybe it wasn't H3. But if not, what was he doing crouching by a fence near a little girl?

And why had Jelena's sister left a three-year old out here alone in the first place? Yeah, it was her backyard, but the light was failing and the temp was dropping. Where was the slovenly aunt? Inside watching *Fixer Upper*?

Jack extended the weapon as the overcoated figure lifted a hand over the fence and held it out to the girl.

Watch it . . . watch it . . .

The girl smiled and said something Jack didn't quite catch, then high-fived the proffered hand. The hooded figure turned and glided into the shadowy bushes. Jack blinked and it was gone.

On the tracker the blip was moving away. That had to be H3 but—

The little girl waved. "Bye, doggie!"

Doggie?

Holy Christ, that had to be H3, but what—?

She turned and started skipping toward the back door. Jack watched her disappear inside and was about to start after H3 when another figure stepped out of the trees and approached the fence

Who the hell was this? Another player?

As he paused to watch, the new guy vaulted over the fence and approached a rear window. He worked a small pry bar between the upper and lower sash, gave it a twist and then hurried back over the fence and into the trees.

What the hell? He pops the lock on a window and then leaves? What's he up to?

Whatever it was it could wait. Jack was on the trail of H3 now and—

A glance at the tracker showed a dark screen. The blip was gone. H3 had gone to ground again.

Shit!

Jack resisted the urge to smash it against a tree.

Instead, he took some deep breaths and considered his options. With the light just about gone, searching for a trail was a waste of time. He'd have to wait for the blip to reappear. He didn't think he'd have to wait long. H3 had to eat.

He headed back toward his van. Curious as he was about the identity of the new guy, he couldn't let the van sit too long in the scrub. Calls would be made and cops would come calling.

Once he was rolling again, he thought about what he'd seen. H3 had been more manlike than he'd anticipated. But the child had seemed unafraid . . . and called it "doggie."

But according to Hess and Monaco, H3 hated Quinnell, killed him, and might be after his family.

Wouldn't be the first time they'd lied.

He drove a few blocks to Cross Bay Boulevard and pulled into the Stop & Shop lot. Time to call Abe and see what he'd learned.

10

When Albert returned from locking the front door behind Hill, the boss motioned him close to his wheelchair. He looked worse than ever—worse than a just a few minutes ago. Had he been putting up a front for the Indian?

"I need your help, Albert." His voice was more like a scraping sound than ever.

"What can I do?" He meant that.

"Bring me the Bagaq."

"I'm trying, but what's that gonna—?"

"It will cure me."

Cure? Was the boss off his head? He'd had an aunt once with cancer that spread to her brain. Made her loony.

"But I thought you said the treatments were working."

"They are. They're making me sick unto death, but the doctors say the chemo is working."

"Then what—?"

"They also tell me I'll never be cancer free. All this agony will give me only a respite. They can't say how long, but they have little doubt the cancer will reemerge and they might not be able to stop it then."

"Oh."

"That's a terrible thing to live with, knowing that the instrument of one's demise is smoldering within." He grabbed Albert's arm in a claw-like grip. "I want a cure, Albert. A *cure.*"

His breath was rank. Albert tried not to wince. "And—and the Bagaq's gonna do that?"

"It has powers. If one knows how to use it, it can cure any ill."

"Wow."

Imagine what something like that would be worth.

"Yes. 'Wow.' But if you don't know how to use it, it's just a lump of metal. I know how. And so does the Madame. That's why she won't give it up, won't even *lend* it to me. She wants to keep all the Infernals and all their powers to herself."

"Bitch."

"Yes. Most definitely. If she is truly in Egypt or headed there, she is out of reach. But the Bagaq is not. You must secure it for me, Albert. You must."

"I will." He tried to sound confident but he knew he couldn't guarantee it.

"Hill could be a problem, however."

"You mean him being a softy and all?"

"That, yes. But I don't trust him."

"You mean you think he's workin' for the bitch?"

As much as Albert hated Tonto's tight-ass superior attitude, he couldn't see him working both sides of the street.

"No, I do not. But once the Bagaq is in his grasp, I fear he might hold it for ransom."

Unease gripped Albert as he listened. The same plan had occurred to him: Find the Bagaq and dangle it for a monster payday.

"Hey, no worry about that, Mister Apfel," he said quickly. Not too quickly, he hoped. "I'll be there to keep him on the up and up."

"That's good to hear, Albert. Because I will never accede to blackmail. I would rather die than be forced to pay for what is rightfully mine."

The boss didn't really mean that, did he? Sure as hell sounded like it, though. Which meant if Albert wanted to keep the cushy deal he had here, maybe he'd better keep this fucking Bagaq thing on the up and up.

"No worry, Mister Apfel. Never happen. Not on my watch."

"I know that, Albert. And you will be well compensated for the successful completion of your mission."

"Thank you, sir."

He had a feeling the bonus would be generous. The bucks flowed when the boss was happy.

"But one thing greatly concerns me, Albert. Hill knows of your loyalty to me. And because of that I fear he might do something drastic to you. You are a very important part of this household, and I would hate to see you come to any harm."

Albert's throat tightened—just a little. The boss cared, he really cared.

"So, you're telling me to watch my back."

"Yes, most certainly watch your back. But more than that. Once the Bagaq is secured, I think you should make a pre-emptive strike."

"You mean, take him out before he takes me?"

"Exactly."

"Yeah. Good idea. I can do that."

As a matter of fact, he'd kinda enjoy it. Watch Tonto's smug expression turn all scared and beggy in his last moments.

"And the stranger—Jack. When he's served his purpose and given up the Bagaq, he should be eliminated as well. The fewer who know about the Bagaq, the fewer who can point to me."

"Got it." Made lotsa sense.

"Because you don't want anything happening to me, Albert. I take good care of you, don't I?"

"Absolutely, sir. The best."

Without the boss he wouldn't just be out of a job, he'd have no place to live. The thought of being homeless made him sick.

"And I fully intend to maintain our present arrangement indefinitely, but I have to be alive and free to do that. Understand?"

"Absolutely. You can count on me."

Yeah, he'd enjoy taking out Tonto. On the other hand, he had no beef with Jack. But if the boss wanted him gone, consider him gone.

11

"Okay, everybody, listen up."

Jelena recognized Junior's voice and so she rose from her chair to peer over the top of her cubicle divider. Junior stood at the rear of the room before the two executive offices—six-two, broad shoulders, square jaw, perfect hair. And a perfect jerk. Robert Tibbett, Jr., the "Son" in Tibbett & Son. Always "Robert" to his face. Behind his back he was "Junior" to most and "Mr. Hands" to others. Jelena was one of the others.

"With the storm coming, things are dead. People are out clearing the store shelves of milk and bread. Personally, I'm going to be stocking in lots of beer."

Polite laughter. Jelena forced a smile. Early close meant she'd lose a couple of hours' pay. Every penny counted, especially this time of year.

"And again, if the storm's half as bad as they say it will be, tomorrow—Christmas Eve eve—will be a washout too. Or maybe I should say a 'white-out.' And as you all know, tomorrow was going to be our holiday party."

Groans, the loudest from Jelena. She'd run through her paid days off, so she wouldn't get paid for the snow day.

"And since we were only planning for half a day on Christmas

Eve anyway, that looks like a white-out too."

Shit!

"So, I guess we can say that Christmas starts early—like, right now. Have a merry, everyone!"

Jelena slumped into her chair and bit back a sob.

This totally sucked. The story of her life lately. Things got bad, and then they got worse.

Like the bank taking her house. She had no way to prevent it.

She and David had bought it with a big initial mortgage, but he'd had a solid job with a good salary. But then he'd started gambling. He gambled away their savings, then he gambled away a second mortgage. And then he started borrowing from the wrong people, which led to agreeing to do a drug buy to erase the debt, which led to a DEA agent's death, which led to a life sentence in Canaan Federal Penitentiary.

The bank had been patient but had reached the end of its tether. Even with housing on the upswing, her little place was far enough underwater that selling wouldn't help. If the market held up another year or two, she might break even, but she had only a month or two: The bank had started foreclosure proceedings.

She jumped as hands landed on her shoulders.

"A little wound-up today, are we, Jelena?" Junior's voice. Mr. Hands. The hands started kneading the muscles. "My, your shoulders are tight."

"My shoulders are fine, Robert. Please don't do that."

He didn't stop. "Just looking out for the employees, Jelena. Speaking of which, some of us are going over to Work for some holiday cheer—y'know, to make up for the busted Christmas party. Why don't you come along?"

Work . . . the snidely named neighborhood dive bar down the street.

Hi, Hon. I'm gonna be late. Yeah, stuck at Work.

"I can't. Cilla's with her sitter and I need to get home. And please take your hands off me."

The hands released her shoulders but she didn't turn.

"You know, Jelena," he said, leaning around her left side, "you need to be more of a team player."

"I'm not a bar person."

"Well, just a little heads up: Business is off and we may have to lay off a couple of people."

Now she turned. A mix of fear and fury made it hard to keep her voice down, but she managed.

"Are you threatening me, Robert?"

He straightened and backed up a step. "Hey, no, I—"

"Are you saying that if I don't go and hang out at a bar with you, I might lose my job?"

"Forget it," he said, his expression hardening. "You're hopeless."

He turned and stalked away.

Oh, God, what have I done?

She'd thought things couldn't get worse, but if she lost her job . . .

12

It took Abe a while to return his call. Something about inventory.

"Hey," Jack said. "What've you got?"

"Whose call am I returning? The bagel man? I got cream cheese here pining for a bagel."

Playing games? Okay.

"This is the burrito man from this morning."

"Is it now? He's the one wants to know what I got? Okay, what I got I'll tell him. On that reverse phone lookup, I got an address in Wantagh. At least that's where the Verizon bill goes. You want it now?"

"Sure. Shoot." Jack wrote it down as Abe dictated. "Great. Now for the other—"

"The other! You want to know what I got on the other? I got mishegoss is what I got."

Jack was fuzzy on mishegoss but knew it wasn't good.

"Meaning?"

"Meaning I floated inquiries toward people I know who have connections to that investigative wing in that department you wanted me to check into."

Abe always assumed his phone was tapped so Jack was used to his verbal tiptoeing and sidestepping.

"And what did they tell you?"

"They say they've got no one named Quinnell—not David, not John, not nobody."

Why am I not surprised? Jack thought. *I'm dealing with pathological liars.*

"What about the people at the address I gave you?"

"In that house, Quinnells you've got. Two of them. At least for now, anyway."

"What do you mean?"

"The mortgage is in arrears and the bank has started foreclosure proceedings. Mother and daughter will be out on the street soon."

Jack hated to hear that sort of thing.

"These Quinnells . . . they wouldn't happen to be related to anyone from—"

"That organization you mentioned? No. However, related to the woman and child you've got a father and ex-husband named David Quinnell."

"The one who killed the DEA agent."

"Also, the one who claimed self-defense."

"Wouldn't you?"

Jack figured he'd claim all sorts of things in that position.

"According to my source, Quinnell might well have been telling the truth when he said the agent tried to kill him after he made the buy."

"Oh?"

"This agent had a rep as a paskudnik."

"Paskudnik . . . that's a new one on me."

"Like a momzer only a lot worse."

Jack had heard momzer before and it wasn't a compliment.

"So, Quinnell could have been telling the truth about self-defense?"

"Truth, shmooth. What does truth mean when you kill a fed, no matter how bad he was? An example they want to make. So, they made one."

"Swell. Truth or not, he'll end his days in Canaan."

"Already they've ended."

Whoa!

"He's out?"

"Out, yes. But as for enjoying his freedom, probably not so much. He's dead."

TUESDAY—DECEMBER 23

1

Snow.

Swell.

The weather folks had been promising it for days, getting all worked up over wind-chill factors and how many inches and how few degrees, but Jack had thought it too cold to snow. Showed how much he knew. Snowmageddon had arrived. Dark, cold, and overcast one minute; dark, cold, overcast, and blizzardy the next. Anywhere from four to eighteen inches predicted depending on which way the storm tracked. One thing was sure: Whatever came down was going to stick. A good inch had accumulated in no time.

Jack yawned and kept cruising the perimeter of Aqueduct Racetrack. The dash clock said 1:12 and he was overdue for some coffee. If he were in the city, no problem. But pickings were slim out here in the boonies of Queens. At least the Cross Bay Diner was open twenty-four hours. Maybe later. Jack wanted to stay on the north side of the Belt Parkway for now.

Because H3 was on this side.

A tunnel . . . H3 had to have access to a tunnel—or more likely a number of them. Jack couldn't think of any other way its blip could appear and disappear the way it did.

Made sense. The racetrack was called "Aqueduct" for a reason.

He'd DuckDucked it and learned that conduits built by the Brooklyn Waterworks in the 19th century funneled water from eastern Long Island through here to the Ridgewood Reservoir. Although the Brooklyn Waterworks was gone and the reservoir decommissioned, he'd bet one of his Little Orphan Annie decoders some of those conduits remained.

Just after Jack's talk with Abe, H3's blip had reappeared—but on the far side of the Belt Parkway. The only way it could have done that was via a tunnel. No way was Jack about to go hunting for its entrance in the dark, but come morning . . .

In the meantime, he had to sort out what was true and not true about David Quinnell. Lots of possible permutations here. Jack didn't care how good Abe's contacts might be, if the Defense Intelligence Agency didn't want anyone to know they had an agent named Quinnell, they'd deny his existence. Simple as that.

So, there might indeed be an Agent David Quinnell and there might indeed be a convicted murderer with the same name who had died of cancer while in Canaan.

But H3 was drawing a connecting line between the two Quinnells, and Jack had yet to make sense of that. If—

A blip lit on the tracker screen—south end of the racetrack grounds. Jack hit the accelerator, but before he'd traveled a hundred yards it disappeared again. Same as last night.

I know where you're headed.

He kept up the pace, swerving onto North Conduit, then onto Cross Bay and back into Howard Beach.

Yep. H3 was headed back to the Quinnell place. Jack could think of only one possible reason at this hour: to wreak some havoc.

He parked the van in the same spot as before and, tranq gun loaded and ready, headed back into the woods. Lack of sunlight made threading through these brambles and avoiding the trees a whole different experience. He'd brought along a mini Maglite but didn't want to give himself away, so he took it slow, waving his free hand back and forth before him. At least the traffic noise from the Belt, loud as ever, covered his passage. Belt traffic ran hot and it ran cold, but it never ran thin, even with snowmageddon in progress.

Jack froze as the Quinnell backyard came into view. Light from Cross Bay Boulevard and the Belt was bleeding and refracting through the snowy air to provide enough faint, ambient illumination to reveal a figure fooling with a rear window—the same window someone had jimmied earlier. Details were hard to scope through the snow, but whoever was at the window was wearing a short jacket instead of an overcoat.

Jack didn't understand what was going on, but he'd bet that window opened into the little girl's bedroom. He didn't care who was fooling with it, the guy was *not* getting inside.

Starting forward for a closer shot, Jack removed his right glove for a better feel on the trigger, but stopped as movement from another quarter caught his eye. An overcoated figure darted from the trees, flowed over the fence, and attacked the figure at the window, taking him down from behind. After the briefest of struggles, the overcoat rose and stared down at the still form at its feet. Some strange drama was playing out here but Jack couldn't imagine what. According to the tracker, one of those blips was H3, but which? Had to be the overcoat. So, who was the other?

Jack watched to see what would happen next.

Abruptly, H3 lifted the prone figure, slung it over its shoulder, then carried it over the fence with the same flowing grace it had shown on its arrival. A large dark splotch marred the fresh snow under the rear window. Blood?

Yeah. Had to be. That big a puddle could only mean a severed carotid. H3 was carrying a mean blade.

Jack worked his way through the brush to where it had taken the fence. He had enough light to make out dark splotches within the disturbed snow.

Decision time. H3 seemed to know its way around the area. The idea of following it in the dark seemed foolhardy at best—downright stupid when you got down to it. But this was his chance to find H3's tunnel. These tracks would be smothered in half an hour. Less.

Okay, he'd follow the trail and would not—*not*—enter the tunnel once he'd found it.

Jack didn't have far to go. The tracks followed the edge of the tree line on the Belt Parkway side. Lots more light here as cars on the Belt rolled through the slush not fifty feet away. Jack had worn a brown jacket and brown twill pants—usually an inconspicuous getup, but not against snow. Anyone looking his way would see him.

The swirling flakes blurred outlines and features, but still . . .

So, he was delighted to find the tracks terminating at a clump of bushes—entering the clump but not emerging.

A dark shape lay unmoving within that clump. Jack inched forward. Still no movement. A little closer and no doubt: a body. Hidden well enough now in the dark, and after a few more inches of snow, it could stay hidden for days. A week, maybe, if the deep freeze held—hard as a rock with no odor to attract scavengers.

But who the hell was it?

He'd need light to get a good look at this guy. He pulled out his mini Mag and, cupping his free hand around the lens, gave a brief flash.

"Whoa!"

He'd seen enough. The victim was all human, no resemblance to the photos of H3 Hess and Monaco had shown him. After seeing the blood on the snow—no doubt already covered with a fresh layer—Jack had assumed H3 had a knife. Maybe he did, but it hadn't been used here. No slice. This guy's throat had been torn out. In that brief flash Jack had seen the stumps of the trachea and both carotids. No wonder the kill had been so silent: his voice box was somewhere in the Quinnell backyard. Never knew what hit him.

Slipping around the body, Jack carefully parted the bushes and found a hole in the ground—an open manhole with a six-inch-high rim. He pushed his way forward and took a quick peek into the steel maw. Nothing but featureless blackness down there. He wanted oh so much to flash his little Maglite to see how deep it was but didn't dare.

H3 was down there. Probably not right *there* there, but somewhere in the conduit, no doubt headed back under the Belt Parkway to the Aqueduct area where Jack suspected it had access to another tunnel, maybe one running under the racetrack itself.

An impulsive part of him clamored to go down there and follow along.

Uh-uh. No. He had the tracker. He'd wait for H3 to reappear on this side and then nail him with a tranq dart.

Back to the dead man. Why had he jimmied a rear window on the Quinnell house, and why had he been trying to get in tonight—or this morning, rather? Any relation to H3?

Jack went through his pockets and found a wallet. His license said he was Barry Wexler and that he lived two doors down from the Quinnells. From the jacket pockets he pulled out what looked like some sort of leather ball gag and a roll of duct tape. His stomach lurched. The guy was a creep and he'd been after Cilla. No other explanation.

But H3 had taken him out first.

Jack was getting a very sick feeling about this.

2

By six a.m., Jack called it quits. Snow had continued to fall at vary-ing rates. The total had reached four inches and was still piling up. Boredom was pushing him toward sleep at the wheel and the chances of H3 rearing its ugly head diminished as the sky lightened. Add to that the lousy handling of the Econoline in the snow and he had to get off the road.

Home was not an option. Not just because the Econoline was a menace in the snow, but because someone might be watching his place. He'd lost whoever had been following him yesterday, and no way could they know he was in Howard Beach. Why go through all that bother again when he didn't have to?

He drove to the end of Cross Bay Boulevard to the Surfside Motel and took a room for the night. He texted Gia his whereabouts and reassured her he'd make it to her place for Christmas Eve.

He wished he could text Abe to look into Barry Wexler but Abe didn't text. *Text schmext. Anyone can text. A voice I want to hear.*

Then he crashed. But disturbing questions about H3 followed him into the comforting arms of Morpheus.

3

"You eat like this every day?" Tier said as he mixed the runny yolk with the Hollandaise sauce.

Poncia shook his head and spoke around a mouthful. "Nah. I'd be big as a house."

Tier bit back an obvious rejoinder.

Roland had told them to meet for an early breakfast at the mansion and plan out their strategy. Tier had reluctantly agreed—didn't want to spend a second longer with Poncia than absolutely necessary—but now was glad he had. The cook had gone all out with a platter of Eggs Benedict. The eggs expertly poached, the ham tender, the English muffins toasted to perfection. And the Hollandaise sauce . . . delicious.

Poncia put down his fork. "This is missing something." He called over his shoulder. "Hey, Maurice. Bring the Heinz."

The little Frenchman bustled out of the kitchen holding a red bottle.

"Oh, no, Mister Poncia. You're not—"

Poncia held out his hand. "Gimme-gimme."

He took the flat-topped bottle, flipped the cap, and upended it over his plate.

"Please, monsieur. I made the Hollandaise from scratch."

"Yeah, but it needs a little zing."

Maurice watched with a horrified expression as Poncia slathered his Eggs Benedict in ketchup.

"Oh, monsieur."

Poncia then began to cut himself a chunk. With his splinted pinky and ring fingers sticking into the air, he was a parody of elegance— one of the Three Stooges breakfasting at the Hotel Pierre.

Forking a red-dripping portion into his mouth, he declared, "*Now* it's delicious." As the cook retreated, muttering and shaking his head, he added, "I think maybe Maurice thinks you're special because the boss invited you for breakfast. That's why he went all out."

As Poncia paused to drown his hash browns in ketchup, Tier thought maybe Maurice had gone all out because he'd be feeding someone who might actually taste what he'd prepared.

"Okay, here's the situation," Tier said. "Tracking this guy wasn't going to be easy in good weather, but now we've got snow to contend with."

"Yeah. Snowpocalypse."

Tier had taken the subway here. Even though the snow was still falling like a bitch, the streets along his walk from the stop looked to be in pretty good shape, though the sidewalks were largely untouched.

"Our problem, besides the weather, is that there are only two of us, and we have a lot of ground to cover."

"What ground? We got his apartment and the bank—two places, two sets of eyes."

"What about the sports shop?"

"He just dropped off some food there."

"How do you know he didn't drop off the Bagaq?"

"Because I saw him walk out with it."

"You saw him walk out with an unseen object in a plastic bag, which he may have pretended to leave in a bank safe deposit box."

Poncia slammed his hand on the table. "I seen what I seen, and he didn't have nothin' with him when he left that bank. And anyway, why would he pretend?"

"Because he knew he was being followed, which was why—"

"He didn't know shit, Tonto!"

"Which was why he ditched you when you tried to follow his rental."

"I'd still be on him if *I'd* been driving. The cabbie didn't know what he was doing."

Tier sighed. "Whatever. The upshot is we have no idea where he spent yesterday or last night. He could be anywhere."

Poncia grinned. "Could be shacking up with that Medici piece, for all we know. I tell ya, I wouldn't mind hitting that myself."

A flashing image of Poncia pawing at one of the most stylish and stately women Tier had ever encountered—the mind boggled and the gut recoiled.

He regrouped and said, "Just think about it: Jack brought food to the sports shop, which means he has a friend there, which means he may well return there. That makes three locations. The gas station is the obvious fourth."

"Ain't obvious to me."

What an idiot. He struggled to keep his tone neutral.

"If he rented the van there, he will eventually return it there. The problem is that the station is a good forty blocks downtown from the other three locations. I'm going to start there while you make a circuit of the first three."

"Why don't I start there?" Poncia said.

"Because it will be very helpful if we can find out when he's scheduled to return the van. And learning that will require tact."

. . . *and intelligence*, he wanted to add, *both of which you lack*. But again, he held his tongue. He had the high ground and wanted to keep it.

"Well, if I'm making a circuit, I'm doing it from a limo. Cold as a witch's tit out there."

"I'm sure you can expense that to Mister Apfel."

"Yeah. I'll get me a driver. Do it right."

Tier's phone buzzed. Ah, his Word for the Day email: EXIGENT. New one for him.

Exigent
adjective: EK-suh-junt
Definition
a: requiring immediate aid or action
b: requiring or calling for much: demanding

He didn't see that one causing a problem. He was sure that being linked with Poncia all day would eventually involve some situation requiring immediate aid or action.

4

Jack awoke shortly before noon, refreshed after a solid five-plus hours of shuteye. For the past few months he'd been sleeping later and waking less refreshed. Having a reason to get up and moving seemed to make a big difference.

He washed up but didn't shower because he didn't have a fresh change of clothes. Next task: coffee and sustenance.

He was glad he'd backed the van into its parking slot last night. The motel lot had been plowed sometime during the night, but the snow was still falling and had added another couple of inches. Even so, the van had a tough time getting over the small mound the plow had left in front of it.

He skipped the Burger King and the Cross Bay Diner and pulled into the McDonald's. He had a weakness for sausage Egg McMuffins. Plus their coffee, formerly the worst in the world, was now pretty decent.

The short drive up slushy Cross Bay Boulevard to Mickey-D's was all it took to convince him that he had to dump the Econoline. The rear-wheel drive had him swerving all over the road every time he accelerated. He'd never find the north end of H3's tunnel in this mess if he had to depend on the van. Needed four-wheel drive.

Settled at a corner table with his coffee and McMuffins, he began making his calls. The first was to Gia because he always called her. The second was to Abe to give him Wexler's name.

And last to the BP station.

Yeah, they had a Jeep Laredo they'd hold for him. Laredos weren't built for frigid weather, but he'd take it. See them in an hour or so.

5

Tier stuck his head inside the BP station's office door.

"Me again. Hate to be a pest but ... "

He'd stopped in here first thing after breakfast this morning to inquire as to the availability of the Econoline van he said he'd been seeing parked on the lot when he'd pass by. Cole—or so the patch on his coverall said—had told him it was out on a rental. The renter hadn't known how long he'd need it so Cole didn't know when to expect it back. Maybe today, maybe tomorrow. He'd suggested Tier try Hertz or Avis but, no, Tier told him he liked to deal with local businesses.

Between alternating watches with Poncia on Jack's apartment, the sports shop, and the bank, Tier kept making sporadic visits to the BP station. On his mid-morning visit he'd heard the same story, so now he was trying lunchtime.

"Hey," Cole said around a mouthful of meatball sub, "I was hoping you'd come back. The van's coming in."

Ohhhh, yes.

"Really? Today?"

Cole swallowed. "Not just today—now. On its way."

Perfect.

He'd call Poncia and the two of them would wait for an

opportunity to grab Jack when he was on foot again. An unfeasible plan in clear weather, but the snow hadn't let up. With visibility down, the sidewalks largely unshoveled, and few pedestrians out in the storm, it became eminently feasible.

He pulled out his phone. "Do you have an ETA?"

"'Soon' is the best I can do." Cole waved a hand at the weather beyond the big glass windows. "You may want to think twice about renting it in this mess. Those vans suck in snow."

"Yeah?" Here was a way to get out of the rental.

"That's why he's bringing it in." Cole waved a handful of forms. "He's swapping it for the Jeep."

Tier's elation took a dive. That was going to complicate plans. But those forms . . .

Tier sidled toward the desk. "A pain in the ass to make a swap like that?"

"Two cars means two rental agreements which means twice the paperwork."

"Complicated?" He leaned over the desk and spotted *John Tyleski* on the renter line.

John . . . Jack . . . yeah, it fit. At last he could get a line on this guy.

He'd spent too much time last night in a fruitless search for info on him. He had his address but no last name. Usually the address was enough for the investigative sites he subscribed to, but they'd yielded nothing when it came to identifying the renter–owner, maybe?–of that third-floor apartment. He wasn't listed anywhere.

Cole shrugged. "No biggie once you've got the hang of it."

Tier put on a worried look and stepped to the window.

"Yeah, maybe you're right. Maybe I should take a raincheck on the van."

Cole laughed. "You mean a *snow* check, dontcha?"

Turning, Tier winked and pointed at him. "Good one. Catch you later."

Not.

As soon as the door closed behind him, he called Poncia.

"Get down to the BP station. He's bringing the van in any minute."

He ended the call without waiting for Poncia to make some inane comment.

The only Jeep on the lot was a copper-colored Laredo. He dug into his messenger bag as he headed for it and pulled out one of his GPS transmitters. Not the model he'd attached to the de Medici Maybach. This had a one-kilometer range which would prove adequate for today's purposes.

He turned on the module and slipped it into its magnetized case, then stuck it inside the rear bumper. As he was walking away, a white Econoline van pulled into the lot.

He's here. But where's Poncia? Where the fuck is Poncia?

Tier walked up to the unshoveled corner and scanned Eleventh Avenue for the limo. He couldn't see all that far through the falling snow, but he should have been here by now. Probably stopped off for some burgers or maybe a few beers. Just what he needed now: Dealing with a half-lit, obnoxious —

Oh, wait. There he is.

Tier waved the Lincoln Continental around the corner and got in the front passenger seat, leaving Poncia alone in the back. Sharing a car with two other people . . . the proximity put his teeth on edge. Could have been worse — could have been four people. Might as well make the best of it.

He extended his hand to the dark-skinned, black-suited driver without acknowledging Poncia.

"Tier. And you are . . . ?"

"Marley," he said with a Jamaican accent. His cheeks were sunken and he was cadaverously thin.

"Like the reggae singer?"

He smiled, showing yellowed teeth. "Yes, but it is my first name. My mother was a fan."

Tier sniffed. "Is that ketchup?"

"What of it?" Poncia said from the backseat.

Tier twisted and saw him sucking on a foil sleeve of ketchup. Two more, flattened and empty, littered the seat beside him.

"You're eating straight ketchup?"

"Great snack."

Tier turned back to Marley and patted the dashboard. "How's this beast handling in the snow?"

Marely shrugged. "Not bad, considering the conditions. The tires be pretty new and she got front-wheel drive."

Tier pointed to the BP lot. "We're going to be tailing that Jeep, so be ready to move when it moves."

"Not a problem."

Tier wasn't so sanguine. Following a four-wheel-drive in this lumbering limo, front-wheel drive or not, might prove a very real problem. Tier's Honda bike was out of the question in the snow, so they'd have to make do with the equipment at hand.

The GPS transmitter would level the playing field. He hoped.

Tier pulled his tablet from the messenger bag. Might as well put this time to good use by nailing down John Tyleski's identity. So far, they'd been hunting a ghost. Tier intended to resurrect him as flesh and blood.

6

Jack had spotted the limo idling by the gas station; made a mental note of it but hadn't attached much importance to it. He'd been anxious to get back to Queens and on the prowl for H3. Yeah, the creature was nocturnal, but it might use the cover of the falling snow to forage before sunset.

After all the papers had been signed and they'd done the obligatory walk-arounds on both vehicles, Cole had finally handed him the keys to the Jeep. He kept an eye on the black Continental as he pulled out onto Eleventh Avenue and headed uptown, and noticed it move in behind him. Following?

He made a right onto Fiftieth Street and headed west. The limo stayed behind.

Well, well, well . . . first time he'd ever been tailed by a limousine. He could make out two in the front and maybe a third in the rear. One of them had been smart enough to keep an eye on the PB station. Not likely the guy who'd followed him here yesterday. Somebody else, somebody with better bird-dogging chops was involved.

For the most part, Fiftieth Street had been plowed but the sparse traffic was crawling. Damn near impossible to work any evasive maneuvers under these conditions. No matter. He was headed for Queens and, if the city's sanitation department stayed true to form, the side streets over there would rank near the bottom of the plows' lists. Which meant they'd be in bad shape. He'd strand them there.

He drove all the way east and took the Midtown Tunnel into Queens where, as expected, the storm was staying ahead of the plows. The limo hung back quite a ways, but was still on his tail. Time to get serious.

Jack took a very slushy Twenty-first Street up to Jackson Avenue, and then hung a left onto Forty-sixth Avenue which hadn't been plowed at all. Even the Jeep's four-wheel drive found the eight inches of snow a challenge. He slowed and waited to see if the limo followed. It did.

Thar she blows.

As he accelerated, he bounced over a foot-high mound where someone had plowed his driveway snow into the street. The limo followed. Looked like it was trying to stay in the Jeep's tracks—an impossibility with its wider wheel base and lower clearance. It made it halfway over the mound before its undercarriage got hung up, killing its momentum and robbing all its traction.

Jack didn't slow, but lowered his window and gave them a friendly wave without looking back. He'd leave them spinning their wheels, unsure as to whether or not he'd led them into a snowy trap, and be far away before they dug themselves free.

He circled back to the Long Island Expressway where he was tempted to stomp on the gas and put as much distance as he could as quickly as possible between the Jeep and the Lincoln. But the black-top wasn't in great shape, and though four-wheel drive meant better traction, it didn't help you stop any faster than two-wheel drive. He settled on forty miles an hour. That would allow him plenty of time to set up in H3's stomping ground.

He was determined to end this before tomorrow morning.

7

While Poncia loosed a stream of invective at Marley, Tier watched Jack drive away. He'd led them onto a side street, aware it wouldn't be plowed, knowing that sooner or later—if not on this street, then the next or the next—they'd encounter conditions the Jeep could handle but the Lincoln couldn't. He'd been right, of course. But instead of taunting them by flipping them the bird, he'd given an insouciant wave, and simply driven off. Hadn't even looked back.

As if to say, *I know your job is to follow me, but my job is to lose you. Just another day's work.*

Tier could almost like this guy.

But Jack had no idea he'd been tagged.

Time to shut up the noisemaker in the backseat before he got out of hand.

"Can it, Poncia!"

"Fuck you, Tonto! This guy's supposed to know how to drive!"

That makes three Tontos, Tier thought.

"And he's been doing just that. But tell me: Did he choose this Lincoln?"

"No, I—"

"Well, you chose the wrong car. Did you happen to miss the fact that it's been snowing like a bitch since last night? If you had half a brain you would have hired a four-wheeler. But no. Mister Bigshot wanted to be seen in the backseat of a limo. So here we are, spinning our wheels, literally and figuratively, while our guy drives off into the sunset."

"Hey, you can't—"

Tier opened his door. "Get out and let's see if we can push our way out of this."

Poncia nodded toward Marley. "Let this jerk push and I'll drive."

"He's not heavy enough. We need extra pounds and you've got 'em."

Poncia hesitated, then complied. Tier had him sit on the hood to put extra weight over the drive wheels. After a combination of rocking and reversing, they finally moved the Lincoln off the snow hump and had her ready to roll again.

"Well, we're pretty well fucked," Poncia said, huffing in the back seat as the Lincoln started moving again, "but at least we won't have to walk home. Sure as hell ain't gonna catch up to that asshole now."

"Don't be so sure," Tier said. "I attached a GPS transmitter to his bumper."

"No shit?"

"None at all."

Poncia grunted. "Maybe we're not so fucked after all."

Using the app that came with the transmitter, Tier had been monitoring their course on his iPhone—all across Midtown and into Queens. He saw now that Jack was on the LIE headed west. He put Marley on a course to the expressway—not far as the crow flies, but the snow-clogged side streets kept them moving at a crawl.

"Push it," he told Marley. His frustration was growing as he watched the blip they were chasing inch toward the limit of the transmitter's range. "We're going to lose him."

Poncia said, "How we gonna lose him if you got him tagged?"

"The transmitter's range is a kilometer, so—"

"What's that in American? Like how many miles?"

"Six tenths or so."

"So, you're telling me if he gets much more than half a mile lead, we lose him?"

"That's right. And he's almost there."

"Ain't that just great. Here I was almost thinking you might know what you're doing. Joke's on me."

Tier had never needed more than a kilometer range because he'd never let his quarry get that far ahead. He might have offered this to Poncia as explanation, but Poncia didn't deserve an explanation.

Marley reached the entrance ramp to the LIE and accelerated. The front-wheel drive pulled the car along with no fishtailing. The snow was falling as hard as ever, the pavement slick and slushy, and visibility sucked, but at least traffic was light. Jack's blip was still on the screen but just barely.

"Fast as you can without killing us," Tier said.

Marley nodded, his expression grim. "I hear you."

Tier admired his stoicism. Not a single complaint out of him. He deserved a hefty tip when this was over.

"How we doin'?" Poncia said from the rear.

"Still got him. And we're closing."

They were passing through Cemetery Land now—First Calvary Cemetery on the right, then Calvary on the left, followed by Mount Zion. Acres and acres of priceless real estate devoted to the unappreciative dead.

Tier told Marley, "Slow down a little. He's about a quarter mile ahead. That's a good distance."

With the snowfall limiting visibility, Jack was out of sight ahead, which meant they were out of sight behind. No matter how many times he checked his rearview mirror, he'd never see them. They were as good as invisible.

On they went, through Maspeth and Elmhurst.

"Where the fuck's he going?" Poncia said. "Could be headed all the way to the Hamptons or Montauk for all we know."

Yep. He could. Tier couldn't know the answer so he didn't bother offering one.

"Hey, detective," Poncia added. "Who *is* this guy? You figured that out yet?"

"He's nobody."

"The fuck's that supposed to mean?"

Tier had explored all the usual proprietary sites he frequented when he was on a hunt and didn't like the picture he'd pieced together.

"Just what I said. The name on the rental agreement said John Tyleski."

"There you go. That ain't nobody. That's somebody."

"Is it? The name John Tyleski is on two credit cards and he has an excellent credit history with both of them. But no bank accounts—not checking, not savings—and no loans."

"Then how does he pay off the cards?"

"Money orders, I imagine. The bills for his credit cards go to an address that doesn't match his Upper West Side apartment. I checked and it's a mail drop."

"So what?"

"I'm totally convinced that our guy is not John Tyleski. That the real Tyleski is probably long dead or, if alive, has no idea his identity's been stolen. This Tyleski has no employment history. He's a ghost."

A ghost in the machine . . .

Hard to do these days, but not so hard to maintain once you achieve it—*if* you stay careful. The real Tyleski might have died as a child and this Jack appropriated his Social Security number. If he never borrows and if he pays off every bill as it comes in, no one's going to give him a second thought. MasterCard or Visa see him as the perfect customer—well, he'd be more perfect if he made minimum installment payments instead paying off the balance every month, but they had to prefer his type to all the deadbeats they dealt with day in and day out.

Only two kinds of people stay under the radar like that: a spy or a criminal. And spies usually had intricate legends behind them.

Which meant Jack was a criminal.

Why would Madame de Medici entrust the precious Bagaq to such a man? Did she know him? Or was it because a man who has managed to hide his true self is the perfect choice to hide other things.

Tier checked the map on his phone. According to the app they'd started to close on Jack.

"Slow a little more," he said. "We don't want to catch up just yet."

Jack was definitely slowing. The map showed him nearing the Woodhaven Boulevard exit. That might be his plan . . .

"Stay to the right. I think he's getting off."

Sure enough, his blip moved onto the off-ramp.

"Okay, Marley. Exit Nineteen it is."

As the sign loomed out of the snow, Marley eased farther right and—

"Shit!"

Three cars ahead, a pickup swerved from the middle lane toward the ramp. It slipped sideways and hit the yellow plastic containers protecting the divider. Amid an explosion of sand, the truck rolled over and slid onto the ramp on its side. The car it cut off T-boned it. Marley managed to slow the Lincoln into a controlled skid along the shoulder, stopping just shy of the car ahead.

No collision.

Tier was releasing a sigh of relief when something crashed into the Lincoln's rear.

8

Jack's tracker beeped.

So soon? Excellent.

Woodhaven Boulevard had become Cross Bay Boulevard and he'd just entered Ozone Park. H3 showed due south—straight ahead. Cross Bay ran past the restaurants and fast food joints along the boat basin in Howard Beach.

Probably hungry, Jack thought.

Cross Bay Boulevard and the upper end of its row of food joints were a thousand feet or so from the entrance to H3's underground conduit. A quick run from there, hit a few Dumpsters for leftovers, then back to the safety of the tunnel in no time.

Not sunset yet—at least by the clock—but who could tell? The low clouds and the snow swallowed the light. The roads were damn near deserted. Anyone with half a brain was huddled indoors. And the kids were probably miffed that a storm that would have guaranteed a snow day or two was happening during Christmas break.

A good time to go foraging through the restaurant Dumpsters. But would H3 find any food? How many places were open in this mess? If your workers couldn't get in . . .

Not Jack's problem. His problem was finding H3 and bringing it down. Hess and Monaco were out of the equation right now. Jack had questions about H3—lots of them—and he was determined to find the answers. The Plum Island pair would figure into all this again, but right now Jack was in it for his own reasons.

He crossed the Belt Parkway into Howard Beach where the Cross Bay streetlights were going strong, their glows diffusing and fusing in the snow-filled air. H3's blip was nearing center screen, so Jack pulled into the lot by New Park Pizza. The place was closed but its lot had only four inches or so of snow, which meant a plow had been through sometime earlier in the day.

He rolled down his window and listened to . . . nothing. The falling snow muffled all sound. But dumpsters were noisy bastards and sooner or later H3 would give itself away.

A *clang* echoed from behind the pizza place.

Gotcha.

Jack gunned the Jeep around the corner and angled the headlights into the rear area.

There! An overcoated figure leaping off the Dumpster into the shadows on its far side.

Tranq gun in hand, Jack jumped out and gave chase. The snow made following easy. H3's tracks led over a fence and across the parking lot of a Chase branch—also closed—toward a brightly lit Stop & Shop still open for business. Its *Pharmacy Open* sign lit up the night. Yeah, people still needed their meds no matter what the weather.

A box truck faced him, filling the rear alley while a guy lugged cartons through the back door. Whoever he was, the storm hadn't stopped him from making his deliveries.

Good on you, fella.

The truck's presence hadn't deterred H3. His tracks led around its front toward the rear. Jack had just reached the front fender when the driver emerged from the store. He stopped dead in the doorway.

"Hey!" he shouted. "Hey, what—?"

Jack hid the tranq gun just before the guy looked his way.

"Was that someone in an overcoat?" he said.

The driver had flat, Toltec features which at the moment were casting a suspicious look Jack's way. "Yeah. You know him?"

Jack ad-libbed. "Tried to break into my car back at the pizza place. I chased him here. What kinda food you hauling?"

"Food? He took something, but if he's after food, he's shit outa luck."

"What's that mean?"

"All I got's toys, man."

Pocketing the tranqer, Jack walked around to the open rear of the truck. A box had been ripped open and a bunch of doll clothes lay scattered across the floor.

The driver joined him. "Shit! That shipment's ruined."

But Jack was tracing the retreating tracks into the buffer trees at the rear of the store. H3 had beat it.

"Who needs doll dresses that bad?" the driver was saying. "I mean, really?"

"Thought it was something else maybe?"

"Check out the box, man. Big drawing of the dresses right there. Big as life."

Yeah . . . big as life. Jack had been nursing a bad feeling about H3 and it just got worse.

"Whoever he is, he's gone," Jack said. "I'm heading back to my car."

Halfway across the Stop & Shop lot he paused and checked the tracker. Just as expected, H3 was on its way back to the conduit. When the blip disappeared, Jack hurried back to his Jeep. Maybe he could catch him on the far side of the Belt.

Sticking to local streets—he'd become familiar with them the past couple of days—he worked his way to Cohancy Street and over the Belt to the racetrack area, found a place to park, and waited.

Didn't take long for the blip to reappear. H3 had resurfaced somewhere between Jack and Aqueduct Racetrack and was heading for the track.

The track? Really? How—? Never mind.

He jumped out and followed.

H3's tracks appeared as if by magic outside a clump of bushes much like the clump on the south side of the Belt. Jack checked and, yep, another manhole. And within the bushes, flanking the opening, two oblong, snow-covered lumps. Jack brushed the snow off the near end of one and found . . .

A head.

Oh, shit.

After a little more brushing, Jack ignored the danger and pulled out his key ring flash. A quick flick on and off revealed a young face and a ruined throat. Same with the other.

Aw, man. The two missing kids—had to be. H3's doing. No doubt. But why? No sign they'd been eaten. So, if not for food, what? This looked like the work of a psycho killer.

He put away the tranq gun, pulled out his Glock, and got moving.

Even in the failing light, the broken snow of the tracks stood out against the surrounding unmarred surface.

He followed the trail to a broken section of cyclone fence and through to the huge parking lot on the other side. He felt exposed out here, but he pushed on, following the diagonal path that led straight toward the dark, empty grandstand. Aqueduct operated through the winter, but no thoroughbreds would be running tonight. Or tomorrow.

Jack was panting when he reached the grandstand. Running in eight or nine inches of snow, even when following in someone else's tracks, was hard work. But here the snow ended and so did the trail. H3 had kept on going, right into the inky shadows under the grandstand.

He edged into the blackness. Glock ready, he used quick flicks of his keyring light to follow the snow H3 had dragged in from the lot, but soon that petered out, leaving Jack lost.

Where the hell had H3 gone?

He didn't want to use his flash much more for fear of giving himself away—if he hadn't already. H3 could be crouched back there in the shadows, ready to spring. Well, two could play that game.

He found a dark corner, pulled the lower end of his parka under his butt, then sat with his back against a wall. Bundled up as he was, and out of the wind and snow, he could hang out here for a good while. Not all night, but he didn't think H3 would wait that long to forage again. It hadn't snagged any food last trip. It had to be hungry.

He checked his phone and found a succinct voicemail from Abe, who hated voicemail almost as much as texting.

"Info I got. Call me."

So, Jack called.

"This person of interest for you," Abe said without preamble and

without mentioning Barry Wexler by name. *"Such a fine human specimen."*

"He registered?"

"He is. Grabbed a little girl off the street but someone had been watching from a window and called it in. He got caught before he could do anything nasty. Said he was just giving her a ride home. But his home computer—oy, such a load of kiddie porn they found. He pled, did three of a five-year sentence, and had been a model parolee since his release."

"Not so model."

"What I figured since you were asking. He was being a bad boy?"

"Not any more. He's changed his ways for good."

A heartbeat or two of silence, then, *"Jack, Jack, Jack . . . "*

"Not me!"

"Ah, those impetuous brothers are at it again, are they?"

He was referring to the Mikulskis, but . . .

"No. A new player."

Looked like H3 had done the human race a service, whether it knew it or not. But that was all the more reason for Jack to keep up his guard.

He pulled out the tranq gun and settled it in his left hand. The Glock remained in his right. He'd leave which one he used up to H3.

9

"Come on!" Poncia said from the back seat. "Get this rustbucket rolling!"

Finally, they were moving again, but not moving well. Tier couldn't say what, exactly, but something was wrong with the rear axle.

They'd lost a good hour and a half dealing with cops, showing ID, Marley trading insurance info, conferring with the limo service office, waiting for tow trucks to remove the disabled vehicles behind them, convincing the cops to let them reverse out and get back on the LIE. No way the Woodhaven Boulevard exit would be clear anytime soon.

Tier had used the time to stand out in the snow. He found weathering a blizzard preferable to sitting in a car with two other people, especially if one of them was Poncia.

"This 'bout the best she do," Marley said. "She hurtin'. I'm gonna have to take her back in."

Tier didn't want to hear that.

"You're sure?"

He nodded. "I push her, she crap out sure. Even doing thirty like this I'm no sure she make it back to the city."

They could *not* go back to the city—especially not at thirty miles an hour. The waste of time was unacceptable.

Tier opened his phone and searched for car rentals.

"Okay. Get off on the Grand Central exit and head south. There's an Enterprise place there. I'll call ahead. We'll rent us a four-wheeler." He turned and glanced at Poncia. "If we'd had one all along, we'd have been far away when that pickup made its asshole move."

"Fuck you, Tonto."

That was number four.

10

Leaving the Allard behind, Madame de Medici walked up Central Park West through the snow. As much as she hated the cold, she loved the way a snowfall painted everything white, hiding the litter, making a dirty city appear clean and new.

She'd looked for Tier Hill in his usual spot across the street from the Allard, but hadn't seen him. He didn't strike her as the type who would be scared off by a snowfall, even a blizzard.

Maybe her ruse had worked. If he'd reported to Roland that he'd found no trace of the Bagaq in her apartment and that she was headed for Egypt, Roland might have sent him elsewhere.

And that elsewhere might be . . . watching Jack's place. Hill knew where he lived because she had deliberately led him there. Jack had a reputation for leaving a certain amount of carnage in his wake, and she had use for that.

So, she'd decided to take a walk uptown to see what Jack was up to. Had he kept the Bagaq in his apartment or taken it someplace more secure?

As she crossed Columbus Avenue onto his block, she spotted a big bearded man in a brown homburg and overcoat—the same man she'd seen from Jack's apartment window. She remembered the look on his face, as if he'd recognized her.

He made a sharp turn and started slogging away through the snow. She was sure he'd seen her. Was he trying to avoid her?

"Excuse me, sir!" He ignored her. "Excuse me!"

Still no sign that he'd heard. No, he'd quickened his pace. He'd heard her, all right, and was trying to escape. Which only intensified her desire to confront him.

She increased her own speed. Running in this snow was not an option. She sensed he was already moving as fast as he could—he looked old and that walking stick probably wasn't entirely for show. She easily caught up to him.

"Excuse me, sir," she said as she tugged on his sleeve. "*Sir!*"

He stopped and turned to face her so abruptly she almost bowled into him.

"What do you want, woman?"

He seemed bigger close up, bordering on massive, at least compared to her slight frame. Despite his age and slightly stooped shoulders, he looked strong enough to break her in two. Snow coated his homburg and the shoulders of his overcoat.

"You know me! You recognized me on Sunday."

"I haven't the slightest idea what you are talking about. Now, if you'll excuse me—"

"And if you know me, I must know you ... "

She stared. His beard and the hair not covered by his homburg were gray, but his olive skin—it hadn't always been so wrinkled—and his pale blue eyes ...

No. It couldn't be.

"Glae—!"

His gloved hand shot out and sealed her mouth.

"I am called Veilleur these days," he said in a low voice. "Gaston Veilleur."

Him, really him ... Glaeken in the flesh. But ...

"You're *old!*"

"How observant of you. Far more astonishing is that you are not. You should be long, long dead. And yet you haven't aged a day since I last saw you. Explain how this can be."

She'd spent millennia wondering that herself.

"Anything can be," she said. "You ought to know that by now. But as to how ... " She shook her head. "I was at the flashpoint of the cataclysm—what they nowadays call 'ground zero'—and yet I miraculously survived. I do not use the term miraculous lightly. Perhaps that's *why* I survived. Whatever the reason, I went on surviving and surviving. When I—"

Glaeken held up a hand and furtively scanned their surroundings.

"If we are going to discuss our past, we shouldn't do it out in the open."

She looked around. Not much of a risk of being overheard with hardly anyone out in the storm, but she didn't want to stand here in the blowing snow anyway.

"Yes. It's too cold. Let's find a bar or a coffee shop."

"Coffee shop? That's even worse."

"Not if we use the Old Tongue. You do remember it, don't you?"

He almost smiled. "Some things one never forgets, no matter how much time has passed."

They trudged through the snow up to Amsterdam Avenue where she spotted a Korean buffet between a nail salon and a Japanese restaurant.

With the lunch crowd gone—if the place had had any sort of crowd on a day like today—and the dinner folks yet to arrive, the space was virtually empty. Though not hungry, they each piled a plate with one of the varied offerings from the tray array—she some kimchi, he some sea-leg salad—to justify their presence to the watchful owners. In the rear seating area, they found a rickety table against the back wall. Glaeken doffed his hat and loosened his overcoat.

She remembered that big body pressed against hers during the First Age, when his skin had been smooth and his hair a red flame. They'd been lovers for a short while, but their lives hadn't meshed. They'd parted friends and remained close until the Cataclysm.

She stayed buttoned up—the cold had reached her bones—and switched to the Old Tongue once they were settled.

"As I was saying, I keep on living. I don't know why. I don't sicken, I don't age, I don't gain or lose weight. When cut I bleed, but I do not scar. I simply keep going."

She used chopsticks to try the kimchi and found it quite good. Glaeken's surimi salad sat untouched before him.

"I was once like that." He stared hard at her. "And you . . . you look the same, but you've changed."

"Really?" Of course she had. "How so?"

"I sense a deep bitterness within. This is new for you. You were always upbeat and now you seem almost . . . despondent."

"You know what it was like after the cataclysm. Amazing how little time it took once our civilization vanished for everything to devolve into barbarism. Brute force ruled the day. The reign of the thugs. If you'd been beaten and raped as many times as I, you'd be bitter too. I've come to see most men as little better than beasts. Present company excluded."

"I'm so sorry."

"And so are they. I never forgave, never forgot. I waited for my chance—time was on my side, after all—and then I struck."

Glaeken raised his eyebrows and drew a finger across his throat.

"Oh, no," she said. "That was too quick." She held up her chopsticks, one in each hand. "A sharpened stick into each eye. You can imagine what life is like for a suddenly blind bully and rapist in those times. They never lasted long, but in the days before they died they paid heavily for their depredations."

"Yes, you've definitely changed."

"But not you, I think. I still sense the same thoughtful barbarian beneath the wrinkles."

"Had I known you lived, I would have sought you out and stayed by your side."

"I searched for you between my enslavements, but never found a trace."

"I was tasked with containing the One. After witnessing the atrocities in his wake, even the worst people seem like angels." He leaned forward, forearms on the table. "But let me ask you: Do you ever get tired of it? Living on and on, I mean?"

"Absolutely not. You read tales about immortals where they suffer crushing ennui and are looking for ways to end it all. But those fictions are written by mortals. One thing the authors can't appreciate is how fast time begins to pass. After the first century or so, the years fly by. Then the decades. And then the centuries. At least that's the way it's been for me. It must have been the same for you."

He nodded. "Exactly. You were quite a celebrity back in our day, yet now you stay anonymous."

"That's the way it must be, and I don't mind. I'm enjoying this life.

In the intervals between the times when they sicken me, I find our species endlessly amusing."

"'Species'?"

She hadn't meant to sound like that.

"You know how it is. Over the millennia you become more removed."

"Only if you disengage. Which I suspect you have."

"I view it as a defense mechanism. Anyway, I can't wait to see what we do next if we're given a chance. I have more wealth than I'd ever dreamed. I just hope for enough time to enjoy it. I'm sure you're well off too."

Another nod. "With time comes perspective. You can spot trends and anticipate where they're headed." A smile. "And after all, we've seen it all before, haven't we?"

Yes, she had. In many ways the progress of this, the Second Age, mimicked that of the First Age of their youth.

"But what happened to you? I'd heard that when the Ally chose you as Defender, it made you immortal. And yet now . . . "

"Just like you, I was enjoying my immortality. The only downside was watching loved ones—lovers, children, grandchildren—age and die. I never got used to that."

Neither had she. The repeated heartbreak . . .

"I never had children, but I had many lovers. The solution is to not get too involved. To disengage, as you say."

"I was never good at that."

"I know. Do you have a woman now?"

He nodded. "Magda. But she is not well. Her mind . . . "

How terrible for him.

"Perhaps the Bagaq . . . ?"

A quick shake of his head. "No-no. It's rare that any true benefit issues from an Infernal, and when it does, it usually comes with a terrible price tag. The present is an ever-shifting mystery to Magda, so she lives mostly in the past. I've learned to deal with that. The Bagaq might only make matters worse."

Poor man. Poor woman. "Do you ever regret losing your immortality?"

Another head shake. "I've watched too many intimates grow old and die. Magda is the first I've grown old with. There's something to be said for taking that journey together. But back when I was immortal . . . the will to go on living, to see what happens next, never left me. Which was why, when I trapped the One back in the sixteenth century and had a chance to end his malevolent existence, I chose instead to lock him away in a prison I had built in a remote corner of the Transylvanian Alps."

"You imprisoned Ra—?"

His hand shot up. "Don't say his name."

"But—"

"Just don't. Back then, I feared if he died, so would I. So, I locked him away." A reminiscent smile curved his lips. "You might be interested to know that I sealed away a lot of so-called 'forbidden' books and scrolls in the keep at the same time. Among them was one of the few remaining copies—perhaps the only remaining copy—of the *Compendium of Srem*."

"How wonderful of you! Is that the broken one in Jack's apartment?"

"The same. Back in the days of the Spanish Inquisition it fell into the hands of the Grand Inquisitor, Tomás Torquemada. He tried to destroy it—burn it, tear it apart, slash its pages—but as you well know, it's virtually indestructible. So, he buried it. But more than that, he designed and built a monastery over the spot—the Monastery of St. Thomas in Avila—where he spent his final years."

"How he must have hated it."

"Fear was his motivating force. The book terrified him. But the *Compendium*'s guardian at the time saw to it that Torquemada buried a decoy. The real one passed to me and I kept it hidden away in the keep for five hundred years until after the war. Alexandru, one of the keep's caretakers, found it along with the other books kept there, and sold them to an antiquarian dealer in Bucharest who in turn sold the *Compendium* to an American collector. A tortuous trail led it to Jack. But it would be locked away still if the damn German Army hadn't interfered and compromised the integrity of the keep. I had to kill the One before he could escape. That was in 1941. The Conflict here appeared over and settled, so the Ally released me. As a result I began to age—slowly, but age nonetheless."

This made no sense.

"But if you killed Ras—"

The hand up again. "Please. He hears and comes looking. Call him the One."

The One . . . in the beginning they had numbered seven—the remorseless Seven who served the Otherness. But Rasalom couldn't tolerate being one of seven. And so, through deceit, treachery, and plain and simple murder, he eliminated them singly and in pairs until only he remained. And thus the Seven became . . . the One.

"But if you killed him, how can he hear me?"

"He found a way back. In 1968 he was able to infuse himself into a unique, newly conceived embryo."

"Are you sure? Knowing him, he'd surely have made his presence known by now."

"He's working behind the scenes, staying off the radar, so to speak."

"Why?"

"Fear of me."

What?

She hid her shock and said, "No offense intended, Glaeken, but in your present state it's nigh impossible to see you as any sort of threat to him."

"Your powers of observation continue to amaze," he said with a sardonic twist to his lips. "Of course, I'm not. But he doesn't know that, and my greatest worry is that he'll discover the truth. If he learns I'm old and mortal, he'll realize he's unopposed here. He'll waste no time reshaping the Earth to accommodate the Otherness, which means making it a living hell for humanity."

This was what she'd been feeling. Her foreboding was no longer nameless.

Burbank's mantra echoed in her brain: *Twilight has come . . . night will follow.*

"His time is coming, isn't it?"

"I fear so. And soon."

"But wasn't there supposed to be someone to take your place should you . . . should something happen to you?"

"The Heir."

"Yes. The Heir. Did something happen to him?"

He gave her a strange look. "Are you playing with me? This is not a matter to be taken lightly."

She felt her mouth go dry. "I'm not sure what you mean." But she had a growing feeling . . .

Glaeken scowled. "Come now. You were in his apartment yesterday."

She closed her eyes. *That* was what she'd sensed about him. "Jack? Jack is the Heir?"

"Yes, but you knew that."

She opened her eyes and stared at him. As the millennia had passed, she'd developed a sense for people and their potentials. "I knew there was something about him, but I couldn't put my finger on it. I sensed he was more than simply an urban mercenary, but I had no idea he was . . . "

"He keeps himself closed off. He's good at that."

They sat in silence a moment. She knew Glaeken was thinking the same as she.

"What are the odds?" he said.

She swallowed. "It seemed like such a natural progression. Earlier this year a piece from my Heracleion collection surfaced in New Orleans. I wanted it back. I asked around and Jack's name came up. I involved him—indirectly, I should add—and he did a brilliant job. I was so satisfied that when another problem of a similar nature arose, I called on him."

"How long ago did you lose this Heracleion piece?"

"The city sank a little over two thousand years ago, so, about that long."

"And suddenly your trinket resurfaces. You didn't question that?"

"Well, another piece—a large inscribed sapphire close to my heart—had surfaced early in the twentieth century, so I wasn't terribly surprised when I heard about this one. The 'trinket' in question is the Cidsev Nelesso."

"Ah. An Infernal. Even more suspicious."

"It had once been part of my collection."

"I'm assuming this current problem of 'a similar nature' involves another Infernal?"

This was looking worse and worse.

"Yes. The Bagaq. Someone stole it from me during the so-called 'Arab Spring' and I recently stole it back. Another collector is in pursuit. I asked Jack to hide it for me."

"That's all?"

She couldn't meet his gaze. "I led one of the collector's men to his home."

The table jumped as Glaeken thumped it with his fist. "He's being set up! And you're complicit! Why would you do such a thing?"

The few other diners in the place—a total of three—paused their chewing to stare a moment, then went back to eating.

"I had my reasons. But I had no idea he was the Heir, or even that an Heir was needed. Had I known, I would have found another way. But even so, from what I've heard and seen, Jack is plenty capable of taking care of himself."

A quick, sharp nod. "He is that. Misdirection, dissimilation, and legerdemain are his stocks in trade. Catch him if you can. But the situation is obviously being manipulated from Outside. The Otherness can't find me, so they're going after the Heir—with the goal of eliminating him. He's at a disadvantage if he doesn't realize that."

She put down her chopsticks. She'd lost her appetite.

"The man I led to him . . . I didn't know it at the time, but he's not an ordinary man."

Glaeken frowned. "How so?"

"You know how it is, when you've been around as long as we, you sense things about people. This Tier Hill . . . he's a Mohawk and he can hear the signals."

"That's extraordinary right there."

"He wears a sense of destiny. Where it will take him, I don't know."

She gasped as a thought came: What if his destiny was to kill the Heir?

"What's wrong?"

She couldn't tell Glaeken what she feared.

"I have to find Jack and warn him."

"Exactly. When he's finally and officially the Defender he'll have greater strength and resistance to injury, but he's not there yet. Until then, he's still as mortal as the next man." He tapped the table, frustration large on his face. "If I were my old self . . . " He jabbed a finger at her. "You're responsible for this and it's up to you to make it right."

"I will. I—"

"Excuse me," said a man two tables away. "Do either of you speak English?"

"Who are you?" she said in English.

"I'm a linguistics professor at Columbia and . . . " He shook his head. "I know a lot about languages and I've never heard anything like what you're speaking. Can you tell me—?"

"It's our own language," she told him. "My father and I here made it up in my childhood. Now do not interrupt us again."

Glaeken wore an amused expression. "Your *father?*"

Reverting to the Old Tongue, she said, "Well, I couldn't very well say we were the same age."

"This is absolutely fascinating," the professor said. "How did you—?"

"*What part of 'do not interrupt us again' was unclear?*" Glaeken said in a voice that shook the walls.

The professor seemed to shrivel in his seat and became very interested in his food.

"I'll have to find Jack," she said.

"Don't bother with his apartment. He's not home."

"Do you have his cell number?"

"He carries a variety of disposable phones, none of which he keeps long. When I want to contact him, I leave a message at his apartment."

On the night before she'd visited him, Jack had called her back, wanting to arrange a meeting elsewhere. Did she still have that number?

"I'll track him somehow."

"Please do. Forces are aligning to bring him down."

"I said I'd find him. But a favor, Glaeken."

"I'm listening."

"When next you see him, don't say anything about me. Don't even mention that you saw me."

"Why not?"

"I like being Madame de Medici. It can't go on forever, but for now it's who I am. Though six months from now it probably won't matter."

His eyebrows rose. "You know something I don't?"

"The signals . . . their frequencies are almost aligned."

His expression slackened for a heartbeat or two, then tightened. "I receive the reports from Burbank, but with no activity for so long, I've neglected them. How long before they reach synchronization?"

"They started speeding toward synchronization this summer, but now their progression has slowed to a crawl."

"But still progressing." He nodded as if that made sense. "The One's forces have killed the Lady twice—first time in Florida and the second right here in Central Park just this past summer."

"But she persists?"

"Just barely. She lost the dog in the last attack."

The Lady without her dog . . . she began to understand how dire the situation had become.

"The signals . . . you think they're waiting for her third demise?"

He nodded. "The third will be the end of her. She's linked to the Noosphere and the Noosphere is our last defense. I'm doing everything I can to protect her. And to prepare Jack for his destiny. Where do you live?"

"Many places. Here in New York I have an apartment in the Allard."

"The Allard? We're practically neighbors."

"I wanted to stay close to Burbank."

"Hard to believe he's still alive."

"I've been helping him with that, but I don't know how much further I can take him." Something Glaeken had said came back to her . . . dates. "Earlier you mentioned 1941. I've never asked Burbank because I never thought it mattered, but he told me the other day that the first signal began in 1941."

She saw Glaeken stiffen. "Did he say when in 1941?"

"He knew the exact minute: 8:56 p.m. Eastern Standard Time on April Twenty-third."

Glaeken leaned back and rubbed his eyes. "That was just about the time the German soldiers released the One from his solitary confinement and let him loose in the keep. He couldn't leave the structure, but he could roam free within its walls."

"You also mentioned 1968. He said the signals stabilized on February eleventh, 1968. Does that date mean anything?"

A weary nod. "That was the day the One was reconceived in human form. No question about it now: The signals are related to the

Otherness. Do you have a safe place you can go?"

She was the only living person who knew the location of her ref-
uge—or that it even existed. Should she tell him?

Of course she should. This was Glaeken.

"I have a hidey hole in a remote corner of the Qattara Depression."

His smile was grim. "Which makes it doubly remote. It's secure?"

"I can survive there for a long time."

But six months from now, if things had gone all to hell, would she
want to survive?

"Good. You will need it."

"Is there no way to stop it—the apocalypse?"

He shook his head. "It appears inevitable. One way or another,
the Otherness will make its move. Sapience attracts attention. The
showdown has been brewing since sentient life took hold here. I
don't know what exactly will trigger it, but I've no doubt it will happen. And soon."

"Burbank says it will begin in the heavens."

"And so it shall. Only the outcome is in question. And right now
our side is at a distinct disadvantage." He gave her a pointed look.
"And at an even greater disadvantage without a Defender. Find Jack."

"I will. But this storm isn't going to help."

Glaeken's expression was grim. "This storm may not be entirely
natural."

That hadn't occurred to her.

"Aimed at him?"

"I'm beginning to think so. He's a creature of the city . . . it's his
domain. But a storm like this alters the terrain, reduces his advan-
tages by blunting his instincts, slowing his movements, constricting
his awareness."

Possessed by a sudden urgency, she rose and he rose with her.
After a heartbeat's hesitation, they embraced.

She spoke against his chest. "We may not see each other again."

His arms tightened around her. "We may not. I have only a few
years left but you will go on—at least I hope you will—for many,
many more."

But will it be a world I wish to live in? she wondered as she broke
away and hurried toward the street.

11

Jack jerked awake.

Movement . . . he'd caught it out of the corner of his eye. Over to his left, by the opening to the outside. Had H3 got away?

He eased to his feet and sidled toward the opening where he was rewarded with a strange sight. Not the strangest thing he'd ever seen—he'd have to go some for that—but up there on the list.

A figure was racing across the parking lot. Not running upright like a man but on all fours like an animal . . . like a dog or a wolf . . . and wearing an overcoat.

Jack raised the tranq gun but H3 was already out of range and fading into the falling snow.

How had this happened?

The cold had been seeping into his bones, making him drowsy. Had H3 seen him or had it been so focused on getting back outside it had missed him? Had to be the latter. Jack had placed himself deep in the shadows. And after seeing what H3 had done to those other three bodies, he doubted it would have left him untouched.

He shook himself and jumped up and down, trying to restore full circulation to his cold limbs. And as he did, he realized he'd been presented with the perfect opportunity to catch H3 in its lair—hit it with a no-miss tranq or two, then call the Plum Island boys and get this over with.

And maybe then he'd get some answers. Because he had questions about H3—big ones.

Maybe he wouldn't have to wait. With H3 across the Belt and out and about over on the commercial strip, here was Jack's chance to learn a little on his own. H3's lair was somewhere in here under the grandstand. It wouldn't be back for a while, so . . . why not?

Maglite in one hand and Glock in the other, he moved to the rear of the deep recess and searched along the steep angle where the concrete support met the concrete floor. Leaves and food wrappers, blown in from the parking lot, littered the corners. But one spot, darker than the rest, stuck out.

Jack approached and found an area of perfect blackness. A heavy steel grate had been moved aside, leaving a dark, empty square in the floor. Here was where H3 did its disappearing act.

He flashed his light down and saw foot rungs imbedded in the concrete wall. Jack didn't expect H3 back soon but had no doubt it would return, so he couldn't waste what time he had. Holstering the Glock, he slipped through the opening and clambered down the rungs.

Another tunnel but unlike the usual drainage pipe. Bigger, a comfortable six feet in height, and of more recent vintage than the one running under the Belt. Its floor was flat but its walls and ceiling angled this way and that. Like a German expressionistic design without a true vertical anywhere. He could imagine Dr. Caligari's somnambulist wandering by. Drainage from the main parking lot and the grandstand had to go somewhere. Maybe through here. But that wouldn't be a concern until the weather thawed.

The question now: which way to go? He sensed a slight incline to his right and decided to try uphill first.

The tunnel curved to the left ahead of him. A half dozen feet around the bend his beam reflected off some plastic packing on the floor. Closer inspection revealed a *Star Wars* action figure: Ridley. Beyond that another plastic pack, this one with a doll's dress. The one stolen from the Stop & Shop truck?

What was going on here? What was H3's attraction to these toys?

A few feet past that Jack found a cubic battery pack loaded with four D cells; a switch jutted from one end and wires trailed off into the dark from the other. A few feet away Jack's flash picked up a tiny bulb jutting from one of the wires.

Lights?

Weirder and weirder.

Feeling a little reckless, he flipped the switch.

The alcove-like space ahead of him came to life, brightening with multicolored lights. It took him a moment to recognize what he was looking at. And then—

"Aw, no!"

12

The limo had limped into the Enterprise lot where Tier learned they had a Ford Explorer with four-wheel drive. He claimed it. Marley arranged to leave his limo on the lot for eventual towing while he rented a car to return to the city.

As Tier was signing the rental papers, Poncia said, "Hey, Tonto, I'm hitting the head to take a dump. Don't leave without me."

Five, Tier thought.

"Why you let him talk you like that?" Marley said when Poncia was gone.

Tier knew exactly what he was talking about, but put on a puzzled expression. "Like what?"

"He call you 'Tonto.' Me, if I you and he call me that, I straighten him right quick."

"Tonto was a loyal partner, a brave friend, a standup guy. I should take it as a compliment, don't you think?"

"You believe me, mon, he no mean that as a compliment. He think he insulting you."

"Well, Marley, for an insult to mean anything, you have to respect the source."

Marley considered this, then shrugged. "I still not let him get away with it. Just because he white, he think he can speak any way he please to you and me."

"I know plenty of whites who wouldn't think of speaking that way. He's a bad person, a man of no worth. He'd be the same no matter what color his skin. But his whiteness allows him to think he can say whatever he pleases with impunity."

"Why you work with him?"

"It's a short-term thing. He works for a man who hired me. We've been temporarily thrown together. I expect us to go our separate ways tomorrow. After that I will never see him again."

Which was true in more ways than one. Tier had decided to break his rule about no more killing and gut Poncia when this was over.

"Still, you should make him stop calling you 'Tonto.'"

"He has called me 'Tonto' five times already today. I'm sure there will be many more."

Marley's eyes narrowed. "You've been counting?"

"Of course."

Yes. Let Poncia keep it up. The total would decide how many times he stabbed his piggy body before he let him die.

13

Jack stared at the miniature Christmas tree and its blinking lights . . . and all the presents piled around it.

And he knew.

"Those sons of bitches! Those rotten, lying, evil sons of bitches!

The suspicion growing in him since he'd watched H3 with little Cilla Quinnell in her backyard yesterday had just bloomed into an inescapable fact.

H3 was David Quinnell . . . or at least had been at one time. And now he ran on all fours. How much human was left in him?

Apparently enough to remember his daughter . . . and that Christmas was near.

Rage combined with wonder and stirred in more rage. How had they managed this? How had they got him out of prison? How had he been declared dead? And how the hell had they turned him into H3?

They'd talked about stem cells treated with some mystery substance. Melis. Had any of that been true? Might have been the only true thing they'd told him.

Jeez, what had he gotten himself into?

Get back in the game . . . it'll do you good . . . start slow . . . track down a lost beastie . . . no emotional involvement there . . . it's just an animal . . . no sweat . . .

Sure.

Whatever the truth about his origin, H3 was a killer. The dead perv and the two dead teens were ample proof of that. And since Quinnell had been sent up for murder in the first place, the conclusion wasn't such a stretch.

Remembering H3 crouched across the fence from Cilla Quinnell, Jack stared at the blinking tree, at the girly toys, and didn't like at all what he saw developing.

Crap.

He wanted nothing more to do with this whole bizarre, rotten situation, but he couldn't walk away and leave H3 out there. The blood and blame for what H3 had done to this point were on Hess and Monaco's hands. Any blood from now on would be on Jack's as well.

He worried about little Cilla. David Quinnell might want only the best for his daughter, but rejection was a real possibility, and H3 might not take that too well.

Time to improvise. And Jack hated to improvise.

Okay . . . one—get the hell out of here before H3 came back. Jack wanted room to maneuver when he dealt with it and the conduit provided very little.

Two—decide on that after he'd completed one.

He took one last look at the surreal scene of the blinking Christmas tree and the presents centered on a *Caligari* set, then turned off the lights and made his way back up to the space under the grandstand. The snow storm hadn't let up yet. Faint light suffused the flake-filled night air over the parking lot.

Using his flash, Jack searched for the darkest spot available with a clear view of the entrance to H3's hidey hole. He settled into an angled corner with the tranq gun in hand and the Glock cocked and ready on his lap.

He didn't think he'd have a long wait. And he was right.

H3 arrived under the grandstand in a rush. The snow muffled everything, so Jack hadn't heard it coming, but he'd caught sight of it as it rounded the barrier along the parking lot. It had been running on all fours in the lot but rose to a slightly crouching upright posture once it hit the dry surface. Jack's big worry was how well it could see in the dark. That turned out to be a nonissue because it headed straight for the opening without looking around. Must have been pretty sure it had the grandstand to itself.

Jack sat with his back against the wall and his knees up, the tranq gun in a two-handed grip and his wrists resting atop his knees. Taking a breath, he fired a dart at H3's silhouette. He couldn't see the dart land, but the way H3 jerked and spun told him he'd scored a hit. If H3 felt it, that meant the needle had penetrated and injected the neuromuscular agent. With no idea how fast it would work, Jack immediately reloaded.

H3 turned Jack's way and snarled. Could it see him? It answered the question by heading straight for him. Jack fired another dart and once again H3 reacted by jerking to a halt. But only for a heartbeat. As it moved closer, Jack grabbed the Glock.

But before he could pull the trigger, H3 stumbled and dropped to its knees. Jack held his fire as H3 struggled back to its feet. But instead of continuing its charge, it wheeled and staggered back to the hole.

Jack held his position as it disappeared into the floor, then he rose and waited a little longer. He tucked the tranqer away and, with the Glock extended, made a slow approach.

A few peeks into the opening with the flash showed an empty passage below. A cautious descent put him on the floor. He stood and listened. From up ahead, where he'd found the Christmas tree, came a dragging sound, and heavy breathing.

Jack stalked forward, found the little light switch, and flipped it.

H3 sprawled in the middle of the floor, trying to drag itself away. Finally, it lay still, panting. A feral face glared at Jack from within the hood and from under the cap bill. It bared sharp teeth as it growled—a weak growl. It had taken two darts, but whatever the Plum Island boys had put in those darts had worked its magic. H3's muscles had turned to silly putty.

"Hello, David," Jack said. "When was the last time anyone called you that?"

14

"They can put up all the *Jackie Robinson Parkway* signs they want," Poncia said, "it'll always be the Interboro to me."

They'd left the Enterprise office and headed west on the Jackie Robinson—AKA the Interboro Parkway. Usually two lanes each way, it had been reduced to one, and that lane in lousy shape. But the Explorer handled well in the slush.

Hours ago—was it only hours?—Jack had turned south off the LIE onto Woodhaven Boulevard. Tier's plan was to head back toward Woodhaven via the Interboro and then follow that south. He'd taken the wheel and put Poncia in charge of watching the phone to see if they got a hit on the Jeep. Chances were near nil along this stretch through Forest Park.

"Y'hear me?" Poncia said.

"I'm concentrating on the road. Looks like they plowed it once and forgot about it."

"I'm betting you like Jackie Robinson better."

Tier sensed where Poncia was going with this—try to make it racial.

"Helluva a ball player."

"Hey, no argument there. But I remember driving this with my dad as a kid—before he took off for parts unknown. It was called the

Interboro then and it should be called the Interboro now."

"Got something against change?"

"Not if it's for the better. But usually it ain't. Look at the Queensboro Bridge. It's now the Ed Koch. Same with the Triboro—renamed it after Robert Kennedy. Fucking guy was born and raised in Massachusetts. Those are changes but they ain't improvements. What next? No more Brooklyn Bridge? Gonna be the Bloomberg Bridge? The DeBlasio Bridge?" He made a gagging sound.

As much as he hated to be on the same page as Poncia about anything, Tier had to agree. He found renaming landmarks after politicians offensive. He preferred the descriptive names. The Triboro Bridge connected three boroughs. The Interboro ran between the boroughs of Brooklyn and Queens. But he couldn't bring himself to openly agree.

Poncia ripped open another foil ketchup packet—his second since the Enterprise office—and began sucking on it.

"How many of those do you have?" Tier said.

"Plenty. I like to play this little game with the 7-Elevens and convenience places. I buy a sandwich and then I ask for ketchup and they point me to the bins where they keep the packs of mayo and mustard and shit. And I say, 'Okay if I take some?' And they say, 'Sure.' And I say, 'Sure?' You see, I'm waiting for the magic words, and so I keep it up until they say, 'Help yourself.' And that's it. I go over and empty all the ketchups into my pockets. And if somebody says something, I say, 'You said I should help myself so that's what I'm doing!'"

Poncia laughed like this was the funniest damn thing.

"I get 'em every time!"

"What a scallywag you are," Tier said.

How much longer would he be trapped in the car with this asshole?

"Yeah, whatever. What are we doing here anyway? Seems like a total waste of time."

"I'm open to a better idea."

A safe offer because Poncia wouldn't have one.

"Like looking for a needle in a haystack."

"Can't argue with that. But we'll hit Woodhaven soon. We'll ride back up toward the LIE, then come back down. If he's stopped anywhere within a half mile along the way, we'll get a ping."

"And if he's not?"

"Then we improvise. Just keep your eyes on that screen. We don't want to miss him."

"Don't worry, Tonto. I ain't gonna miss nothing."

And that made six.

15

The flaccid Quinnell offered little resistance beyond growls when Jack used a set of Monaco's cuffs to shackle his left arm to one of the pipes running through the space. His hands had shortened and thickened to semi-paws, but he still had enough wrist to make the cuff effective.

Jack seated himself against the opposite wall. He placed the tranq gun on the floor nearby but kept the Glock in his lap within easy reach.

"You're supposed to be dead, you know," Jack said. "I mean, Canaan lists you as dead."

Quinnell gave him a dull stare.

"Can you speak?" Jack said.

Quinnell growled and shook his head.

Okay, so he'd lost the power of speech—due to changes in the brain or in his throat? Jack guessed the latter since he seemed to understand easily enough. But damn the loss of speech. Jack had so many questions. He'd have to go the Twenty Questions route and frame them for *yes* or *no* answers.

"First off, I've got a very good idea why you killed the perv. But why those two kids?"

Quinnell growled and bared his teeth as he briefly raised the sleeve of his overcoat. He hadn't the strength to hold it up long, but from across the space, even in the dim, multicolored blinking light, Jack could make out the scorched area.

"They tried to burn you?"

A nod.

Wouldn't be the first time some sicko set fire to a homeless man. Sometimes they survived, sometimes they were too drunk or drugged to wake up in time. He couldn't imagine what possessed two middle schoolers to take that leap. Probably heard about it and thought it would be—what—fun? Or maybe their civic duty? Whatever, if they were expecting a helpless victim, they couldn't have made a worse choice.

Stupid kids . . . well, after he'd settled the H3 fix, he'd make an anonymous call about where to find the bodies. The families needed to know. But for now . . .

Jack waved his hands at Quinnell's body, trying to indicate his changes, his overall condition. "How did this happen?"

Quinnell simply stared at him. No way he could explain without words.

"Okay, okay," Jack said. "Let's try this: I've met Monaco and Hess and—"

The loudest growl yet from Quinnell.

"Yeah, not my favorite people either. They sent me to find you and bring you back."

More growling, accompanied by violent shaking of his head.

Jack could see he should leave going back to Plum Island out of the conversation. At least for now.

"What I'm trying to fathom is how this came about. They told me they injected you with something. That right?"

A nod.

Okay. At least that much was true. Jack couldn't be sure about anything those two had told him.

"But did you let them or were you forced?" No, wait. That wasn't a yes-or-no question. "Were you forced?"

A head shake.

"You *let* them?"

A nod.

Jeez.

"Why?"

Oh, hell, that wasn't yes or no either.

But before Jack could rephrase, Quinnell scratched something on the floor with one of the claws on his free hand. Careful to stay out of reach, he leaned over to see.

$

"Money?"

A nod.

"I hope it was a lot." A helluva lot.

Quinnell scratched something next to the dollar sign. The effort seemed to exhaust him. Yeah, the agent was still working.

$500K

"Five hundred thousand bucks?"

A nod.

"A lot of money, but then not a lot of money at all when you wind up not human and unable to spend it.

He pointed to himself and gave his head a vigorous shake. Then picked up one of the Barbie dresses and waved it.

"Ah. For your family."

Kind of noble. No, insanely noble. David Quinnell abruptly soared in Jack's estimation.

"But even so . . . to sacrifice your humanity . . . "

Quinnell made a slashing motion across his throat.

"You want me to shut up?"

A head shake and a repeat of the slash, then a claw digging into his stomach.

Jack raised his hands in a not-following-you gesture.

Quinnell did a retake . . . and then Jack got it. The throat slash . . .

"You were dying?"

A nod.

When Hess had been spewing his line about sticking human stem cells into a wolf, he'd said the wolf had had cancer and that the stem cells had cured it. Did he mean . . . ?

"You were dying of cancer."

Another nod.

"According to Hess, whatever they've been doing to you cured the cancer. Did you know that?"

A nod.

Jack leaned back. What a bloody mess. David Quinnell had considered himself a dead man, and so he'd sold his dying body to those two devils to let them do whatever they wanted in exchange for half a mil for his wife and daughter. And now he was cured but no longer David Quinnell.

"You've got to go back. You know that, don't you?"

Vigorous headshakes.

"David, you've gotta see that there's no place for you out here. They've turned you into a . . . " He'd been about to say "freak" but thought better of it, even though Quinnell was every inch a freak now. "I don't know what you've been turned into, but the only place for you is Plum Island."

The headshakes became continuous.

"You could be the answer to cancer." Damn, he hadn't meant for it to rhyme, but why not go with it? "Think about that, David. The answer to cancer. You could be it. And who knows? Maybe someday down the line Cilla might need the cure you're carrying. Think about that."

The headshakes stopped for a few heartbeats, then resumed.

Poor guy. He'd thought his days were numbered so he didn't care what they did to him. But now he was going to live and he wanted what he'd had. But that could never happen. He'd traded his humanity . . .

Wait.

Hadn't Abe said the Quinnell mortgage was in arears and the bank had started foreclosing? That didn't jibe with Mrs. Q receiving a half-million-dollar windfall.

Unless . . .

"Oh, shit. Oh-shit, oh-shit, oh-shit, oh-shit, oh-shit."

Quinnell gave him a questioning look.

The sons of bitches. Had they kept the money for themselves?

"I don't think Jelena ever got the money."

Jack instantly regretted his blurt. But the mendacity, the sheer, unalloyed, unabashed avarice had propelled the words past whatever filters he possessed.

Quinnell stared at him, mouth agape for maybe a full fifteen seconds, then went into a wild, thrashing, roaring, full-tilt berserker rage. Looked like the neuromuscular agent was wearing off. To the cuffs' credit—and the pipe's as well—they all held. No doubt the residual effects from the muscle relaxer helped.

When Quinnell finally ran out of steam, Jack said, "I'm going to find out what happened to your money."

A questioning look: *Why? Why do this for me?*

Good question. Jack didn't have a good answer.

Okay, yeah, he did. Hess and Monaco . . . that they could do something like this—that *anyone* could do this—offended him beyond all reason. His fingers itched to close around someone's throat.

An old mentor's words echoed from the past: *There are certain things I won't abide in my sight.*

"I have a few questions of my own for Doctor Hess. I'll add in one about your money. And I'm not talking about tomorrow or the next day. I'm talking tonight. Now. Because I have the fucker's address."

16

"If he got on a plane we're royally fucked," Poncia said.

"But he didn't."

"Oh, and you know that how?"

"Because JFK's been shut down most of the day."

"But we should still check it out. He might have a ticket and be sitting there waiting for the storm to stop."

"Big 'might be.'"

"Mister Apfel will want to know that we checked everywhere for this guy, Tonto—*everywhere.*"

Number seven. Keep it up.

Strange how little it bothered him now that he knew Poncia was a dead man.

They were making their way through Ozone Park where Woodhaven Boulevard renamed itself Cross Bay Boulevard. Aqueduct lay off to the left, Howard Beach straight ahead. The trip down from the LIE had taken longer than Tier ever could have imagined. And to no avail. No pings.

Where was Jack?

Here was what he knew: Jack had been heading west on the LIE and then he'd turned south onto Woodhaven. No chance that he was playing them with misdirection because he hadn't known he was being followed at the time. As far as he knew, he'd ditched his tail on a snowy side street in Queens.

Because of all that, the best odds placed Jack's destination south of the LIE and either along Woodhaven or west of it. JFK Airport lay in that quadrant.

Tier wanted to cover all possibilities, but the chances of Jack renting a Jeep just so he could leave it in one of the JFK lots seemed slim to none. But what if he had? It wouldn't take them long to do a circuit of the long-term and short-term lots. If the Jeep was anywhere on the JFK site they'd get a ping. He just wouldn't hold his breath.

But on the plus side, Howard Beach was down by JFK. After running around the airport, he could use the opportunity to check it out.

"The airport it is," Tier said.

"Good thinking. Otherwise I'd have to rat you out to the boss. You know, as my duty."

Tier followed the JFK arrows onto the Belt Parkway where the going was slow.

"We could be out all night at this rate," Poncia said. "You got a squaw waiting up for you?"

Tier decided to count that as a "Tonto." Number eight.

17

The address Abe had given him for Hess was a mile or so south of the Southern State Parkway in Freeport which, though in the next county, wasn't all that far from Aqueduct—maybe 20 miles west. A half-hour trip in good weather along the Sunrise Highway, miles to the south, but Jack didn't know how much plowing had been done down there. The Southern State was bigger, busier, and more important. But even so, only two of its three lanes were drivable. Took him almost an hour to reach the West Seaman Avenue address.

The Freeport sanitation department was doing a better job on the local streets here than New York City was doing for its outer boroughs. But then, NYC had more streets.

Hess's place was a side-by-side, two-family Dutch colonial with a mansard roof. Both halves were lit. His street looked like it had been plowed recently—not down to the pavement by any means, but enough to offer solid footing for the Jeep's four-wheel drive. His driveway was untouched and the plows had built a solid berm along the curb. Jack parked in the street. He couldn't see the plows coming back anytime soon.

He climbed the berm and slogged through a good eighteen inches of snow on the lawn to the double doors located front and center. The one on the right bore the number 922A, with 922B on the left. Hess's address had an "A," so Jack tested the storm door on the right and found it locked. A quick twist of the blade of his folder knife fixed that. He hated to treat his Spyderco that way, but when Hess opened the inner door, he needed to believe he still had a barrier between him and whoever was on the front steps. Jack rang the bell and a few seconds later saw a silhouette peek through a front window. Could have been Hess himself, or maybe his wife if he had one. If Hess himself, he wouldn't recognize Jack in his hoodie.

Jack rang the bell again and this time the door opened. The shock of recognition was just lighting Hess's expression through the storm-door glass when Jack pulled it open and pushed him back into his living room.

"Jack! W-what are you doing—?"

"Who else is here?"

"No one.

"No wife, kids?"

"I'm divorced, no kids. Look—"

Excellent. Okay, down to business ...

"Where's Quinnell's money?"

His eyes widened. "Have you gone insane? Quinnell ... " Jack could almost hear Hess's mind racing. "Quinnell is dead!"

"Cut the crap. I've got him."

Now Hess's eyes went from merely wide to double wide, verging on Tex Avery bug-out. "Here? You brought him *here?*"

"No. But I can go get him if you want."

"No-no!" Then the eyes narrowed. "Wait ... you pulled this on me already. Fool me once—"

"He told me about the money. About everything."

Hess relaxed and managed a laugh. "Now I know you're lying. He can't talk."

Jack stepped closed. "You just told me he was dead."

"Well, I ... " Sputter-sputter, then, "Yes, well, of course: Dead men can't speak."

Enough of this. Jack pulled out the Spyderco and used the thumb hole to flick open the four-inch blade. "You've heard of the Death of a Thousand Cuts, right?"

A shaky laugh. "Oh, come on. You don't have it in you."

Hess was right. Well, probably. But Jack was pissed enough to get started. He remembered something Burkes had told him when they'd met in Julio's the other day.

"Didn't Burkes warn you about me? About collateral damage."

Hess shook his head but his expression said otherwise.

"I'm thinking I should change your name to 'Collateral.' And if you think I won't damage you after seeing what you did to David Quinnell—"

"He knew what he was getting into! Full disclosure—we told him exactly what we were going to do—or try to do—and he agreed!"

"But not for free, right? He wasn't doing it for the sake of humanity or the advancement of science. He was doing it for his family—for half a million dollars to go to his wife and daughter."

The wide-eyed look again. "How can you know this?"

"He told me."

Hess's voice rose to a shout. "But his hyoid bone regressed to nothing. He can't *speak!*"

"No, but he can still write by scratching letters."

Hess's expression said he'd never thought of that.

"Okay, okay! But we paid his wife. We gave her half a million in cash—a whole suitcase packed with stacks of hundreds."

"Really? Then why's the bank foreclosing?"

After years and years of fixes Jack had learned that there comes a point in any battle, whether of wits or bullets or fists, when one side senses that the momentum has shifted the other way, never to return. Jack saw that in Hess's face. He'd run out of lies.

"Tell me the story from the beginning," Jack said. "The abridged version. And no lies."

Hess let out a sigh that could have come from his toes. He backed into an easy chair and sat hard.

"We'd hit a wall injecting the human stem cells. We'd get impressive physical alterations but all the animals would die before we could test their intelligence."

"That lysis thing you mentioned."

"Yes. Cellular lysis. Agent Greve was getting impatient and—"

"He's your Defense Department handler?"

"Was."

"Was? The one Quinnell killed?"

Hess shook his head. "That was Monaco's fiction. H3 didn't kill anyone on Plum Island."

"You call him 'Quinnell' now. No need to continue that 'H3' fiction either."

"H3 was his official designation and, as he began to change, we both found it easier to call him that. It became uncomfortable—at least for me—to think of him as 'David' and 'him.' So he became 'H3' and 'it.'"

"'It rubs the lotion on its skin.'" Jack singsonged.

Hess looked genuinely confused, but Jack didn't want to get into a sidebar on Jame Gumb.

"Not important. So, this Greve guy . . . ?"

"He was our DIA overseer. He held the purse strings and we were afraid he was going to cut off our funding if we couldn't show some results soon—real soon. For years Monaco had been itching to reverse the protocol: inject animal cells into a human. He mentioned it in passing at one of our monthly meetings with Agent Greve, and—"

"And he jumped on it."

"With both feet."

"Sounds like a swell fellow."

"A scary fellow. But he became all excited. Human intelligence would already be onboard. If the treated stem cells could confer animal properties to make the subject a more effective warrior or scout, we'd have what he called 'a home run.' The problem was finding a volunteer. Our candidate would obviously need to be someone desperate, say, terminally ill, with nothing to lose long term."

"Seems like a waste of time. If you make changes in someone who's already knocking on death's door, what use can they be to Defense?"

"We needed an initial trial just to see if the process had any effects at all on a human. You know—a feasibility test. If the human subject's immune system rejected the stem cells, there'd be no point in going any further. But if we saw changes—*any* changes—then we'd design a whole new protocol."

"But still . . . a tall order finding someone."

"Greve thought otherwise. He said the Federal penitentiaries would make an excellent source. The max security pens are full of murderers and rapists and terrorists and other human detritus who'd be mourned by no one. He started researching potential sub-jects and came up with David Quinnell.'"

"Who had cancer, right?"

"Yes. Advanced pancreatic cancer for which he was refus-ing treatment. He preferred to die rather than stay a prisoner. He was perfect. So Greve made him an offer he couldn't refuse and he volunteered."

Sure, Jack thought. Help his family and maybe do some good with his death. Hard to refuse.

"Did you tell him you were going to turn him into a wolfman?"

Hess made a supplicating gesture. "How could we? We had no idea this would happen—we didn't know if *anything* would happen. We sure as all hell didn't know the stem cells would be killing off the cancer cells within months of starting therapy. He's cancer free now. That's why it's important we get him back."

"You cured him of cancer?"

Hess shrugged. "As scientists we can't say that. We can say that Quinnell's cancer went into remission during the stem cell therapy, but without a clinical trial we can't say it *caused* the remission."

"And no clinical trial is going to happen because curing cancer isn't on the Defense Department's agenda."

"No. But it might be on *our* agenda."

"You and Monaco?"

A vigorous nod. "A couple of more successes like H3—I mean Quinnell—and we can take it to NIH. And from there the sky's the limit."

"Meaning you become famous."

"Right. But not necessarily rich."

Ah, Jack thought. Here we go.

"And there's the rub. That's why you stole from Jelena Quinnell."

"It's not stealing! She never had it—didn't even know about it. And Greve gave it to *us*, not Quinnell!"

"Why would he do that?"

"Because he didn't want any of his men involved with Quinnell's family. The money was in a suitcase. We were supposed to present it as airline luggage that had been found in a storage area. It would have Quinnell's name and address on it. We were to have it delivered to his wife as lost property and then vanish."

Not a bad plan.

"So Greve gave it to you with the understanding that you'd fun-nel it to Quinnell's family. But you didn't. I don't get it. I mean, half a mill isn't a life-changing amount for two federal employees."

"It's a start. With Quinnell's success, we could see more suitcases coming down the line. And hey, we can do a lot of good with that money. Quinnell doesn't deserve it. If anything, he owes us for mak-ing him cancer free. He's alive because of us."

"But he has to live as a wolfman. And his wife and daughter get kicked out of their home."

"A home that was bought with money Quinnell made in whatever illegal scheme he was involved in."

That did it. Jack suddenly had his fill of this self-righteous bas-tard. He was still holding the Spyderco. He didn't allow himself to think about it. He raised it and plunged the blade well into Hess's leg. He put a good amount of force behind it. He had to go through his slacks and his skin, and human skin is tougher than most people imagine. But Jack kept his blades honed. Stabbed him mid-thigh—through the center of his quadriceps, far away from any major artery, but down to the bone.

Hess cried out, twisted in his chair, and tumbled to the floor. Not Jack's idea of fun, but he hid his reticence as he watched Hess writhe on the rug, clutching his thigh.

"Hurts like hell, doesn't it?"

"Are you crazy?" Hess said through pain-clenched teeth.

"No, Mister Collateral. I'm simply pissed off. Make that *very* pissed off. That's cut number one. Nine hundred and ninety-nine to go."

"No!" His expression said he was a believer now. "What do you want?"

"I want the money. And don't tell me it's in a bank, because that won't fly. No way you could go on record with that kind of cash. The DoD would know. Which means you've hidden it. Where?"

"Monaco has it."

"Really? Why am I not surprised? That means you're gonna call him and tell him to bring it over here. Now."

"But he won't bring it! He won't give it up, no matter how you threaten me!"

Jack wiped the blade on Hess's slacks. "Then I guess that means you'll have to find a way to convince him. And to provide inspiration we'll start with cuts number two and three and—"

"Wait!" That defeated look had invaded Hess's features again. "He's next door."

"What?" Jack hadn't seen that coming. "You guys share the place? Are you a couple or something?"

Hess gave his head a quick shake. "Me and Monaco? Are you crazy? Nothing like that."

"Then why?"

"Once we decided to keep the money, like you said, we knew we couldn't spend it without Greve getting wind of it. We also knew we had to stay close."

"Why don't you just come out and say it: You don't trust each other."

"Would you trust Monaco?"

No love lost there, Jack thought.

"My Trust List is very short."

"Yeah, well, as Monaco said, keep your friends close and your enemies closer."

Sounded like Monaco. Count on him to find a cliché for every occasion.

"You consider yourselves enemies?"

"We're not bosom buddies, I can assure you of that. Neither of us is married, so this seemed perfect. We sold our previous places and bought this."

"You work together. Do I assume you commute together?"

A nod. "But beyond that we go our separate ways."

"But you let Monaco keep all Quinnell's money?"

"He insisted. And he can be relentless."

"I'll bet." Jack figured it wouldn't hurt to make it look as if he were edging onto Hess's side. "Where's he stash it?"

"In his half of the basement."

"Just sitting there?"

"Of course not. It's behind a wall."

"Well, then, let's go see Monaco."

He indicated his bleeding leg. "I can't."

The bleeding had slowed to an ooze, but had created a big red stain on Hess's jeans. A perfect persuader for Monaco.

"Sure you can."

Jack yanked him to his feet and propelled him toward the front door. Hess moaned as he hobbled outside and made the four-foot trek across the front stoop to the door of 922B.

"Good man," Jack whispered as he knocked without waiting to be told.

Swapping the Spyderco for his Glock, Jack stayed to the side and made sure Hess was positioned front and center at the peephole when the overhead light came on.

Monaco opened the inner door and said, "Edward?"

"I'm hurt."

"I thought I heard a strange noise." He unlocked the storm door. "What—?"

Jack was on him then, jamming the Glock against his chest to push him back into a front room configured in a mirror image of Hess's. He pulled Hess in behind him.

"What the hell?" Monaco cried.

He wore vertically stripped pajamas and brown leather slippers. Obviously, he hadn't been intending to go out tonight.

"The basement!" Jack said, poking Monaco again. "Let's go!"

"Edward?"

"Do as he says," Hess said.

Then Monaco's gaze dropped to the bloodstain. "You're hurt!"

"H-he stabbed me!"

He looked at Jack. "You—?"

"Yeah, and you're next. Although I may just shoot you since I like him better. Now let's get moving."

Monaco got the message. He led the way to the stairs, flipped on a light, and started down. Jack made Hess follow while he brought up the rear. The three of them wound up in an unfinished basement. Totally unfinished—as in bare cinderblock walls.

He did a quick recon: naked incandescent bulbs among the exposed beams and struts in the ceiling, concrete floor, a line of lally columns supporting a central I-beam. Furnace, hot-water heater, washer and drier, a red tool box along with scattered miscellaneous junk. The only outlier was a long-handled sledge hammer.

When Hess had said *behind a wall*, Jack had expected to pull off wallboard and find the cash stacked between the studs. But this . . .

"I'm not seeing Quinnell's money."

"Finders keepers," Monaco said with a sly grin.

"What's that supposed to mean?"

"If you can find it, you can keep it."

Jack shot the floor by Monaco's slippered feet, spraying him with concrete chips and making him dance a little two-step as it ricocheted away.

"Okay, okay! Jesus!" He pointed to the rear cinderblock wall, next to the water heater. "It's behind there."

"That's an outer wall."

His tone dripped scorn. "No, that's a sealed-off alcove."

"Yeah? Who was the mason?"

"Moi."

Impressive. No clue that it wasn't an outside wall.

"Nice job, Montresor. Might you have sealed up some sherry along with the money?"

A confused look. "What? No, why would—?"

"Never mind." Sheesh. "Kind of convenient you've got a sledge down here to use against the wall."

"That's why it's here . . . in case I had to get at the money fast."

Jack waggled the Glock's barrel between Monaco and the sledge. "Well, then, get to work, Montresor. I haven't got all night."

"It's Monaco, not Montresor. Why are you—?"

"You wouldn't understand. Just get hammering."

Sometimes Jack's brain insisted on reminding him of his three-year stint at Rutgers as an English major.

As Monaco started swinging the sledge at the block, Jack unfolded a beach chair leaning against the wall. He pushed it toward Hess and indicated he should sit. With a puzzled yet grateful look, Hess dropped into the chair.

Not a kindness. His wounded thigh would make it hard for him to get out of that chair, so he was effectively on injured reserve, allowing Jack to concentrate on Hess's more spritely and arrogant partner in crime.

"This isn't fair, you know," Monaco said as he took another swing. The block was crumbling nicely.

"Fair? You mean playing by the rules? Like you?"

"Hess and I deserve this money. It would be locked away in some secret DoD vault if not for us."

Monaco broke through into the space beyond. Demolition would go faster now.

"You mean if not for Quinnell, don't you? He's the guy who sacrificed his humanity and his life for it."

"His life?" Monaco snorted. "He had no life. He was terminally ill in a federal prison. We got him out and cured his cancer."

"Turning him into a wolfman in the process."

"That was the deal, yes. And as a result, he can't spend the money anyway."

Jack shook his head at Monaco's *Cirque du Soleil*-class moral contortions.

The hole was now big enough for a man to poke his head through. Jack wasn't about to take a peek, though—not with Monaco holding a sledgehammer.

"How's the money stored?"

"In a suitcase."

"Half a mill fits in a suitcase?"

"A hard-case carryon."

Was that all it took? Jack had no feel for the bulk of half a million bucks. He'd have thought it would need a full-size at least.

Finally, the hole looked big enough to admit a man.

"Okay. You can stop. Now you switch parts and play Fortunato."

"What's that supposed to mean?"

"You crawl in behind the wall."

Monaco threw down the sledge. "Like hell!"

Was he going to have to come up with more threats?

Jack spoke softly. "My dear Fortunato—"

"Stop calling me that!"

"Let me relate my state of mind. You promised that money to Quinnell's family if he let you experiment on him. He held up his end of the deal, but you didn't honor yours. Now his wife and daughter are about to be kicked out on the street. That pisses me off, Fortunato. Pisses me off like you wouldn't believe."

"But—"

"No-no-no. You listen. Now I tell you how this interlude ends: I walk out with the money. What happens between now and then is up to you. You can crawl in there and shove the suitcase out, or I can shoot off both your kneecaps and get it myself, then push you through and leave you in there. Your choice."

Monaco clenched his teeth, balled his fists, then shook his head and crawled through the dark opening.

Half a minute later, when nothing happened, Jack said, "Well?"

"Come and get it, fuck face!"

Really?

Figuring Monaco was crouching somewhere to the left or right, Jack fired straight into the opening and heard the bullet ricochet around inside. He fired again and heard Monaco cry out in pain.

"I'm hit!"

"Just a ricochet," Jack said. "One won't kill you. But two or three . . . "

He fired again.

"Stop! Stop!"

A black hard-shell suitcase scraped through the opening and fell to the floor. Monaco's foot quickly followed.

Jack gave the shin a hard rap with the Glock's barrel. "Not so fast, Fortunato. Let's see what we've got here." He rolled it over to Hess. "Open it."

Hess laid it on its side, worked the zippers, then flipped it open to reveal rows of banded stacks of 100-dollar bills.

"That'll do."

After Hess had zipped it shut again, Jack lifted it—not heavy at all—and started toward the steps.

"Hey, Fortunato. Can you say 'For the love of God, Montresor'?"

From within the hole. "Are you going to shoot again?"

"I have a thing for high-capacity magazines."

A pause, then a faint, "*For the love of God, Montresor!*" from within.

Jack headed up the steps. "You just made my day."

18

Albert had pretty much given up watching Tonto's phone. It hadn't shown a single goddamn blip this whole trip, and it sure as hell wasn't going to start way out here in Nassau County. The Southern State Parkway had only two plowed lanes, and they must have been done a while ago because the road needed another pass. Needed it bad.

"We're out in Hempstead, for fuck's sake," he said. "How long we gonna keep this up?"

They'd made the circuit of the JFK parking lots–Christ, there were a lot of them–with no hits. Same with their drive through Howard Beach. So, over Albert's protests about how they were wasting their time, Tonto had got on the Belt and then the Southern State to head west into Nowheresville.

Tonto shook his head. "Not much longer. I thought for sure . . . "

"Yeah, well, like I told you before: You thought wrong, Tonto. *Way* wrong."

Tonto said nothing, just kept focused on the road straight ahead.

What did it take to get a rise out of this guy? To get under his red hide? "Tonto" didn't seem to bother him. Rolled right off his back. Albert had asked about his squaw, figuring that'd piss him off. But he didn't even blink. Didn't nothin' bother this bastard?

He'd heard of wooden cigar store Indians—though why an Indian would be selling cigars was beyond him—and Tonto here had about as much expression as you'd expect from one of those.

All of which would make snuffing out Tonto's life so much more fun. He just wished they'd find that fucking Bagaq so he could get down to it. When he—

A red dot appeared top left on the phone screen.

"Hey-hey-hey! We got something!"

Tonto leaned over for a look. "Yep. That's him. Must have finished up whatever business he had out here and now he's on his way back. Good thing we kept going or we'd have missed him."

Was that a dig? Fuck him.

The blip was moving along the left side of the screen.

"He's going the other way! Make a U!"

"Glad to. Where?"

Good question. The median between the eastbound and west-bound lanes was wide and piled high with plowed snow. They'd have to wait until the next exit.

"We're losing him!"

"I'm driving as fast as I can. He may go off the screen, but we'll catch up to him. We've got him now."

Said with all the confidence in the world.

Had to hand it to the fucker, he'd been right, insisting back at the airport that if Jack had gone anywhere, he'd gone east. Somehow, he'd put everything together and made the right prediction. How did someone *do* that?

His father's words came back to him: *You're like me, Ali-boy. You ain't gonna amount to much on your own. You gotta hitch yourself to someone with ideas and earn your keep by helping make them happen.*

That was what his dad had done. Worked as driver and all-pur-pose go-to guy for one of the old-money bankers in the city. Dad always called him "Ali-boy" and said neither of them was good with coming up with an idea, but they was good at making those ideas happen. Give Dad a job and he got it done, no matter what. Same with Albert. He'd hitched himself to Roland Apfel and life had been good.

But that good life would last only as long as the boss lasted.

The blip slipped off the bottom of the screen.

"Shit! He's gone!"

"Not to worry. Here's an exit."

The exit ramp had been plowed sometime earlier but was under a good six inches of snow again—and ran uphill to a stop sign. Instead of slowing to exit, Tonto gunned the Explorer and kept gunning it up the ramp. It swerved left and right and began to lose momentum but they reached the top where he blew through the stop sign to skid into a left turn onto the overpass. They crossed over the parkway and hit the onramp on the far side. Just as much snow there but they made the downhill run no sweat and were back on the Southern State heading west.

"There!" he said. "Now we'll catch him."

Albert clenched his teeth. How could he be so fucking sure?

"We goddamn well better. The boss needs that fucking Bagaq."

"'Needs'?"

Shit. Had to watch his mouth. The boss hadn't wanted anyone to know. But why not? Tonto didn't matter. He wasn't going to last the night anyway. And maybe it would light a fire under his red ass.

"He says it'll cure him."

"Of his cancer? Really?"

"Really."

And then Tonto did the unexpected. He laughed. The fucker *laughed*.

"What's so funny?"

"That's the most ridiculous thing I've ever heard! You believe that?"

"I don't have to believe, Tonto. Ain't a matter of what *I* believe. If the boss believes it, that's good enough for me. I'll go and get him the fucking Bagaq. If it works, it works. If it don't, it don't. Either way, I held up my end."

Tonto gave him a thoughtful look.

"What?"

"I didn't expect that from you, Poncia."

"Expect what? What're you talking about?"

"A work ethic." As Albert tried to decide how he should take that, Tonto added, "Don't worry. It's a compliment, albeit left-handed."

What the fuck?

Albeit? What did that mean? And what made a compliment

left-handed—or right-handed, for that matter? Another thing he hated about this guy. Half the time he didn't know what he was saying. Oh, he heard him good enough, but what did he *mean*?

Christ, he hated Tonto's airs and fancy words. Couldn't wait to stop his rotten little Indian heart.

19

"Burkes here."

"At last! You're a hard man to get hold of."

"Who is this, may I ask?"

"Oh, sorry, I thought they would have told you. This is Doctor Monaco."

"And just who might Doctor Monaco be?"

"You connected my associate and I with a fellow named Jack."

"Oh, aye-aye. I remember now. What happened? Didn't show up?"

"Oh, he showed up, all right. But you neglected to tell us he's completely insane."

"Now why would I say that, pal? His methods might be a wee unorthodox, but he's one of the sanest blokes I know."

"No. Quite the opposite, I assure you. Just moments ago, he threatened our lives and robbed us at gunpoint."

"What's insane about that?"

"He's supposed to be working for us! We paid him half of his outrageous fee in advance!"

"Let me ask you this: Were you straight with him?"

"What do you mean?"

"Y'ken damn well what I mean. Did you tell him the truth or feed him shite?"

"We told him what he needed to know."

"Ah, there you go. Now you've done it."

"Done what?"

"You've pooched the deal."

"I have no idea what you mean."

"If he says he'll do something, that's what he'll do. It's a contract. Unless you play games with him. Then the contract's dead and he plays it any way he sees fit. If you've put him in a black mood and wound up on his shite list, you—"

"'Shite list'? What—?"

"Figure it out. If you're on that list, anything can happen. My best advice, chief, is sit quiet like a bairn with folded hands and wait. You've already wound him up. You don't want to set him off."

"I'm not asking your advice. I want to know if you can recommend anyone we can send after him."

"For what?"

"To get our money back, for one thing."

"I dinnae ken anyone I dislike that much."

<click>

"Hello? Hello?"

20

Lugging the suitcase against the driving snow across the parking lot had been no picnic. The wind had picked up and swept a few spots clear, while piling the drifts higher in others. Typically, none of the clear spots had been along Jack's path.

Cold and panting, he arrived in Quinnell's lair to find him where he'd left him, still cuffed to the pipe. Jack had suffered visions of an empty space, or worse: a free Quinnell lying in wait.

"That took longer than I thought," he said, wheeling the suitcase into the center of the space and tipping it over onto its side. He worked the zippers and flipped it open. "Voila!"

Quinnell gave him a questioning look.

"It's the money they never gave to Jelena."

Quinnell growled and shook the manacle.

"Yeah, I know. They're sonsa bitches. They were afraid to spend it yet, so they bricked it up inside a wall."

Quinnell waved his free paw at the money, then pointed to Jack.

"What am I going to do with it? I'm going to get it to Jelena. Tonight."

Jack couldn't read Quinnell's features all that well, but he was pretty sure he was seeing shock.

"You want to ask me why, right?"

A slow nod.

He didn't want to let Quinnell in on the ultimate reason, so he shared the most obvious.

"Because it belongs to Jelena and Cilla. You earned it for them—paid a hell of a price so that they could have it—and then you all got cheated. I'm gonna fix that."

Quinnell growled and turned away as best he could with his arm chained to a pipe.

"You don't believe me?"

A no-look, dismissive wave of his paw.

"Okay. I can understand that. Can't say as I blame you, either. You've been lied to once, David, so what's gonna stop me from saying I'm gonna deliver it and just stick it in the back of my Jeep instead? But it's already been in the back of my Jeep and I could have left it there and told you Hess and Monaco had already divided it up and spent it."

He was starting to look interested. Just a little. What would turn him around?

An idea struck Jack then. A really stupid idea. But sometimes you had to dare to be stupid.

"All right, I don't see any way you're gonna be convinced unless we deliver the dough together."

The interested look became a dubious look. At least that was how Jack interpreted it.

"We're gonna need conditions, though. Heavy conditions."

The dubious look continued.

"You've been altered. You've got wolf genes running around inside you. But fundamentally you're still a man, still David Quinnell, right?"

A nod.

"Okay, then. This may sound hokey—I know it does to me—but I'm gonna ask David Quinnell for his word as a man that he will not try to harm me if I uncuff him from that pipe. Not only not try to harm me, but he will not try to escape while he's free, and that after we've delivered the money he will come back here with me and allow himself to be cuffed to that pipe again."

The dubious look had morphed to . . . what?... incredulous?

"Yeah, I know what you're thinking—This guy must be crazy,

right? Wouldn't be the first time I've been called that. Won't be the last, I'm sure. But the way I see it, after what you've been through, it won't be enough for you to believe that money's gone to your family. You'll need to *know*. Right?"

A nod.

"Okay. Just so we're both clear on this: I free you up long enough to witness me giving your wife that suitcase, then you're back here and reattached to the pipe. And in between you don't attack me or try to escape. Agreed?"

Quinnell only stared.

"Are we agreed or not?"

Finally, a nod.

Quinnell rose to his feet and stood swaying.

"Still feeling some effects from that dart, huh?"

A shrug. What did that mean? Not much, or just a little?

Quinnell stuck out his free hand or paw or some come combination of the two. It happened to be his right one.

Am I crazy? Jack thought. I gotta be crazy to do this.

This had to be the riskiest gamble he'd ever taken during a fix. He sensed most of Quinnell's humanity still intact under that changed hide. Jack was appealing to that humanity right now. He wanted Quinnell to believe he could trust him, and to solidify that belief he had to see that Jack kept his word and was on his side.

Because nothing good was going to come of this whole situation. Every outcome would end badly for someone. Jack had made it his business to steer things toward the least bad. He wished someone else were available for the job. Even though he'd opted into this position based on a pack of lies, he felt obligated to see it through. Because no one else was going to step up. And deep in his gut he knew no one else *could* step up.

He gripped Quinnell's paw-hand and shook.

Then he stuck the Glock into his waistband.

"I'm going to bring this along. I don't know you well enough to trust you completely. And after all"—Jack pointed to Quinnell's clawed hands—"you're bringing some built-in weaponry."

He fished the cuff keys from his pocket and eased over toward Quinnell. He had a grip on his forearm as he unlocked the cuff from the pipe. He felt the muscles under the overcoat sleeve tense as if readying to strike, then relax. Jack quickly cuffed Quinnell's wrists together in front of him. Would have preferred behind his back but the guy needed his hands to climb those rungs.

"Good man."

Just then the lights dimmed.

"Your batteries appear to be running out," Jack said. "Got spares?"

Quinnell nodded toward the power box. Jack stepped over and found a pile of D batteries.

"Looks like you thought of everything."

He swapped fresh ones for the used and the lights brightened. He moved to the suitcase. As he zipped it up, Jack spied the tranq gun and its darts leaning against the far wall. Take it or not?

Not. If Quinnell became violent, the neuromuscular juice would take too long to slow him down. Jack would need 9mm slugs on his side.

He was counting on it not coming to that.

He grabbed the suitcase handle and said, "All right, my friend, let's go."

21

She stepped into Burbank's lair and found him where she always found him: seated before his microphone.

"Good evening, Burbank."

"Twilight has come, Madame," he said, his voice barely audible. "Night will follow."

"So I've heard. How are you feeling?"

"Perfectly fine, dear."

"Now the truth."

"Failing, I'm afraid. I don't know if I can sit here much longer. I may have to lie down."

"Why don't you?"

"Because I'm not ready yet."

"Are you well enough to do me a favor? I hate to impose but—"

He swiveled in his chair to face her. My, he looked ghastly.

"You cannot possibly 'impose' on me, Madame. My debt to you is far too great to deny you anything. What is this favor?"

"I'm trying to locate someone and all I have is his phone number."

He smiled. "Is that all?"

22

Jelena lowered her toothbrush and listened. She thought she'd heard the front doorbell. She had to be hallucinating. No one could be—

There. She heard it again—definitely the front door. She couldn't imagine who would be at her door at this hour on *any* night, let alone *this* night, in the middle of Snowmageddon.

Her heart picked up tempo as she grabbed the ratty old terry-cloth robe hanging on the back of the bathroom door and pulled it on over her flannel PJs. Nothing good could come from a late-night caller. Someone was either up to no good or bringing bad news.

Tihana? Had she got herself into trouble again?

She turned on the over-door light and peeked through the peep-hole. A guy stood there. He had his parka hood up and not a whole lot of his face visible, but none of what she could see looked familiar. A strange guy on her doorstep at ten-fifteen during a snowstorm. This couldn't be good. No way could this be good.

"Yes?" she said through the door, and hated how her voice wavered.

"This the Quinnell house?" he said, pronouncing it wrong.

Oh, shit. He knew their name.

"Y-yes. Is something wrong?"

"Got a suitcase for ya."

"A *what?*"

"Suitcase. Jet Blue found it in storage at Kennedy."

Jet Blue? This was crazy.

"I don't understand. I haven't been traveling at all."

"Oh, this isn't recent, ma'am. I could tell that from the dust I had to clean off it. This thing's been lost a long time."

Lost luggage?

"And it's got my name on it?"

"Got *David Quinnell* on the tag and this place is listed as the address. He does live here, don't he?"

Never a good idea to let a stranger know there was no man in the house.

"Yes, he does, but he's sleeping."

"That's okay. Hey, I can understand you not wanting to open the door. As long as I know I've got the right place, I'll just leave the suitcase here on your front stoop, okay?"

"Okay."

A wave of relief washed over her. She'd had such a bad feeling about this being a scam of some sort. Not that this was the sort of night for running a con, but still . . .

"Don't leave it too long," he said. "Snow might get inside, or someone might grab it."

"Yes. Sure. Thank you."

She felt bad about not tipping him after coming out on a night like this, but the situation was so bizarre. David was dead and had never mentioned losing a suitcase. He'd been involved in some pretty shady goings on before his arrest, and this might or might not be related. No way to know, so no way was she unlocking her door for a stranger.

She sidled to the front picture window and watched the stranger trudge out to a Jeep idling in the street, climb in, and drive off. She had an impression of someone else inside, watching from the passenger seat.

When he was gone, she pressed the side of her face against the glass and could make out a medium-size hardshell suitcase sitting on her unshoveled front stoop. Okay. It seemed safe to grab it now.

She undid the safety chain, then the deadbolt, then quick like a bunny pushed open the storm door, grabbed the suitcase, and pulled it inside. Not terribly heavy. After relocking everything, she checked out the luggage tag. Sure enough: *David Quinnell* followed by this address.

How strange. How long had this thing been sitting in a warehouse? She was a little afraid to open it. Really, anything could be inside. Maybe things she didn't want to see, didn't want to know about. Though most likely not. Most likely dirty old clothes.

She knelt on the carpet, tipped it onto its side, undid the double zippers . . . then paused.

Why all these nerves? Just do it, Jelena.

Holding a breath, she lifted the upper half and let it fall back.

And stared . . . and stared some more . . . it looked like . . .

Money.

Lots of money. Banded stacks of one-hundred-dollar bills, and each band printed with *$10,000.*

No. No-no-no-no-no. This couldn't be real, had to be a joke, a cruel joke. Counterfeit bills. Had David been into that too? Funny money? Those goddamn bookies took over his whole life.

She fanned through a couple of stacks. All hundreds. And not new bills. These seemed well used and—

Wait. The stacks contained three different types of hundreds— some with a little Benjamin Franklin in a circle, some with a big Franklin in a circle, and some with Franklin and no circle at all. If they were fakes, real funny money, wouldn't they all be the same design?

"Oh, Jesus, Jesus, Jesus!" she whispered. "It's real. It's *real!*"

She stiffened at a noise outside. Had the delivery man returned? She ran to the front window and peered out. The street remained empty—no, a plow was trudging along from her right with a loud, scraping noise. Clearing her street. Not that it mattered. She hadn't any place to go.

Giving in to a spasm of paranoia, she pulled the shades. When she turned and saw the suitcase crammed with money again, she couldn't resist a happy dance—a little one, brief and silent.

Then back to the suitcase where she unzipped the top half. More stacks of hundreds. She wanted to scream.

Hard to believe nobody had looked inside. Obviously, no one had or it never would have reached her.

Her hands shook as she did a quick count. Forty-eight stacks. Just shy of half a million dollars. The amount gave her the shakes. This solved so many of her problems. She could get right with the bank—catch up on the payments and stop the foreclosure. She could quit her job—flip the bird to Mr. Hands and go to school, get that accounting degree, become a CPA . . .

Be somebody. Somebody who could provide for Cilla, get her the help she needed.

With no warning, Jelena began to cry. Huge, wracking sobs. "David . . ."

She didn't believe in Santa Claus, so it had to be David. Somehow, he was behind this. Somehow, he'd reached out from the grave and saved her and Cilla. But how? He'd never mentioned this money while he was alive. Had he thought it lost or stolen? He'd cut himself off from everyone after they locked him up, and now he was gone, so asking him wasn't an option.

It simply didn't make sense. He got into all that trouble because he owed a fortune to the wrong people. If he'd had this money available, he wouldn't have owed . . .

Get a grip, Jelena.

She stifled the sobs. No use in trying to make sense of it. Life had stopped making sense years ago. The money was here, right in front of her. She had to deal with all this cash. She doubted very much it was clean money, but no matter. Right now, it was *her* money—hers and Cilla's—and she was going to make sure it stayed theirs.

Which meant she couldn't put it in a bank. The government would want to know where it came from, and sure as hell the IRS or the FBI or somebody would find a way to take it from her. She couldn't tell anyone about it. Especially not Tihana. She'd get high and blab it to the world.

My little secret. Okay, my big secret.

And the suitcase made the perfect hiding place. Just stick it up in the attic with that old leather bag she never used.

She zipped it up and wheeled it to her bedroom. Then she crept to Cilla's room and knelt beside her bed.

"We're gonna be all right, honey," she whispered as she brushed back her angel daughter's bangs. "You're gonna be all right, I'm gonna be all right, everything's gonna be all right."

23

They were closing in on midnight when a blip appeared at the top of the screen on Tonto's phone.

"Hey, we got him!" Albert shouted. "We got the fucker!"

Tonto glanced over and nodded. "I won't say I told you so. Then again, perhaps I should: I told you so."

Oh, was it going to be fun to off this guy. Good thing he hadn't given him some sort of shit-eating grin or nothin', because Albert was not at all sure he could have held back doing him right here in the car.

Yeah, all right, Tonto *had* said they'd find this Jack guy again, but for the longest time it seemed they wouldn't.

Back when they'd arrived at the end of the Southern State, they'd had a choice of either heading south on the Belt or north on the Cross Island Parkway. Since they'd already done the Belt, they decided— somehow they'd actually *agreed*—to try the Cross Island. When that didn't pan out, they'd headed back to the Belt.

Albert studied the screen. The map on the phone put them in South Jamaica at the moment, and Jack . . .

"He's straight west of us. Looks like he's over by Aqueduct."

Tonto accelerated. "Let's see if we can catch up."

"Damn well better catch up."

The goddamn snow wasn't letting up. They'd been listening to the radio off and on along the way and the weather geeks all had hard-ons over how the storm had gone against all predictions and stalled off the coast where it kept on pounding the area with inch after inch of snow.

The glowing dot of the Jeep crept toward the center of the screen.

"Hey, you know what?" Albert said. "I think he's stopped moving."

"Excellent. Guide us to him."

"You gonna let him see us?"

"He doesn't know what we're driving. Last time he saw us we were in a Lincoln Continental. Remember?"

The way he said *remember* set Albert's teeth on edge. He didn't trust himself to answer so he just started giving directions to the dot. They moved off the beaten path onto an unplowed road. Fresh tracks ahead of them. Jack?

Pretty soon the dot arrived dead center on the screen.

"Voila," Tonto said, pointing straight ahead.

Sure enough, the Jeep sat parked at the end of 96th Place near a train stop.

"The fucking end of nowhere," Albert said.

Tonto took them on a slow pass close by it.

"Looks empty," Albert said.

Tonto nodded. "It does. But where could he go? The nearest house is . . . "

"Yeah." Albert looked around. "Gotta be a hundred yards away."

"Right. But even so, I didn't see any tracks leading from the Jeep."

Albert laughed. "So, where'd he go? Ain't nothin' goin' on at the track, so . . . " They looked at each other. "You don't think . . . ?"

Tonto rounded a curve and pulled over about a hundred feet past the Jeep. He turned out the headlights and said, "Only one way to find out."

"What're you doing?"

"Going to follow his tracks."

"Have fun."

No fucking way was Albert going out in this mess.

"It's better if you stay here in the car anyway. Just in case he returns by a different route."

"What you gonna do if you find him?"

Tonto pulled out his revolver and flicked off the safety. "I'm going to find out where he's hidden the Bagaq."

"And if he ain't talking?"

"I'll bring him back here and we'll combine our persuasive efforts."

Not a great plan, but as long as it didn't involve him slogging through the snow, Albert was cool with it. He didn't care if Tonto found the Bagaq. Didn't matter who found it. All that mattered was who delivered it to the boss. And that would be Albert.

"One other thing," Tonto said. "There's a chance I might need some help once I find him. If I do, I'll call you."

"How you gonna call me if I got your phone?"

"I always have a backup."

With that he jumped out and walked away.

"Enjoy your last night on Earth, jerk," Albert whispered.

He turned up the heater and settled back to wait. Nice and comfy. If only his finger didn't throb like a bitch. Should've brought along some Vikes.

CHRISTMAS EVE

1

Even with his hands cuffed in front of him, Quinnell had seemed to prefer to lope along on all fours as they'd slogged through the snow to the grandstand. Jack had let him go first through the opening to the underground.

So far, so good. No way Quinnell couldn't trust him now, see him as a straight shooter.

"Now we see if I'm a dumb ass or not," Jack said as they reached the lighted area.

Quinnell gave him a look that Jack interpreted as puzzled.

"We see if my faith in you keeping your word was justified."

Another stare, and then Quinnell held out his wrists. Jack nodded and unlocked the left manacle. But when he went to replace it around the pipe, Quinnell snatched it back.

Uh-oh. Don't do this . . .

They stared at each other.

"Really?" Jack said, edging his hand toward the Glock in his belt.

Quinnell shook his head.

"I get it," Jack said. "I wouldn't want to go back to being chained up either. But we have a deal. And we need to talk about a heavy decision you've got to make."

More unreadable staring, then Quinnell extended his left hand toward the pipe. Repressing a sigh of relief, Jack quickly snapped the manacle around it.

For someone only partially human, Quinnell was more of a mensch than too many full-blooded *Homo saps* Jack knew.

Quinnell slumped to a sitting position on the floor. Jack did the same, leaning against the opposite wall.

"Much as I hate to say it—and surely not as much as you hate to hear it—you've got to go back, David."

A violent shake of his head.

"There's no place for you out here in the everyday, workaday world ... except maybe as a circus freak. Hell, they're shutting down the circuses, so even that's not an option. And even if it were, you know the people behind Plum Island will be coming after you. Not just Hess and Monaco, who think you're key to a cure for cancer—"

A growl.

"Yeah, I wouldn't want anything further to do with those two low-life scumbags either, but it's not just them who'll be after you. They've got the Department of Defense and Homeland Security behind them. We're talking major heavy hitters there. So, I don't see any other option. One way or another you're going to wind up back on Plum Island, or wind up dead."

Another growl ... fainter.

"And ... maybe you *do* carry a cancer cure. That'd be one helluva legacy."

Quinnell didn't respond.

Jack waited. He hated the thought of turning him over to Hess and Monaco, but no way could he let him run free. He'd already killed three people. The two kids . . . maybe they'd asked for it by burning him, but hell, they were just kids. The perv, well, okay, he'd been put down to protect Cilla, but no one but Jack knew that. As soon as the city became aware of the deaths and the existence of a creature called H3, he'd be hunted down and killed.

Easy enough for Jack to hit Quinnell with a couple more tranq darts and call the two Plum Island clowns to come and pick him up. But he wanted Quinnell to make the decision himself.

Jack kept waiting for a response, but Quinnell remained quiet and immobile.

"Hello? You still with us?"

Quinnell tapped the side of his head.

"You're thinking about it? Well, I can see that."

He pointed to his mouth and then his stomach. He began to drool. Not a pretty sight.

"Hungry?" Jack realized he was starving—nothing since those Egg McMuffins. "Yeah, I could use some food too."

He wondered if the Stop & Shop was still open. Doubtful. Midnight had just passed.

"Happy Christmas Eve," Jack said.

Quinnell's head snapped up as if that meant something. But the subject was food. When Jack had eaten at the Cross Bay Diner the other day, the signs had said the place was open 24 hours. He doubted the late shift had made it in, but just the same, the middle shift probably couldn't make it home.

"I hope you don't insist on raw meat."

Quinnell shook his head.

"Good. Because I think the diner might be open. I'll grab you a steak."

A vigorous nod.

The Cross Bay Diner was less than a mile away. Jack might grab a couple of burgers for himself. And then once their bellies were full, they'd have to come to a decision.

2

Tier eased the explorer's door closed and stood for a moment, reveling in the solitude. Trapped in that car with someone, anyone, for so damn long, was torture for him. But when that someone was Poncia . . .

Then add to that the stench of ketchup and the whole front of the car littered with empty packets . . .

He shook it off. Time to move.

As he edged along the shoulder toward the Jeep, he stuck close to the line of bushes buffering the chain-link fence, making sure to fill his tracks by shaking the snow off the branches after he passed.

He stopped a half dozen feet from the Jeep and checked it out. Someone had exited on the passenger side as well as the driver side. The two of them met on the passenger side, then slipped through a hole in the fence and took the steps down to the train station.

Stepping into the existing tracks, Tier flashed his light into the Jeep interior. Typical of a rental, it lacked the clutter of a personal car. No sign of a Bagaq-size object.

He followed the tracks through the fence, down the steps, through another fence, and onto a huge, windswept parking lot. He stopped and gave the tracks in the snow a closer look. Something odd about them. He faced away from the grandstand and spread out his coat to either side to hide the quick shot from his flashlight. Which only served to increase the odd factor.

One set was just what he'd expect from the heavy work boots he'd spotted on Jack's feet back at the gas station. But the other . . . worn sneaker soles landed at an odd angle—like the wearer was walking on his toes—and then other marks that looked like . . . hands? But strange hands. Was Jack's companion walking on his hands and feet? Like an ape?

No-no-no. You can't go there.

The snowfall had tapered off to flurries, but that had happened before. It meant either the storm was finally moving off or just another gap between snow bands. The light filtering through the air from the surrounding human hive revealed a vague remnant of disturbed snow stretched across the lot like a fresh scar. The pavement lay bare in some areas but no question where the tracks headed: straight toward the dark, empty grandstand.

Why? Tier wondered.

Nothing going on here. The racetrack equivalent of a ghost town. At least for the time being. Totally deserted.

But maybe that was the attraction.

He needed to learn what had brought Jack here. A hiding place for the Bagaq? Tier had to be honest—Aqueduct Racetrack was the last place he or anyone else would look for an ancient artifact. Which meant he had to check it out. But he needed to take a more circuitous route to the grandstand.

He started walking the periphery, hurrying across the bare spots when they presented themselves, and slogging through the drifts when he had no other choice. He figured if Jack decided to return to his Jeep, he'd follow his old, more direct path: the diagonal across the lot. Tier's tracks would be invisible from out there in the middle. But right now, he was highly visible. He tended to wear dark clothes, all the better to blend into the shadows, but out here, against all this white, he felt totally exposed and obvious. Like a fly on a wedding cake.

When he completed his long way 'round to the looming flank of the grandstand, he saw the other tracks entering its dark underbelly. Stepping cautiously, keeping to a low crouch, he crept into the shadows and stopped, listening as he searched the darkness for signs of life or light. But no flashlight beam pierced the gloom.

The tracks dragged snow onto the dry shielded pavement and trailed away into the black. Tier made sure the snow he tracked in landed with the rest as he followed to ... where?

He couldn't see, and he feared to risk his flash. So, he started feeling along the wall. Had to be a door here somewhere. Jack couldn't simply vanish into thin air. He—

Tier froze at a sound to his left. It seemed to be coming from ... the ground? Some sort of tunnel or drainage pipe below. Of course—the only explanation for how Jack had seemingly disappeared.

It sounded like someone approaching from below. Here was where Tier's dark clothing would serve him well. He was skilled at blending into the background, and here he'd blend with the shadows. He took a deep breath and held it as someone come out of an opening in the floor and took off across the parking lot without a look back.

Jack. Tier recognized his parka.

He waited until he was well on his way before releasing his breath and moving to the opening. Jack had not arrived alone, yet he'd been the only one to leave. That meant ...

He aimed his flashlight into the opening and flicked it on and off. Rungs in the wall. Much as he hated the idea, he had to go down. If Jack had hidden the Bagaq down there ...

He checked Jack's whereabouts again: Three-quarters across the lot. He pulled out his backup phone and called Poncia.

"Jack's on his way. If you've got the engine running, turn it off and hunker down so he won't see you. If the Bagaq is here, we're done with him. If it's not, we go after him."

He killed the call before Poncia could respond. The less he heard from that man, the better.

Tier pulled his .38, slipped through the opening, and clambered into the down-below. As his feet hit bottom, he spied dim light off to his right. Revolver out ahead of him, treading as softly as he was able, he headed for it. He heard a growl as he rounded a corner and—

"Holy—!"

Something not human but wearing an overcoat thrashed by the wall but didn't charge him. And then he saw the handcuffs and knew why.

"What the fuck are you?" he said in a low voice.

The creature rattled the cuff against the pipe and swiped at him with its free hand. Tier had never seen anything like it. All his primal instincts screamed that this was *wrong-wrong-wrong* and pushed him to get the hell out. But he had to make a search.

But first he took a closer look at it. Was it a dog-faced man, or a man-faced dog? Its body had human proportions but its teeth were all wrong and its fingers were stubby and ended in claws.

What corner of hell had spawned this thing?

An even bigger question: What was Jack doing with it? The toys, the lights, the mini-Christmas tree . . . totally surreal and unsettling.

Okay, okay . . . eye on the prize. The thing, no matter what it was, couldn't get to him. So . . . focus. Did any of this have anything to do with the Bagaq? That was what mattered—all that mattered right now.

Keeping his distance from the creature, he made a quick search of the space. Very quick. The angled concrete walls and ceiling provided zero hiding places. He did find a strange little air gun with syringe darts. He'd never seen a tranquilizer gun, but what else could this be?

Had Jack used it on the dog man? Most likely.

Tier pocketed the pistol and the darts. Might come in handy to use on Jack. Or maybe even mad-dog Poncia, for that matter.

He took a last look at the creature and noticed it digging one of its claws into the keyhole of the handcuffs. Trying to pick the lock?

How much intelligence? he wondered

It hadn't made a single sound that remotely resembled speech, but its eyes . . . the eyes had a knowing look.

Jack's problem, he thought as he headed back to the exit. Not mine.

As soon as he'd climbed topside, he called Poncia again.

"What's the story?"

"He showed up and took off."

"I'm on my way."

He ran back in Jack's tracks and found the Explorer sitting and idling. He slipped in behind the wheel.

"Is he still on the map?"

"Yeah. Headed across the Belt."

Tier put the car in gear and started rolling. "Not onto the Belt but across it?"

"Ain't that what I said?"

If he didn't need him to monitor the tracker, Tier would be delighted to pop Poncia with one of the tranquilizer darts right now.

"Looks like he's taking Cross Bay into Howard Beach."

Tier banged on the steering wheel. "Excellent!"

"Why's that excellent?"

"Because there's water on three sides. Unless he's headed across Jamaica Bay, we've got him cornered."

3

Well, no surprise, the Stop & Shop was closed.

Jack noticed a landscaper's pickup plowing the parking lot, so he made a sharp right and pulled in. After a quick, tight U-turn he stopped and faced the street, waiting to see who would pass.

Cross Bay Boulevard remained empty. Pretty much what he'd expected at one A.M. on Christmas Eve at the tail end of a major blizzard.

But dammit, he couldn't shake the feeling of being followed. Obviously, he was wrong, but the feeling persisted.

Shrugging it off, he pulled back onto the street and continued south to the Cross Bay Diner's lot. The sign was lit up, including the boxed OPEN 24 HRS—*WE DELIVER.*

Yeah, you say you deliver, but will you deliver to the tunnel under the Aqueduct grandstand?

He wouldn't bet on it.

The lights were on inside but all the cars parked in the lot were under mounds of snow. The front steps, however, had been shoveled. A good sign.

He parked and trotted up to the front door. As soon as he stepped inside, he was greeted by cheers from the five workers, three men and two women, seated at the counter.

"What's up?" he said.

"A customer!" someone cried. "Been hours since we seen one."

"I need a steak and burgers to go. Can you handle that?"

More cheers.

"How do you want that steak?" said a woman on the end.

"I'm thinking rare. Very rare."

4

"He's going to a fucking diner?" Poncia said.

They'd been hanging back, way back. Good thing too. Jack had pulled into the parking lot of a closed grocery store for no good reason Tier could see other than to scope out whether he was being followed. Did he suspect? No way could he have seen them.

"Maybe he's hungry," Tier said.

Maybe he was going to bring back food to feed that thing he had chained in the underground.

Tier hadn't mentioned the creature to Poncia. Not worth the effort to explain. Hell, he couldn't explain it to himself. How was he going to make a cretin like Poncia understand?

He killed the headlights and turned into the diner's north lot where he pulled up close to the side of the building. Jack had parked in the south lot.

Off to the left, behind the diner, sat the boat basin. It ran most of the length of Howard Beach and was crammed with boats all summer. Empty now. Had a funny name that eluded him at the moment. Shellbank . . . that was it: the Shellbank Basin.

Tier watched the big diner windows. They'd been painted with seasonal images like giant green holly leaves with red berries. He didn't see any sign of customers inside. Jack was either eating or picking up food to go. Best case scenario: He'd head back to Aqueduct and they could grab him on that isolated street where he'd parked before. Worst case: He'd drive back to Manhattan where he'd turn in the Jeep and disappear.

"We've got to take him here," Tier said.

"You mean go inside and drag him out?"

What an idiot.

"Too many witnesses."

"So? That's why they invented guns. Corpses tell no tales. Can't have much of a crew working the graveyard shift on a night like this, so we're talking, what?—three losers at the most." He grinned and made a soft *heh-heh* sound. "Graveyard shift. We can make it a real graveyard shift."

Tier looked at him. What was it with this guy?

"They're innocent working people, with families. And it's Christmas Eve."

"So, you'd rather leave them to get together with an Etch-A-Sketch cop and have our faces all over the place in a couple hours?"

"Don't you have any sort of code?"

"What're you talking about? You mean like Morse code?"

Talking to this guy was like… like… like talking to a houseplant.

"I mean a code of behavior. You know, like I'll do this, this, and this, but I won't do that."

Poncia made a face. "You mean like that Meat Loaf song? Are you talking about a fucking Meat Loaf song?"

"Forget it."

Hopeless!

"No, let's not forget it. We're getting philosophical here and that's good. I like that, 'cause I'm a philosophical kinda guy. I just need a better clue as to what you're talking about."

… *a philosophical kinda guy* … was he serious?

Okay. One more try.

"I'm talking about self-imposed obligations to behave in a certain way. Like in my Army unit, we had a rule—part of our code—that we never left anyone behind. If someone got hurt or even killed, we'd do everything in our power to bring them back with us."

"Oh, I getcha. Yeah, for me, it's do whatever Mister Apfel tells me.

He wants something done and I do everything in my power to get it done."

"No matter what he tells you to do?"

"Yeah. That's my job. He pays the bills and I do what he wants done."

"What if he told you to kill a mother and child?"

He shrugged. "Well, yeah, sure."

"Seriously?"

"Well, I assume he's got a good reason and they probably deserve it. So y'see? I do have a code."

More like an obedient dog. No, wait. Even dogs had a better set of ethics than this . . . this fucking automaton.

Tier pulled out the dart pistol and inspected it.

"The fuck's that?"

"Shoots tranquilizer darts."

Poncia pulled out a semiautomatic. "This shoots bullets—nines."

"This doesn't kill. We—"

"Is that it? You're afraid of killing someone? How can an ex-army guy be afraid of killing?"

Tier did a slow count to three as he thought about the crowd of Taliban up there with Allah who were wishing he'd been afraid to kill.

"If you'd let me finish: We want information from him, remember?"

"I can shoot him in the legs."

"And make one hell of a racket in the process."

"I got a silencer."

He switched the pistol to his splinted left hand and dug out a four-inch cylinder from a pocket with his right. He began screwing it onto the end of the barrel.

"It's called a 'suppressor,'" Tier said.

"I call it a 'silencer.'"

"Ever done any shooting with it?"

"Yeah. Course."

"Was it silent—that is, made *no* sound?"

"Course not."

"I rest my case. Plus, suppressor or no, if you hit the wrong part of a leg, he can bleed out in less than a minute." He held up the dart gun. "This is quiet and leaves him alive."

Poncia grumbled as he shoved his pistol back into his shoulder holster.

"Okay," Tier said. He'd have much preferred leaving Poncia in the car but knew he'd need a second pair of hands to move Jack once he was down. "Here's the plan: We sneak around back and wait for him to come out. We shoot him up with a dart, then carry him back here."

"Then what?"

"Then we take him somewhere private and search him for that safety deposit key. If it's not on him, we wait till he wakes up and then persuade him to tell us where we can find it. I'll leave the persuading to you."

He hoped very much it wouldn't come to that, but he was throwing Poncia a bone, giving him something to look forward to.

"What's the matter, Tonto? No stomach for it? I thought you Injuns got off tying white folks to ant hills."

And that was number . . . what? He'd lost count. Not that it mattered. As soon as they secured the Bagaq, ridding the world of Albert Poncia would become a priority . . . an *exigent* priority.

Yes!

Poncia would never make it back to Roland's house. Tier would leave his body in a roadside snow drift. Might be a week before he was discovered. If then.

"Let's go."

They jumped out and hurried around the rear. Lights across the basin shimmered off its mostly frozen surface. A few spots here and there remained liquid. Salt water was stubborn that way. A bare bulb in a metal cage glowed over the diner's back door. Snow had drifted against the rear wall, covering the big steel garbage bin, forcing them to walk close to the bulkhead.

When they rounded the corner into the south lot, Tier wanted to cheer. He'd been worried about not finding any cover to take his shot, but a handicapped ramp running up to a side door made a perfect blind. Even better, Jack had backed in to park, putting the driver door less than a dozen feet away.

The downside was they had no view of the front door, so they'd have no warning he was coming until he rounded the corner.

The minutes dragged. Five . . . ten . . . fifteen . . .

"I'm freezing my nuts off." Poncia said, rubbing his hands together. "What the fuck's he doing in there?"

Tier had been wondering about that himself, but dared not take a peek.

"Zip it," he whispered. "He could hear you."

Poncia glared at him but said nothing more.

What *was* he doing in there? Waiting for takeout, or chowing down on a three-course meal?

5

Jack sat with his back to the counter and sipped coffee as he watched the deserted Cross Bay Boulevard through the painted front windows. He felt marginally refreshed after washing up as best he could in the men's room, and the caffeine was perking him up a bit, but overall, this fix was weighing on him like few others.

Where was the solution for David Quinnell? Jack couldn't blame him for not wanting to return to Plum Island, but he had no place else in the world. He'd made a lot of bad decisions in his life and the system had made him pay for them. He'd made one good decision for his family, and was paying for that as well—a hellish price. Like that old Albert King song: If not for bad luck, he'd have no luck at all.

What would I do if I were Quinnell?

The guy's situation might be reason enough to choose the final exit. But could Quinnell make that decision? Did his part-wolf brain have the capacity for that?

"Here y'go," said a voice behind him. The waitress was pushing two paper bags across the counter. "T-bone steak rare and two cheeseburgers."

Jack checked inside. Foil-wrapped burgers in one, a cardboard like clamshell box in the other.

"The steak?" he said, indicating the box. "No Styrofoam? It's gonna get cold."

She shook her head. "Styrofoam's banned. That's called bagasse. Made from sugarcane leftovers or something like that. I wrapped the steak in foil inside it."

The bill came to forty bucks. He left her sixty, figuring she wasn't going to see many tips tonight.

"Enjoy," she said as he headed for the door. "Stay warm."

"I'll do my best."

He hurried down the front steps. The snow was definitely tapering off but the wind blew as cold and stiff as ever. As he opened the Jeep's rear door to place the bag on the floor, he felt a sharp sting in the back of his right thigh, followed by a burning sensation. He twisted to look and—

A dart? That looked like one of his. How the—?

He yanked it out and looked around. Two men emerged from behind the handicapped ramp, moving his way. Fast. He recognized one of them as the stubby, inept bird-dogger. The other was a stranger, taller with ruddy skin and strong, sharp features.

Jack slammed the rear door and reached for the driver door handle but his right leg gave out. Balancing on his left, he pulled the door open and tried to climb in but now his left leg wouldn't move, and then it wouldn't hold him, and then he was down in the snow.

As the men grabbed his arms from behind, he tried to fight them, but with the whole lower half of his body dead, with all his major muscles next to useless, he had no leverage. And soon his arms were gone too. He couldn't use them worth a damn, could barely *feel* them.

And now they were dragging him through the snow, around to the backside of the diner. Jack tried to call out for help but all he could manage were faint croaks.

"I'm gonna have to borrow your dart gun sometime, Tonto," one said. "That shit works fast."

Tonto? That meant the tall one was a Native American?

"Drop him here," he said. "I want to check his pockets before we get him to the car."

Jack couldn't resist him. He ground his teeth in frustration. At least he could still do that.

6

"Well, you've led us on a merry chase, haven't you," Tier said as he inverted the parka's pockets.

He was guessing that dart hadn't contained a tranquilizer, because Jack's eyes were open and alert but his limbs were like overcooked linguine. Had to be some sort of paralyzer or super muscle relaxer. The guy was totally helpless.

A key ring tumbled out a pocket. He held it up for Poncia to see.

"House keys . . . they'll get us into his building quick and quiet."

Unlikely that the safety deposit box key was among them. If Jack didn't have it on him they could find it in his apartment. But the keys wouldn't get them past his apartment door. They'd need the combination to that lock.

Tier rolled him onto his belly and came upon a nice Spyderco folder. He dropped that on the ground. And then a compact Glock. Sweet. That went on the ground too. Pulled the wallet from a rear pocket and went through it. He found a folded piece of paper jammed in with the bills, and within that . . .

"Here's the safety box key—with the receipt and everything."

"So . . . we got everything we came for?"

"Well, we still don't have the Bagaq."

"But if it ain't in the bank box, it's in his apartment, right?"

"I think that's a safe assumption."

Tier had a feeling where this was going.

Poncia said, "Then what do we need him for?"

"Insurance. It being Christmas Eve, the bank will have limited hours. I'll be there when it opens in a couple of hours. I have his wallet and all his ID, I have the key and the receipt for the box. With all that I'm ninety percent sure I'll be able to bluff my way in. But if the Bagaq isn't in the box, we'll need him to get into his apartment."

"We got his keys."

"He's got a combo lock on the door. We'll need to get the combination out of him."

"Yeah? And where do we stash him while all this is going down?"

"We'll find a place. Help me lift him."

They each grabbed him under an arm and hoisted him off the ground. His feet dragged like a marionette's with its strings cut. Suddenly Poncia cried out in pain and dropped Jack's arm as he staggered around, clutching his thigh.

"What's—?" Tier began, then saw the knife sticking out of his thigh. The Spyderco . . . How—?

"Fucker cut me!"

Somehow Jack had grabbed the Spyderco, thumbed it open, and stabbed Poncia. More a supreme act of will than anything else. Jesus, if the guy could do that in a paralyzed state, what was he like at one hundred percent?

With another hoarse cry of pain, Poncia yanked out the blade, then hurled it out over the basin.

"Fuck this!" he said.

Without warning he grabbed Jack's arm. The move caught Tier by surprise. In one violent move he wrenched Jack free from his grasp and shoved him over the edge of the bulkhead. But instead of a splash, they heard nothing.

"You gotta be kiddin' me!" Poncia shouted, standing on the bulkhead. "You gotta be fuckin' kiddin' me!"

Tier joined him at the edge. Just a few feet below them, Jack lay face down in a snowbank on the frozen basin. As usual, Poncia hadn't been paying attention.

Tier had to laugh. "Can't you get anything right?"

"Yeah?" He pulled out his pistol. "Let's see how right this is."

"Hey, wait—"

But before Tier could stop him, Poncia fired. The suppressor kept the noise down as Jack's body bucked with the impact of the bullet in his upper back. Then Poncia turned and aimed the pistol at Tier.

"Hey, what?"

He smiled. "Remember when I asked you what we needed Jack for? Same goes for you. We got the safe deposit box key ... so whatta we need you for?"

"Whoa! Whoa! Your boss told you to—"

"To what? Take orders from you?" He barked a laugh. "That was just for show, dumbass! In private he told me to let you find what he needed, then take you and Jack outa the picture. He doesn't want any loose ends. And you, Tonto, are a very loose end. So, this is from Mister Apfel. But even if he hadn't said a word, I'd be doing this on my—"

Before Poncia could fire, something leaped through the air with a deep growl and buried its fangs in his neck.

With a shocked cry, Tier fell back as the thing shook its head and came away with a piece of Poncia's throat in its mouth. It promptly spat out the chunk as Poncia dropped the pistol and crumpled, clutching at the pumping ruin of his throat.

Tier recognized it then—the thing from underground. Somehow it had got free of the cuff. He reached for his revolver as the thing came for him but it was too fast. He managed to turn and partially deflect the charge so that its jaws closed on the side of his neck instead of square on his throat, but he couldn't help crying out at as the teeth pieced and tore.

"Forget him!" said a woman's voice. "Get Jack."

The creature left him and leaped off the bulkhead. Tier dropped to his knees and pressed a hand against his bleeding neck. No pumper there, but a lot of blood.

Poncia lay on his back, his hands on his throat, but they'd gone limp. He might have had some life left in him, but what little remained was making a speedy exit.

Nearby stood a dark-haired woman. It took Tier a moment to recognize Madame de Medici. Gone were her Cossack hat and fur coat. Instead she stood bareheaded on the bulkhead wearing a snug leather jacket, jodhpurs, and leather boots. Her gaze was fixed on the basin.

Suddenly Jack appeared, limp as a rag doll, being pushed up from below by the creature.

"This wasn't supposed to happen!" she said, turning to Tier, her amber eyes flashing with anger. "Mister Hill! You poisoned him and then you shot him?"

Tier struggled to speak. "Not poison . . . and I didn't . . . "

"This never should have happened. My fault. I am too reckless in my old age. If I'd known it would turn out like this I never . . . ." She seemed to be talking to herself, then she refocused on Tier. "Do you know how important he is? He is the Heir. The *Heir!* And look what you've done! Look what *I've* done!"

Tier had no idea what she was talking about. She'd been so calm and rational in her apartment. Now she'd obviously gone crazy.

"Please," he rasped. "Call 9-1-1."

"I'll deal with you in a minute," she snapped. "He comes first. Open his shirt," she told the creature.

Oddly enough, the creature obeyed her. Tier had opened Jack's parka before, so now the creature ripped open his bloody flannel shirt amid a spray of buttons. A gaping exit wound oozed below his right clavicle. Poncia's bullet must have passed straight through, puncturing the lung. Was he conscious? Was he even alive? Hard to tell. Whatever had been in that dart had rendered him as limp as a fresh corpse.

Madame reached into her bag and produced a dull bronze-colored lump of metal.

The Bagaq? How . . . ?

She pressed it against Jack's bloody chest. As Tier watched, it seemed to melt, its metal turning liquid and spreading out over an area the size of a serving platter.

What the—?

As she rose and began to pace, Tier searched for his phone with his free hand. Had to get help.

She deftly kicked it out of his hand. "Do not call anyone. Your turn will come."

My turn? My turn at what? Dying?

He glanced over the edge of the bulkhead. A red splotch marred the drift where Jack had fallen.

Jack coughed up a spray of bright red blood. Oh, hell. That

couldn't be good. A second cough, dry this time. At least he was still alive. But for how long? That chest wound was—

Wait. Where'd it go? He'd had an oozing hole in his upper chest a moment ago. Now ... where was it?

The bronze sheet of the Bagaq began to contract then, scrunching back into that same rough ovoid shape as before. Jack groaned as Madame plucked it from his chest. Briefly he lifted a forearm and let it fall back.

Madame turned the Bagaq this way and that in her hands, examining it.

"It's not full yet," she muttered, then turned to Tier. "You ... if you had no destiny I'd let you fend for yourself, but it's not full yet and I need your wounds."

She was making absolutely no sense.

"Lie back and bare your chest."

"What? No."

"Do you want to keep bleeding? This will stop it."

How? By healing the wound as it had Jack's? Well, why not? What did he have to lose?

"Why ... why help me?"

"Because I despise conflict. I wish to live in peace, so I resolve all conflicts. I need you to resolve this one."

He lay back, unzipped his coat, and pulled up his sweatshirt. The wind chilled his skin. Inanely he found himself fixating on her jodhpurs ... who wore jodhpurs unless they were going horse riding? And what idiot would be riding a horse in this weather? Madame de Medici, that's who. Had to admit, though, she looked pretty hot in them.

What was he thinking? Had to be the blood loss affecting his brain.

But then she placed the Bagaq on his sternum. As soon as it touched him it grew hot. He watched it melt and form a metallic layer on his chest, like frosting on a cupcake. Then hotter. *Too* hot.

He tried to lift his hands to peel it off but his arms wouldn't move. Same for his legs. And then light filled his vision as men and women, all bare chested, all with wounds or sores or growths, floated past. He wanted to scream with the pain but then the heat vanished like flipping a switch.

He looked down and saw the Bagaq contracting and bunching up as it had on Jack. When it had resumed its former shape, Madame plucked it from his chest and again turned it over and over in her hands. Its color seemed to have darkened.

He checked his neck. The bleeding had stopped and the torn area was now closed over. It didn't feel like normal skin, but the opening had been sealed. He sat up, still probing his neck. Things like this didn't happen—couldn't happen—and yet the wound was gone . . . healed.

Madame was muttering again. "It's full. At last it's full. But at such a price." She turned to Tier. "Why did you hurt him?"

"I didn't. I had no intention—but wait-wait-wait! What just happened?"

"How can you ask that? You just experienced it firsthand. Your wound was healed."

"No, okay, I realize that, but I mean *how* did it happen?"

"The Bagaq, of course. The word means 'sponge.' It absorbs diseases and injuries."

"Nothing can do that."

She looked at him with a bemused expression. "And the signals cannot exist, and no one should be able to hear them, right? Listen to yourself! Can you really be saying that?"

"I guess I shouldn't be. It cures. That's why Roland sent me for it."

"Obviously."

"He's sick."

"I know. And you were tasked with finding this for Roland, yes?"

"I was."

She held out the Bagaq, now a gleaming black. "Then give it to him."

Tier couldn't believe what he was hearing. "After all you've put us through? We've got a dead man there." He pointed to Poncia—no loss to humanity in his case—then to Jack. "And another over there who would have been dead if you and that . . . wolf thing hadn't intervened."

"He's not a *thing*. He was once like you. But I am tired of this. As I told you, I despise conflict. I do not wish to be looking over my shoulder. I cannot live life like that. So here . . . take it."

Tier grabbed it from her outstretched hand but felt no sense of victory. "If only you had done this last Friday . . . "

"Why should I give up what is mine? Thieves stole it from me, and I was angry. I'm still angry, but tell Roland to use it with my blessing and not come looking for me. Tell him he may keep it as long as he lives. But I want it back. When he is on his deathbed, I will show up to reclaim it. Be sure to tell him that."

Tier struggled to his feet and staggered a few steps to the side. Dizzy. Blood loss?

"You will tell him?" she said, her tone insistent.

"I will."

He hefted the Bagaq. This was the thing Roland had been so hell bent on finding, the thing he thought would cure his ills. It looked like a worthless hunk of lava now. What was that Sam Spade line? The stuff dreams are made of . . .

"Now get moving and do your duty," Madame de Medici told him.

"Gladly. But . . . " He nodded toward Poncia. "What about him?"

She turned to the creature. "Young man, please dispose of that trash."

Young man, is it? And here I thought tonight couldn't get any more weird. Stupid me.

The creature rolled Poncia's corpse over the edge where it landed with a thud on the ice. As good a place as any for him.

Tier zipped up his coat and staggered toward the parking lot. When he rounded the corner, he saw a Hummer idling a couple dozen feet from his Explorer. A tall turbaned man in a long overcoat stood by the rear passenger door. He nodded to Tier as if to say, *You may proceed.*

Oh, I'll proceed, all right. I'll proceed right the hell out of here.

This job could not be over soon enough.

7

Jack realized with a start that he was back in Quinnell's lair.

He remembered the terrible impact of the bullet hitting him in the back, of finding it increasingly hard to draw a breath, then being pulled—or pushed, rather—from the frozen basin onto the bulkhead. Madame de Medici pressing the Bagaq against his chest, then warmth and comfort. He remembered some—but not all—strength returning to his muscles but coordination eluding them, half-walking, half carried to a Hummer, driven through the snow by a silent Sikh, ending up somewhere else . . .

He sprawled against a familiar concrete wall, saw familiar blinking lights, a little Christmas tree . . . Quinnell sitting across from him, and next to Quinnell . . .

"Madame de . . . ?"

"Hush. You're still feeling the effects of the poison."

"Neuromushclar agent." Jeez, he sounded drunk.

"Whatever it was, the Bagaq could not reverse all its effects. How do you feel?"

"Ever drink a quart of tequila and follow it with IV fentanyl with a Shoma chaser?"

She deadpanned: "Every night before dinner."

His laugh muscles didn't seem to be working so he said, "A

shenshe of humor too."

"You will be helpless for a while yet."

"No . . . I'm fine."

He tried to stand but his legs wanted no part of it. He managed to raise his butt a few inches before dropping back to the floor.

"Give it time," she said.

Questions surfaced in the muck of his brain. "How . . . how did you find me?"

"Your phone. I had its number on mine from when you returned my call the other night. A friend helped me track it." She pointed at Quinnell. "But your friend here . . . he arrived and dashed ahead of us as we pulled into the diner lot. I followed him around to the back."

Quinnell?

He noticed the empty cuffs handing from the pipe. Oh, right. Jack had mentioned going to the diner. But what about . . . ?

"The Bagaq . . . I heard you . . . you gave it t'your enemy?"

"I despise conflict. I—"

"I know. I heard you talkin' a the tall guy."

"That would be Mister Hill. Yes, Roland and I have a conflict. I decided to resolve it. It's as simple as that."

"But—"

"You have more questions, I know, but I have an errand I must run. Fear not, I shall return, and I will explain all when I do."

She hurried down the tunnel, leaving Jack and Quinnell staring at each other. Quinnell looked spent.

"Y'okay?"

A nod.

"You don' look sho hot. Not that I've met lotta guysh in your condition, but you looked a li'l more with it before."

A shrug and then a waggling point at Jack.

"Oh, wha'? You think *I* don' look sho hot. I know that. Bud I know zactly why: I got hit with a doshe of that neuro shtuff myself. Only half a wha you got an' I'm shtill wiped out. Don' know how you came outa it sho fasht."

Another shrug.

Jack half-raised a leaden arm to point at the empty cuffs hanging on the pipe.

"How . . . ?"

Quinnell held up a taloned finger.

"Picked it? More power to you, buddy."

New questions kept popping up. Chief among them was how Madame had got hold of the Bagaq. Had she persuaded Abe to give it to her? Or had she sent some of her people to take it by force? He remembered a turbaned guy driving her car . . . if she'd hurt Abe . . .

Had to call him.

It took massive effort to slip his hands into his pockets only to find them empty. Then he noticed the pile of paraphernalia on the floor beside him: his wallet, Glock, keys, and yes, his phone. He spider-walked his hand over to it, thumbed it on and . . . *No Service.*

Shit-shit-shit.

He'd have to wait till Madame de Medici got back from wherever she'd gone.

8

Tier was feeling a little stronger by the time he reached the city. He'd found an open 7-Eleven along the way where he'd picked up coffee and a couple of glazed donuts. The coffee wasn't fresh and the donuts were a day old, but not stale yet. The carbs and caffeine gave him a much-needed boost.

Alone in the car . . . he embraced the solitude.

But still he'd driven in a daze of sorts. Reality had taken a left turn through a back alley into a neighborhood he hadn't known existed. In his workaday world, ugly lumps of metal didn't melt onto skin and suck up diseases and heal wounds. That was the stuff of Harry Potter stories or *Lord of the Rings* or whatever, not the world where he was born and raised. Oh, sure, the old men and women of the tribe had told their share of fantastic tales, but he'd never believed them. In fact, he'd always doubted that even *they* believed them.

Less than two hours ago he'd been wounded, and bleeding badly. But now the wound was gone. He'd been healed. By Magic.

The wonder of it enveloped him all the way into Manhattan where he found the streets pretty well plowed. He hadn't a prayer of finding a legal parking space so he double-parked outside Apfel's house. At this hour, he doubted anyone would complain. Besides, he didn't intend to spend much time here.

The cars along the curb had been completely plowed under. No way to pass between them so he resorted to climbing onto a hood and jumping into the knee-high snow of the untouched sidewalk on the far side.

He slogged up the front steps and rang the bell again and again. Apfel had round-the-clock help so Tier knew someone eventually would answer.

A sleepy-looking man in his thirties, clad in green scrubs with *A. Lindo, LPN* on his name tag, opened the door. Tier didn't give him time to speak.

"Hill here to see Mister Apfel on urgent business."

"But—"

He pushed his way in. "Tell him I have what he's been looking for. I'll wait here." When Lindo hesitated, Tier shouted, "*Go!*"

"Is that Poncia?" came a faint voice from upstairs.

"No, it's me. Hill."

"Bring him up, Tony."

The nurse motioned Tier to follow him up the wide staircase. For no particular reason, Tier dragged a dozen feet behind Tony. His earlier energy boost was wearing off.

He found Apfel in the master bedroom, hooked up to one of his tubes. The only light in the room was a gooseneck reading lamp attached to the headboard. The dramatic lighting made the bed look like it was floating on an inky pond.

"Where's Albert?"

"He didn't make it."

Apfel frowned. "As in, he is merely indisposed, or gone for good?"

"The latter."

Tier didn't want to get into the depredations of the wolf thing— the "Young Man," as Madame de Medici had called it.

"That's too bad."

"I'll have to disagree with you on that. He was a psycho."

A thin smile. "Psychos have their uses. But to the reason for your visit: You have it?"

"I do."

His expression turned avid. "Well, where is it?"

Tier pulled the Bagaq from a pocket and held it up. He watched

Apfel's eyes light. Yeah, the stuff dreams are made of, all right. Then the eyes narrowed.

"The color has changed."

"So it has. It darkened right after it healed two people."

Apfel straightened off the pillow. "It what? When?"

"Less than two hours ago."

"What happened?"

"It made a bullet wound go away. Saw it with my own eyes."

For some reason he held back on his own healing bout with the Bagaq. A part of him wanted to keep that to himself. Nobody else's business, really. And of course, then he'd have to get into the wolf thing too.

Still the suspicious look. "How do I know you're telling the truth? You could be lying and that could be a fake. And do you really expect me to believe you know how to use the Bagaq?"

"I don't. Or at least I didn't. Madame de Medici—"

He slammed the mattress with his right hand. "*She* was there?"

Tier nodded. "She brought the Bagaq to the party. Showed up out of the blue after Poncia shot a paralyzed guy—"

"Paralyzed?" Apfel *tsk*ed. "That sounds like Poncia."

"—in the back."

"Of course."

"Well, the de Medici gal took this and placed it on the guy's bare chest. A minute later the entry and exit wounds had closed."

In truth, he hadn't seen the post-Bagaq entry wound, but felt he'd made a safe assumption.

"But how did you take it from her? Does she share Poncia's unfortunate condition?"

The gleam in his eyes said he wouldn't find that the least bit unfortunate.

"No. Here's where it gets really strange: She gave it to me."

"Do you really expect me to believe that?"

"I don't give a damn what you believe, Mister Apfel. But she wanted me to tell you a few things."

"Conditions?"

"Depends on how you look at it. She said for you to use it with her blessing, but don't come looking for her. You can keep it as long as you live, but eventually she wants it back."

"Hell will freeze over first!"

"She wanted me to tell you that when you're on your deathbed she'll show up to reclaim it."

He grinned. "With the Bagaq at my disposal, I plan to live a very long time." He stretched both arms toward Tier. His grasping fingers made his hands look like a pair of spiders doing the backstroke. "Now give—give it here!"

"Not so fast."

His expression hardened. "I was afraid of this."

"Of what?"

"Blackmail, of course. Well, how much do you want?"

Tier shook his head, sick of this man. "I don't do blackmail. But once this gives you back your health, you may decide to welch on the deal."

"You insult me!"

"Just pay me the rest of my per diem and the finder's bonus, and we're done."

"That's all?"

"No more, no less."

Apfel gave him a long stare, then said, "Tony, get my checkbook."

Tier said, "A checkbook? No Paypal or Venmo?"

"I'm old school. But let me ask you, Hill: How would you like to work for me?"

"Take Poncia's place? Not interested."

"I could put you on a generous retainer."

How did he tell this man that he'd rather have cancer than work for him?

"I prefer to spread my work around."

Tony returned with a checkbook. Apfel did some scribbling, then tore off a check. As Tier stepped forward to take it, Apfel held it back.

"Now it's my turn to say 'not so fast.' How do I know that's the real Bagaq?"

"I just told you—"

"An interesting story, but the color is way off, so how do I know it's true?"

Bastard.

"Fine." He dropped it on the bed. "Only one way to find out, I guess."

Apfel placed the check on the nightstand and grabbed the Bagaq. "My sentiment, exactly. But I wish to have some privacy for this, so please step outside. Both of you."

"Mister Apfel," Tony said. "I don't understand what's—"

"You don't need to understand, Tony," he said in an icy tone. "You need only to do as you are told."

Tony flushed. "Yessir."

Tier followed him out into the hallway where the nurse closed the door behind them.

"Just what is going on?" Tony said. "I can't be a party to—"

"Not your worry, Tony."

"But you talked about that rock healing a bullet wound. How is that—?"

"Possible? I have no idea, Tony. And I'm too tired to care. If I never see your boss and that 'rock,' as you call it, again it'll be way too soon."

That seemed to shut him up. They waited in silence, which was fine with Tier.

And then that silence was split by an agonized scream from the bedroom. With a cry, Tony yanked open the doors and rushed in. Tier followed at a more leisurely pace. He remembered it hurting—burning—but not that bad. Maybe Apfel had a low threshold of—

Another scream—this time from Tony. Tier stepped closer and felt his gorge rise when he saw what lay on the bed.

"What happened?" Tony was shouting. "Great God, what happened to him?"

Roland Apfel was barely recognizable. His face was ravaged with tumors and what looked like shingles across his forehead and into his right eye. The Bagaq, in its ovoid form, lay on the sheet beside his chest. But his chest . . . more tumors, plus pustules and blisters and goddamn if he didn't have an exit wound exactly like Jack's a couple of hours ago. And the left side of his throat sported a bloody tear, right where Tier had been bitten. Was that what his wound had looked like before the Bagaq had worked its magic?

What the hell happened here? The Bagaq was supposed to cure. Tier was living proof. But it seemed to have the opposite effect on Roland Apfel.

"What did you do to him?" Tony cried.

"Me? Nothing. You were with me out in the hall."

"It's that thing you gave him."

Tier didn't like the way this was going.

"You mean, the thing he paid me to find."

"You killed him!"

Okay, time to turn this around.

"Listen, buddy-boy, I'm not the one who was hired to keep him alive. This isn't exactly going to be a high point on your resume."

Just then, Roland opened his eyes and took an agonized breath. Tier nudged Tony. "He's still alive. Better call 9-1-1. Pronto."

As Tony pulled out his phone and began punching in numbers, Tier stepped to the nightstand, picked up his check, and pocketed it. The banks would be open in a few hours. He'd have to cash it ASAP.

Blabbering into his phone, Tony hurried from the room. Was he going to wait by the door for the EMTs? Tier had a feeling it might take them a while to get here through the snow.

Apfel's lips moved but no sound came. Tier leaned closer.

"That woman . . . " His voice . . . if sand could talk, it might sound like this. "She . . . " His voice gave out.

"She pulled a fast one on you, I think."

"How?"

"No idea. You're the expert—you and Madame. You should ask her."

His eyes widened in fear. "Here?"

"Not that I know of. At least not yet. But I've a feeling she will be."

A questioning look.

"Well, she did promise to visit you on your deathbed."

Nothing she'd said upon handing him the Bagaq had made sense at the time, but it all made terrible sense now. He stared at the Bagaq where it lay next to Apfel on the rumpled sheets. Its color had returned to the original bronze.

Tempting . . .

But no. That wouldn't be wise. It belonged to Madame de Medici. It did not seem a good idea to place oneself between that woman and what she wanted.

"I can't say it was a pleasure doing business with you, Roland, because it was anything but. And to top it off, Poncia told me just before he died how I was a loose end you wanted him to eliminate."

"No . . . "

"He thought he had the upper hand, had his gun pointed straight at me, point-blank range, so he had no reason to lie."

He turned at a sound behind him and expected to see Tony. Instead, Madame de Medici sauntered into the room.

"And this is my cue to leave. You two deserve each other."

He gave Apfel a little salute and walked toward Madame de Medici, intending to pass her without a word.

"Don't go too far," she said, barely glancing at him. Her amber gaze was fixed on Apfel.

"Why not?" Not that he'd been planning a vacation.

"Burbank might be calling."

"What for?"

"That will be between you and him."

He couldn't imagine what the old guy could want with him but he said no more.

They both walked on.

Downstairs he found a very cowed-looking Tony sitting on one of the padded benches in the foyer. The tall Sikh stood next to him with a gentle hand on his shoulder. He gave Tier another *You-may-proceed* nod, and Tier did just that.

The frigid air slapped his face as he stepped out onto the front steps. It felt wonderful.

9

Madame de Medici stopped by the side of the bed and looked down at the ruins of Roland Apfel.

"Well, here we are," she said, keeping her tone flat. Mocking him at this juncture was beneath her.

His mouth moved but no words came forth.

"Last week I asked you if you knew the meaning of *bagaq*. You didn't. That is the trouble with you dilettante collectors. You don't research thoroughly, if at all. You simply want-want-want. Bagaq means *sponge* in the Old Tongue. And if you had done your homework, you would have known what the change in color meant."

She picked up the empty Bagaq and turned it over in her hands. Was it lighter in weight as well as hue, or just her imagination?

"The Bagaq is an Infernal that absorbs diseases and injuries. But like any sponge, it becomes saturated and must be squeezed before it can be useful again. The color change is a warning that it is full. The Bagaq was designed to squeeze itself when full. Woe to the first to use it after it reaches the saturation point. It empties all the diseases and injuries it has absorbed into that unfortunate person. And tonight, Roland Apfel, that person was you."

A groan from the bed. His breaths were coming further and further apart. One of his exhalations sounded like "Lied."

"'Lied'? Of course I lied. Not about stealing it, because how could I steal what was mine to begin with? My Cairo apartment was looted in 2011 during the 'Arab Spring' and the Bagaq was taken along with everything else. You may have purchased it from the thieves, but that did not make it yours. I did lie about having it because I didn't want you hounding me. But when I saw your man posted outside my apartment building, I knew I would have no peace until I resolved our conflict. Which I have done."

She watched him take a breath, then waited for the next. When it didn't come, she slipped the Bagaq into a pocket and turned to leave.

Wait.

She stepped to the pedestal and retrieved the bronze cup from the valley of Gohar Rud. She ran a finger over the rim, remembering again how it had come to be dented. Yes, sentimental value.

She gave Roland's still form a last look as she passed.

Conflict resolved.

10

Jack awoke with a dry mouth and a tongue that felt like old leather. He hadn't realized he'd fallen asleep. He recognized the Quinnell lair, but ... was that music? Sounded like Bing Crosby ... yes, definitely Bing Crosby singing "I'll Be Home for Christmas."

Okay, he'd fallen asleep and was still asleep, but dreaming he was awake.

And then he heard a child sob. And sob again.

He sat up. After fighting off a swirl of vertigo, he found the source.

"Oh, no." He said it softly, not wishing to make matters worse.

Cilla Quinnell huddled a few feet away, wrapped in a blanket. The toys David had stolen had been arranged around her. Quinnell himself sprawled against the opposite wall, looking like hell.

Cilla turned her tear-streaked face toward Jack but didn't quite look at him as she sobbed again.

"It's okay, honey," he said as he scooched closer. "No one's gonna hurt you here."

As least he'd stopped slurring his words.

"I want my mah-ha-ha-hommy!"

Jack sat next to her and wrapped the blanket more tightly around her before pulling her against him. She was shaking like an epileptic.

"I know you do, and we're going to get you back to her as soon as possible."

This earned a growl from Quinnell but not much else.

"Doggie Man," Cilla said.

He remembered seeing her talking to him in her backyard. Her expression then had showed a mix of fear and fascinated affection. Maybe she sensed the paternal feelings this creature had for her. Maybe a bond had been forming. But pulling her from her bed and her home and bringing her here had shattered that.

"Right, Cilla. Doggie Man. Doggie Man loves you and would never hurt you. Right, Doggie Man?"

A whine from Quinnell. Jack had never heard him whine.

"You know," Jack said to him, "I was afraid this was on your mind. Soon as I saw the little tree and the lights and the toys, I thought, he's planning on bringing Cilla here. I was almost afraid to think it, and I was even more afraid to warn you off it because I feared if this crazy idea wasn't already in your head, I just might put it there."

Quinnell made no sound, simply stared. He looked exhausted.

"What were you thinking?"

Quinnell gestured at the tree and the toys.

"One last Christmas with her?"

A nod.

Jack's heart went out to him, but more to little Cilla. Her tremors spoke of her terror.

"She's scared to death, Dog. And I'm not going hip-hop on you, I just don't want to say your name. You've got to end this."

A growl.

"What happens when her mother goes in to wake her to see what Santa Claus brought? Do you hate Jelena that much?"

Another whine.

"Then I'm taking her back."

This brought Quinnell to his feet. He swayed as he faced Jack. Jack struggled to his own feet. Damn, his knees were still weak.

"We're going to have a fight? In front of her? You really want that?"

Quinnell crumpled to his knees. A sound like a sob escaped him. Poor bastard.

But it didn't seem like simple resignation. More to it than that . . .

something else going on. Was the cellular lysis Hess and Monaco had mentioned catching up to him? Was David Quinnell dying? Had he known that all along?

He was in no shape to stop Jack, but neither was Jack in any shape to carry Cilla back through the snow to—

"Oh, Christ!"

He had the keys but the Jeep was still in the diner's parking lot.

Just then sounds started echoing down the passageway.

Now what?

Madame de Medici appeared.

"Jack, I'm so glad—" And then she saw Cilla and gasped something unintelligible.

"Exactly how I feel," he said.

She pointed back and forth between Cilla and Quinnell. "Are they . . . ?"

"Yeah."

"But—"

"Before we go any further," he said, "you've got to tell me how you wound up with the Bagaq." He was still worried about Abe.

"It never left me. The one I gave you was a fake—a decoy."

Okay. That was a relief—but only as far as Abe not being in danger.

"So, you lied to me."

"Surely you expect that from your clientele."

Yeah, he did. But . . .

"Why the charade?"

"You of all people must understand misdirection: draw attention to the right hand to hide what the left is doing?"

"Yeah, yeah, I get all that. What irks me is, I've been guarding a fake and you wind up giving the real one away. I damn near got killed for nothing."

"No, not for nothing. You proved quite useful. I was able to use the Bagaq on you. And I have it back."

"You were counting on me getting hurt?"

"Not at all. I never dreamed you'd be hurt. I was counting on the trail of carnage that seems to follow you. I intended to saturate the Bagaq with that carnage. But you unexpectedly wound up being part of it. It all worked out, however. After helping you and

Roland's hireling, the Bagaq was full."

"With what?"

"Disease and injury."

"And that's a good thing?"

Her amber eyes flashed. "Not for Roland."

"I take it the Bagaq didn't help him?"

"Not in the least."

"Does that mean you've resolved your conflict?"

A smile. "Yes. Quite satisfactorily. Plus, the Bagaq is mine again and no one is trying to take it from me."

Something scary about that smile. Especially when he remembered how she'd promised she'd visit Roland on his deathbed to reclaim it.

"Let's put that aside for now," he said. "We have a more immediate problem."

She fixed her gaze on Cilla. "I've gathered who she is, but what is she doing here?"

"Well, as I see it, Christmas is a time families tend to get together, and our friend here thought . . . well . . . "

Madame de Medici got the message.

"It used to be a time," she said, "when people gathered to celebrate the passing of the winter solstice and the lengthening of the day. Now it's been overlaid with so much else. But none of that changes the fact that the child must go back immediately."

This brought a growl from Quinnell.

Madame stepped over to him and bent to get in his face.

"This is not up for debate, young man. No matter what the time of year, this child needs her home and her mother." She turned to Jack. "Do you know where she lives?"

He nodded. "I was about to take her there but my Jeep's—"

Her eyes widened. "You? Have you looked at yourself?" She shook her head. "No, of course you haven't. How could you? You're a bloody mess, Jack."

He looked down at his punctured, bloodstained parka and shirt. The Bagaq may have healed the wounds, but he'd done a lot of bleeding before it went to work.

"Oh, yeah. That."

"Yes, that. My car is waiting. I'll take her back. I'm sure her mother would rather open the door to a cultured, well-dressed woman than a bloodied, bedraggled man."

. . . a cultured, well-dressed woman . . . certainly no self-image issues there. But she had an excellent point.

He looked her up and down, jodhpurs and all. "Will she open it for someone who looks like she just came from the race track?"

"I shall be back in fur when I call on her."

"How will you explain having Cilla?"

"I'll think of something. I'm an excellent liar."

"Practice makes perfect, right?"

She didn't respond but her sidelong glance spoke volumes.

And then Quinnell did a slow slide from sitting against the wall to sprawling on his side. Jack scuttled over and knelt beside him.

"What's wrong?"

He mustered a whine. His eyes were cloudy and yellow, his breathing shallow. Jack had no doubt he was dying.

"Okay, listen: Cilla's going home. Understand?"

A nod.

"And then I'm going to call the bastards to pick you up."

A shake of the head.

Jack figured Cilla was listening—little kids heard everything—so he chose his words carefully.

"Seriously. If your, um, remains are found here, the authorities will do all sorts of testing on you. Your DNA is in the system. You could be identified. Do you want that to be part of your legacy—and your offspring's as well?"

No immediate response, then a shake of the head. Quinnell looked at Jack. His rheumy eyes were hard to read, but Jack sensed a *thank-you* there.

He motioned to Cilla to come over. She hesitated, then approached with her blanket wrapped around her shoulders.

"Doggie Man isn't feeling well. He's going to stay here while we take you home. But before you go, maybe you can say good bye and thank-you for the presents."

Cilla didn't hesitate. "Bye-bye, Doggie Man. Thanks for the presents."

Jack was reaching out to lift her when she bent and kissed her father on the head.

Quinnell made that soblike sound again. Jack tried to speak but realized his throat had locked. He wrapped the blanket around Cilla and lifted her into his arms.

Madame de Medici was staring at them, her amber eyes glistening. She shook it off and said, "You're still weak from the poison. I'll have Sochai—"

"Who's Sochai?"

"My driver."

"I've got her."

His legs were feeling stronger now and he'd be damned if he'd walk along emptyhanded while her driver carried this child. Not gonna happen.

Climbing the wall rungs with her proved a challenge because he was afraid she'd slip from his grasp, but after that, the trek across the parking lot was doable.

Sochai was holding the fence open for them when they arrived. Then he hurried ahead to open the Hummer's passenger door for Madame.

"I'll take the rear with the child. You sit up front with Sochai."

The interior was warm and comfy. A minute after they started rolling, Madame de Medici announced, "She's asleep."

11

Edward Hess was on his third spiced rum and Coke–the alcohol took the edge off the throb in his thigh–when the phone rang.

"At this ungodly hour," Monaco said, "that can be only one person."

Neither of them had been able even to think of sleep, so they'd sat up together in Edward's place, plotting how to get their money back. Before his first Captain and Coke–a stiff one, just like those that followed–every idea had sounded impossible; as he approached the end of his third, more and more were sounding feasible.

Monaco didn't drink. Twit.

Monaco was reaching for the cell but Edward snatched it away. "My phone."

"But you've been drinking."

"I'm not affected."

Well, maybe a little. But he could deal with this.

Monaco gave one of his impatient glares. "We won't argue the point. But put it on speaker."

Fair enough.

"Hess? Jack. Your guy's ready for pick up."

"Our 'guy'?" Edward said.

"You wanna play games, the conversation's over."

"Wait," Monaco said. "You've got to understand, we've got trust issues here."

"The issues are on this side—as in, I don't trust a word either of you says."

"All right, then. Where is it?"

Still calling Quinnell "it," Edward thought.

He'd reverted to "him."

"Aqueduct."

"The race park?"

"You got it."

Edward had heard of it but had no idea where it was. He threw Monaco a questioning look.

"Queens," Monaco whispered. "Near H3's old place in Howard Beach." Then he raised his voice. "That's a pretty big 'where.'"

"He found a spot under the grandstand. I'll walk you in. But I gotta tell you: I just left him and he's not doing well."

"What's that supposed to mean?"

"He looks like he's dying. The whites of his eyes are all yellow."

Edward slumped back in his easy chair. "Oh, no."

Yellow eyes . . . Quinnell's liver was failing . . .

"I think it might be that lysis you told me about."

"We'll be the judge of that," Monaco said testily.

"Well, then, better do your judging soon. He doesn't look like he can hang on much longer. Either of you have wheels that can get in here through the snow? That Odyssey's not gonna cut it."

"I've got a Highlander," Monaco said.

"That'll do. Drive to the Belt Parkway and take it to the Aqueduct exit. Call this number when you get there and I'll talk you in. Bring flashlights and dress warm. You have some walking to do."

"Can he walk?" Edward said.

"No way."

"Well, we don't have a stretcher."

"Bring a rug to wrap him in. And don't forget the other half of my fee."

The line went dead.

Monaco's face twisted in rage. "His fee? The fucking nerve! He steals half a million from us and still wants his *fee?*"

Edward's rum-fogged mind wasn't thinking about fees. It had focused on the rest of what he'd said.

"Rug?"

"We happen to have a body bag," Monaco said, rising.

"What? Why?"

"I put one in the back of the van last week in case someone killed H3 before we caught it."

"Oh." Okay. That was taken care of. But . . . "Where will we get the money for his fee?"

"He's not getting his goddamn fee! He's getting something else instead." He stomped toward the door. "We'd better get moving."

He hurried out, leaving Edward to gulp the rest of his drink. When finished, he pulled a heavy overcoat from the closet. He had no boots—who had boots?—so he slipped into a worn pair of sneakers. Not warm, but at least they had rubber soles. He searched out a scarf and some knitted gloves. He checked his flashlight and it still worked.

All right. Ready to go.

By the time he got outside, Monaco had burst his Highlander through the mounded snow at the bottom of the driveway and was waiting for him. Edward slogged across the drifted front yard and climbed into the passenger seat. Usually he drove, but not tonight.

"God, it's cold out there."

"Good thing, too," Monaco said. "If this had been a wet snow, I never would have made it out of the driveway. But it's like powder."

As the SUV lurched forward, Edward noticed a pistol resting on the console.

"What's that for?"

"It's Jack's fee."

"No, seriously." And then it hit him. "Oh, no. You're not thinking . . ."

"Of shooting a few holes in him? Goddamn right I am. But not right away. He'll help us with the lifting and hauling. But as soon as we have H3 settled in the back here, I'm going to find out where Jack stashed that suitcase."

"What if he's already given it to Quinnell's wife?"

Monaco laughed. "*What?* I can't believe you're so naïve. Do you really believe he has any intention of giving that pile of cash away to some woman he's never met? If you do, I've got this nifty bridge for sale. No, no, my friend. As sure as night follows day, he's keeping every penny for himself. I guarantee it."

"I don't know. He seemed genuinely outraged."

"All an act. And even if by some insanely remote chance he meant it, he wouldn't go deliver a suitcase full of cash in the dead of night in a blizzard. Not a chance. He'd wait until daylight. Have no fear: He has our money and we're going to get it back. And then ... "

Ed waited, but Monaco let it hang. So ... "And then what?"

"He knows too much, Ed. You slipped about 'melis.' And we both know—just *know*—he's going to Google it when he has time. And then they'll come looking for him. And when they find him, he'll point to us."

"You're making a lot of assumptions, the first being that he even remembers the word, the second being that he cares what it means."

"Oh, he cares. We made a big deal out of not mentioning it, and then you go blurt it out. There's that old movie line that goes, 'If I tell you, I'll have to kill you.' Well, you told him, so now ... "

Ed's stomach did a turn. A little sick from the rum and coke? Or from the subject matter?

"He doesn't deserve to die just because he heard a word."

"Okay, then, how's this? He knows all about H3 and the project. If he blabs about that, we're ruined. I've already mentioned the melis issue. And last but not least, *he stole half a million fucking dollars of our money!* That's three strikes. In my book, three strikes and you're out. He signed his own death sentence."

What's happened to me? Ed wondered.

His life's course had been set: He was supposed to make discoveries about animal diseases, help cure or prevent them, make the world a better place. Then Agent Greve had shown up with his container of goddamn melis and everything had gone to hell. But slowly. So slowly that Ed had never noticed the old Edward Hess eroding away, leaving a shell captivated by the magic of that infernal substance.

Nausea threatened to overwhelm him. "I never signed on for this."

"Well, neither did I. But a man's gotta do what a man's gotta do."

12

The sound of a bell woke her.

Jelena snapped upright in bed when she recognized it.

The front door.

She checked the clock on her cable box: *4:28.* For real? Who on Earth would be knocking on someone's door at four-thirty on Christmas Eve?

"Oh, no!" she whispered.

They've come back for the money

"No-no-no-no-no!"

Fighting panic, she leaped from under the quilt and ran around her bedroom, looking for clothes. She couldn't go to the door—even if she didn't answer it—in a T-shirt and panties. She found a pair of sweatpants and pulled them on. Leaving the lights off, she tiptoed to the door. She realized she'd forgotten to turn off the front stoop light. Bad for the electric bill but good for seeing who was out there. If she saw that guy who'd delivered the suitcase, she'd pretend no one was home.

She peeked through the peephole and saw an attractive, classy-looking woman in a white fur coat and fur hat. Definitely overdressed for this neighborhood. She had some sort of blanket-wrapped bundle in her arms. Was she lost?

"Hello?" Jelena said through the door. "Can I help you?"

"I have something I believe is yours," the woman said.

What was going on tonight? First the suitcase, and now . . .

"What is it?"

"A child."

What? It sounded like she'd said—

"Oh, God!"

She ran back to Cilla's room and flipped on the light. Her bed was empty! Jelena couldn't help the panicked screech that escaped her as she raced back to the front door and yanked it open.

When the woman pulled back a flap of the blanket to reveal Cilla's peacefully sleeping face, Jelena felt her legs begin to fail her. She clutched the doorframe for support.

"Yours?"

Jelena managed a "Yes."

"I found her wandering in the snow and—"

Jelena regained her voice and screamed, "Give her to me!" as she grabbed for her.

"Of course," the woman said calmly as she released the bundle. "That is why I'm here."

She clutched Cilla against her, wanting to sob and wanting to scream again. How could this be?

The child stirred in her arms and murmured, "Doggie Man."

"What? What was that?"

"She's been saying that ever since I found her," the woman said.

Jelena pulled the blanket open—the blanket from Cilla's bed. Cilla was still dressed in her favorite pajamas and looked fine . . . perfectly fine.

"I don't understand," Jelena said. "I put her to bed and . . . how could she . . . ?"

The woman shrugged. "That is not for me to answer. I found her a block away, standing in the snow and staring up at a streetlight. I took her into my car and asked her where she lived and she guided us here."

Staring up at a streetlight . . . so Cilla . . .

Jelena saw the Hummer idling in the street. Her mind whirled. None of this made sense. Was she dreaming?

"All's well that ends well, I guess," the woman said and turned to go.

"Wait. I don't understand."

"Neither do I," she said without turning back. "But please keep a closer watch on your child in the future."

The admonishment stung. She *did* keep a close watch. Cilla was never alone.

A turbaned man got out of the Hummer's driver seat and opened the rear door for the woman.

"Wait!" Jelena called. "I don't even know your name!"

The mystery woman waved as she seated herself in the rear. The driver closed the door, got back in, and drove off.

"Thank you," Jelena said softly and closed the door.

She gave Cilla a gentle shake, and kept shaking her until she opened her eyes.

"How did you get outside, baby?"

"Doggie Man." And then she closed her eyes again.

Jelena checked the back door: double locked; the dead bolt could be turned only from the inside. But in Cilla's bedroom the one window was unlocked. Jelena knew she'd locked it as soon as the weather turned cold and kept it locked. Had she crawled out the window?

Oh, God, this was awful. For the millionth time she wished David were here.

She hugged Cilla tighter and carried her toward her own bedroom.

"You're sleeping with me tonight, baby."

Cilla mumbled "Doggie Man" in her sleep. Again.

What on God's Earth did that mean?

13

"That looked like it went pretty smoothly," Jack said as Madame de Medici ascended into the rear of the Hummer.

"Yes, of course it did. She had no idea her child had left the house. For a moment I thought she might swoon."

Swoon?

As Sochai climbed behind the wheel and got them rolling, Jack twisted in the passenger seat to face Madame.

"That was a good thing you did there."

A smile. "You sound surprised."

"I'm always surprised when someone does something totally out of character."

She gave a soft laugh. "Yes. 'Totally.'" She looked at him. "Do you really have such a low opinion of me?"

"After the way you set me up—what do you think? *La Belle Dame Sans Merci.*"

She smiled. "I accept '*La Belle Dame*,' but as I've already said, I did not intend for you to be injured. I expected you to injure others. That's usually the way it works for you. Do we have a conflict here?"

He waved a hand. "No conflict." Not if Roland was an example of how she resolved conflicts. "I only wish I'd had a heads-up that a Native American was following me."

"You mean Mister Hill, the Mohawk? I'm still familiarizing myself with New World things and peoples."

"Yeah, well, whatever. I'm sure you have Mrs. Q's undying gratitude. Why *did* you do it?"

"I can be quite ruthless—I have enough self-awareness to know that—and I admit it. But I am not '*Sans Merci*.' Besides, I did it for you."

"Me?"

"A small compensation for your injuries. As we have already discussed, had a bloody, bedraggled-looking man such as you appeared on her doorstep, she would have immediately called the police. But me . . . a stylish *Belle Dame* . . . " She shrugged.

Had to hand it to her: She said it like she saw it. He looked back at the Quinnell house. All the lights were on.

"Where'd you say you found her?"

"Wandering a block away."

"And the mom bought it?"

Another smile. "Simple lies are the best. The listener tends to fill in the details. Only later do questions arise."

Jack thought about that. Yeah, that was how it usually worked. He—

Wait . . . words from half a moment ago trickled back: *New World*? Who the hell said *New World* in this day and age?

"Who are you? I mean really."

"I've told you: Madame—"

"Yeah-yeah. So you say. What's your first name?"

"Madame."

"Can I get a serious answer here?"

"I've had many names. This one seems to have stuck. I've been Madame de Medici the longest of all."

"And how long is that?"

"A long time."

Jack clenched his teeth. The woman was impossible.

Despite no hope of a straight answer, he asked anyway: "How old are you?"

"Mmmm . . . let me see . . . how does that expression go? As old as my tongue but a little older than my teeth."

Jack shook his head. "I can't help it—I keep looking around for your dog."

"As I've already told you: I am not her."

"But you know her?"

"I know *of* her. We've never met face to face."

Try another tack: "Got any family?"

"Once. All gone now."

"So you're alone?"

"Alone but not lonely. I have my treasures."

"Things . . . no people?"

"I prefer 'things.' Things possess a permanent state of being: They are what they are and stay what they are. They don't change, they don't disappoint you, don't betray you. They don't . . . die."

"But . . . " Hell, what was the use? "Okay, change of subject: What next for you? You've secured your nasty little Infernal. Gonna stick it with your other *things*?"

"Yes. I've been keeping my Infernals in the New Orleans house— to which I cannot wait to return and get out of this weather. I'm not suited to the cold." She lifted her hand bag. "I have a spot reserved for this. Right next to the *Cidsev Nelesso*."

A weird name he'd never forget . . . the bracelet-like Infernal he'd encountered in New Orleans. But she'd said . . .

"So, you *do* have it. You told me you didn't know where it was."

"I lied."

Jack couldn't find a hint of guilt in her tone. "As you said, you're excellent at it. How do I know you're telling the truth now?"

"You don't. But I knew you only by reputation last week. I know you better now. By the way, I also have the arm it adorned."

That jolted Jack. "Chastain's?"

She nodded. "Of course. Who else?"

"His *arm*?"

"Well, not his *whole* arm, of course—just the hand, wrist, and lower half of his forearm. You may recall, in a sudden frantic need to be rid of the *Cidsev*, he hacked it off."

Jack recalled. He'd seen Chastain and his bandaged stump in a NOLA hospital. He made a face. "And you kept it? Won't it rot?"

"Not if properly preserved—and I have people who know the old ways. It seems an appropriate mount for display, don't you think?"

"Never let a good body part go to waste, right?" Sheesh. "Your personal version of Feng shui?"

She laughed. "I doubt a master would approve, but the pairing appeals to me."

The woman was scary—very scary. He glanced at his watch. "Gotta go. Need to be there when Burke and Hare arrive."

"You still wear a watch?"

"Old school, I know. But phones make clunky timepieces."

"And after you deal with the scientists . . . a Christmas Eve celebration with the family?"

"That's a dozen hours away—after some shut-eye and a couple of showers. And as for family, all the blood relatives I know of are dead."

Mom, Dad, Kate, Tom . . . all gone.

A spear has no branches . . .

"The same for me." She gave him a long look. "You have a woman?"

"'Have'?" He laughed. "I don't think she's the sort of woman you 'have.' More like she has me."

"That sounds like a woman I would like to meet."

Was she angling for an invitation? Well, why not?

"It's at her house—eight Sutton Square. If you'd like to stop over, you'd be more than welcome. Sochai too."

He and the Sikh had done a little bonding while his Mistress was returning Cilla. Jack had sensed a deep loyalty there.

"I am deeply appreciative," Sochai said, "but I do not celebrate Christmas."

"Neither do I," Madame said. "But I may take you up on your offer. Tell me: Your woman . . . she would not mind your inviting another woman, especially one as desirable as I?"

He had to laugh. "You kill me. Not in the least. Her name's Gia, by the way, and she's got no insecurities where I'm concerned. She knows me. But she's the type who hates to think of someone with no place to go on Christmas Eve."

"That is very kind of you—and her—but I may be prevented from coming because I must help an old friend tonight."

"Older than you?" he said, hoping to catch her off guard. But she didn't bite.

"Who said I was old?"

"Sorry."

"For a number of years, I have assisted him with his health, so to speak, and he has had a long life, but he no longer responds. I fear this might be his last day."

"Will you miss him?"

"He performs a vital service. But I am working on a replacement."

Jack noticed how she evaded a direct answer but let it slide.

"Well, if you can make it, please don't hesitate to show up. As for now, how about dropping me at the diner so I can reclaim my rental?"

14

Jack squatted beside Quinnell who'd managed to push himself back up to a sitting position while Jack was away.

"Cilla's back with her mom, safe and sound."

Quinnell gave a nod.

"You look a little better. Feeling any better?"

He shook his head.

"Listen, I called Hess and Monaco and they're on their way in."

Jack had expected some sort of protest but Quinnell only stared with his yellow eyes.

"Did you hear me? They're coming to take you back to Plum Island."

Instead of the usual insistent head shaking, Quinnell gave a halfhearted shrug.

He'd given up. Yet, despite that, Jack had an inexplicable feeling that Quinnell was clinging to what remained of his life with everything he had. He supposed that was very human.

It saddened Jack.

He looked around at the tree, the lights, the stolen presents that Cilla had had to leave behind. On the surface it seemed like all that effort had been for naught, but then again . . .

David Quinnell had known it was his last Christmas, and he'd wanted to be home for it, wanted to spend that last Christmas with his daughter. And he'd nearly made it.

Jack coughed to relieve the growing tightness in his chest.

"All right, my friend," he said, waving his phone. "I'm going up to where I can get a signal. The scumbags should be getting close by now and will never find their way here without help."

Quinnell didn't respond.

Jack watched them get out of the Highlander... watched them closely. Had to be prepared for the unexpected with these two. Especially Monaco.

"Where on Earth are we?" Monaco said as he headed for the rear hatch.

"Right where you need to be."

He'd guided them in via phone along a twisty-turny route from the Belt Parkway.

The rear hatch slammed and Monaco returned with a folded body bag, saying, "Is he still alive?"

"Barely."

"When did you last see him?"

Before answering, Jack played his flash beam over Monaco's ski jacket and spotted a suspicious bulge in its right pocket.

"Just before I got on the phone to you. Still able to sit upright at the time, but I don't know how much longer." He waved his beam toward the opening in the fence. "Let's go."

As they trudged across the parking lot, Jack kept to Monaco's right where he could watch his right hand. He wanted early warning if the scientist tried to pull a weapon. He wasn't worried about Hess who looked a little loopy and disconnected and hadn't said a word yet. Jack didn't think either of them would try anything before they had Quinnell. After that, though, all options were open and anything could happen.

Under the grandstand they balked at descending into the conduit.

"How do we know it's not waiting down there to maul us?" Monaco said.

"He can't stand—can't even crawl."

"So you say."

Giving them no warning, Jack fairly leaped into the opening and scrambled down the rungs. Monaco was not the sort he wanted at his back.

He waited for them at the bottom, then led them to the lair.

"Good God in heaven!" Hess said when he saw the Christmas tree. "Did he do this?"

"Well, it wasn't me," Jack said.

But Jack was more interested in Quinnell who had fallen on his side again. Jack shook his shoulder.

"David . . . David, it's Jack."

No response. Communicating with Quinnell had been difficult when he was up and about, but damn near impossible in his present semi-comatose state.

Behind him he heard Monaco say, "Well, well, looks like you two have bonded."

A second later Jack had him by the front of his jacket and was in his smirking face. "Shut it!"

Monaco said nothing but the smirk vanished.

Hess had taken Jack's place at Quinnell's side and was looking him over, prying open his eyelids, looking for a pulse.

"Severe sclericteris. Looks like hepatic coma."

"Damn it," Monaco said, moving to Hess. "Of all the luck. Let's get him in the bag and move him to the car."

As they busied themselves spreading and opening the body bag, Quinnell opened his eyes and looked at Jack. He gave a slow wink, then closed them again.

What . . . what was he up to?

Jack decided it best to leave these three alone and watch how things played out from a distance.

15

Ed wanted out of this place. He'd never been claustrophobic, but he felt like the walls were closing in on him. All the Christmas trappings made it worse. Quinnell dressing up this little space for the holidays . . . why? The children's toys were the most upsetting. For his little girl? It made Ed feel like a total shit for calling him H3 all this time when a husband and a father – a *man* – still lived among all the wolf cells.

But most of all he dreaded lifting Quinnell. His back had become unreliable lately – downright cranky was more like it – and he didn't know what he'd do if it went out on him.

Once the body bag was spread out, he said, "How about giving us a hand?"

"Yeah," Monaco said, "your new best friend is going to be heavy."

When Jack didn't answer, Ed looked up but he was nowhere in sight. "Where'd he go?"

Monaco leaped to his feet and looked around. Pulling his pistol he hurried back toward the access port.

"Shit! Shit! Shit!" echoed down the passage.

"No sign of him?" Ed said when he returned, though he'd already guessed the answer.

"He's gone. The son of a bitch took off and left us."

"Without the rest of his money?"

"I don't like this," Monaco said, his pistol still drawn as he turned in a slow circle. Did he think Jack would pop out of a wall? "Something fishy going on. He's planning something."

Edward thought about that and didn't buy it.

"If he was going to harm us, he could have done it when we got out of the car, or after we arrived down here."

"Then what game is he playing?"

"Maybe he doesn't want to hurt his back lifting. Maybe he doesn't want any more to do with us. What difference does it make? Either way we have to lug Quinnell up to the surface and back to the car. So, let's get to it."

Quinnell's dead weight would have been pure hell to maneuver even without Ed protecting his back, but they managed to move him to the body bag and zip him in. That turned out to be the easy part. If not for the sturdy handles sewn into the fabric of the bag, they never would have been able to wrangle him up the rungs and through the opening.

Exhausted, they both sat on the frigid ground, panting to catch their breaths. Ed looked around for Jack but saw no trace of him. Was he waiting for them back at the car?

"All right," Monaco said. "Let's get this over with."

Instead of lifting him, they each took hold of one of the bag's head-end handles and dragged it atop the snow. Halfway across the parking lot, the bag rolled onto its side.

"What the hell?" Monaco said.

Ed stopped, panting. "I need a breather anyway. I'm so out of shape."

New Year's was a week away. Time for a resolution: hit the gym. Make it a habit.

Right. Like he'd stick to that.

"Help me flip this back," Monaco said.

As they bent over it, something looked wrong.

"The zipper's down," he said. "And Quinnell's arm's out."

Monaco leaned closer. "Now how the hell—?"

The arm moved—fast—as extended talons ripped into Monaco's throat. Ed froze in shock. How—? And then the talons swung his way and he felt the impact against his larynx, heard its cartilage crack, felt the skin tear. Agony enveloped him as he fell back and saw a dark jet arc away through the air.

16

Jack had been waiting for it, expecting it as he watched from the fence, and still it surprised him when it happened. It ended almost as soon as it began.

He took his time walking toward the three dark shapes splayed on the snow.

Lots of blood looking black on the white. He didn't bother checking Hess and Monaco, but he squatted by Quinnell and shone the light in his face. He watched for a hint of breath to fog the air, but none came. His semi-animal features looked at peace. And why not? He'd settled his scores.

Jack had sensed that Quinnell had been hanging on for a reason. He hadn't been sure why. Maybe because life was so short to begin with and you simply had to hold onto every last minute of it. But when he'd seen that slow jaundiced wink, he'd known this was coming. It told him to stay out of the way, and he had. Not his place to interfere.

He searched the pockets of Hess's overcoat and found his phone. He used it to search out the DIA's public affairs number. He didn't know where its 202 area code was located but called anyway.

He listened to a metallic woman's voice telling him the office was closed but he could leave a message.

"Hi, folks, just wanted to let you know that I'm standing here in one of the Aqueduct Racetrack parking lots by three fresh corpses involved in a DIA matter related to Plum Island. The matter in question is something I'm sure no one in DIA will want explored in the local papers. Don't sit on this. Someone in DIA will know what I'm talking about. I'll leave the phone here so you can trace it. Have a merry Christmas."

He wiped down the phone and tossed it onto the body bag. He'd called Hess on it a number of times but always had made a point of using one of his burners. He'd destroy those before dawn.

He looked down at the three bodies. What a mess. Four days ago, he'd signed on to find a missing animal, never dreaming it would all end like this.

No winners here.

Well, maybe Quinnell. The money had finally reached Jelena and Cilla. They'd have a better life because of it—just what David had intended when he sold his body for research.

Oh, yeah. And a fourth body in the boat basin. Jack didn't have a name for him. Would anyone connect that to Quinnell? Not that it mattered.

And wandering through it all, unscathed, untouched by human hand or human emotion . . . Madame de Medici. Where was she now? And where was Hill, the Mohawk?

One helluva night.

And on Christmas Eve, no less. Didn't seem right.

Whatever happened to peace on Earth, good will toward men?

17

Tier was working on his second whiskey when his phone rang. He ignored it.

One of the things he liked about Manhattan was the truth in its city-that-never-sleeps rep. No matter what the hour you could find, depending on your needs, an open bar or coffee shop ready to serve you. His need had been for a bar and he'd found this Irish pub in the East Forties. He'd barely registered the name as he'd pushed through the door. O'Somebody's . . .

Three or four other men had scattered themselves along the impressive length of the bar, watched over by a solitary, tired-looking bartender. The lights were too low to make out more than rudimentary features on the faces of his fellow drinkers, none of whom exhibited the slightest interest in engaging him in conversation. Perfect. In deference to the ethnicity of the environs, Tier had ordered a double Jameson's on the rocks.

It didn't help much. He still couldn't push what he'd seen—what he'd *experienced*—out of his head. Two deaths, two miraculous healings. He sensed a balance there but didn't pursue it. He could fabricate all sorts of meanings but, with no one to tell him whether or not he was on the right track, they'd be of little solace.

So, he ordered another Jameson's. Too bad Poncia wasn't here to make a "firewater" crack . . . so that Tier could kill him. A shame how that pleasure had fallen to the dogman. Tier was sure he would have enjoyed it more.

His father's words came back to him as they always did in the low times.

Find your place . . .

Maybe his place was here, or someplace like it . . . as a barfly. With Spartan needs and no one else to spend on, he'd built up a healthy bank account. He could fund a barfly life for a good long time. Big question: Could his liver outlast his savings?

His phone rang again. Who the hell—?

He checked the number and didn't recognize it. Madame de Medici had said Burbank might call. He didn't know if he should answer. Oh, why not? He thumbed the *TALK* button.

"Yeah?"

"Twilight has come," said a barely audible voice. "Night will follow."

"Hello, Mister Burbank. How are the signals?"

"Just 'Burbank,' please. I wish to speak to you."

"I believe you are doing that right now."

"In person."

"I'm sorry, I'm not—"

"It's important. Very important."

Tier wasn't sure Burbank was all there. Could a guy who slept in a coffin and devoted himself to sitting alone in that penthouse monitoring weird-ass signals all over the globe be all there? But he seemed harmless enough.

"Okay, when?"

"Right now."

Oh, hell.

"Can it wait till after the holidays?"

"Do you have family you need to see for the holidays?"

"Well, no . . . "

"After Christmas will be too late, I'm afraid. Please . . . "

Something in the breathless way he spoke that last word . . .

"Okay. Let me finish this drink and I'll be on my way."

Tier ended the call and shook his head. What was he getting into?

18

Jack parked the Jeep in the same twenty-four-hour garage where he kept the Crown Vic. He'd return it to the BP station later.

"You okay?" said the lone attendant when he saw the blood on Jack's coat. "You hurt?"

"Just a bad bloody nose."

His ebony features were a study in doubt. "I've had my share of bloody noses but they never made a hole in my coat."

"Let's forget the blood and do me a favor: fifty bucks if you can find some sort of a GPS tracker hidden on this thing."

He'd given the question a lot of thought on the drive in from Queens and could come up with only one explanation for how those two guys had tracked him to the diner. He was sure they were the same two in the Town Car he'd left stuck in Queens. No way could they have caught up to him in Howard Beach without a tracker.

So, he wasn't surprised when, after a mere five-minute search, the attendant found it inside the rear bumper. Had to be the easiest fifty bucks the guy had ever earned.

But how had it got there? Jack had walked out to the Jeep with the BP manager, done the walkaround, and driven off. No chance for anyone to—

He'd driven off in the only four-wheel rental on the lot.

Of course . . . they'd tagged the most likely vehicle while he was in with the manager. Maybe they'd tagged more than one, but the Jeep would have been their best bet.

Okay, score one for them and shame on him. He'd bet it had been Hill's idea. The stubby guy hadn't struck him as very brainy—most likely his genius idea to rent a limo in a blizzard.

Jack walked home through the empty, snow-laden streets, stripped off all his bloody clothes, and stood in the shower for a long, long time. He searched his right upper chest for some sign of an injury—a reddened area, a new scar to add to his collection, *something*. But found nothing.

He stuffed his bloody parka and shirt into a garbage bag for incineration sometime soon—didn't want any of his blood *anywhere*. Then crawled into bed. Before conking off, he texted Gia. She'd be asleep still—dawn was still hours away—but he wanted to let her know he was okay and would see her tonight. And that they might have a guest.

19

The Allard's glass front doors were locked but a doorman—not Simón—waited just inside.

"Burbank's expecting me," Tier said.

The guy swung one of the doors open for him.

"He left word. Take the middle car all the way to the top."

Tier knew that but simply nodded.

Up top, the elevator doors opened to reveal the scene exactly as he's left it—the stacks of dusty old books, the racks of equipment blinking in the dark, the overhead Tiffany—except no Burbank. His chair was empty.

Tier walked to the console and looked around, trying to pierce the darkness. Had to be a light switch somewhere—

"Over here," said a faint voice from the direction of the coffin.

Oh, right. He sleeps in the coffin.

Tier approached it and found Burbank staring up at him. Pale as candle wax. He looked dead. And then he took a breath and spoke too softly for Tier to hear.

He dropped to one knee beside the coffin. "Say again?"

"Thank you for coming."

"You said it was very important."

"Twilight has come. Night will follow. My night is here. I am dying."

After 118 years, hardly unexpected.

"I sensed that." Though he was already pretty sure of the answer, he had to ask. "Want me to call an ambulance?"

"No. Please, no. They can't change things, just cause me misery. I've lived here, and I wish to die here."

"I understand perfectly. Then why did you want me here? Just to sit with you? I can do that."

Tier would be perfectly happy to die alone, but most people probably weren't like that.

"Thank you," Burbank rasped. "Very kind of you. But what I really need is your help with the reports. I'm expecting a run of them soon and I'm just . . . not up to it."

Why the hell not? Didn't have anything better to do at the moment.

"Yeah, I guess I can handle that. For a while."

"You sit in the chair, and when a call—"

"I watched you the other day. I've got a pretty good idea of what to do."

It appeared to take all Burbank's strength to bend his elbow and raise his hand. "Thank you."

Tier grabbed the hand and squeezed. "'Sokay."

Burbank didn't let go. "Twilight has come. Night will follow."

"Right. I think I've got that."

"The signal frequencies are important. Don't neglect them. You—"

"*Sector seven-two-nine reporting.*"

Burbank released his hand. "There you go. And remember: It will begin in the heavens and end in the Earth."

Tier vaguely remembered the rest. "Something about rules?"

"But before that, the rules will be broken."

Whatever.

As Tier moved to the seat, the monitor showed a rapidly undulating sine wave. He tapped in 7-2-9 and the number appeared on the screen. He found a button on the base of the mike and pressed it.

"What's the frequency, seven-two-nine?"

"Burbank?"

"He's taking a break. What's the frequency?"

"Oh. Well. Three hundred-and twelve, that's three-one-two kilohertz."

He typed in *312 kHz*, then hit ENTER. "Got it."

"You're supposed to say, 'Recorded.'"

Christ. "Recorded."

He rotated his chair toward the coffin. Burbank wasn't visible from this angle. "How'd I do?"

Before Burbank could reply, another sector reported in. He took care of that. And then another.

He kind of liked this. Burbank had it made. Swank building, lots of electronics, tons of books, and best of all: no people.

"He's gone," said a woman's voice behind him.

Tier swiveled and wasn't surprised to see Madame de Medici looking down into the coffin.

"'Gone' as in 'no longer breathing?'"

"I'm afraid so. Such a strange man. So devoted to the task."

He joined her beside the coffin. She fascinated him and scared the hell out of him at the same time.

"You took care of him for a long time, I take it?"

She looked up. "I wasn't his caretaker, merely a neighbor who looked in on him occasionally."

"What are we going to do with him?"

"'We'? 'Do'?"

"We can't just leave him here to rot."

"He told me that when he dies the original owners of the coffin will come to take it and him away."

"The South American native tribe you mentioned?"

"I believe so. Except I've never seen them and I don't know how to contact them, so how will they know to come?"

Tier shrugged. "You're asking the wrong person."

"We'll have to trust that somehow they'll know."

Questions leaped immediately to mind but Tier brushed them off. Burbank's body couldn't wait *too* long, that was obvious. But not his problem. Or was it? He felt strangely connected to the old guy.

He posed another question instead: "Did you have something to do with his living so long?"

She frowned. "Why would you say that?"

"I saw the Bagaq at work. What it did for me wasn't what it did for Roland Apfel."

"Out of ignorance, he chose the wrong time to use it."

"Well, because of it—and you—I'm still alive. I don't believe I thanked you. I don't think I had the opportunity."

"You have a destiny, Mister Hill. I could not allow that to be thwarted."

Destiny . . . mission . . . here we go again. *Find your place . . .*

"And what might that destiny be?"

She gestured around. "Why, here, of course."

No-no-no.

"Hell, you say. I don't think so."

"What else do you have in your life that is more important?"

Good question.

"Well, my investigative work, for one."

"The world is chock-a-block with investigators. But only one is destined to replace Burbank."

He waved around. "You really expect me to spend the rest of my life here?"

"If things go right, it won't be anywhere near the rest of your life. Six months to a year at most."

"And if things go wrong?"

"Then it most likely *will* be the rest of your life . . . if you get my meaning."

Burbank's last words came back . . .

We're property . . . one of them owns us but may lose us to a competitor. That will not be good for us.

Yeah, he got her meaning. *Twilight has come. Night will follow.*

"So . . . you will try it?"

"What if I say no?"

She shook her head. "There is no one else."

Shit.

"Why can't *you* take over?"

Another shake of her head. "I am still searching for my destiny. This is not it. But it *is* yours." She gestured to the chair. "Just for a little while?"

"Sorry, I–"

"*Sector four-eight-three reporting.*"

"You'd better take that."

"No–"

"For Burbank?"

Damn her.

He dropped into the chair and banged *4-8-3*, then hit the mike button.

"What's the frequency, four-eight-three?"

"*Two-point-two gigahertz.*"

He typed it in. "Recorded." As he was swiveling his chair . . .

"*Sector five-twenty-two reporting.*"

Okay . . .

"What's the frequency, five-twenty-two?"

"*Seven-twenty-seven kiloHertz.*"

"Recorded."

When he turned, Madame de Medici was gone.

"*Sector eight-ninety-two reporting.*"

Oh, hell . . .

20

They hadn't been doing it long enough to call it a tradition, but they each opened one gift on Christmas Eve. For Jack and Gia, their only gift. Jack always told her he had everything–emphasizing *thing*–he needed or wanted. Yeah, sounded hokey, but he meant it.

But Gia always managed to find some little treasure for him.

They'd settled in the living room by the piano; Jack had started a blaze in the fireplace about an hour ago. Vicky went first, of course. Gia had bought clothing gifts, and had split them up with "From Mom" and "From Jack" labels. But Jack always insisted on at least one toy of some sort. He'd bought her a drone last year but its lifespan had been hours. This year . . .

"The new *DNA Wars!*" she screeched as the wrapping paper tore away.

"Yep," Jack said. "*The New Generation.*"

He'd cleared it with Gia first. She had her reservations about videogames, and he shared them. But he'd played the original *DNA Wars* and tried this one as well. The emphasis was on preparation–designing your start-up genome was crucial–and strategy and stealth, rather than twitch shooting. Plus, along the way, by osmosis, you learned a ton of genetics and how to manage the laws of conservation of mass and energy.

"Can I play it? Can I play it now?"

"Don't you want to see what Jack's got?"

"I saw it already." To Jack: "It's really neat, Jack. Soooo cool!" Back to Gia: "Can I, Mom? Can-I-can-I-can-I?"

Gia surprised him by laughing and saying, "Oh, go ahead. Try it for half an hour—but half an hour only."

And *bam*, she was gone.

Gia went to the bar and returned with two short glasses. She handed him the fuller one.

He sniffed. "The Balvenie?"

"Yes. I can't help remembering last Christmas Eve."

"Yeah. Tom."

"By rights I should have had the memorial service today, but Christmas is Vicky's time and I don't want to mix in death and disappearance. But now that it's just you and I: a proper toast to Tom, the reason you're still with us."

Now he understood why she'd let Vicky run off.

He raised his glass. "To Tom."

Jack sipped while Gia tossed off her wee dram.

"Ugh!" she said with a shuddering grimace. "I had to get that over with. Does anybody really enjoy this stuff, or do they just pretend?"

Jack took another sip. "Nectar of the gods." And meant it.

Gia poured herself some white wine and returned to his side. They leaned together in silence. Here was what it was all about, here was the one true thing in the mendacious façade that surrounded the rest of his life. Here he could be just plain Jack, that guy with Gia.

And to that end . . .

He handed her the little wrapped package he'd been hiding. "Do you mind if we put this under the tree?"

She put down her glass and frowned as she checked out the label. "'Emma'?"

"Yeah. I just thought . . . "

Jack wasn't sure what he thought. Last January Gia and Vicky had been the target of a hit and run assault. They weren't supposed to survive, but they did. Both came out of their comas with no residual damage. Not so the baby Gia had been carrying. She'd been in her sixth month . . . they'd known she was a girl . . . they'd decided to name her Emma . . .

Emma had possessed a beating heart, a fully sensing nervous system. She'd felt the impact that tore her placenta loose and stopped her heart. Jack had exacted revenge but that hadn't filled the empty place inside him.

He'd become a father figure to Vicky, and he loved that, but she was already seven when they'd met. He'd been so looking forward to being with Emma from day one.

"I get it," she said, her voice thick.

"I just want to make her part of the three of us ... make it four of us. Am I making any sense?"

A tear ran down Gia's cheek as she nodded. "Perfect sense." She wiped the tear and slipped her arms around him. "Every time I think I have you pegged and you can't surprise me, you do something like this."

They clung to each other for a long time, then Gia straightened and said, "Where's this guest you texted about?"

Jack checked the mantle clock. "If she's coming, she should be here soon."

"Who is she again?"

"Calls herself Madame de Medici."

"*Calls* herself'?"

"Well, are we supposed to believe that's her real name? Anyway, I just did a fix for her and she's all alone in the city and I just thought, you know ... "

"That I don't like the idea of someone being alone on Christmas Eve?"

"Exactly. I don't know if she'll even show. She was iffy about it."

"Well, if she does, she's welcome."

21

Madame de Medici watched through the window.

Jack and his woman—*Gia* he'd called her—sat and talked as they sipped their drinks. She'd known that sort of domestic bliss a few times in her life. But all so transient. She'd lived on while the latest love of her life had withered and died, often hating her toward the end for her persistent youth.

No, she wouldn't go in. This was their last Christmas like this. By this time next year their world would be a different place, where Santa Claus and tree decorations and pretty lights would be far from anyone's thoughts. Relics of the past. They didn't need a stranger intruding tonight.

She wondered if Gia knew she was consorting with the Heir. Did she have even a hint of the terrible responsibilities he would have thrust upon him when things started to go to hell? A better question: Did *he?*

Before leaving the Allard, she'd written a note just to let him know she'd been by and to offer a hint as to who she was. She'd asked Glaeken to say nothing but she'd had a change of heart. After all, he was the Heir. If she couldn't reveal herself to him, then whom? She was sure he was bright enough to catch the hidden message.

So sorry you were injured, Jack.
Roland's hireling was a wild card.
Eventually you will forgive me. Everyone does.
Madame de Medici

She tucked the envelope, secured with a disk of red wax with her scarab seal, into the space between the jamb and the door, then returned to the car.

22

Jack heard a car door slam outside on the street.

"That's probably her."

He opened the front door and saw an envelope drop from the door jamb. He snatched at it but the wind off the East River caught it and carried it toward Sutton Place. He chased after it and might have caught up if a snow plow hadn't trundled by at that instant and buried it in its blade.

He slid to a halt and watched it rumble from sight. Who could have left the envelope? Madame de Medici? No sign of her on the street.

He'd never know.

He hurried back to the warmth of the house.

23

In the Allard's penthouse she found Tier Hill still in Burbank's old chair, hunched over the microphone.

She heard him say, "Recorded," as she walked in.

"All is well, Mister Hill?"

"When I'm sitting here, Madame," he said without turning, "you can call me Burbank."

Ah, yes. Burbank. When–? She was startled to see the coffin missing.

"What happened to . . . ?"

He swiveled in his chair. "They came and took it."

"The tribesmen?"

"Four of them. Never spoke a word. Just showed up, bowl hair-cuts and face paint, fitted the lid into the top, and carried him out."

He turned back to the big monitor and began adjusting the settings.

"Twilight has come, Burbank."

"And night will follow," he said.

Satisfied that all was as it should be up here, she headed down-stairs to her apartment.

THE SECRET HISTORY OF THE WORLD

The preponderance of my work deals with a history of the world that remains undiscovered, unexplored, and unknown to most of humanity. Some of this secret history has been revealed in the Adversary Cycle, some in the Repairman Jack novels, and bits and pieces in other, seemingly unconnected works. Taken together, even these millions of words barely scratch the surface of what has been going on behind the scenes, hidden from the workaday world. I've listed them below in chronological order. (NB: "Year Zero" is the end of civilization as we know it; "Year Zero Minus One" is the year preceding it, etc.)

Scenes from the Secret History is FREE on Smashwords

THE PAST
"Demonsong"* (prehistory)
"The Compendium of Srem" (1498)
"Wardenclyffe" (1903-1906)
"Aryans and Absinthe"* (1923-1924)
Black Wind (1926-1945)
The Keep (1941)
Reborn (February-March 1968)
"Dat-Tay-Vao"* (March 1968)
Jack: Secret Histories (1983)
Jack: Secret Circles (1983)
Jack: Secret Vengeance (1983)
"Faces"* (1988)
Cold City (1990)
Dark City (1991)
Fear City (1993)
"Fix" (2004) (with Joe Konrath and Ann Voss Peterson)

YEAR ZERO MINUS THREE
Sibs (February)
The Tomb (summer)

"The Barrens"* (ends in September)
"A Day in the Life"+ (October)
"The Long Way Home"+
Legacies (December)

YEAR ZERO MINUS TWO

"Interlude at Duane's"+ (April)
Conspiracies (April) (includes "Home Repairs"+)
All the Rage (May) (includes "The Last Rakosh"+)
Hosts (June)
The Haunted Air (August)
Gateways (September)
Crisscross (November)
Infernal (December)

YEAR ZERO MINUS ONE

Harbingers (January)
"Infernal Night" (with Heather Graham)
Bloodline (April)
The Fifth Harmonic (April)
Panacea (April)
The God Gene (May)
By the Sword (May)
Ground Zero (July)
The Touch (ends in August)
The Void Protocol (September)
The Peabody-Ozymandias Traveling Circus & Oddity Emporium
    (ends inSeptember)
"Tenants"*
The Last Christmas (December)

YEAR ZERO

"Pelts"*
Reprisal (ends in February)
Fatal Error (February) (includes "The Wringer"+)
The Dark at the End (March)
Signalz (May)
Nightworld (May)

* available in *Secret Stories*
+available in *Quick Fixes–Tales of Repairman Jack.*

ABOUT THE AUTHOR

F. PAUL WILSON is an award-winning, bestselling author of 60 books and nearly one hundred short stories spanning science fiction, horror, adventure, medical thrillers, and virtually everything between. His novels *The Keep, The Tomb, Harbingers, By the Sword, The Dark at the End,* and *Nightworld* were *New York Times* Bestsellers. *The Tomb* received the 1984 Porgie Award from *The West Coast Review of Books*. *Wheels Within Wheels* won the first Prometheus Award, and *Sims another; Healer* and *An Enemy of the State* were elected to the Prometheus Hall of Fame. *Dydeetown World* was on the young adult recommended reading lists of the American Library Association and the New York Public Library, among others. His novella "Aftershock" won the Stoker Award. He was voted Grand Master by the World Horror Convention; he received the Lifetime Achievement Award from the Horror Writers of America, and the Thriller Lifetime Achievement Award from the editors of Romantic Times. He also received the prestigious San Diego ComiCon Inkpot Award and is listed in the 50th anniversary edition of *Who's Who in America*.

His short fiction has been collected in *Soft & Others, The Barrens & Others,* and *Aftershock & Others*. He has edited two anthologies: *Freak Show* and *Diagnosis: Terminal* plus (with Pierce Watters) the only complete collection of Henry Kuttner's Hogben stories, *The Hogben Chronicles*.

In 1983 Paramount rendered his novel *The Keep* into a visually striking but otherwise incomprehensible movie with screenplay and direction by Michael Mann.

The Tomb has spent 25 years in development hell at Beacon Films. Dario Argento adapted his story "Pelts" for *Masters of Horror*.

Over nine million copies of his books are in print in the US and his work has been translated into twenty-four languages. He also has written for the stage, screen, comics, and interactive media. Paul resides at the Jersey Shore and can be found on the Web at www.repairmanjack.com

Curious about other Crossroad Press books?
Stop by our site:
http://store.crossroadpress.com
We offer quality writing
in digital, audio, and print formats.

Enter the code FIRSTBOOK
to get 20% off your first order from our store!
Stop by today!